F... ...

Wars of ...

Ravenspur: Rise of the ...dors

'Iggulden is a master storyteller and makes our blood flow faster'
Sunday Express

'Superbly plotted and paced' *The Times*

'It's been said that *Game of Thrones* is the Wars of the Roses written as fantasy: this is the real thing, more glorious, more passionate and far, far more gritty' Manda Scott

'Absorbing and bloody. Iggulden handles the origins of the Tudor dynasty with great panache' Antonia Senior

'Iggulden breathes new life into the darkest and most dramatic of times, with a flair for both the huge scale and human interest of it all' *Star*

'A page-turning thriller' *Mail on Sunday*

'Pacey and juicy, and packed with action' *Sunday Times*

'Energetic, competent stuff; Iggulden knows his material and his audience' *Independent*

'Exceptionally well-written and gripping' *Stylist*

'Compelling reading' *Woman and Home*

ABOUT THE AUTHOR

Conn Iggulden is one of the most successful authors of historical fiction writing today. Following the *Sunday Times* bestsellers *Stormbird*, *Trinity* and *Bloodline*, *Ravenspur* is the concluding book in his superb series set during the Wars of the Roses, a remarkable period of British history. His previous two series, on Julius Caesar and on the Mongol khans of Central Asia, describe the founding of the greatest empires of their day and were number one bestsellers. Conn Iggulden lives in Hertfordshire with his wife and children.

www.conniggulden.com

Also by Conn Iggulden

THE WARS OF THE ROSES SERIES

Stormbird

Trinity

Bloodline

THE EMPEROR SERIES

The Gates of Rome

The Death of Kings

The Field of Swords

The Gods of War

The Blood of Gods

THE CONQUEROR SERIES

Wolf of the Plains

Lords of the Bow

Bones of the Hills

Empire of Silver

Conqueror

Blackwater

Quantum of Tweed

BY CONN IGGULDEN AND HAL IGGULDEN

The Dangerous Book for Boys

The Pocket Dangerous Book for Boys: Things to Do

The Pocket Dangerous Book for Boys: Things to Know

The Dangerous Book for Boys Yearbook

BY CONN IGGULDEN AND DAVID IGGULDEN

The Dangerous Book of Heroes

BY CONN IGGULDEN AND
ILLUSTRATED BY LIZZY DUNCAN

Tollins: Explosive Tales for Children

Tollins 2: Dynamite Tales

Wars of the Roses

Ravenspur: Rise of the Tudors

CONN IGGULDEN

PENGUIN BOOKS

PENGUIN BOOKS

UK | USA | Canada | Ireland | Australia
India | New Zealand | South Africa

Penguin Books is part of the Penguin Random House group of companies whose addresses can be found at global.penguinrandomhouse.com.

First published by Michael Joseph 2016
Published in Penguin Books 2017
004

Typeset by Jouve (UK), Milton Keynes
Printed in Great Britain by Clays Ltd, St Ives plc

A CIP catalogue record for this book is available from the British Library

ISBN: 978–1–405–92149–7

www.greenpenguin.co.uk

To my mother

Acknowledgements

After the death of my father, I hoped my mother would recover and grow strong once again. Instead, she was gone within the year. I would like to acknowledge her here, in the first of my books she will not read.

Her love of words and particularly poetry was a huge influence on me. She told me that history was a collection of stories about real people, with dates. I miss her advice every day, because she used to give me advice every day.

> A ship spreads white sails into the morning breeze. I stand and watch until she hangs as a speck between sea and sky – and someone says: 'There. She is gone.'
>
> And at that moment, as someone at my side says, 'She is gone,' there are other eyes watching for her arrival – and glad voices are raised to shout: 'Here she comes. There she is!'
>
> Henry Van Dyke

Map and Family Trees

Family Trees

England at the time of the Wars of the Roses

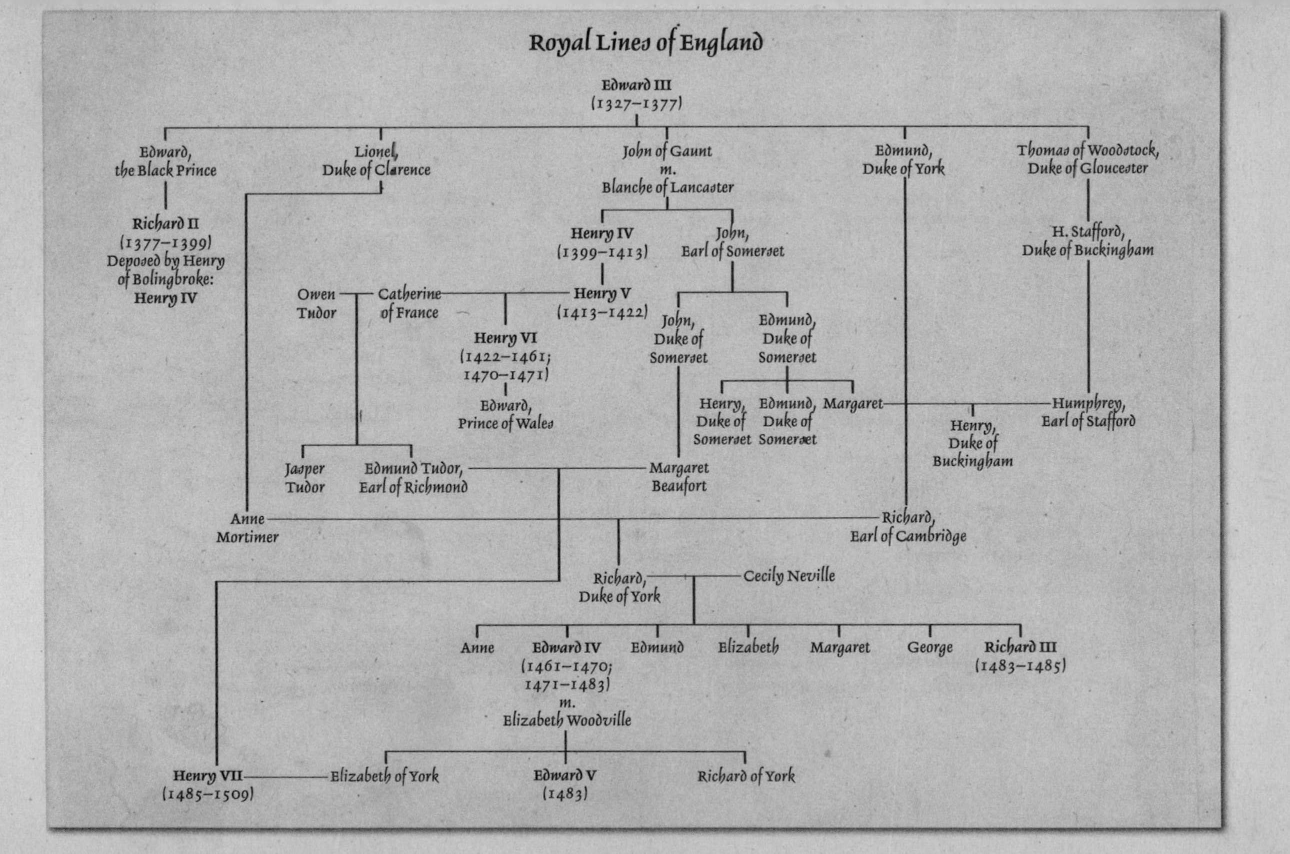
Royal Lines of England
Edward III
(1327–1377)
Edward,
the Black Prince
Lionel,
Duke of Clarence
John of Gaunt
m.
Blanche of Lancaster
Edmund,
Duke of York
Thomas of Woodstock,
Duke of Gloucester
Richard II
(1377–1399)
Deposed by Henry
of Bolingbroke:
Henry IV
Henry IV
(1399–1413)
John,
Earl of Somerset
H. Stafford,
Duke of Buckingham
Owen
Tudor
Catherine
of France
Henry V
(1413–1422)
John,
Duke of
Somerset
Edmund,
Duke of
Somerset
Henry VI
(1422–1461;
1470–1471)
Edward,
Prince of Wales
Henry,
Duke of
Somerset
Edmund,
Duke of
Somerset
Margaret
Humphrey,
Earl of Stafford
Henry,
Duke of
Buckingham
Jasper
Tudor
Edmund Tudor,
Earl of Richmond
Margaret
Beaufort
Anne
Mortimer
Richard,
Earl of Cambridge
Richard,
Duke of York
Cecily Neville
Anne
Edward IV
(1461–1470;
1471–1483)
m.
Elizabeth Woodville
Edmund
Elizabeth
Margaret
George
Richard III
(1483–1485)
Henry VII
(1485–1509)
Elizabeth of York
Edward V
(1483)
Richard of York

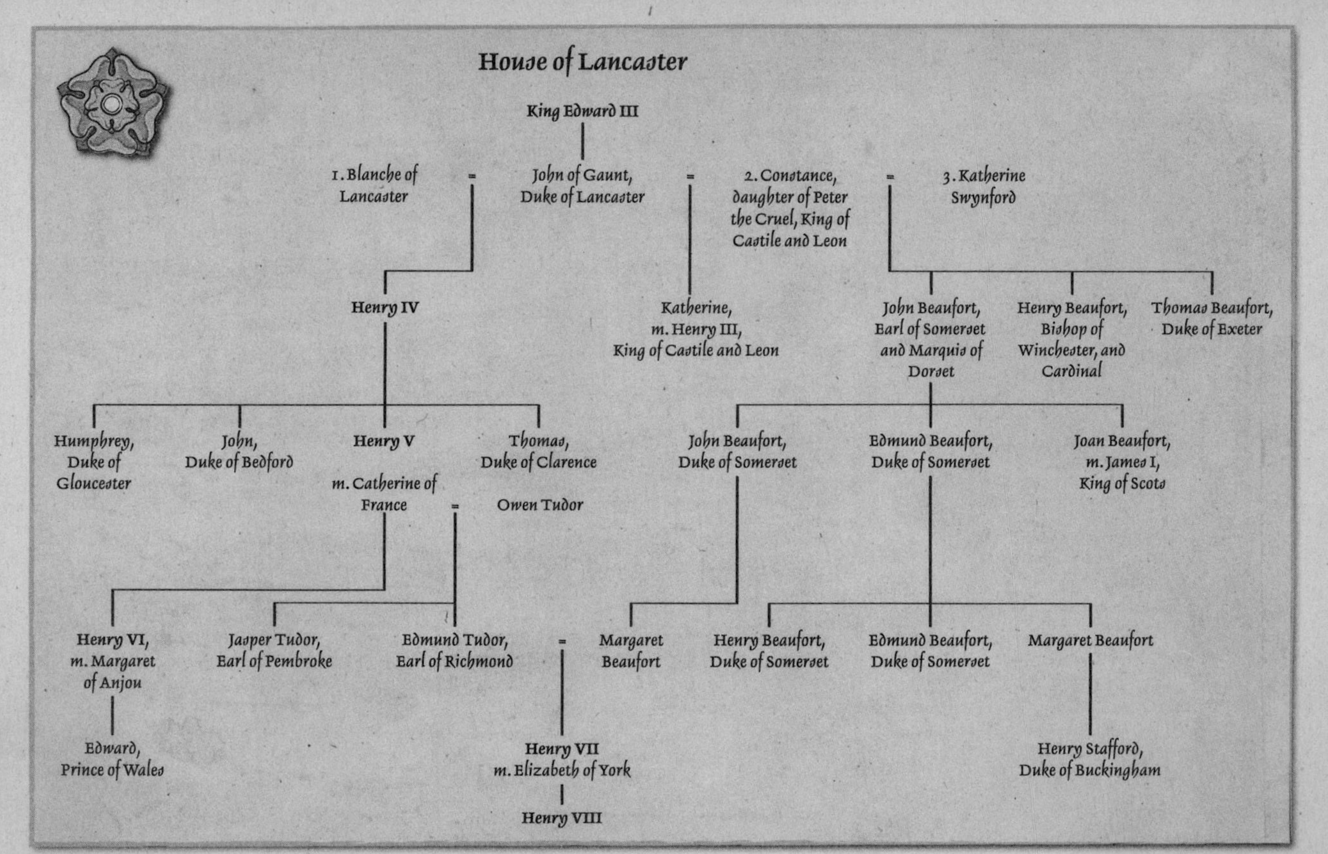
House of Lancaster
King Edward III
1. Blanche of Lancaster
=
John of Gaunt, Duke of Lancaster
=
2. Constance, daughter of Peter the Cruel, King of Castile and Leon
=
3. Katherine Swynford
Henry IV
Katherine, m. Henry III, King of Castile and Leon
John Beaufort, Earl of Somerset and Marquis of Dorset
Henry Beaufort, Bishop of Winchester, and Cardinal
Thomas Beaufort, Duke of Exeter
Humphrey, Duke of Gloucester
John, Duke of Bedford
Henry V
Thomas, Duke of Clarence
m. Catherine of France
=
Owen Tudor
John Beaufort, Duke of Somerset
Edmund Beaufort, Duke of Somerset
Joan Beaufort, m. James I, King of Scots
Henry VI, m. Margaret of Anjou
Jasper Tudor, Earl of Pembroke
Edmund Tudor, Earl of Richmond
=
Margaret Beaufort
Henry Beaufort, Duke of Somerset
Edmund Beaufort, Duke of Somerset
Margaret Beaufort
Edward, Prince of Wales
Henry VII m. Elizabeth of York
Henry VIII
Henry Stafford, Duke of Buckingham

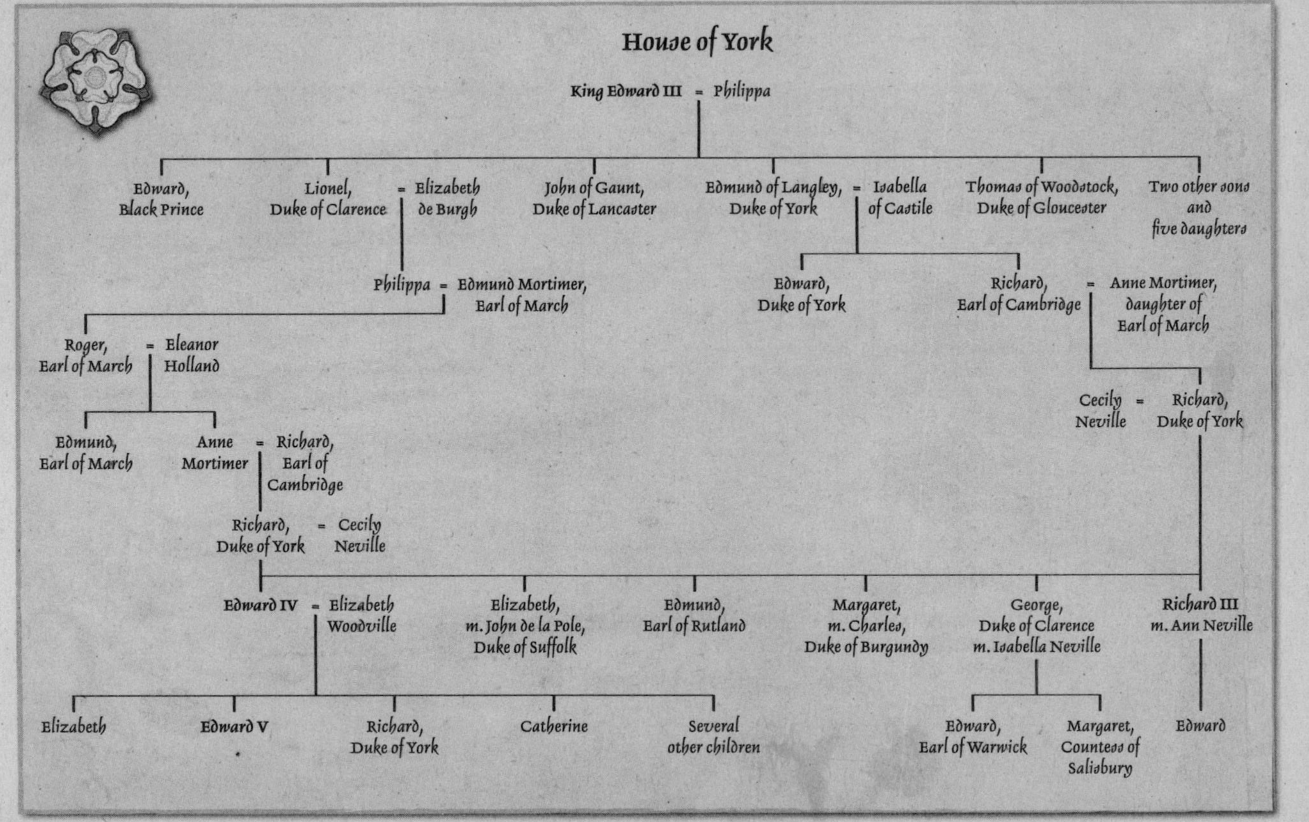
House of York
King Edward III = Philippa
Edward, Black Prince
Lionel, Duke of Clarence
= Elizabeth de Burgh
John of Gaunt, Duke of Lancaster
Edmund of Langley, Duke of York
= Isabella of Castile
Thomas of Woodstock, Duke of Gloucester
Two other sons and five daughters
Philippa = Edmund Mortimer, Earl of March
Edward, Duke of York
Richard, Earl of Cambridge
= Anne Mortimer, daughter of Earl of March
Roger, Earl of March
= Eleanor Holland
Cecily Neville = Richard, Duke of York
Edmund, Earl of March
Anne Mortimer
= Richard, Earl of Cambridge
Richard, Duke of York
= Cecily Neville
Edward IV = Elizabeth Woodville
Elizabeth, m. John de la Pole, Duke of Suffolk
Edmund, Earl of Rutland
Margaret, m. Charles, Duke of Burgundy
George, Duke of Clarence m. Isabella Neville
Richard III m. Ann Neville
Elizabeth
Edward V
Richard, Duke of York
Catherine
Several other children
Edward, Earl of Warwick
Margaret, Countess of Salisbury
Edward

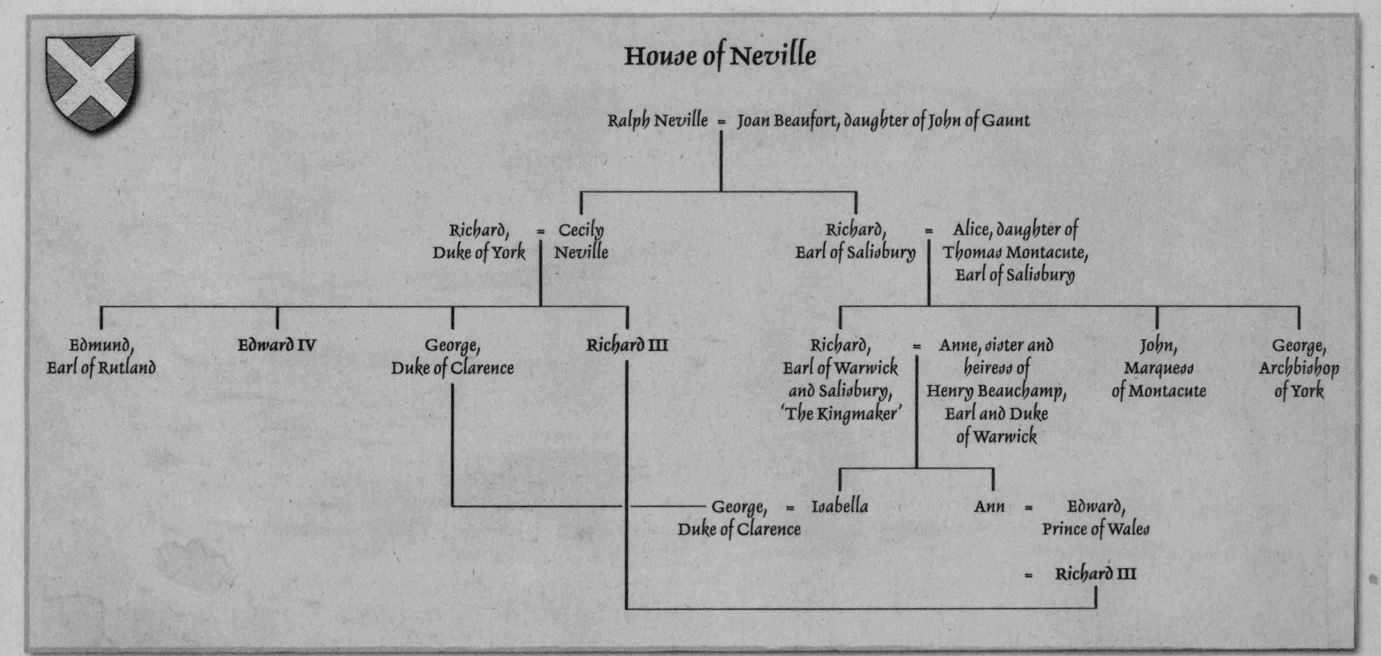
House of Neville
Ralph Neville = Joan Beaufort, daughter of John of Gaunt
Richard, Duke of York = Cecily Neville
Richard, Earl of Salisbury = Alice, daughter of Thomas Montacute, Earl of Salisbury
Edmund, Earl of Rutland
Edward IV
George, Duke of Clarence
Richard III
Richard, Earl of Warwick and Salisbury, 'The Kingmaker' = Anne, sister and heiress of Henry Beauchamp, Earl and Duke of Warwick
John, Marquess of Montacute
George, Archbishop of York
George, Duke of Clarence = Isabella
Ann = Edward, Prince of Wales
= Richard III

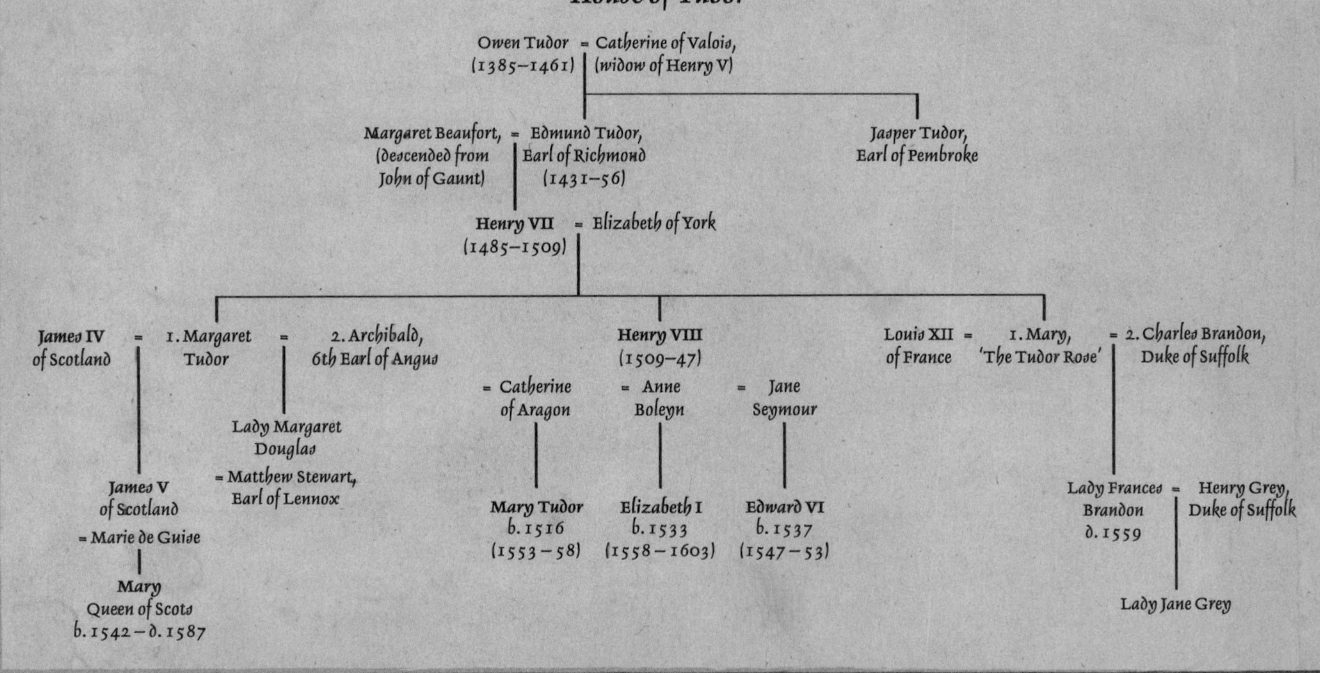
House of Tudor
Owen Tudor (1385–1461) = Catherine of Valois, (widow of Henry V)
Margaret Beaufort, (descended from John of Gaunt) = Edmund Tudor, Earl of Richmond (1431–56)
Jasper Tudor, Earl of Pembroke
Henry VII (1485–1509) = Elizabeth of York
James IV of Scotland = 1. Margaret Tudor = 2. Archibald, 6th Earl of Angus
Henry VIII (1509–47)
Louis XII of France = 1. Mary, 'The Tudor Rose' = 2. Charles Brandon, Duke of Suffolk
= Catherine of Aragon
= Anne Boleyn
= Jane Seymour
Lady Margaret Douglas
= Matthew Stewart, Earl of Lennox
James V of Scotland
= Marie de Guise
Mary Queen of Scots b. 1542 – d. 1587
Mary Tudor b. 1516 (1553 – 58)
Elizabeth I b. 1533 (1558 – 1603)
Edward VI b. 1537 (1547 – 53)
Lady Frances Brandon d. 1559 = Henry Grey, Duke of Suffolk
Lady Jane Grey

List of Characters

- *Queen Margaret/Margaret of Anjou*: Wife of Henry VI, daughter of René of Anjou
- *Lady Margaret Beaufort*: Great-granddaughter of John of Gaunt, mother of Henry Tudor
- *Thomas Bourchier*: Archbishop of Canterbury
- *Derry Brewer*: Spymaster of Henry VI and Queen Margaret
- *Henry Stafford, Duke of Buckingham*: Supporter of Richard, Duke of Gloucester
- *Charles le Téméraire (the Bold), Duke of Burgundy*: Enemy of King Louis XI, and backer of Edward IV
- *George, Duke of Clarence*: Brother of Edward IV and Richard, Duke of Gloucester
- *John Courtenay, Earl of Devon*: Supporter of Queen Margaret and the Prince of Wales at battle of Tewkesbury
- *Edward IV*: King of England, son of Richard Plantagenet, Duke of York
- *Edward V*: Elder son of Edward IV, one of the princes in the Tower
- *Henry Holland, Duke of Exeter*: Supporter of Henry VI and Queen Margaret
- *Richard of Gloucester*: Brother of Edward IV and George, Duke of Clarence, later King Richard III
- *Lord Baron William Hastings*: Lord Chamberlain to Edward IV
- *Henry VI*: King of England, son of Henry V

– *Edward of Lancaster*: Son of Henry VI and Queen Margaret, Prince of Wales
– *Louis XI*: King of France, cousin of Queen Margaret
– *Jacquetta of Luxembourg*: Mother of Elizabeth Woodville
– *John Neville, Baron/Marquess Montagu*: Brother of Earl Warwick
– *John Morton*: Bishop of Ely
– *Ann Neville*: Daughter of Earl Warwick, wife of Edward of Lancaster, then of Richard of Gloucester
– *George Neville*: Archbishop of York, brother of Earl Warwick
– *Isabel Neville*: Daughter of Earl Warwick, wife of George, Duke of Clarence
– *John de Mowbray, Duke of Norfolk*: Supporter of Edward IV and Richard III, formerly supporter of Henry VI
– *Henry Percy, Earl of Northumberland*: Head of Percy family, reluctant supporter of Richard III, formerly a supporter of Henry VI
– *John de Vere, Earl of Oxford*: Supporter of Henry VI and Queen Margaret, and later of Henry Tudor
– *William Herbert, Earl of Pembroke*: Guardian of Henry Tudor in Pembroke Castle
– *Anthony Woodville, Earl Rivers*: Brother-in-law to Edward IV
– *Edmund Beaufort, Duke of Somerset*: Supporter of Queen Margaret and Edward of Lancaster
– *Lord Thomas Stanley*: Royal treasurer and stepfather to Henry Tudor
– *Sir William Stanley*: Brother of Lord Stanley and captain to Lord Hastings; fought with Edward IV, and later Henry Tudor
– *Robert Stillington*: Bishop of Bath and Wells

- *Rhys ap Thomas*: Welsh captain, supporter of Henry Tudor at Battle of Bosworth
- *Edmund Tudor*: Husband of Margaret Beaufort and father of Henry Tudor; died of the plague in 1456
- *Jasper Tudor*: Brother of Edmund Tudor, uncle of Henry Tudor
- *Owen Tudor*: Father of Edmund and Jasper Tudor; killed after Battle of Mortimer's Cross
- *Richard Neville, Earl of Warwick*: Head of the Neville family after the death of the Earl of Salisbury, later known as the Kingmaker; formerly supporter of Edward IV, restored Henry VI to the throne
- *Baron Wenlock*: Supporter of Margaret and the Prince of Wales
- *Elizabeth Woodville*: Wife of Edward IV
- *Earl of Worcester*: Supporter of Edward IV and Constable of England
- *Anne, Bridget, Catherine, Cecily, Mary and Elizabeth of York*: Daughters of Edward IV and Elizabeth Woodville
- *Richard of Shrewsbury, Duke of York*: Younger son of Edward IV, one of the princes in the Tower

The Road to This Place

In the fifteenth century, two great houses of England were bound by blood. The older line, Lancaster, held the throne for three generations – until King Henry VI fell ill. The lesser line, York, snatched up the reins then – and war followed.

There could not be two kings. Edward of York joined with Earl Warwick to settle the issue on the battlefield in 1461. The house of Lancaster was defeated. Queen Margaret fled to France with her son, leaving her husband, Henry, to be held in the Tower of London.

King Edward IV married Elizabeth Woodville, who turned him against Earl Warwick. After endless provocations, Warwick snapped and captured Edward, holding him prisoner. Warwick also allowed the king's brother, George, Duke of Clarence, to marry his daughter.

Though Warwick freed Edward in the end, their friendship never recovered. Edward acted on accusations of treason against Warwick, sending men to arrest him.

At the end of the events in *Bloodline*, Warwick ran. He left England with his heavily pregnant daughter and his son-in-law, George of Clarence. Denied safe harbour, the child was born and died at sea. Warwick and Clarence were made exiles in France, rejected by friends and family.

The French king, Louis XI, saw a rare chance. He gave Warwick and Clarence an army of mercenaries – and the ships to land them. They returned to the coast of England in September 1470. Leaves of gold and red and white had been swept up in a great gale, so that no one knew how they would land. The season of vengeance had begun.

PART ONE

1470

Trust not him that hath once broken faith.

William Shakespeare, *Henry VI, Part Three*

I

The river bent a tail around Pembroke Castle. Winter sun shone red against the walls and the keep rose above the rest, tall as a cathedral, and about as proud.

On the path by the gatehouse, the stranger rested his hands on his saddle pommel, rubbing a thumb along a line of broken stitching. His horse was tired, the animal's head drooping as it found nothing to eat on stones. Compared to the guards staring down, Jasper Tudor was as dark as a shepherd. His hair was thick with road-dust, like matted cloth. It hung to his shoulders, keeping his face in shadow as the sun set and the day began to die around him. Though he was weary, his eyes were never still, watching every movement on the wall. Each time a guard turned his head to the inner yard, or glanced at an officer below, Jasper saw and listened and judged. He knew when news of his presence had summoned the master of the castle. He knew how many steps that man had to climb to reach the outer gate, barred in iron and just the first of a dozen defences against an attack.

Jasper counted under his breath, distracting himself from the anger he felt just at being in that place. He imagined each turn of the stone steps within and his mouth quirked when he saw William Herbert arrive on the crenellations. The young earl looked down at him, strong emotion making him mottled. The new master of Pembroke was just seventeen years old, a red-faced brawler, still reeling from the death of his father. It seemed Earl Herbert did not much like the sight of the dark and wiry man looking up at him. That much was clear from his expression and the way he gripped the stone with his thick hands.

Jasper Tudor had been the Earl of Pembroke once, a dozen years before. It was hard not to bristle when a man half his age looked down upon him in arrogance from his own walls.

Earl William Herbert merely stared for a time, his eyes pinched small as if he had swallowed something that irked him. The younger man had a wide head, not fat but broad, topped by sleek hair cut straight across. Under that gaze, Jasper Tudor inclined his head in greeting. It would have been hard enough to deal with the father, had the man lived.

The older Herbert had not died well, giving no new honours to his family line. He had not lost his life in some valiant action, but had been cut down without thought when Warwick had captured King Edward. That small loss, ignored at the time, had been eclipsed by the greater sin of Warwick laying hands on the king. In Pembroke, it had meant an entire town in mourning.

In the gathering gloom, Jasper Tudor swallowed nervously. Glints of light appeared and vanished in stone slots along the walls, as men in armour shifted their weight. He knew he had gained no advantage by spotting them. No one could outride a bolt.

Clouds drove across the sky, lit from beneath by the last of the sun. Above, the new earl lost patience at last with the silence. For all it cost him a slight advantage, for all his grief and dominance, there were not many seventeen-year-olds who could have matched the stone-like calm of a man at forty.

'*Well?* What do you want here, Master Tudor?' The young earl seemed to find some small pleasure in the lack of a noble title. Jasper Tudor was King Henry's half-brother. He had been raised high by the house of Lancaster, and in return he had fought for them. He had taken the field against the eighteen-year-old Edward of York, the giant still weeping in rage for the death of his father. Jasper repressed a shudder at the memory of that monster in red armour, carmine as the sun on Pembroke walls.

'I give you God's good day and recommend me to you. I have sailed from France to this coast, running ahead of all news. Have you heard yet from London?'

'Does it so stick in that Welsh throat to call me lord?' William Herbert demanded. 'I am the Earl of Pembroke, Master Tudor. If you're at my gate to beg for food or coin, you will be disappointed. Keep your news. Your Lancaster mobs and your ragged, *prisoner* king have no claim on me. And my father gave his life in defence of the *rightful* king of England, Edward of York.' The young man's mouth turned up on one side, twisting his face. 'While you, Tudor, I believe you were *attainted*, losing all honour, titles, property. I should have you struck down at this moment! Pembroke is mine. All that was my father's, is *mine*.'

Jasper nodded as if he had perhaps heard a point worth considering. He saw bluster in the young man, covering weakness. Once more, he wished he could have dealt with the old earl, who had been a man of honour. Yet that was the way of it, when wars began. Good men died and left their sons to follow them, for better or worse. Jasper shook his head, swinging the clotted locks of his hair. He was one of those sons himself, perhaps a lesser man than his father, Owen. Worse, in the years of his exile, Jasper had found no wife nor made sons of his own. If the French king hadn't granted him a stipend as his cousin, Jasper thought, there was a chance he would have starved to death, alone and penniless. Yet he had remained loyal, to King Henry, and to Queen Margaret of Anjou, in all her despair and her fall.

Jasper looked down for a moment, his hopes fading under the earl's scorn. Yet he stood before Pembroke, and that old place had been his. It still rang with an aching familiarity and gave him some strange comfort just from being there, tempting him to reach out and touch the stone. He could not allow himself to be shamed in sight of those walls. He raised his head once more.

There was still one whom he loved within the fortress, as well as any father loved a son, and the real reason for his visit. Jasper Tudor had not come to Pembroke for accusations or vengeance. The tide of men's affairs had called him home from France and he had asked permission of Warwick to take the time for a private errand. As the great fleet braved the open sea, his ship alone had set off into the west.

Jasper looked along the length of the battlements and saw no sign yet of his brother's son, kept for fourteen years as a ward, or a prisoner.

'I used to think Pembroke was a different world from all the busyness in London, all the doings and the trade,' Jasper said, raising his voice to carry. 'Two hard weeks on the road, with a string of horses. It can be done, but it is no easy task. And in the winter, the roads are such a quagmire, it is better to sail round the Cornish coast, though it takes at least as long and is more perilous. For myself, I fear those winter storms that can tear a ship's hull open and drown all those who risk their lives on deep waters, God bless their souls.'

The words flowed from him, making the eyes of the earl grow glassy until the young man shook his head in confusion.

'You will not enter here, Master Tudor,' Earl Herbert snapped, losing the last threads of his patience. 'Play no more of your Welsh games; I will not open my gate to you. Say what you have come to say and then go back to your damp woods and your camps and your poaching of hares. Live like the grubby, starving brigand you are, while I enjoy Pembroke and roast lamb and all the comforts of King Edward's trust.'

Jasper rubbed his jaw with the back of his thumb to keep a flash of anger from showing. He loved Pembroke still, every stone and arch and hall and musty storeroom, filled with wine and grain and preserved haunches of sheep and goats. He had hunted the land all around and Pembroke was home to him in a way that had a greater claim than anywhere else in the world. It had been a dream as a child that he might one day own a fine lord's castle. When it had actually come true, Jasper Tudor had been satisfied. There was no greater dream, not for the son of a soldier.

'Whether you have heard or not, *my lord*, the tide is turned. Earl Warwick has come home with a fleet and an army.' Jasper hesitated, searching for the right words. The young earl watching him had leaned right out on hearing that name, gripping the stones so hard it looked as if he wanted to break a piece off and hurl it at him. Jasper went on slowly, making the words fall far from the gatehouse.

'They will restore Lancaster, my lord. They will lay a hot iron over the wounds, ending York. I speak not to threaten, but to give you the good word so that you may choose a side, perhaps before anyone asks again with a sword in their hands. Now, I have come for my nephew, my lord. For Henry Tudor, son of my brother Edmund and Margaret Beaufort. Is he well? Is he safe within?'

As the Earl of Pembroke opened his mouth to reply, Jasper saw movement along the wall at last, a white face, surrounded by thick black hair. The boy, surely, not yet with a man's growth. Jasper gave no sign he had seen.

'*You* have no claim on him,' William Herbert snapped,

showing his teeth. 'My father paid a thousand pounds to gain a ward. I can see the ragged edge of your cloak, Tudor. I can see the grease and dust on you from here. Can you return that thousand pounds to me?' The young man's sneering grin vanished as Jasper Tudor reached behind him to a parcel of canvas and leather strapped to the small of his back. He pulled it out and shook it to jingle the gold coins within.

'I can,' he said, though there was no triumph in his voice. He could see the scorn in the earl and he knew it would not matter.

'Oh yes? Do you also have . . .' William Herbert's mouth worked as if some thick clot of rage had closed his throat '. . . *the years* spent on his training in that bag of yours? Do you have my father's time? His trust?' The words spilled out faster, his confidence returning. 'It looks too small for all of that, Tudor.'

The young earl's will would prevail, no matter what was said, or who had the better of the exchange. One man could not force the door of Pembroke. Ten thousand could not.

With a sigh, Jasper shoved the pack out of sight once more. At least the French king would not own him once he had returned the loan. He rubbed his forehead as if in tiredness, hiding his eyes from the man thirty feet above him so he could flicker a glance at his nephew. Jasper did not want the boy seen and sent away. If he addressed him directly, he sensed enough spite in William Herbert to make his nephew's life a misery, or even put it in peril. When Jasper spoke again, it was as much for the ears of Henry Tudor as it was to the new earl in Pembroke.

'This is a chance to earn a little goodwill, my lord,' he called up. 'The past is the past, all our fathers gone to tombs. You stand now where once I stood as earl – and Pembroke is yours. The years turn, *my lord*, and we cannot take back a day, or return one *hour* to make a better choice when we had the chance.' He took heart from the earl's silence, feeling that the young man was at least not yelling curses and threats.

'Edward of York is away in the north, my lord, far from his armies and palaces. And now it is too late for him!' Jasper went on proudly, making his voice ring out for all ears. 'Warwick is returned to England! With a vast host raised in Kent and Sussex, aye, and France. Men such as he have even kings bend close to listen when they speak. They are a different breed to you and me, my lord. Look you, Earl Warwick will bring Henry of Lancaster from the Tower to rule again. *There* is your rightful king – and he is my half-brother! Now, I would like to take my nephew to London, my lord. I ask you to pass him into my care, in good faith and in trust of your mercy. I will repay your father's investment in him, though it be all I have.'

While they had spoken, torches and shuttered lamps had appeared along the walls, seeming to snatch away the last of the day's light. Lit by a flickering gold, William Herbert waited only an instant when the entreaty came to an end.

'No,' he called down. 'There's my answer. No, Tudor. You'll have nothing from my hand.' The earl was enjoying his power over the ragged man at his gate. 'Though I might have my men take your coins from you, if that was not one of your lies. Are you not a brigand on my road? How many have you robbed and murdered to gather so much coin, Tudor? You Welsh hedge-lords are all thieves, it's well known.'

'Are you so much a *fool*, boy?' Jasper Tudor roared up at the younger man, making him splutter in outrage. 'I have told you the tide has turned! I came to you with an open hand, with a fair offer. Yet you bleat at me and threaten me still, from behind the safety of your walls? Is that your courage then, in the stone under your hands? If you will not give up my nephew, then open your ears, boy! I will put you under the cold ground if you harm him in any way. Do you understand me? Deep under the earth.' Though he spoke in apparent rage, Jasper Tudor shot a glance to the fourteen-year-old nephew watching him from the battlements further down the wall. He held his nephew's gaze until he sensed William Herbert craning round to see what had caught his attention. The face vanished. Jasper could only hope his message had been understood.

'Serjeant Thomas!' the young Earl of Pembroke called in imperious tones. 'Take half a dozen men and ride down this brigand on my road. He has not shown sufficient respect to a king's earl. Be thou *ungentle* with this Welsh bastard. Spring a little blood from him, then fetch him back to me for punishment.'

Jasper cursed under his breath as great thumps and cracks sounded within the castle gatehouse, along with the rattle of enormous chains. Soldiers raced up to the walls on all sides to check the environs for any force in hiding. Some of them carried crossbows and Jasper Tudor could feel their cold gazes crawling over him. It did not matter that one or two might have been his own men, from years before. They had a new master. He shook his head in anger, wheeling his horse and digging in his heels so that the animal bunched and lunged down the open road. No bolts sprang after him into the darkness. They wanted him alive.

Leaning out as far as he dared between the stones, Henry Tudor had stared at the rider, thin and defiant before the gatehouse of Pembroke, sitting like a beggar on a dark horse and yet daring to challenge the new earl. The black-haired boy had no memory of his uncle and would not have been able to pick him from a crowd if William Herbert hadn't called him Tudor. All he knew was that Uncle Jasper had fought for King Henry, for Lancaster, in towns so distant they were just names.

Henry had drunk in the sight of his blood relative, risking a fall to hear every word, gripping the rough stones he knew so well. He had been born in Pembroke, both he and his mother coming close to death, so they said. He'd heard it was surely a miracle that a woman so tiny had survived at all. Not twenty feet from the gatehouse wall where William Herbert stood, Henry had come into the world, his mother just thirteen years old and half-mad with fear and pain. He had been given to a wet nurse and little Margaret Beaufort had been spirited away to marry again, her only child and dead husband to be forgotten and left behind. When the Yorkists took Pembroke and his uncle Jasper had been hunted as a Lancaster traitor, Henry Tudor had been left utterly alone.

He was convinced it had made him strong, that isolation. No other lad had grown up without a mother, without friends or family, but instead with enemies on all sides to hurt and scorn him. As a result, in his own mind, he had been made about as hard as Pembroke. He had suffered a thousand cruelties from the Herberts, father and son, but he had endured – and he had watched, all the years of his life, for one single moment of weakness or inattention.

There had been shameful times, when he had almost forgotten the hatred and had to nurse and blow upon it to keep it alight. Before the old earl had been killed, there had even been days when Henry had felt more like the man's second son than the mere coin he truly was, to be hoarded and spent at the right time. He'd found himself wanting to earn some word of praise from William, though the older boy never missed a chance to cause him pain. Henry had hated himself for his weaknesses then, and clutched anger to his breast as he slept, curling in on it.

On the road below, he heard his uncle grow stern. The man's stream of words caught at Henry like a barbed line snatching across his throat. '. . . under the cold *ground* if you harm him.' It was the first concern for his well-being that Henry could remember and it shook him. At that instant, as he understood in wonder that a man cared enough to threaten an earl, his uncle Jasper looked directly at him. Henry Tudor froze.

He had not known his uncle had spotted him creeping closer. He was pierced by the gaze and his thoughts shook suddenly, skipping a beat ahead. *Under* the earth. *Deep* under it. Hope soared in Henry's chest and he ducked back inside, away from his uncle's eyes – away too from a Herbert earl who had long taken out his hatred of Lancasters on the weakest end of a distant line. Henry Tudor had taken no sides in the wars, at least beyond the colour of his blood, as red as any Lancaster rose.

The boy ran, clattering along the walkways that rested on beams beneath the battlements. In the flickering torchlight, one of the guards put out a hand to stop him, but Henry knocked it away, making the man swear under his breath. Old Jones, stone-deaf in his right ear. The Tudor boy knew every man and woman in the castle, from those who lived within the walls and tended to the Herbert family, to the hundred or so who came up from town each morning, bringing supplies and carts and their labour.

He leaped down steps, throwing himself against the outer post with all the carelessness of youth so that he thumped hard into the rails but lost no speed. He had raced across the castle grounds a thousand times, building his wind and his agility. It showed then, coupled with a purpose that had him casting off all caution and running like a scalded cat through Pembroke grounds.

In near darkness, he scrambled through a workshop erected on the main yard, raising himself on his arms as he jumped across piles of crates, thick with the briny green smell of the sea. On another day he might have stayed to see the silvery fish or oysters unpacked, but he had a path to follow and a burning need to know that he had not been mistaken. Across the open ground, he could see the setting sun had dropped beyond the walls, casting an odd light as he reached the stone halls around the keep, the massive tower that stretched five storeys above the rest of the castle and could be sealed against an army. Pembroke had been built for defence, though it had one weakness to those who knew it, one secret, kept well hidden.

Henry skidded as he reached the lower feast hall. He saw the earl's constable there, a florid man in earnest conversation with one of the castle factors, both poring over a scroll as if it held the meaning of life and not just some record of slates broken or hundredweights of oak and beech. He slowed to a stiff-legged walk as he crossed the end of the hall furthest from them. Henry could sense the men looking up, or perhaps he imagined it, as they did not call out. Without even a glance back, he reached the door and opened it into the heat of the kitchens beyond.

Pembroke had two dining halls, with the kitchens running beneath the grander of the two. Staff and unimportant guests ate in the first. Henry had spent many evenings chewing bread and meat in near darkness there, begrudged even the cost of a tallow candle. He'd sat alone, while reflected light and laughter spilled from the windows above, the greater hall where the earl entertained his favoured guests. Henry would have risked a beating even to enter that place, but that night he was concerned with the kitchens themselves – and what they concealed.

The maids and serving staff barely looked up as he entered, assuming the skinny boy was bringing back a bowl, though he usually ate off a trencher and took the slab of hard bread away with him to gnaw or to feed to the jackdaws on the towers. Even so, Henry was familiar to them and he could not see the cook, Mary Corrigan, who would have shooed him away with her big red hands and a flapping apron. In the steam from bubbling pots, the air was thick and there was bustle on all sides as the staff dug into piled ingredients and measured them out. The sight made him lick his lips and he realized he had not eaten. Should he wheedle a little food from the cooks? His gaze flickered over a pile of peeled apples, already turning a honey brown. Slabs of cheese bobbed next to them, in a pot of watery whey. How long would it be before he ate again?

As he stood there, with the clatter and smells and sheer hard work of the kitchen going on all around him, he could sense the door on the far side. Set into the stone wall, it was narrower than a man's chest, so that a soldier would have to turn to pass through. An oak plank blocked the doorway, resting on thick iron braces in the mortar. Henry could feel it there as he looked anywhere else but directly at it. He knew every stone of Pembroke, in winter and summer. There was not a storeroom or an attic or a path he had not walked, though none of them had gripped his attention as had that single door. He knew what lay beyond it. He could feel the dampness and the cold already, though his skin was sheened in sweat.

He walked across the kitchen and the staff parted before him like dancers, carrying pots and trays. They would feed six hundred men and some eighty women that evening, from the high table in the great hall and those closest to the young earl right down to the falconers and the priests and, in a later sitting, the guards and the boys who mucked out the stables. Food was a vital part of the compact between a lord and his people, a duty and a burden, half symbol, half payment.

Henry reached the door and lifted the bar with a heave, staggering under its weight as it came free. He spent precious moments steadying the plank against the wall. Breathing hard, he took the key from where it hung, and as he inserted it, he felt a hand on his shoulder. He turned to see Mary Corrigan peering at him. She was no taller than he was himself, but seemed three times his weight in meat and bone.

'And what are you after?' she said, wiping her hands on a thick cloth. Henry could feel himself flushing, though he did not stop working the key until the ancient lock clicked open.

'I'm going down to the river, Mary. To catch an eel, perhaps.'

Her eyes narrowed slightly, but in disdain rather than suspicion.

'If Master Holt or the constable saw you using this old door, they'd skin you, you know that, don't you? Honestly, *boys*! Too lazy for the long way round. Go on with you, then. I'll lock it behind. Be sure you put the keys back on their pegs. And come back to the gatehouse. I won't hear you knocking here, not with all this noise.' To Henry's surprise, the big cook reached out and ruffled his hair with fingers strong enough to bend an iron ladle.

He felt his eyes threaten tears, though he could not remember the last time he had wept, not in all his life. There was a chance he would never set foot in Pembroke again, he realized. What passed for his family were all within the walls of that castle. It was true Mary Corrigan had beaten him three times for stealing, but she had once kissed his cheek and slipped an apple into his hand. It was the only act of kindness he could remember.

He hesitated, but recalled the dark figure of the rider. His uncle had come for him. Henry's resolve hardened and he nodded to her. The door opened with a draught of cold air and he closed it on Mary's bright cheeks and perspiration, hearing the lock click and the woman grunt as she lifted the bar and put it back. Henry steadied himself, feeling the cold seep into him after the thicker air of the kitchen.

The stairs turned immediately, so that no one who came up them would ever have room to brace himself and swing an axe. They dropped away into the cliff under Pembroke, twisting sharply. The first few steps were lit by cracks in the door, but that dim gleam lasted only to the second turn. After that, he was in blackness, thick as damp linen pressed against his face.

No one knew if the cave had been discovered after the castle was built or whether it was the reason the first wooden fort had been raised in that spot, centuries before. Henry had seen chipped flint arrowheads recovered from the cavern floor, formed by hunters from a past too distant to know. Roman coins too had been found, with the faces of dead emperors set into blackened silver. It was an old place and it had delighted Henry when he'd found it first, during a winter of solid rain when every day had been a misery of tutors, bruises and damp.

Some change in the echoes of his steps warned him before he struck the door below. It too was locked, but he felt for the key there and found it on a leather cord. It took all his strength to force the door open after he'd unlocked it, thumping his shoulder against the swollen doorjamb over and over until he fell into a much colder darkness. Panting from exertion and not a little fear, Henry shoved the door closed behind him and held the cold key in his hand, wondering just what to do with it. It didn't seem right to take such a vital thing. He could sense the huge cavern overhead – a different world, though he stood directly under Pembroke. The silence was broken by flutters of pigeons on the high stones, reacting to his presence in their mindless way. He listened harder and heard the river's gentle breath.

The darkness was complete as he stepped out, immediately knocking his shin on the keel of a rowing boat, no doubt dragged into the cave to be repaired. The existence of the cave was not the secret of Pembroke. The secret was the hidden door back in the gloom, that led to the heart of the castle above. Henry cursed and rubbed his leg, feeling the key once again. He hung it on the prow of the boat where it would be found and edged his way past on a floor that was as smooth as a riverbed.

The last barrier to the river was of iron, a gate set into stone walls built over the natural mouth of the cave. Henry collected another key and worked it in the lock until he heard a click. He stepped through and stood outside in the darkness with his back to the river, relocking the gate and tossing the key back beyond reach. He did not do that for William Herbert, with all his scorn and cruelty. He did that for Pembroke – and perhaps for Mary Corrigan. He would not leave Pembroke's secrets to be discovered by others.

He could not go back. Henry heard himself breathing hard before he summoned his will and slowed his heart, forcing calm like cream poured into bubbling soup, so that all became still. The heat was still there, but hidden, or drowned.

He turned to the river then and understood that he had been hearing the muffled sounds of a boat, somewhere close. Though there was no moon and the river was almost as black as the cave, he thought he could still make out some deeper blot, barely twenty feet long. He whistled in its direction, hoping he was not wrong.

Oars plunked and creaked, sounding loud in the night. The boat came gliding across the current and Henry Tudor stared in fear. Smugglers, fishermen, poachers and slavers – there were a number of men with reason to go out on the waters in the dark. Not many of those would take kindly to being hailed by a boy.

'Well done, lad,' came a voice from the darkness. 'And didn't your tutors say you were clever?'

'Uncle?' Henry whispered. He heard the man chuckle and began to scramble down, half falling into the boat until a dark figure grabbed him by both arms and proceeded to crush the air out of him with surprising strength. Henry felt the man's stubble rasp against his cheek and he could smell sweat and green herbs, and the odour of horses driven deep into his uncle's clothes. There were no lamps lit, not with Pembroke's walls looming above. Yet after the blackness of the cave, stars and the moon were enough for Henry to see surprisingly well as he was guided to a thwart to sit.

'Well met, lad,' Jasper Tudor said. 'And I only wish my brother could have lived to see this. Half the guards seeking me in the town, the rest following one of my men with a burning brand, while I am here – and you remembered the cave under Pembroke. Your father would be so proud of you.'

'He would not know me, Uncle,' Henry said, frowning. 'He died before I was born.' He felt himself retreating from the warmth of the man, his tone and his embrace, pulling back in all senses, finding an old comfort in coldness. He inched a fraction clear along the plank, feeling the boat rock. 'Delay no further for me, Uncle. There must be another boat, a larger one. I heard your words to William Herbert. Are we to London?'

Henry did not see the way his uncle Jasper stared, obscurely deflated. They were utter strangers, both becoming aware of it in the same moment. Henry had never known a mother or a father. Waiting in strained silence, he supposed it was not so strange that his uncle might retain some family feeling for his brother's only son. He felt no answering need in himself, only a black chill as deep as the river under them. Yet it felt like strength.

Jasper cleared his throat, shaking off the stillness that had held him.

'To London, yes. Yes, boy! My ship is moored at Tenby and this little bark is far too frail for the open sea. I have horses though, waiting a mile up the river. Can you ride, son?'

'Of course,' Henry said curtly. He'd had the training of a knight, or at least as a squire to William Herbert. It was true he'd had more in the way of cuffs and scorn than proper instruction, but he could stay in a saddle. He could handle a sword.

'Good. Once we are out of sight of the castle, we'll mount up and ride to the coast. Then London, boy! To see your namesake, King Henry. To see Lancaster restored. By God, I'm still taking it in. We are out! To roam like free men, while they search the woods for us.'

The boat moved on the current, the oars employed with little noise. For a long time, the only sounds were from the water and the harsh breath of working men. Jasper shook his head at the continuing silence of the boy. He had expected a chattering jackdaw. Instead, he had rescued a little owl, watchful and still.

2

Warwick's mouth tightened in worry. King Henry stood before the London crowd, looking across the city from the height of the Tower walls. There was a cold wind up there and Warwick repressed a wince at how frail the king had become. Henry of Lancaster had been broken, emptied by the years of his life. Though the king had been dressed that morning in fine embroidered cloth and a thick cloak, Warwick knew the poor fellow was just bones underneath. In fact, the cloak seemed to weigh the king down, so that he was more hunched and bowed than ever. Henry shivered constantly, his hands shaking as if he had an ague or an old man's palsy. When the cloak fell back to his elbow, it revealed no swell of muscle but a forearm of uniform width, just twin flattish bones, sheathed in skin and veins.

Standing by Warwick and the king, Derry Brewer stared down at the heaving crowd. Like the king himself, the spymaster was not the man he had been. He walked with the aid of a stick and peered at the world from just one, gleaming eye. The scars that had replaced the other were hidden by a strip of boiled leather. In turn, that had rubbed away Brewer's hair as it moulded itself to his scalp, so that it creaked and shifted against bare skin. Warwick shuddered to look at the pair of them and Brewer sensed it, turning his head and catching the edge of a younger man's disgust.

'We make a fine sight, don't we, son?' Brewer said softly. 'Me with one eye ruined, one leg that don't work and so many scars I feel like I'm wrapped in cloth, the way they pull. I don't complain though, have you noticed? No, I'm like a rock, me, like St Peter. Perhaps I'll change my name to remind people. Here stands Peter Brewer – and on this rock I will rebuild my kingdom.'

The king's spymaster chuckled sourly to himself.

'And King Harry Sextus here, still about as unmarked as a newborn lamb. No! I recall one. He took a wound up on the hill at St Albans, do you remember that, my lord?'

Warwick nodded slowly, knowing Brewer was prodding at him for old times.

'You do?' Derry said, his voice hardening. 'You *should*, seeing as it was your order – and your archers that made the shot. You were the enemy then, Richard Neville, Earl of bleeding Warwick. I remember you.' He shook his head in irritation, recalling a better year than the one he knew lay ahead, with every day begun in pain.

'Beyond that scratch, I don't believe King Henry has taken another scar, not in all the years I have known him. Is that not strange to think upon? A king wounded only once, but the arrow was yours – and it broke him, I'll tell you now. He was cracked all over like an old jug, woken from his stupor, but weak and frail, barely able to stand in his armour. That arrow of yours was like dropping that jug on to a stone floor.' To Warwick's discomfort, the king's spymaster touched his hand to his missing eye, scratching an itch or rubbing away a shine of tears, it was impossible to tell. Brewer went on in sudden anger, gesturing at the crowd.

'Oh, these cheering people! They make such a bloody noise! Yet they are calling out to an empty man. I tell you, Richard, I would rather have all my scars and one good eye than lose my wits. Eh?'

Warwick nodded in response, wary of the man's bright gaze.

'Perhaps you and King Henry make one man between you,' he said. 'Your wits and his form.'

Derry Brewer blinked at him.

'What's that? You saying I'm not a man? That I'm less than a man?'

'No . . . I meant it lightly, Master Brewer.'

'Oh yes? I'm willing to give you a turn right now, if you think you're more a man than me. I'll knock you *out*, son. I have a few tricks yet.'

'Of course you have,' Warwick said. 'I meant no insult.' He could feel his cheeks growing warm and of course Derry Brewer noticed that as well.

'Don't be afraid, my lord, I wouldn't hurt you. Not now you're on the right side.'

Warwick frowned, then saw the spymaster had a wry expression that revealed his humour. Warwick shook his head.

'Have a care, Master Brewer. This is a serious business.'

The king had made no movement as they'd talked. Henry stood like his own effigy in wax, resembling those sent to shrines in times of illness, or the mannequin of Caesar Mark Antony had once shown to a mob in Rome. When Warwick took the king's hand, it was almost a surprise to find the flesh warm and pliant. He winced as swollen knuckles shifted in his grip, the veins like cords. Henry looked slowly round at the touch, his eyes showing no recognition. There was blankness there, and a trace of sadness. All else had gone.

Slowly, Warwick raised the king's arm with his own, a gesture for all the eyes on them. The crowd roared and stamped below, but Warwick still heard King Henry gasp and felt him tug back, too weak to break the grip. It was pitiful, but Warwick could only maintain the hold, turning the king back and forth as he held his hand high.

'It hurts!' Henry muttered, his head drooping. Warwick

lowered his arm as the man began to sag, sensing it could only get worse. Tower guards stepped past Derry Brewer then, taking the king's weight. Warwick glanced at Henry's hand as he let go. The nails were black with dirt and he shook his head.

'Find gloves for His Majesty!' he called after the guards. There were servants to tend the king at the Palace of Westminster. They would restore and bathe him. Perhaps the royal physicians might even bring a little life back to the man.

Derry Brewer's voice interrupted his thoughts.

'Poor old sod. I look at him now and I wonder if he even knows you've freed him. Or if he's the right . . . foundation stone for this rebellion of yours, if you understand me.'

'I understand you. It is not a matter of right and wrong, Master Brewer. He is the king.'

To his irritation, Brewer laughed out loud.

'The guards have gone, my lord! Those below can't hear us, up here on the wall. Perhaps they believe a king's blood runs a deeper red than theirs, I don't know. But you . . .' Derry shook his head, smiling in wonder. 'You saw Edward of York make himself a king. They say it was your suggestion that pricked him to it. And yet you deny him now. Perhaps *you* are the St Peter here, my lord, claiming you don't know your master, over and over until the old cock crows.'

'King Henry of Lancaster is the king of England, Master Brewer,' Warwick said softly. For the first time in their conversation, Derry saw the man's hand rest on the knife in his belt. He could not feel a true threat from the earl, just an awareness. Nonetheless, Derry shifted his weight and adjusted his grip on his cane. It was weighted in lead and he had surprised a couple of men with it in the years since Towton.

'You can give him any name you like,' Derry replied. 'It

will not mean anything. See that crowd below? All staring up at us in hope of one more glimpse? You want my advice?'

'No,' Warwick said. Derry nodded.

'Good for you, son! My advice is to show the king in a few places. To let them see Henry alive and freed. Then put something in his food that will take him out of the world, so that he sleeps but doesn't wake up. No pain or blood, mind, not for a man who never had the wits to do harm except by his own weakness. Let him go quietly. His son will make a good king. By Christ, that boy is the grandson of the victor at Agincourt. He'll make us all proud.'

Warwick narrowed his eyes, tilting his head as if he was seeing something he could hardly believe.

'You think that is my intention!' he said. 'You can believe that of me? That I would murder the king? For some boy I hardly know?' To Derry's surprise, Warwick laughed suddenly, a harsh sound in the wind that blew at that height. 'Edward of York said something like that to me once, when we went to visit Henry in his cell. He said he wished him forty years of good health, so that there could be no new young king over the water. He *understood*, Master Brewer. Just as I do now. You do not need to prod and poke at me with your suspicions. King Edward turned away from me and I have burned my boats with him. There is no return to that fold. I swear it on Mary, the Mother of God, on my oath and on the lives of my daughters. There now. I have raised an army to overwhelm him, like a cloak thrown over his head. Caesars *fall*, Master Brewer. *That* is what I have learned in my years.'

Derry's one-eyed gaze had not wavered as Warwick spoke, judging and reading the man for the first hint of a lie or a weakness. What he saw eased some of the tension in his shoulders. He reached out slowly so as not to startle the earl, patting him on the arm.

'Good lad,' he said. 'You know, you've done great harm, in your time. With your father and with York. No, let me speak. Just about the only thing you ever did well was fight against Jack Cade's rebels. Remember that? That was a night that still wakes me sometimes in a sweat, I tell you true. Now you have a chance most men *never* get – to undo some part of all the hurt you caused. I just hope you take it by the throat when it comes. God knows there won't be another.' As Warwick stared, Derry Brewer turned away, limping after the king he had followed and protected his whole life. In that moment, Warwick understood that Brewer was the closest thing to a father King Henry had ever known.

Left alone, a glance over the wall reminded Warwick of the stakes. There were thousands of men and women filling the streets around the Tower of London, stretching further as those beyond came in as soon as they heard the news. King Henry had been freed. Lancaster was restored. There had been some fights and scuffles at the start, but those few willing to yell in anger for York had been battered silent, made to run or left to bleed. London was not a soft city, not a place to cross. Warwick knew that well. He needed the dockmen and fishermen, the bakers and smiths, the poachers and the knights and the archers. He needed the mercenary swordsmen he had been given by the king of France, despite the resentment they caused amongst the English. Despite the chests of silver it took to keep them loyal. He needed them all to keep his momentum, or his fate would be as if he fell from a galloping horse: dashed down and broken to pieces on the road north.

The south was Warwick's heartland and always had been. Kent and Sussex of old, Essex and Middlesex too: the ancient kingdoms where Edward of York was still whispered to be a usurper and a traitor. Cornish and Devon men had come to join him as news spread, with entire villages setting out together to restore the rightful king. Warwick had made London a stronghold to give them time to walk or ride to him, knowing he would need every one to defeat King Edward in the field.

The mere thought of facing Edward brought fear – and jarring recollections of Towton to his mind: a Goliath in silver armour, fast and enraged and unstoppable. Yet so fragile as well, so prey to the whims of angels that he could be felled by a snagged foot, or by a single stone flying true. Warwick too had been at Towton. He had seen how easily good men could die and how little sense of right there was to it.

As he stared out over London, Warwick saw the wide south of England in his mind's eye, narrowing with every mile north. He imagined it as the head of a spike he could hammer in, struck from France against the white cliffs, driving an iron point into Edward of York in all his arrogance and youth. It did not matter what had gone before, whatever Derry Brewer thought. Not one night's candles could be unburned, not even if kings and bishops prayed for it. Warwick patted the old stones of the Tower with his gloved hand. If it came to survival, of Edward of York at his mercy, he would not hesitate. Brewer had seen that in him and it was true. Warwick had captured kings before. He saw them as mere men.

He thought perhaps there was not another in England who understood the world so well as he did then. If an earl could create a king, he could not love him too.

Warwick smiled to himself, turning away from the fevered tumult of the crowd below. In that sea of faces, in their yelling and their murmuring, it was easy to think of chickens in a coop, or perhaps the buzzing of hives. Yet they were men and women, once chosen to tend a garden, with foolishness and pride enough to steal the one fruit forbidden to their hand.

Warwick followed the guards down to the waiting coaches. As he did so, his smile twisted, growing bitter. Perhaps there *were* no kings, not without men to follow them. Men dreamed such things from dust – and then forgot that they were dreamers. They put foxes in with chickens and then just laughed and laughed as blood was shed.

As soon as his footmen saw him in the shadow of the Tower gatehouse, they stepped in smartly with lowered staves, pressing the crowd away to let the earl through to his horse. A dozen knights in full armour waited on horseback, watching for the first sign of violence in the heaving mob, ready to charge, glowering around them at anyone who strayed too close. King Edward was loved. God knew it and so did Warwick. For all his excesses and cruelties, that giant in his armour, still only twenty-eight, could turn a crowd to his side with one grand gesture or one call to battle. There would surely be some there who might give their lives for such a master. Warwick's followers were twitchy and nervous, seeing threat in every drunken shout.

On a black gelding, a young man waited with them, blade-slim and hardened over the previous year. George, Duke of Clarence, leaned over his saddle pommel as he idled away the time, resting on his forearms and staring over the heads of the people, as far as he could see beyond. London was clotted with houses, guilds, inns, workshops and storehouses, all crammed in along a river that carried goods to lands most of them would never see. Lenses were ground there, clocks made, glass blown, stone carved, meat sliced and dried. It was a busy place, as a forgotten leg of pork can be busy in the hot sun, giving life to all those within it.

George of Clarence did not look pleased at whatever he saw, though Warwick could not discern whether it was the press of the commons or some internal thorn that pricked at him. Warwick forced a smile as his son-in-law glanced over and straightened.

'They made me think of lions or bears with their roaring, when I was up on the wall,' Warwick said. 'I can hardly imagine what it must have been like down here.'

His daughter's husband began to shrug, then reconsidered, remembering his manners.

'They are loud enough, my lord, and brash, these Londoners. None too clean, either, some of them. I have been offered a dozen different kinds of food for coin and there are beggars and urchins and . . .' He waved a hand, lacking the words to describe the variety all around them.

'Be thankful they are cheering along with us,' Warwick said. Like his guards, he did not enjoy the swell of the crowd, so like the movement of a tide that might snatch a man away into its depths, or rise in a great wave with no awareness for whoever was swept up into it.

'I have seen them roused to rage and hatred, George, as when Lord Scales poured wildfire down upon their heads, not a dozen yards from where we stand today.' Warwick shuddered at the memory of men and women on fire, their screams rising until their lungs drew only flame. Lord Scales had not survived that night. His gaolers had stood aside and let the mob into his cell.

'Did you speak to the king, sir?' George asked carefully. He was not used to the word, not for Henry of Lancaster. Warwick turned away from the festivities and clapped his son-in-law on the shoulder.

'I did,' he lied cheerfully. 'He was mortally weak from his imprisonment, but I told him of your service to me and he agreed. When there is a new Lancaster seal to set to a bill, you will be made second heir to the throne, after his son, Edward of Lancaster.'

George of Clarence was twenty years old and had witnessed the death at sea of his firstborn only months before. He blamed his brother King Edward for that death, with a clean anger that suffused and filled him to the edges, so that it seemed at times that there was room for nothing else. He bowed his head at the news.

'Thank you, sir. You have honoured our agreement.'

'Of course,' Warwick replied. 'My daughter's husband! I need you still, George! Not least for the men you can put in the field. You are the Duke of Clarence. Your brother – well, if he is no longer the king, he is still the Duke of York for now. I will not mistake his threat. Every day we lose here is one more for Edward to raise an army. And I would rather ride out with half the men and catch him unprepared than fight another Towton. God save us all from that.'

Warwick saw his son-in-law's expression grow distant as the younger man imagined meeting his brother once more. There was a depth of hurt and rage there, all focused on the man who had called him a traitor and forced them to run. Warwick's daughter Isabel had given birth in sea spray and lost her daughter to that cold. Warwick saw no forgiveness in George, Duke of Clarence, and for that he was thankful.

'Be patient,' Warwick said, his voice lower. George looked across at him, seeming to understand. Bringing the true and rightful king of Lancaster from his captivity was like a mummer's scene performed for the crowd – a glowing brand to hold above the city and set alight the torches of the mob. Now it was done, they could race north and catch Edward, out of place and out of luck.

Queen Elizabeth of York gasped, pursing her mouth to a small moue and breathing hard, almost whistling as she rushed along the path close by Westminster Abbey. Her daughters scurried alongside, the three girls looking afraid and close to tears, taking their cue from their mother.

The queen's pregnancy was so far advanced that she had to support her swollen womb with a hand and roll her gait, more like a drunken sailor than the wife of King Edward. Her breath was harsh and cold in her throat, but she still used part of it to curse her husband at intervals. The child kicking in her womb would be her sixth. She knew how perilously close she was to giving birth and she puffed as she lurched along, feeling again the differences that told her it would be a boy. Her daughters had all grown in perfect serenity, but when she bore sons, Elizabeth vomited so hard each morning that she had tiny starbursts of blood in her eyes and mottling along her cheeks. She dared to hope for a prince and an heir.

Her mother, Jacquetta, looked back every time she overheard Elizabeth hiss an angry word, tutting and frowning at her in reproof. Thin-haired and pale at fifty-five, she had outlived two husbands and borne fourteen children, but in the process lost neither the manners nor the accent of her childhood in the duchy of Luxembourg. Elizabeth rolled her eyes in exasperation, biting her tongue.

'We are nearly there, my pigeon,' her mother said. 'Just another hundred yards, no more. We will be safe, then, until your husband comes for us.'

Elizabeth had no breath to reply. She looked ahead to the squat building of grey stone built in the grounds of the Abbey. Sanctuary. It frightened her, looking like a fortress or even a prison, despite the ivy that covered the walls. She had hardly noticed its existence before, but it had suddenly become her only chance for safety.

She had kept her wits as Warwick arrived in the capital with an army of brigands and foreign soldiers. Without fuss or fanfare, Elizabeth had summoned her barge and brought her children and her mother to the river's edge, taking to the water to be rowed upstream, just as Warwick entered the Tower to free King Henry. It made her heart thump painfully to think of how close it had been – and what a prize Warwick would have made of her. Yet she had not panicked and, as a result, she had reached the only place they dared not come.

The little fortress had not been built to give hope, but only the barest comfort in the direst need. Yet the protection of the Church was what Elizabeth desperately required, with a child so close to being born and her fool of a husband out of place and unable to defend her. Elizabeth hissed a longer breath at that thought, pausing to rest her hands on her knees and just gasp, feeling the heat build in her face. A drop of sweat ran along her jaw and darkened the stone of the path. She could only stare at it.

'We are almost there now,' her mother cooed to her. 'Just a little further, *ma cocotte*, my little hen. See, there is a young brother waiting at the door. Come, dear. For your father's memory.'

The monk's eyes widened as he took in the sight of the queen, her mother and three young princesses in little dresses, all panting as if they had run a mile. His gaze drifted over the great bulge of Elizabeth's womb and he blushed and looked at his feet, radiating warmth.

'I claim sanctuary,' Elizabeth said formally, between breaths, 'for myself, my mother and my daughters. Grant us entrance.'

'My lady, I must summon my master, from where he prays in the Abbey. Please remain here while I run to him.'

'*Non!*' Elizabeth's mother said forcefully, poking him in the chest. 'You are the brother of the door. Write our names in your book, allow us to enter! After that you may fetch whomsoever you desire. *Now, monsieur!*'

Elizabeth closed her eyes, feeling dizzy and relieved that she could let her mother's temper handle the details. She leaned against the doorpost as the young monk stammered and acquiesced, bringing out a large leather tome with ink and a quill. Handing them to Jacquetta, he scurried back in for a desk.

Elizabeth looked up, her senses sharpening at a shout from the river. It could have been a boatman hailing the shore. Or it could have been pursuers, tracking her from her rooms that morning. Perhaps they had not expected a queen of England to move so quickly, without servants or bags. She was ahead of them and so close to safety she thought she might weep or faint.

'Mother, they come,' she said. Her mother dropped the book to the ground and half tore pages as she flicked through the vellum sheets, the record of centuries. When she found a blank page, the old woman dipped a quill and scattered droplets of black in her haste as she scrawled the names and titles of their small party of five. As she wrote, the monk came out with a writing desk on a pedestal, struggling under the weight of cast iron and oak. He stared nonplussed at the small woman sitting like a child on the grass to write, then put the table down and accepted the book from her.

Elizabeth heard another shout and looked up to see a group of running men, all in mail and bearing swords on their hips.

'Sanctuary has been granted now, yes?' she demanded of the monk without taking her eyes off the approaching men.

'As long as you remain on consecrated ground, my lady, yes, from now until the end of time. No man may enter here, from this moment.' He spoke the last in full awareness that his voice could be heard by the group who had slowed and fanned out around them. Elizabeth ushered her daughters and mother inside the open door before she looked back from the gloomy interior. The young monk showed surprising courage, she thought, as he continued to speak. His faith made him brave, perhaps.

'Any man who breaches holy sanctuary will be made criminal and excommunicated from the Church, never to take the Sacred Host, or marry, or be buried in a churchyard, but instead to suffer alive and in hell for all eternity, damned in this world and set afire in the next.'

The threats were all for the men who glared through the doorway at Elizabeth. When she was certain they would not dare to follow, only then, she turned and left, vanishing into the gloom. The pangs of birth began before she had gone a dozen yards and she had to stifle a cry before they heard.

'I will not forgive Edward for this,' Elizabeth hissed as her mother took her arm and tried to support some part of her weight. 'Where is he, the cursed fool?'

'Shh, my hen. Your husband will be doing all he can against these armies, you know it. Such a fine man! You are safe now; that is what matters.'

Her mother had been resting a palm on the bulge of Elizabeth's womb as they walked deeper into the fortress of Sanctuary. With a gasp, she pulled it back as if she had been stung.

'Is the child . . . ?'

'Coming? Yes, I think so. It was the running, wrenching at him.'

To Elizabeth's surprise, her mother chuckled.

'Your big husband *deserves* a son. I pray it is a boy. Now, I will send that monk for the Abbot. We will need a midwife and a private room for the child to be born.'

‘I am afraid,’ Elizabeth said, her voice breaking.

‘Why? Have I not had fourteen children born alive? I know as much as any midwife, my pigeon.’

‘It is the strangeness of this place. It is so cold and dark.’

They had reached a door and Jacquetta guided her daughter through it, not caring what they would find as long as there was more light than in the corridor. The noise of Elizabeth’s daughters grew as they entered a wood-walled study, comfortable and smelling of polish, tallow and sweat.

‘This will do, I think,’ Jacquetta said. ‘And this place is not so strange. Remember it is consecrated ground, my love. To be born in Sanctuary must be a very great blessing.’ Elizabeth gasped as another tightening came, giving herself over to her mother’s care.

3

With bustling market crowds on either side, Jasper Tudor jumped down from his horse and walked away without looking back. A red-faced butcher shouted that he couldn't just leave his horse in the middle of the bloody road, but was ignored.

'Follow me, lad,' Jasper called over his shoulder. 'Quick now.' Henry tossed his reins to the butcher, seeing the man's small eyes swim with confusion and bad temper.

'Oy! You can't . . . Hey!' Henry dismounted quickly, determined not to lose his uncle in the crowds. Jasper was already getting ahead, his long-limbed stride and grim expression parting the early-morning traders of Tenby. They were everywhere as the sun rose, carrying trays of hot bread or baskets of fish brought in from the first catch of the day. They seemed to sense Jasper would go through or over them if they didn't move sharply.

Henry heard new shouts behind him, different to the traders' cries, rising in excitement as if hunters had him in sight. He ducked his head and hunched his shoulders, making himself small. He had assumed they were safe in the crowds. Cobbles were no help to trackers, after all. He felt his stomach twist in fear when he looked back and saw the bobbing heads of men in mail with swords drawn. Cries of outrage and a clatter of falling stalls seemed close on his heels. Henry imagined he could feel the first hand clapping him on the shoulder and bringing him to a halt.

There was still a very good chance they would both be killed, he forced himself to admit, just as he had begun to feel they would escape. With his life in peril, there was no room for wishes and fantasies. He could not allow that form of weakness, that had poor men dreaming of justice even as they walked up the steps to the scaffold, even as the rope rasped against their necks. He would not be such a fool. Those chasing them were brutal, remorseless men. He knew they would rather go back to the earl with a broken body than empty-handed, a thousand times over.

Panting, Henry pressed on. His uncle Jasper had no protection in the law for his past estate. As a common man, Jasper could be arrested and put to torture by any king's officer. It was true a judge and jury would eventually be called to hear his accusers, but with Earl Herbert to speak against him, there was only one possible outcome.

It was far more likely that his uncle would be cut down in the pursuit or take an iron bolt in the back. Henry jogged along after the man, a stranger in all but their shared name, weighing the odds of being killed as his companion. There would be chances he could take, he thought, before the end came. There would surely be a moment when he could just step aside and melt into the crowd, or even to surrender to one of the guards, who would know him by sight. To his surprise, Henry found himself struck by discomfort at the thought. Yet he would not choose death for a man he barely knew, not if there was a chance to live and plan again.

Henry kept his eyes on his uncle as they wove through the crowd, passing close enough to an apprentice carrying a pig carcass to make the man stagger. As the butcher's boy turned to shake his fist, Henry slipped around his back, amusing himself by slapping the pig loudly on its haunch. The apprentice began to turn the other way in rising indignation, but Henry was past, barely in time to see his uncle vanish into the gloom of an apothecary shop.

Henry hesitated as he reached the door, looking back along the busy street. The guards were still there, not far behind. They seemed determined to continue the chase and he thought he could hear them shouting. He felt as if he could lead them a merry dance all day, but he had no special desire to be run to exhaustion. The harbour was a few hundred yards away, behind the cliffs and the row of shops at their foot. The apothecary was surely just a rathole, with no way out. The guards would find them. Henry took a deep breath, calming himself. Perhaps it was time to surrender to Earl Herbert's men. He'd take a beating, but he'd survived those before.

His thoughts were interrupted as a wiry arm reached out from the shop door and snagged his collar, yanking him in. Henry grunted, his hand dropping to his belt dagger until he felt fingers tighten over his and he looked up at his uncle.

'Can't have you standing out there like a signpost, can we, lad?' Jasper said. He was panting and flushed, but he smiled on one side of his mouth and his eyes were bright with amusement. 'Come on.'

With his uncle's hand on his arm, Henry stumbled across the wooden floor of the shop, between rows of glass jars and vials on either side. The shelves were so crammed with goods that there was barely an aisle and his uncle had to turn and sidestep to reach the counter. The place smelled strongly of vinegar and something else at least as bitter. Henry held his nose in his fist as a sneeze built, still half trying to listen for their pursuers. He looked up when his uncle spoke to the owner.

'Master Ambrose? I give you good day and God's blessings. Do you remember me? Do you know my name?'

'I believe I do, my lord,' the apothecary replied, not looking particularly happy about it. The little man was completely bald, his scalp a pale and freckled white from all the years spent in the sunless shop. He looked a little like one of the strange fish peering out of the glass-stoppered jugs on the high shelves. When he smiled, Henry saw he had very short teeth, worn to nubs that barely cleared the gums.

'This is my nephew, Ambrose, not much older than I was when I was last in this shop of yours.'

Henry and the old man exchanged wary glances. The action was enough to bring the apothecary's courage to the surface.

'The . . . new earl is said to be a vengeful young pup, my lord,' the old man said, sucking at something in his mouth so that his entire face twisted. 'If I am accused of sheltering an outlaw, my life, my shop, everything I own will be forfeit. I am sorry, my lord. I knew your father well and I know he would want me to do right by his boy, but . . .'

Jasper lost patience with the slow speech.

'Master Ambrose, I ask no favour of you – except that you turn the other way as we use your entrance to the tunnels.'

The pale brow wrinkled in consternation.

'That old door has been boarded up nigh twenty year,' he said, rubbing a hand over his face where sweat had begun to shine.

'Even so. There are men following me, Master Ambrose. They will have the harbour roads well guarded. This is my way past them all. I have a ship waiting. You will not hear from me again, unless it is to reward you for your sealed lips. Now, please. Step out of my way.'

The old man shuffled to one side and bowed slightly as Jasper flipped up the hinged countertop and rushed through with Henry a step behind.

'Tend your shop, Master Ambrose. I was not here.'

Jasper pushed through rows of sacks and wooden crates

ready to be opened. He snatched up a bit of strap iron used as a lever, spinning it in his hand as he walked.

The shop went back a surprising distance. Above, the plastered ceiling became rough stone as if it had been made by burrowing into the cliffs. Henry nodded to himself as he went. He'd heard tell of smugglers using tunnels in Tenby. The old man had certainly not been surprised by the demand.

Jasper reached a wall of old boards blocking their way. Both he and his nephew looked up and froze as they heard loud voices back in the shop, rising into a question.

They were out of time. Jasper jammed the strap iron into a crack and heaved, breaking the boards away from their nails. He pulled the gap open with his free hand and the wood fell into pieces, releasing a cloud of dust and a breath of cool air tinged with green damp.

The tunnel beyond led into blackness, covered in mould and slippery to the touch. Jasper didn't hesitate, plunging into the dark. Henry had time to hear someone call 'There! At the back!' before he was off, breathing so fast he found he was making himself dizzy. It was not time to give up yet, not with an escape beckoning before him.

His uncle raced in, straight and blind for a hundred yards, two, three, as if he knew for certain that there would be no sudden turn or block to knock them cold. Henry had enough of a task just keeping him in sight, though his terror of being left behind gave wings to his feet. It was still hard to keep up. Jasper Tudor was running for his life and he would not be caught for lack of trying.

When the first turn came at last, it was upon them so suddenly that Jasper crashed sideways into rough stone, driving the air out of him with a cry of pain. Henry heard him hiss instructions to himself, then they were off again, into a dark so complete that he could not see his own outstretched hands dipping and swinging in front of him.

Jasper slowed as he counted, his fingers trailing along the wall until they found a gap. The sounds of their pursuers had dwindled and as they turned right once more, the silence of the deep earth seemed to swell upon them. Henry found himself relaxing without distractions. It was a cool, peaceful place that smelled of stone and clay – a place of no life, of no sound, perhaps a place of death, but calm even so. He smiled in the privacy of blackness, realizing he was enjoying himself. His uncle was heaving for each breath by then, but he kept moving, still muttering numbers until Henry became aware of the faintest lines of grey piercing the blackness. There was a light ahead, growing as Jasper broke into a run once again. A tiny door lay before them, its planking cracked and grown all about by ferns and brambles. There was a bar across and Jasper shoved it up and wrenched the door open without hesitating.

The sunlight blinded them both. If there had been armed men waiting for them at that moment, they would have been taken as easily as children. Yet there was no one and Henry gaped at the sight of a shingle beach. The door had been placed at the back of a cleft deep in the harbour cliffs, hidden from any passing eye. Out on the deep water, half a dozen ships rocked at anchor. Gulls called overhead as Henry and his uncle crept to the outer edge and peered along the docks.

There were guards there: four, in the livery of the Herbert family. They were alert enough and bore weapons, but they were facing into the town along the road. Henry felt Jasper's gaze and looked up into his uncle's eyes, seeing amusement and relief.

'You see the boat there?' Jasper said. 'With the stag pennant? That's mine. She'll take us to that glorious ship waiting for us, the one with the low waist. Understand?' He waited until his nephew nodded and clapped him on the shoulder. 'Now, lad, you might have seen two of those guards have crossbows. It isn't enough to just run for it, or they'll walk over and put a bolt in our backs as the oarsmen get going. We'll have to take it slowly, to stroll, maybe one at a time. All right?'

'Why a stag?' Henry asked. He saw his uncle frown in surprise, glancing out once again at the guards waiting just two hundred yards away.

'A hart, lad. I was born in Hertfordshire. So was my brother. Now go on.' He gave his nephew a push to send him out, but Henry resisted, looking stubborn.

'A hart?'

'The county crest! Perhaps a small joke as well, as I have been hunted my whole life. And I am hunted now, in case you had forgotten.' He went to push Henry out again.

'*Wait*,' Henry snapped, jerking away. 'My mother was English. If my father was born in England, how can I be Welsh?'

His uncle's expression grew less stern. For all the madness of it, with soldiers hunting behind them and watching for them on the quays, he chuckled. His brother's son was in earnest, so he answered.

'You don't know this? What does it matter where we are born? You are what you are made – and you are the blood that made you. Where you are born is just . . . for taxes. "Tewdyr" is a Welsh line, son.' Jasper pronounced their name with a heavy emphasis, making it sound odd to Henry's ear. 'It was my father's name. Your ancestors stood with Glendower when he fought the white dragon banners of the English. I honour him for that, though they broke him. They have ever been a hard race. And if birth matters at all, you were born in Pembroke Castle!' He saw the boy looked troubled still and clapped him on the shoulder.

'Look, you have the same blood that runs in my veins – a

little French, some English and some of the finest Welsh ever shed in a good cause. Have you tasted brandy or grain liquor yet?' Henry shook his head in confusion. 'Ah, then I will not talk to you about the fine results to be had from blends. Just remember this: men who carried your blood raised the flag of King Cadwallader, the red dragon, the *Ddraig Goch*. Red like the rose of Lancaster, is that not a fine, poetic thing? It matters, lad. It matters that you do not shame all the men who carried your name and your blood who went before and wait for us both. When we see them, I do not want you to be ashamed.' Henry was astonished to see Jasper's eyes grow bright with the sheen of tears. 'I wish you could have known my father, lad. And there is you, the fine, brave boy – and the last of his line. Be proud of that. Understand? Now, it is time, whether you are ready or not.' His uncle peered out once more to where the sun sparkled on the sand and shingle, glittering on a blue sea. The soldiers had moved a little further along, standing perhaps three hundred yards from where they watched. Jasper smiled.

'Henry, my brother was not a stupid man. He could beat me at chess without even seeming to try. So when I tell his only son to run for the boat, his son will run, is that clear? His son, his fine Tudor boy, will not discuss the order. He will *go*, like the fires of hell are after him – which they will be.'

'You said I should walk,' Henry replied.

'I have changed my mind. If you walk, I think you will start arguing again. I don't think I can bear it.' His eyes sparkled, but there was no answering humour in the frowning young man studying him.

'You should go first. You are tired. If we are seen, you'll be too slow.'

'Thank you for your concern,' Jasper began. Henry shook his head firmly.

'It is not concern. I do not know if your men in the boat will take me without you. You should go first.'

Jasper looked at him in astonishment, his head moving left and right as if he could not believe what he was hearing. In the end he clamped his mouth into a thin line.

'Just go, lad. Now. *Run*, or by God I'll kill you myself.' With an effort, he shoved Henry out into the sunlight and they were off. It did Jasper's temper no good to see how quickly the boy opened a gap between them, going like a hare heading for gorse. Jasper dared not look back at the guards along the quayside. One glance at the noise of running steps was all it would take. There. A shout behind him.

'Cast off!' he shouted ahead to his men. He saw the first mate sawing through a tarred rope holding them to an iron stanchion, the boat almost pitching over as the small crew of six men raced to set the oars. The ship's cutter was narrow in the beam, built for speed.

Ten paces ahead, Jasper saw Henry leap, clearing his own body length in the air before waiting hands caught him in a great tangle. He'd been lucky not to smash straight through the ribs of the boat and sink them all, Jasper thought, his mind working in fear and manic exhilaration. His breath was rasping and his legs were clumsy and slow. He could sense the clatter of boots on stone at his back and he expected a bolt at any moment. When he reached the dock edge, Jasper followed his nephew's example, throwing himself headlong at the boat. He could not swim and it seemed an age in the air.

The rail struck Jasper a cruel blow under the ribs. His legs trailed in choppy cold water as his men cheered and pulled at him. They could not row with his weight hanging over the side. Jasper rolled in against the inner planking, panting and laughing in reaction as he looked up at white clouds scudding overhead.

'Row! And keep your heads down!' he shouted. As he did, he heard the dull clack of crossbows and one of the French rowers gave a sharp cry, clutching at his chest. That oar fell out of time and fouled the next. Jasper felt the boat turn and swore, knowing that they would present a perfect target to the soldiers on the quayside as the bows swung round.

He heaved himself up as his nephew grabbed the dying man and put him over the side, taking the loose oar. Henry settled himself with quick, neat movements and an expression of utter calm, dipping the oar with the others.

The sailor behind shouted in shock and fury, though Jasper noted the man did not stop rowing. They had been friends, clearly. The French sailor seemed caught between outrage and weeping as he heaved with the others, all the while cursing Henry Tudor.

The boat's swinging prow lurched back round and Jasper saw a bolt streak into the water in a bright trail of bubbles, missing them completely. The rowers knew very well the agony and fevers that would await them if they were hit. They bent their wooden oars in huge sweeps, their faces swollen purple as they surged away from the docks.

Jasper Tudor lay wearily back once more, propped on an elbow and a thwart, craning his neck to look ahead to his ship, as she grew before them. *Pembroke* had been named in his honour. Crewed and paid for by the king of France as she was, he had grown fond of her. She was ninety feet and six inches prow to stern, twenty and four in the beam, with a great triangle sail and rowing benches for when there was no wind. The Flemish-built galley was both sleek and fast and he knew nothing on the Welsh coast could catch them.

'Isn't she fine?' Jasper said to Henry, still leaning into his rowing. A part of the older Tudor remained aware of the sullen rage in the sailor staring at Henry's back. He had not come so far and risked so much to lose his nephew to a feud or a stabbing. With a sigh, Jasper fingered a knife in his pocket, a sharp little thing barely longer than his thumb.

In his position at an oar, Henry Tudor was able to look back at the coast as it dwindled away. The young earl's guards were tiny, lonely figures on the docks, still staring and perhaps considering their own futures now that the Tudors had gone.

As Jasper watched, Henry smiled to himself, taking a huge breath to fill his narrow chest. The lad was tiring visibly, but his uncle sensed he wanted to finish the task and he did not interrupt it. As they drew close to *Pembroke*'s hull, the rowers shipped oars together and grappled ropes sent flying down to them. The boat was lashed on, as steady as it would ever be. Jasper beckoned to his nephew and saw the sailor rising behind at the same moment, his face ugly with passion. As the Frenchman reached out, Jasper knocked him off balance with his shoulder, just as the man had intended for the lad. The sailor flailed and went into the sea with a great splash.

'The rest of you go aboard,' Jasper growled. 'And look after this boy, my nephew, who has the blood of kings in him. Keep him safe or I'll see you swing.'

They climbed with ease, barefoot and strong. He noted how they took care to show Henry where to place his hands on the coarse ropes, though the bristles stung his softer skin. Jasper looked over the side and was surprised to see the French sailor there, just paddling away without panic. Not many of his men could swim, but those who had grown up on the coasts sometimes learned to float and dive when they were very young.

There was no longer any anger on the sailor's face. He knew very well who had pushed him in and his temper had been cooled by the sea.

'Milord, I am sorry. I stumbled and I will not trouble you again.'

Jasper realized the man thought he was at fault, as one who had knocked against the captain of the ship, of all people. Not that it mattered what the man thought. For an instant, Jasper considered letting him strike out for the shore, but the earl's guards were still there. The sailor knew their home port, their strengths and supporters. Jasper Tudor put out an arm to help the man climb back into the boat. As the fellow took hold, Jasper reached down with his little knife, catching him in a long slice under his chin. The water bloomed red around him and the sailor fell back and under with an expression of astonishment and betrayal.

Jasper turned away as quickly as he could, tying the blade cord on to his belt once more. He went fast up the ropes, skinning his knuckles on the rough planks but feeling the pleasure of a sea breeze and success. He had gone to rescue his only living blood relative. All the men of Pembroke, all the earl's servants and guards and hunters and soldiers had not been able to stop him. He felt the weight of the French king's gold at his back and patted it. It seemed a shame to just meekly hand it over once again, with London still ahead. A man could make his fortune in London, with a good stake to get him started.

'Raise sail and bear east for Bristol. I command this vessel in the name of King Henry Sextus of England, House of Lancaster.' There were English and Welsh among the crew. They cheered his words. The Bretons and Flemish sailors just shrugged and got on with raising the anchor from where it dragged over the seabed far below.

4

Dressed in black, Richard, Duke of Gloucester, settled himself on the top step of the stairs to the inn landing, his chin held in his palm, above a propped elbow. The hose he wore contained a padded section over each buttock. It had been made for hard riding, but it also served to keep his backside clear of splinters. The doublet jacket was comfortable enough, cut deceptively wide to allow a swordsman to move freely. At intervals, he worked his jaw against the high collar, rubbing the dark-blond bristles against the linen weave. He would have to shave again soon, though the experience left his skin raw as a plucked goose.

His back was hurting. He shifted uncomfortably to ease it, from right to left, increasingly bored and irritated. On a normal evening, he imagined the tavern talk and laughter would have drowned the squeals and rhythmic thumping coming from the rooms above. Yet with King Edward's guards glowering at anyone who moved or spoke, most of the regular drinkers had slipped away. The bloody-minded few who remained were determined not to notice anything. They emptied tankards of ale at a steady rate, keeping their gaze on the rush-covered floor.

The noises above built to an extraordinary crescendo, every note as clear through the thin walls as if they stood in the bedroom with the king. The tavern girls had not been particularly striking, Richard recalled, despite the rumour that had brought the royal hunt to their door. Still, they showed enthusiasm enough when they saw who would take them upstairs. Edward was known to be generous, if he liked a whore and felt he was liked in return. The results were to be heard. Richard wondered if his brother was strangling one of them, by the noise she made. Part of him wished he would, just to keep her from screaming like a vixen in heat.

It was an unworthy thought and Richard sighed to himself. His brother brought out the worst in him sometimes, though the big clod could change his mood with just a smile or a word. Both men and women went in awe of his brother. When Richard stood close by Edward's side, eclipsed and forgotten, he was free to observe their wide eyes and trembling hands. There was no shame in bending a knee, he thought, especially to a king anointed by God. It sometimes seemed to Richard that all men were made to kneel, that all they really desired was a shepherd who would keep them safe and take his cudgel to the wolves that threatened them. In exchange, Edward could have their daughters for his sport and they would not complain.

Richard shook his head, rolling his neck until it cracked and feeling the bunched strength of his shoulders. When he had been a boy, he had suffered terribly with a twisted spine. His father's remedy had been for him to build such a pack of muscle and sinew that he could throw a blacksmith's anvil across a yard. The pain had not gone, nor eased, so that he lived each day with spikes of it running along his flesh and into the bones themselves. Yet he had grown as strong as his father wanted. Just weeks from his eighteenth birthday, there were few of Edward's guards who relished a bout with Richard any longer. Slim-waisted and fast, he was a thinking warrior, always looking for the place to put the blade. None of his bouts lasted long and he knew he frightened older men who felt the touch of winter in their limbs. His spring was still ahead.

Richard let himself slump further. If Edward had wanted, the two sons of York could have led the English and Welsh on a great crusade against the blasphemous Mahometans, or against France, or, by God, to the ends of the earth. The tragedy was that his brother preferred to ignore and to waste all he had gained. Edward was only truly happy in the deep wood or the wild moors, with his dogs and falcons and trusted men all about him.

Standing in the shadow of a king was not quite the joyful experience Richard had imagined when he had been a boy and a ward of Earl Warwick. His brother then had been in real peril, beset on all sides by Lancaster enemies. Only Edward's strong right arm, only his faith and his honour had brought him through, though tens of thousands lay where they had fallen, gone to bones and rust and shallow graves in Towton Field.

Richard sank a fraction deeper into the cup of his hands, trying to ignore the shameless gasping a dozen feet behind him. The struggle to raise the crown and keep it seemed a nobler time, without a doubt. Before Warwick of all people had turned on them, making a traitor of Richard's own brother, George of Clarence, kidnapping King Edward himself and holding him as a prisoner. Warwick had held back from royal murder, which was about all the good they could say of him. Up to that last blush, he had committed all the forms of treason named in law.

A peculiar knocking began to sound, echoing in the corridor at the top of the steps. The young duke raised his head to listen, then raised his eyes to the heavens above. He was not being summoned. His brother had left some part of his armour on and was denting the wall with complete abandon. Richard did not smile as he'd used to. There had been too many nights, no, too many months of drunken tourney bouts, of fighting, wenching and huge feasts thrown down the open maw that was the king of England. Though Edward had not yet seen his thirtieth year, he had become too tight in his old armour and perforce paid fortunes for new sets with room to breathe.

Richard himself remained lean, his waist and back like seamed saddle-leather. When he remarked on the difference between them to his brother, Edward would only grin and pat his stomach and tell him a man needed a little meat. It was infuriating. He did not know whether it was that the rewards of the world had come too easily, or that Edward simply lacked the wit to appreciate and earn his luck. No man for a hundred miles would have begrudged the king a few local girls, nor the huge number of wineskins or jugs of ale he could empty at a sitting. Yet Richard had argued even so for them to return to London, to wait in dignity and calm restraint for his brother's fourth child to be born.

'It will be a girl,' Edward had said, glowering at him on the sparring yard at Windsor. On that day, they had faced only jousting posts of padded oak. It had not been spoken aloud between them, but the brothers made a point of not facing each other. In his most private thoughts, Richard thought he had the skill and perhaps the speed, but his brother was a killing knight. His opponents were often carried from the tourney field, no matter how light the mood had been at first. Edward did not spar well, though he fought like an archangel.

Richard shifted on his step, looking across the tavern. There were a few old soaks wandering in as the twilight sank into darkness outside. Richard watched as three of them spotted the king's guards and stood in indecision, licking dry lips. Their eyes flickered to the jugs of ale and then up to him, the slim swordsman blocking the upper floor and watching everything that moved. One touched his forelock to him on instinct and backed out. Two more decided to stay, the choice visible in the slight rise of their heads and the way their shoulders dropped and settled back. They were free men after all, with coins they had earned. Richard smiled at the sight of their courage, feeling the small act raise his own spirits.

The world was hard and full of pain. He woke each morning with such a band of agony across his shoulders that he could barely move. Only his stretches and exercises could ease it down to the sullen aches he endured the rest of the time. He did not complain, though he had been given much to endure. Men lived with suffering, that was all there was to it. They killed what they ate. They lost their wives as they gave birth and even then, every family rich or poor found children cold and stiff in the mornings, burying them with their grief in frozen ground.

A duke was different again, Richard knew, a man who trained to exhaustion each day against the time he would stand in battle, or perhaps simply face another in armour who wished to take away everything he loved. It was a heartbreak his father had known, beheaded on a field close by his own castle of Sandal.

It was rare for Richard to have hands clear of broken blisters or his body unbruised. When he was weak of will, as his brother was weak, when he wanted to gorge his starving frame or drink himself to oblivion, or simply allow all his bruises to heal to spare himself from pain, he would recite the words a Benedictine monk had taught him for such times: '*Non draco sit mihi dux. Vade retro Satana.*' 'The dragon is not my master. Get thee behind, Satan.' The words had become a talisman and saying them brought him back to calm. Richard lived in pain and his flesh was in opposition to his will. Yet he would prevail, because all flesh failed, whereas the will was a sea deep enough to drown.

As high on the steps to the upper floor as he was, Richard was perhaps the first in the taproom to notice the king's herald slipping through the tavern door as it swung closed. The man wore King Edward's badge of a sun in flames, embroidered on a tabard across his chest. Such as he were required to carry no weapons nor any armour, beyond the authority of their masters. Richard noted the long dagger strapped to the man's wide belt as well as the dusty chain-mail that stretched from thigh to throat as he turned and took in the tavern. Not a trusting fellow then, he thought, his mouth turning up. Away from the cities, the law was a fickle thing.

He felt the herald's gaze flicker across him and then settle. The man took only a single step towards the stairs before one of King Edward's guards was there to block his path.

Richard gestured for the stranger to be let through, though the herald's dagger was removed and left behind. His brother's guards were careful men.

The herald would no doubt have known Richard of Gloucester by sight, even without the white boar embroidered on the breast of his black shirt. Richard saw the man's eyes pass over it as he tried to bow on a flight of steps without sending himself head-over-heels. Good balance, Richard noted. The herald would acquit himself well in a brawl.

'My lord Gloucester, I bear urgent news for His Highness King Edward.'

'Speak then, if you know me. I will pass the words on to my brother.'

The fellow hesitated only a beat. London was arming for a war some two hundred miles to the south. He'd ridden every one of them without rest and had bruised places on his bones he hadn't felt for years. There was no room to stand on details.

'My lord, Earl Warwick has landed and is gathering an army close by London.' The herald's gaze broke and he looked away as he went on, understanding the reaction it would bring. 'The Duke of Clarence is said to be with him, my lord.'

Richard's eyes tightened as he leaned forward.

'My brother George? Well, he was always a fool. Is the queen safe?' he said. The man's skin grew shiny with sweat and he opened his hands in apology.

'There will be others following with such news, my lord. I was sent from London by His Majesty's Chamberlain, Lord Hastings. I believe I am the first to come with the news.'

Richard saw the herald was trembling, though whether it was from fear, or exhaustion or just coming into the warmth from the night, he did not know or care. He stood suddenly, almost sending the man tumbling down the stairs.

'Wait down there while I talk to His Highness. He will have other questions.'

Richard strode along the corridor and knocked at a door even as he opened it, uncaring what he would see after such news. He stopped even so on the threshold, his mouth falling slightly open. A blonde serving girl had been lying naked on her stomach, tapping away at a wall with the heel of her shoe. Richard's entrance interrupted her gleeful cries and she curled up, pulling blankets around her with a shriek.

King Edward the Fourth of England was lying supine on the bed, completely asleep and snoring softly. Another woman lay in the crook of his arm, sprawled with one paler arm across the expanse of his chest.

'He said I should keep going . . .' the girl at the wall said, tossing the shoe away and trying to cover herself. Richard ignored her, stepping in and kicking his brother in the sole of his foot. He did not care what games Edward was playing, any more than he was embarrassed at his brother's lolling nakedness, though he lay like a huge dead fish, thick-thighed and heavy, taking up the entire bed without any modesty. There were other matters to concern them. For a second time, Richard struck out, more savage than he had intended to be in his temper, risking his brother's flesh on the blade of his spur.

'Stop that,' Edward murmured sleepily. He began to turn over, then sensed a man's presence standing over him. Richard saw his brother go from relaxed stupor to awareness in a great spasm. The eyes snapped open and the king pushed the girl away, ready to launch himself from the bed. When he saw it was his younger brother, he blew out the great breath he had taken, chuckling and looking around for the jug of wine balanced precariously on a side table.

Edward began to make some inane comment and Richard spoke over him, irritated and strained.

'There is an army come to London, under Earl Warwick. George is with him, of course. No news of Elizabeth yet, or your girls. I'm sorry. Come down now, would you? I'll clear the inn.'

Without another word, Richard turned and walked out, leaving his brother to stare in dismay, then suddenly roar, reaching for his discarded clothes. The two strumpets were dismissed without being paid, though they made no word of complaint after what they had heard. Over woollen hose and undershirt, King Edward buttoned a thick tunic, still rank with his sweat. He stood swaying by the bed then, pissing long and hard into a pot dragged out from under, then sat once again to pull on his boots, yanking his leg right up into the air with the force of his hands on the leather ties. At the last, he splashed cold water on his face and hair from another deep bowl set into the dresser. Making bear-like sounds, he dipped his face in, then blew and gasped and shook his jowls as he ran his hand over his features. His head was thumping with a dull pain above his right eye. He felt as if he might vomit and two of his back teeth were loose and hot, the legacy of some piece of meat trapped in there for a week. He'd have to have the damned things drawn before they poisoned him, he was certain.

When Edward was ready, he eyed his gauntlets and mail, along with the panels and straps of his leg armour. He wore such a weight of metal on most days that when he went without it, he felt as light as a boy. He patted the bulge of his stomach ruefully. His brother Richard's wiriness was a constant taunt to him, an irritant. Edward sweated more and yes, he knew he was much heavier and slower too. Yet he felt the strength he needed in his arms and back and legs. Was that not his reason for such hunts, to restore the trim waist he had known?

He did not look at the great pile of lamb bones on the floor, where he had kicked away a platter earlier on. A man needed meat, to fight and to ride. It was only common sense. He stood as straight as he could, pulling in his belly and patting it. Better, definitely. Mostly muscle. The room lurched suddenly and he shuddered at the hot bitterness rising in his throat. He ignored the scattered armour, snatching only a sword belt from where he had thrown it. He nodded, satisfied, as he left the room, certain he had not yet let himself grow too fat.

By the time Edward emerged, the tavern had been forcefully emptied. Even the owner and his staff had been made to vanish, the king knew not where. He saw his brother Richard and a herald in York livery rising from a table to kneel in his presence. Only one of his guards remained. Edward squinted down at the taproom. Sir Dalston, yes. Good eye for prey gone to earth, the man had.

Edward felt his thoughts drift, the drink still making him stupid and slow. He shook his head, but the sudden action just brought a fresh surge of acid and made the room swim. Dark depression clamped upon him, stealing away his first rush of confidence.

He knew another few hundred or so of his followers were camped in fields nearby, with greyhounds and bull mastiffs, with the king's gyrfalcon and a score of spare horses. Friends and trusted lords drifted in and out of the great hunt, joining Edward for weeks until the regimen of vast quantities of meat, wine and ale had reduced them to trembling old men. Then they would return to their estates to recover their vitality, to the exasperation of their wives. In comparison, Edward seemed to thrive on the life.

As well as his brother Richard, there were others of high rank in the royal party. The king's brother-in-law, Anthony, Earl Rivers, was present, slightly worn from a week of Edward's drinking games. Barons Howard and Say had joined the hunt, no doubt with some awareness of the favour they might win from having the king's ear. Earl Worcester was the last of the senior men, one with a reputation for savage treatment of the king's enemies. Edward wondered how Worcester would react when news reached him of Warwick's return. As Constable of England, Worcester had overseen the trials and execution of a number of Warwick's followers over the previous months. He would not fare well if Warwick's rebellion succeeded. Edward grimaced at that thought.

In all, he had perhaps a hundred and forty fighting men – and as many servants who could hold a blade, if their lives depended upon it. Edward swore under his breath as he stood swaying on the steps. It was just not a large group, that was the truth of it. Yet he could not take an army with him every time he wanted to ride to the hunt or visit a lonely widow in some far-flung estate. Edward took a moment to run a hand through his wet hair. A king should be able to ride his own land without having to watch for enemies seeking him out. England always seemed so quiet, so unchanging. Yet it was a treacherous place. He looked down at his brother, imagining he could see scorn and angered further by the thought. As boys, they had not dreamed of a crown, nor dukedoms beyond that of York. Edward had won such things for them, raising them up by their belts and their collars, dragging them into the light. He did not deserve such dark glances from his brother. What would Richard have been without him? Some minor baron, he reminded himself, some forgotten man.

'George is with him? Our brother?' Edward said, his voice strained. He cleared his throat angrily, bringing a flush to his cheeks.

Richard winced and nodded.

'Turned against us. With the archers and men-at-arms from his estates, I don't doubt. George can put two or three thousand in the field, or even more. You know Warwick can do the same, without even a levy or a call to arms in the shires. As things stand, we have been caught out of place.'

'I am not out of place so close to York, Brother!' Edward said. He struggled to sound confident, though fingers of drunken darkness seemed to suck at him. 'I called them once.'

Rather than argue, Richard sensed his brother's hurt and confusion. His tone softened a touch as he went on.

'They will come in the king's name, Edward, yes. Of course they will. I have sent our lads out already with your badges to rouse them from their beds. Every hour will bring more to our side, I don't doubt it.'

He did not say it could not be done in time. The London herald had covered the two hundred miles in just two days, changing horses on good roads a dozen times. It had been a fine feat of horsemanship and endurance. Yet Richard of Gloucester had been Warwick's ward and lived in his house for years. He admired many of his qualities – one of which was the ability to move quickly, where others dithered and discussed. It had led to errors in the past – to rash decisions made too quickly. In this case, on this day, it would mean Warwick was already on the road. Richard was certain of it.

Warwick had been at Towton. He had killed his own horse and fought on Edward's right hand, with the young king in all the first flush of youth and strength. Richard of Gloucester knew Warwick would not leave the north to Edward, to a king who could raise armies. No. Warwick would be coming north with all the dice thrown into the air and every man he could call, buy or borrow, to make an ending.

Edward came unsteadily down the stairs, leaning on the banister. Richard swallowed, overwhelmed by the need to move and yet held perfectly still on that spot, by oath to the king, by loyalty to his brother.

Even without armour, even in bagging hose and with his pale belly showing under an open coat, Edward was a huge presence, a weight in the room that was only part due to his physical size. Lowering his great head so as not to crash it into the beams, Edward seemed to fill the tavern as a bear would, so that the guard edged back from him. Without a word, he pulled up a tall three-legged stool and seated himself, swaying and blinking. Richard knew then that his brother was still wildly drunk. No doubt the room was spinning as Edward sat and breathed out sour fumes.

'Fetch His Highness a bucket,' Richard murmured to the guard. Sir Dalston looked offended at the order, but scurried off and found a cracked and ancient leather pail. He deposited it at the foot of the king as if it was frankincense or myrrh, bent right over as he edged away. Edward appeared to watch him, but his eyes were glassy.

Richard's temper surged. He would have slapped or shaken any other man to alertness, but his brother would not forgive such a slight, not ever. Edward was more than capable of rough horseplay with the guards or his knights, but there came a point and it never varied. The king would not allow himself to be humiliated, or dominated physically, in any way at all, no matter how slight. Richard still remembered Sir Folant de Guise, who had made the error of taking the king in a headlock when they'd been in their cups together. Edward had borne it for a single instant, then reached between the knight's legs and practically torn his purse from his body. Richard's lips tightened at the memory of Sir Folant's high shriek.

They stood in perfect silence for a time, three men in a ring facing Edward on his stool, while he swayed and looked at nothing. He had raised an arm along the polished wood of the bar and they all started when he rapped suddenly on the wood with his knuckles.

'Ale, here,' he called. 'To clear my head.'

'*More* ale?' Richard said in exasperation. 'Are you not concerned at the news? Of Warwick marching north? Of George with him?' The last was a needle of spite between them, spoken in part to wake Edward from his slack-jawed state. Their brother had fallen in love with Warwick's daughter some years before. With awe-inspiring lack of foresight, the union had been forbidden by Edward. They had married then in secret. George had been driven towards Warwick by new ties of family and loyalty – and when both men had been accused of treason, they had run together, with Warwick's daughter about to give birth.

Richard of Gloucester watched in distaste as his brother's demand for a drink was met by Sir Dalston, the knight edging around the bar and pulling the stopper from a cask. Sir Dalston was a burly knight who regarded the king with the same uncritical affection as did his mastiff hounds. The knight did not care how drunk Edward was or could become, only that the king had asked for ale. The king would have ale.

Richard watched as his brother was presented with a foaming earthenware jug, dark brown and glossy. His eyes opened wide and his smile was childlike as he grasped it in scarred hands and gulped and gulped, belching ferociously. The king began to beam at them, then leaned over suddenly and vomited on to the rush-covered floor, missing the bucket by some distance.

Richard breathed through his nose, holding a fist so tightly he could feel the muscles of his back draw. That made him open the hand immediately, fearing the first sharp twinge of the hot belt his muscles could become, like ropes pulling at him, or ribs turned and stuck in the wrong spot. With the wrong twitch, he could suffer a pain like a knife for weeks, with no way to shorten the time. His breaths would grow shallow and his shoulder blade would wing out, so that he felt it against his armour.

Richard looked on his brother with scorn and envy, mixed. Edward had driven Warwick away and fate had decreed his daughter would give birth at sea – and that the child would die before she ever reached land.

It should not have been enough to sunder three brothers, Richard thought, not beyond the first fury of tragedy. There were few parents who had not lost two or three children, finding them still in the morning, or watching them fade with fever stealing their life and smiles away. Richard grimaced at the thought. He had no children of his own and he supposed he *would* blame the man who had driven him to sea, if he lost his first as a result. Certainly his letters to George had been returned unopened since then. There was rage there – and as yet no forgiveness.

When Edward sat straight again and wiped his mouth with the back of his hand, some of his wits had returned. He focused on the nervous herald, still standing with bowed head and no doubt wishing he was not a witness to the king's drunkenness. Such things were remembered and not often forgiven.

'You – herald. Tell me of Warwick's rag and tag of whelk-fishermen and . . . bailiffs.' Edward waved a hand in annoyance at his own stumbling words, aware that his thoughts still swam in deep pools.

'Your Highness, as I told my lord Gloucester, I saw only the first morning, as they crossed the bridge in London and came into the city proper. There were thousands, Your Highness, though I was sent north before the full extent became apparent, in number or in strength of arms.'

Edward blinked slowly, nodding.

'And my brother George was there with him?'

'The Clarence banners were sighted, Your Highness, yes.'

'I see. And my wife? What word of Elizabeth? My daughters?'

The herald squirmed, flushing deeply. Although he wished by then that he had waited for news of the royal family, he had been away at a wild gallop as soon as he had his orders.

'I have no word of them, Your Highness, though I do not doubt they are safe.'

'Is there any other thing you can tell me, lad?' Edward said, peering at the man, who was at least a decade older than he was. The herald could only shake his head, his eyes bulging slightly. 'No? Nothing? Then go back down the road to the south and scout for me. Seek out Warwick's rabble and note well how far the man has marched in the days since.'

The herald was worn out, just about dead on his feet, but he only bowed and left quickly.

Richard looked sourly at his brother. He had wanted to question the man a little more thoroughly than Edward's feeble effort, but the opportunity had been lost.

'Another jug of ale here,' Edward said loudly, looking around him. Richard's last thread of temper frayed at that. He turned to his brother's guard.

'Sir Dalston, you will leave us alone.'

'My lord, I . . .'

'Get *out*!' Richard snapped over him. He dropped a hand to his sword, knowing he was taking out his impotent anger on a man of lesser estate, but still unable to control himself. Sir Dalston grew pale and tight-lipped as he stood there, unmoving. Richard had the very real sense that the knight would draw his sword. He knew he would kill him if he did.

'Go on, Dalston,' Edward said, releasing the man from his duty. 'I see my young brother wants a word in private. It is all right. Wait outside.'

Sir Dalston bowed his head, though his eyes remained sharp, even as they avoided the still hawkish glare coming from Richard.

'Off you go,' Richard said to his back, smiling as the man's stride hitched and then resumed.

'That was petty,' Edward said as soon as they were alone. 'Would you force a good man to show you his steel? So I had to hang him? Why? Just to push a thorn into me? I have enough troubles – and too few men to lose one today.'

The words were still slurred, but Richard felt some of his fears ease. He needed his brother alert. Sober, Edward was the sun in flames he wore embroidered on his breast and set into the metal of his armour. He led as if he had been born to be a king – an ability as close to magic as Richard had ever seen.

Richard pulled in a great breath, forcing calm.

'I am afraid,' he said softly. 'You know Warwick as well as I do. We've had no news of armies gathering from France. He must have had his spies working hard since last year, but this is the first I hear of this plot. And here we are, with a few dozen men, with winter almost upon us – and thousands on the road to take your crown.'

'I have fought in winter before, Richard. In snow,' Edward said after a time. He raised the great mass of locks that framed his skull then, tying them into a tail with a leather thong. When he looked up once more, his eyes were clearer.

'A trip to the privy will settle my seething guts. A few hours of hard riding will blow away these pains that make my head knock and thump. We'll visit a few villages, you and I, yes? We'll raise 'em up for the white rose. As they fought for me before.'

Richard saw the need for reassurance in his brother. He wanted more than anything to agree and clap him on the shoulder and ride out, but at the last moment, he found he could not.

'Brother, Towton was not so long ago. What is it, ten years now? But thirty thousand men died. A generation lost their husbands and brothers and sons . . .'

'And those who were boys of twelve then are twenty-two now – and in their prime! The land gives us crops of wheat and hops – and *men*, Brother. Never fear for that.'

Richard felt his brother's gaze. Edward was hugely overweight and so unfit that merely mounting his warhorse could leave him gasping. The truth of it was that the king was a deeply unhappy man, his marriage cold and empty and heirless. Hunting was the only pleasure he retained. It was no accident that had him far away from Elizabeth as she approached the end of her term. The king spent hardly any time at all in her presence.

Yet in that gaze still lay the extraordinary persuasive power of him. Richard did not want to disappoint his older brother. It would somehow cause Richard pain to see the smile fade from Edward's wide face.

He summoned his will to be cruel, to tell Edward they had no choice but to run, that they were in the wrong place, in the wrong season and that Warwick had already won . . . but he did not. Instead, Richard clung to the straws that won Edward all his battles. Men believed in him – and he proved them right to believe. Richard hid his fears and his dismay and he smiled tightly.

'Very well, Edward. I will ride with you, one more time.'

The monks who kept the book and administered Sanctuary were nowhere to be seen, of course. As well as the midwife, Elizabeth herself and her mother, two other serving women scurried around the small room, warming bowls of water on a brazier that would reduce the birth cord and caul to ashes, preventing its use in dark magics.

Elizabeth was calm enough and spoke to reassure them all, even as the midwife rubbed her thighs, easing taut muscles.

'I have borne three healthy daughters and two sons before for my first husband. I will shell another like a pea, I tell you.' She paused, feeling the rising tension that was a spasm of birth. For a time, there was no sound in the room except the swishing of the hands rubbing rose oil into her. The midwife said a prayer to St Margaret, patroness of childbirth. Almost shyly, the woman pressed a stone of polished red jasper into Elizabeth's right hand. She felt the warmth of it and nodded her thanks though she could not speak.

'I see a head,' the serving girl said excitedly. The midwife moved her out of the way and dipped her entire hand into the jar of oil. She waited patiently for the spasm to end before reaching between Elizabeth's legs. Elizabeth looked up at the ceiling while the older woman nodded to herself.

'Head down, squirming. Good. The umbilicus is clear and loose. My lady, it is coming now. Push, dear. Push down as hard as you can.'

Another hour passed and the candles burned down before the child came out in a rush, red and opening its mouth to squall with no sound.

'It is a boy, my lady!' the midwife said. Even for one so experienced, she was delighted to bring an heir to the throne into the world – despite the odd circumstances. A husband driven into exile. The house of Lancaster calling its old claim to the throne. A boy born on sacred ground.

'Edward! I will name him for his father. One day, he will be king,' Elizabeth said proudly, wiping a strand of hair away from her cheek. She was panting lightly, but the relief showed even more strongly in her. Her three girls had not secured her husband's throne. Just one son would.

The midwife bit through the cord to free the child, then licked the boy's face clean and wrapped him in bands of clean cloth before passing him back to Elizabeth. One of the serving girls opened her chemise to reveal a full breast, the young woman's eyes bright with tears for the baby she had lost just days before. The midwife frowned.

'The Holy Virgin suckled her only son, my lady. You know

the Church does not approve the use of wet nurses. Perhaps as we are on consecrated land . . . ?'

'No, dear,' Elizabeth said firmly. 'My husband is hunted, while I cannot set one foot outside these stone rooms without being made a prisoner. I have such anger in me that my milk would make the child a bloody tyrant. Let him be – and let my teats dry.' She took the woman's hand and passed back the stone of jasper, warmed by her skin. Elizabeth's eyes remained on the child as he was wrapped. Her son. Edward's son, at last.

5

Lincoln was a fairly bleak place to lose a crown, Richard thought. Rainwater streamed down his face, disappearing under his mail and tunic and making his cloak feel like a sheet of lead. He did not mind the actual cold, but there was something about damp that hurt his back and made rising each day even more of a misery. He had taken against Lincoln, he decided, though it could have been the company of those riding with him, with their bowed heads and air of defeat. As he rode over the crest of a field and through a small copse of oaks, each panting breath felt like warmth stolen away. Such a rise in the land thereabouts was rare enough, which was why King Edward had pointed it out and driven his ragged band towards it.

The forests and fields of Lincoln could be places of drowsy beauty. The summer was not so far back and to those who recalled long hot days, it felt as if they might see the sun once again, at any moment. Yet the rain continued and the clouds remained unbroken. Country paths once polished to hard clod by cattle became sucking quagmires, mud almost too deep for a man on foot so that he had to plunge and rear. Spots of it were flung up as they rode, until they were all as speckled as blackbird eggs – and almost as blue around the lips.

Richard could see Edward's back hunched just ahead of him, his brother locked into place on the saddle and trotting as if he would go on for ever, making for the hilltop. Every yard of height revealed more of the land around them.

Richard smiled at the idea. A man climbed – and was rewarded with far sight. Those who refused to climb would always live in the shadow of others, and see not much at all.

He could sense his brother's humiliation and seething anger still, in the dipped head and the glower. Edward had cast away his helmet in a temper the night before. When the king had turned his mount, Richard had nodded to a servant to fetch it for the baggage. God knew, they might need it yet.

Three days had passed since the London herald had reached the tavern by York. Each morning had begun in disappointment and seen even flickering hopes fade by the time the sun darkened the western sky once more. Richard could still hardly believe how they had been caught. His brother raged about it when he didn't care who heard him, saying a king should not have to search his whores for knives, or his towns for traitors, or have his food tasted for poisons like some oriental khan. Richard had borne the brunt of such tirades, all the while thinking that perhaps a king should. Perhaps that was what being a king meant. At least for a king who had won his crown on the battlefield.

Richard blew his heat away in a hiss of anger that came upon him like a twitch of sore muscles. There was more than one kind of battle, that was the truth of it. The moment they realized the cause of Lancaster had gained a foothold in the towns once again, the very instant they understood a campaign had been whispered for weeks or months, they should have run to safer ground. When a king of England cannot ride into a town and gather young men to his service, it is time to collect a few bags, coins and jewels and just race for the coast.

They had found empty villages on the first morning, bringing old fears of the Black Death that had left entire communities growing grass in their corpses. Yet there were no bodies in the ditches. Word of the royal hunt had been carried ahead and the people had just gone, slinking away into the deep woods and the high crags of the Yorkshire moors, places so dark and green they had never known the footfall of men before. Richard's face tightened in the cold, feeling it lance into the greater cold within. A king could not rule those who refused to be ruled, that was the secret. All of it, all the sheriffs and bailiffs and judges and lords depended on quiet and enduring obedience, given in exchange for peace. He remembered the stories of Jack Cade coming into London, breaching the Tower. If the people refused to follow, there could be no king.

Of course, Edward had burned the empty villages, riding from house to house himself with a flaming brand. Some of those with him were the sort of men who delighted in destruction, like Anthony Woodville, Lord Rivers. The queen's brother had laughed to see the flames spread, the more so when cats or dogs came scrambling out with fur scorching.

On the second day, they had burned an old man alive in his house. The scrawny old devil had shown himself as they rode past, shaking a fist and cursing Edward for a Yorkist traitor. Rivers had nailed his door shut and they had waited for the old man to try and pull it open once again. The handle hadn't even rattled as the fire spread. The ancient had sat inside without a single cry until the smoke and heat took him.

Word had gone out. From those they met who were still loyal, they heard that men had come into the villages, telling them that Lancaster would rise once more. Letters were left at night, held to the doors of courts and tally-houses by fine daggers. No one saw them placed there, or heard the hammer strike, so it was said. They told of such things almost in holy awe, as if there were dark spirits of vengeance abroad rather than just a campaign by clever men, of letters and bribes and whispers. Each murmuring mouth, each scrawled paper said that King Henry was restored and that Edward was no more than a scabrous whoreson who could not hold what he had stolen. The lies were ugly, simple things. Richard of Gloucester sensed in them the touch of a hand he knew, at least by reputation. Derry Brewer, the Lancaster spymaster. His work.

Richard thought it no coincidence that the letters handed nervously to him were all signed 'Reynard'. In France, the name meant a cunning little fox, who defeated far stronger animals with his wits. Over the cold salt channel between the two nations, Margaret of Anjou and King Henry had an heir, a prince over the water, even a court of sorts, all paid for by the French king, Louis, her cousin. It seemed they had not lost hope in their exile, though they had lost all else.

Edward reined in and Richard looked up once again, seeing a landscape of grey rain threads, stretching into the dim haze. There was morning mist still visible, gathered around the smoking chimneys of houses in a tiny village they could see at a junction of paths in the distance, like a crease in a withered cheek, not more than a dozen homes and a mill race on a fast-flowing stream. The white fog clung to those who lived there, while the king's hunt looked on not a mile away, standing high on the hill and unseen. Not every peasant had run. Not every knight had turned away, in cowardice or ingratitude, from the king who had won at Towton. The royal hunt had gathered almost eight hundred fighting men to its ranks. Amongst those and giving Richard slender hope were forty archers. It was true they were men with too many years gone to their bellies instead of their arms. Still, they could all bend a bow once.

The rain began again, filling the air with wet and the noise that always made Richard think of dried peas poured on to a tin tray. Men in armour under a downpour. Miserable, cold and hungry, he stared into the distance and decided to dismount.

The copse of oaks on the hilltop was young, the trees still slender. He could stare between them even though the leaves still hung gold and red on their boughs. No doubt they had been planted by some farmer who still thought of the pagan ways, before Christians had ever come to the tin islands bound by white cliffs. Richard blinked at the names and old books swimming into his imagination. This cold, wet land had been Cassiterides to the Greeks, Albion and Britannia to Rome. Planting trees in high places was a sign of the old ways, one that Richard recognized. He touched his forelock in respect as he swung to dismount, acknowledging the spirits of the land. He would not be proud, not now he and the king were hunted.

'*There*, to the west,' one of the men shouted, pointing. Richard turned to look over his left shoulder, his heart sinking. They had almost been caught on the second day, lost in their arrogance, going from village to village. He shuddered at the closeness of it and how blind he had been, blaming himself as much as his brother for leaving them so exposed.

Warwick and Derry Brewer had paid men to creep up to village halls and pin vile treasons to oaken doors, but they had also found the time to gather soldiers in the north, ready to sweep down on the king's party. Yet King Edward had moved first, springing the trap early that would have caught him neatly between two armies.

Richard shook his head in anger. In all the mists and endless rain, they still did not know the numbers of those driving them down through the country. More than they could stop and tear into bloody rags, of a certainty. The king's hunt could not break the noose – and every day that they moved south brought Warwick closer, marching up the London road. It was a pincer's grip, Richard thought, prepared by men who knew his brother's strengths and weaknesses. No French tyrant could ever have managed it, not on English soil. That was the very heart of the simmering fury that kept Richard warm in the rain, that only English traitors could have conspired so well, with such a result. In just a few crucial days, Edward had gone from careless revelry to being driven like a stag before hounds. It was a cruel reverse.

In the distance, the fields seemed to move. Three columns of sodden soldiers trudged like spilled oil along the flat land towards them. They were two miles away at most, surely no more in the drizzle and damp. Richard wondered if those ahorse and those marching along with nodding heads would see the king's hunt on the hill. Edward's banners still flew: the white rose and the sun in flames, the three lions of the crown of England. His pride would not allow him to have them furled, though they hung so limp in the rain it was almost the same.

Richard did not think Edward's followers would look too fearsome. The king's hunt was just a smudge on a hill, stretching into a tail of weary, shivering men, sheltering from the wind behind their mounts.

'Walk on, then,' Edward called. 'East again. Look to that small road there. Make for that and hope for stone and gravel over this sucking mud.'

As if in answer, the rain doubled in weight and power, forcing them to bow over their saddles while they remounted, blinded by it, drummed by it, exhausted. There was no exhilaration in having become prey.

Richard looked behind as they reached the flat ground once again, his brother's men a bedraggled column, filing out of the field. The Earl of Worcester had fallen back, he saw, the man so ill with fever and damp that he could not keep up with the rest. Mastiffs and greyhounds lurched along beside and amongst them, muzzled so their barking would not draw in their enemies. Richard shook his head, feeling despair grow in him. The rain had thickened the mists so that he could see no sign of their pursuers. He clenched his jaw and rode on. There were nets out for them to the north, Warwick to the south. All they could do was run east and he knew Edward would be thinking of the Norfolk ports.

The idea was shameful, that the king of England, the victor of Towton, could be made to run, to take ship. Richard considered his own future with increasing bitterness. He would not turn from his brother, that was certain. Yet it would cost him all. If Warwick restored Lancaster, the sons of York would be named traitors and attainted.

Richard shrugged under the weight of mail and his wet cloak. He had no wife or children. All his honour rode with his brother, that enormous great drunkard. Yet he would not abandon Edward, even if they had to leave the land that had fed and grown their bloodline since the oldest times. To his surprise, he found the very idea caused him pain, making his stomach clench. He did not want to be driven away from his home. It was in the bones of him.

Richard had been asleep as he rode, he realized, coming awake with a start and looking all around to see if any of the others had noticed. The rain had returned in sheets, chilling him to wakefulness. Edward still rode slightly ahead, slumped and nodding, as if he were already a prisoner. Richard frowned, wanting to call to his brother to put on a better show. He felt his anger return a little warmth to his frozen hands. Dawn was just a cruel time of day, when all flaws are revealed. With a chance to sober up and a week to send out trusted men, Edward might have had his army. Young men hungry for advancement and glory had always sought him out – knights or lords who enjoyed having a strong king on the throne and cared nothing for the sick line of Lancaster. Yet their enemies had caught Edward in a perfect snare, snapping at his heels in such numbers that he could not gather enough men to stand his ground. Like a bear pursued by dogs, he had not been allowed a chance to rest, but had to endure the nips and lunges pressing him on through the rain.

On impulse, Richard dug in his heels, though he was numb with tiredness, his thoughts leaden. His mount had walked all night through mud and drifts of leaves in the darkness. He assumed he had dozed, but could not remember it. His back was the only hot part of him, so sharpened by lack of sleep that when the horse lurched he had to bite his lip rather than cry out.

As he came abreast of Edward, Richard reached to clap his brother on the shoulder. Edward swayed away from the touch, half aware and as pale as Richard had ever seen him. His face had been leaner once, that was true. The flesh had grown over the ten years since Towton, pink and soft like a cloak to hide the harder man he had once been.

'They will bring me to bay, Richard,' Edward said softly, his voice barely a breath. 'If that is what they want. They will run me down and force me to turn and fight and there will be too many. They will force an ending on me. Perhaps you should leave. Warwick has no cause for anger with you. Let me go. Let me stand. I cannot leave England like a thief.'

Edward shook his head, lost in self-pity that was as irritating to Richard as the armies hunting them down. He clenched his jaw as the pain under his shoulder blade flared and the damned thing started to wing and press against his armour. There would be no ease for it then, he knew. It would be weeks before he could sit comfortably once more. He ground his teeth together and found his tongue working at a small piece of one where it had broken free.

Horns blew somewhere behind, a mournful note like a stag calling. A thrill of fear made Richard turn, but in the morning mists there could be no sign of banners. Still, there was a cold horror in being hunted, even for those who had known battle.

As he stared behind him, Richard frowned. In such a place, in cold and rain and caught between violent enemies, he would not have blamed his brother's followers if they had slipped away in the night. Yet they remained, stubborn as personal oaths and still certain that Edward would come through. Richard thought it was madness as he blinked through blurring rain. He could do much with such loyalty, were it ever his to command.

Earl Rivers rode close by Edward's shoulder, with his usual eye for Woodville advancement, Richard did not doubt. There was one who would be at Edward's side until the last breath, just in case a title or a fortune needed a new owner.

The thought was depressing. Though neither of the two York men had announced it as a plan, they were running east then towards the port of Bishop's Lynn, the final decision coming closer with every milestone. With just eight hundred men, the land was lost. Yet if Edward took sail, it would be an ending in humiliation, on a bitter sea. There would be no more titles or great hunts after that. No York, no Gloucester. Their enemies would have triumphed and the house of Lancaster would rule once more, as if their cousins had never cast them down. Richard shook his head at the thought of the poor broken mute who would wear the crown. They should have killed King Henry, for all his foolish innocence. Warwick could not have used a corpse for his throne.

Richard's horse stumbled. The animal was exhausted and could fall. Had he been asleep again? Edward was a dozen paces ahead of him and Richard reached up to slap himself awake in stinging blows. He had ridden with almost no rest for three days . . . no, four. This was the fourth day. Some had fallen behind, out of sight, but Richard was almost eighteen years old and he would not fail his brother, the king. He would not.

They had begun to pass between a row of ancient thorn hedges, overgrown so that they loomed and stole what little light there was. To the west, horns sounded again, closer; to the east, for the first time, Richard could smell the sea. He found tears springing from him at the thought of leaving. He had to remove a gauntlet to rub his eyes clear, keeping his head low so that no one else could see. As he glanced up though, he saw that he was not the only one. They pushed their horses on for the last mile down to the docks. Edward seemed listless and dull-eyed, too downcast to do anything but stare miserably at the morning sun.

The fishing crews had already gone out and the port of Lynn was quiet. No one seemed to know what to do in their tiredness, their minds made lead. Hundreds of horsemen milled around, talking in low voices and always looking up for those who pursued. Richard glanced to his brother, knowing Edward should have had some word for them. They had not deserted the king, to the end. Yet Edward sat bowed over his saddle, lost and sullen and far from that place.

With a groan at his tortured muscles and stiff joints, Richard dismounted. The pain was just about unbearable and he wanted to curl up in a doorway and sleep. Instead, he peeled off his cloak and left the thing to drip down the flanks of his overheated horse. Richard staggered as he approached a merchant vessel and hailed the master. The man was there to oversee the loading of cargo. He had observed the arrival of the weary band of soldiers and riders with barely hidden fear.

'In the name of King Edward, we demand safe passage,' Richard said. It could not be for all. Eight hundred would need a fleet even if they had a day or two for loading. He wanted Edward to dismiss the men, to say a few fine words and then get on board. His body hurt terribly and he was so tired even death had become enticing, as a chance to just *rest*.

Like a pale ghost, Richard stood blinking at the captain. In reply, the man took a step back, shaking his head before he could even speak and holding up empty hands.

'I am just a trader, my lord. I want no new enemies. I have broken no laws. *Please*, leave me to my business.'

'I will not ask again,' Richard said wearily. He dared not look behind, though his back crawled at the thought of Warwick's men spilling on to the quays. 'Instead I will cut your heart out and leave you dead on this dock. My name is Richard Plantagenet, Duke of Gloucester. My duty is to preserve the king's safety. Do not doubt my intention.'

He knew Edward had come to stand beside him by the way the merchant looked up, then nervously at the white rose of York embroidered on both their tunics. Edward too had left his cloak behind. As well as the symbol of York, his tunic was set on the breast with seed pearls in the design of a sun in flames. The merchant stared at it with wide eyes.

'May I send the horses on board?' Edward asked. The man could only nod mutely. Edward gestured to Lord Rivers and the man began issuing sharp commands, driving the animals to the ramp. The horses clattered on to the deck and the merchant winced at the sound. Richard clapped him on the shoulder.

'There are traitors close behind us, captain. If you have

not cast off and retreated out of bowshot by the time they reach this dock, I do not doubt they will set your ship ablaze with arrows dipped in oil. It is what I would do.'

Richard turned then to his brother. Edward still loomed, but some vital spark had been taken from him. He was red-eyed as he met Richard's gaze.

'Dismiss your men, Edward. We cannot take more than a few.'

Without another word, Richard climbed the ramp to the deck. Behind him, he heard Edward take a breath. When he addressed them, it was without flourish or booming call. He spoke as a man rather than a king.

'You have brought me safe to this place,' he said. 'You have my thanks. God willing, I will seek you out once again and I will reward you for your loyalty. Until then, go with God, my brothers.'

It was all that had held them on the docks and they bowed and remounted, trotting away in every direction. The poor Earl of Worcester would surely have been taken by then, miles behind the rest.

Edward watched the loyal men depart, until there were just a few of his lords remaining with their servants and guards. A dozen men, no more. They walked their mounts on to the ship, leaving Edward to stare at the country he was losing.

Ropes were untied that bound them to the shore. The ramps were pulled in and the sail run up on to the mast. A yard of water appeared between the wooden rail and the stone dock, then two and they were easing away.

'Where is your home port, our destination?' Richard called. The captain was practically weeping at the sight of the bales he'd left behind on the quay. The man stared at him, not daring to give voice to his anger at his turn of fortune.

Richard of Gloucester felt like striding across the deck and strangling him where he stood. A man could suffer greater losses than a mere ship's cargo. Something of that strong emotion in his gaze made the captain look down.

'Picardy, my lord. France.'

'No longer,' Richard shouted over the increasing breeze. 'Set your rudder and sail for Flanders, northern coast. We have friends there still. And look cheerful! You have played a fine part today. Your little ship holds the king of England.'

The captain bowed in response, not that he had any choice at all. If any of his crew had dared to resist, Edward's remaining knights and lords were still fighting men, for all their hunger and weariness.

'Flanders, my lord, as you say.'

The land retreated and, for the first time in days, Richard relaxed, settling into the motion of the merchant cog. Flanders in the north, with Luxembourg to the south. Below those, the duchies of Bar and Lorraine – and then Burgundy itself. He pictured them all in his mind's eye, all disputed territory. Edward had only one ally over the Channel: Duke Charles of Burgundy, avowed enemy of the French king, who ruled from Flanders to his heartland. The duchy had made huge gains while the old French king was weak. Richard rather envied the man his position.

Overhead, the sun was a smudge of light through the clouds, a weak thing that could not warm either brother as they stared at the green English coast, blurring in the distance.

'Earl Warwick came back, Brother,' Richard called to him. 'Are you a lesser man?'

To his pleasure, he saw Edward consider it, his eyebrows rising in surmise. Richard chuckled aloud. For all the failures and disaster they had suffered, there was still something joyous about the sense of a live ship under them, of the salt spray and the morning.

It was a joy that faded quickly when Richard began to belch and feel a sort of clammy sickness steal over him, made worse with each rise and plunge of the ship. After only a short time, his stomach heaved up into his throat and he rushed for the rail, guided backward and downwind by exasperated sailors. He spent the following day and night lashed to the stern, lolling over grey, rolling waves, helpless as a child and sicker than he had ever known was possible.

6

Margaret of Anjou could sense the rise in her status in a thousand ways. It showed in the deference of King Louis's courtiers, men and women who spent their lives with a fine appreciation for the power and connections of those around them. For too long, she had been one of a hundred little *moules* of the royal family. She had heard the word whispered by snide clerks and the fat daughters of French lords. Mussels clung to the belly of ships in clusters, or grew on rocks and gaped for their food like young birds in a nest. She did not know if the comparison stung all the more because of the truth of it.

Her father was still alive, to her daily irritation. Others of his generation had passed sweetly away in their sleep, surrounded by loved ones. René of Anjou remained, made thinner by age, but still a great white toad into his sixties. Though he lived in the castle at Saumur, he had not invited his daughter to join him there. In her private moments, Margaret could admit that if he had, there was a chance she would have smothered him, so perhaps it was not a poor decision. René had offered her a broken old house on the Saumur estate, a cottage fit for a charcoal burner, without even a roof. Perhaps he had intended it as a mark of his disfavour; he had sent her out into the world to marry an English king – and she had come home with a son and little else beyond the clothes on her back.

The thought made anger blaze in her even then, after years. How strange to have the French king show her more mercy and kindness than her own father! They called King Louis the Universal Spider, for all his clever plans and his schemes. Yet he had visited a stipend on Margaret and allowed her to take rooms at the Louvre Palace in his capital, complete with the servants whose manners had changed so abruptly over the last month. She and her son had been little *moules* on his ship of state, it was true. Yet Warwick had kept his word and her husband had been freed from the Tower.

'And Henry wears the crown once more,' she whispered to herself. It was not just the answer to her prayers, it was the result of years of work. She inclined her head, staring out of a window lined in gold leaf, each delicate flake pasted on by a master who did no other work. She could see her own reflection as she focused more closely. Time had stolen the youthful bloom from her skin, clawing at her. She smoothed her hair with a palm as she examined herself, but each day required a little more artistry with paint and powder – and even then her teeth had either been drawn or grown brown. She snorted to herself, irritated at the signs of a weakness she did not feel. She was in no pain, which was a blessing. Forty was the beginning of old age, especially for one who had seen and lost so much in the quarter century she had given to England. Yet she had been given another throw in return.

Even after so long, she did not know for certain that she could trust Warwick.

'Show me,' she had said, when he made his promises, imperious and unbending. His father had been killed by her men, that was what troubled her and made her fear. Salisbury had fallen together with York – and though she'd felt only triumph at that moment, it had been her greatest failure. In bringing down the fathers, she had unleashed the sons.

Could Warwick ever forgive? He had no love for her, she

understood that much. The bare truth seemed to be that he had no other choice, now that he had fallen out with Edward and his precious, traitorous house of York. He said he wished to undo the pain and grief he had caused. As if that was ever possible.

Margaret sniffed, the first sign of the winter colds that plagued her each year for months. A life was lived like paths forking in the deep forest. Each choice was made and a man or woman had to go on, with no opportunity to return and find a way back to some happier time. All they could do was stumble deeper and deeper in, blind and weeping.

Yet Warwick had promised to free Henry of Lancaster, the true king of England – and he had. He had promised to put a crown on Henry's bowed head and her spies swore he had done so. That was why the courtiers who had sneered at her faded finery now looked abashed. Her husband was once again the king of England; her enemies were hunted down. She raised her head a fraction further, feeling the strain in her neck. She had been bowed down, for too long. She could look at herself in a glass, the odd doll of her reflection staring steadily back – and feel no shame.

All Warwick had asked was that his remaining daughter be married to her son. Margaret had laughed when he'd first broached the idea. His oldest daughter was already married to George of Clarence. Seeing a second girl wed to Lancaster would give Warwick a son-in-law in both camps. Some bloodline boy of his could even be king of England when they were all gone. His ambition was greater than she had ever known and Margaret could only sigh at the things she could have told her younger self. The paths all lay behind, the decisions made, for good or ill.

Her son entered the room at the far end, his spurred boots muffled on the carpets. Servants bowed as he appeared and again, Margaret saw that they were suitably respectful. Her beautiful young Edward was once more Prince of Wales.

'Have you heard the news, Mother?' he called in fluent French as soon as he laid eyes on her. Margaret had heard it all hours before her son, of course, though she still shook her head to allow him the joy of telling it.

'My father has been crowned once again in Westminster. It is all over Paris, *Maman*! They say Edward of York has run off somewhere in the north, but he has no more than a few hundred with him. He will be hunted with dogs, they say – and torn apart.'

'It is *magnificent*,' Margaret breathed. She felt tears come and she knew her eyes were shining with them. To her pleasure, Edward came and took both her hands in his. He was well made, with a look more of his grandfather than his father, so she had told him a thousand times. That man had taken the war to the French heartland, defeating them at Agincourt with strength and courage and rage and arrows. This boy would have pleased the battle king, Margaret was certain. Great lines could skip a generation.

Her Edward was taller than his father, though not as tall as the giant of York who bore the same name, more was the pity. From the time her son had learned to talk, he had listened to a thousand tales of loss from her, when there was no one else to see her weep. He loved his mother, and in his youth he simply wanted to make it right once more, to uproot the bad vine on the throne. England had failed her, after all. Prince Edward had worked harder than any man Margaret had ever known to build skill and strength as a knight, though of course it had fallen to the French king to actually make him one.

He stood like a young bull across the shoulders, deep-chested and clear-eyed, his health and seventeen years of perfect youth written on his every movement. She felt tears spill on her cheek and wiped roughly at them. A mother's pride could be overwhelming, even for one who had seen too much of loss.

'When do we leave, Mother?' he said in English. 'I have my dogs and my horses ready. Uncle Louis has said he will send his best men with me if I wish, just so he can say he played his part.'

Margaret smiled. 'Uncle Louis' and his webs had brought about a result he wanted. The French king had persuaded Margaret and Warwick to meet in the first place, taking enormous pains to put them in the same room. Edward of York had no time for the French royals, preferring Burgundy and all their vulgar grasping. No doubt King Louis would be raising a toast to Henry of Lancaster as she spoke.

'There is one task yet to put behind us, my son, before we go rushing back to England. Your marriage to Warwick's daughter. That much I promised him, as earnest of my goodwill and my trust. He has fulfilled his part of our bargain, at least for today. Until King Edward's head is spiked like his father's on the walls of York, I will not sleep soundly in my bed, but for today, it is . . . enough.'

To her pleasure, her son waved a hand as if at a mere formality. He had met the daughter of Warwick a few times once the betrothal was announced, more for the look of it than any great desire to know one another. Prince Edward's heart and hawkish gaze were on England and always had been. Margaret knew he would give anything to set foot there once again. It was her task to rein him back from rashness, to be certain that England would not take her beloved son from her. That cold bitch of a country had taken everything else and all the years of her youth, after all.

'As soon as it can be done, Mother, it does not matter to

me. I want to be at sea! I want to watch those white cliffs grow once again after so many summers riding French coasts and seeing them out there – forbidden to me. I will be king, Mother! As you promised.'

'Of course,' Margaret replied. She had told him so a thousand times, but never been more certain than at that moment.

Warwick stared out over a winter sea. Armed men waited, packing the roads and fields all around. Beyond their grim ranks, the town of Bishop's Lynn appeared utterly deserted, every house barred and shuttered just as they would be for a great storm.

Warwick looked to the two men with him, one bound by blood, the other by marriage. It was hard not to think of sixteen years before, when he had been the least experienced man, when his father, Earl Salisbury, and the Duke of York had contemplated raising banners against a king of England. He had come a long way since that day, though in the cold and the soft rain, it was not hard to imagine himself back on a muddy field by the town of St Albans, with it all to play out.

George, Duke of Clarence, seemed less certain of himself than was usual. Warwick watched him carefully, seeing that the young man had lost some of his confidence. Perhaps he felt Edward being driven out of England as a blow to his status, Warwick did not know. His son-in-law seemed lost in thought as they looked out over the waves. Warwick could hear seals somewhere out there, barking and yelping. He could not pursue Edward, not without a fleet already in place, ready to take up the chase over the trackless ocean.

Warwick dismissed his own irritation even as it surfaced. He could not be right every time and he refused to waste any more of his life on pointless blame and wishing-it-had-been. No. He accepted his errors and put them aside. He would go on.

His brother John, Lord Montagu, rather spoiled the fine feeling of the moment by raising his head and answering a question no one had asked.

'We should have had a few fast ships out on the brine, waiting on him. Yes. We could have strung Edward up on a yard then and not have to worry now about him coming back.'

'Thank you, John,' Warwick said sourly. 'That had not occurred to me.'

'I'm just saying you don't leave a man like Edward of York alive, is all. You know that even better than me. He doesn't stay down, unless you *put* him down. That's what I came to you for, Brother. That's the hunt I wanted. A clean sweep, with all the scraps washed down the drain. Not this. Now I'll be looking over my shoulder for the rest of my life.'

Warwick scowled at his younger brother. John Neville was hard-bitten and dark, the skin of his face drawn tight across the bones beneath. He was one of the most ruthless men Warwick had ever known. John had even been called Edward's hound for a while, until the king took the title of Earl of Northumberland away from him. It had been one of Edward's key mistakes, and all for the whispers and manipulations of his little wife. Warwick made a grunting, growling sound at the thought, looking out to sea once more and recalling his resolution not to let the past bind him.

'Nothing we can do about that now, John. You'll get Northumberland back, just as we agreed. And I will have all the lands and titles taken from me – and denied to my daughters after me. Titles you will inherit, George, eh? When I am gone.'

'And I will be made Duke of York,' George said suddenly, his voice strained.

'Of course,' Warwick replied immediately. 'When Edward is attainted, the title will fall to you as of right.'

'And heir. Heir to the throne,' George went on. He looked mulish and ready for an argument, but Warwick only shrugged.

'As I have said, though after Henry's son.'

'Yes . . . of course,' George replied. He did not seem quite as pleased at that as he had been before. What had been a fantasy was coming true before his eyes. His brother King Edward had been driven from England. Henry of Lancaster was upon the throne once more and George recalled Henry's son had been a fine young man. Still, to be second in line for the throne of England was no small thing. Warwick watched as George shrugged to himself and decided to wear it and wait. It was all he could ask.

'Good lad,' Warwick said, playing the expansive father-in-law to perfection as he gripped the young man's shoulder. 'Go now and see that the captains know to make camp. It's too far to the London road to return to it today. There is something right and proper about keeping a watch, at least for one night. I can do no more now.'

George of Clarence dipped his head, pleased to be given the responsibility. He rode away and Warwick waited until he was out of earshot before turning to his brother, expecting the exact bitterness of expression he saw there.

'We could not have gone faster, John, I swear it,' Warwick said. 'You told me Edward ran early. It saved his life.'

'He'll come back,' Montagu said. He spat on to the cobbles as if the words themselves were bitter.

'Perhaps,' Warwick replied. 'And if he does, we'll be followers of the true king, with Henry and his wife and his son, the Prince of Wales, all safe. Maybe I'll pay for an army to guard them, when Parliament give me back my estates. By God, I will! Why should we raise surly farmers each time we need them to stand? We should have proper soldiers, like the old legions. Men who don't go home to their farms to take in the damned harvest.'

'They say he grew fat,' Montagu said, still grumbling. 'But Edward of York is still the most dangerous man I ever met. He'll come back – unless you move against him. Use the men you have. Derry Brewer for one. That vicious old whoreson has more cunning in him than a dozen of your Parliament fellows. Give Brewer a purse of gold and tell him to make sure Edward of York doesn't bother us again. He'll know what to do.'

Warwick rubbed his chin, sick of the cold and the damp. He recalled the times he had shown mercy in his life and everything that had cost him. The decision was not a difficult one and he felt no sense of regret.

'I will try. No word to young George about it. He is already torn and I want to keep his loyalty.'

'I wouldn't trust him,' Montagu said.

'You don't trust anyone,' his brother replied.

'And that has served me well.'

Jasper Tudor could hardly believe the bustle of London as he rode through narrow streets to the Palace of Westminster. He had spent the previous fourteen years in France and Flanders, surviving and taking on the sort of soldier's work his father, Owen, would have known well. He had been a captain of a troop and a warehouse guard, a sheriff's bailiff and, at one low point, a prizefighter who had been knocked unconscious three times. All of that was behind and he could still hardly believe how his fortunes had changed.

Out on the river, he could see merchant ships and a thousand boats being rowed or poled along in the shallows. Anything the world could provide was being sold right there on the docks. Some of the noise and clamour dwindled as he and his nephew walked their mounts west, but there were houses and roads springing up in the land between the city and its great palace. One day, Jasper thought, the city would swallow Westminster completely. He shook his head, amazed at it all.

Yet it was not the noise of trade that excited him. In the Palace of Westminster, his half-brother Henry wore an old crown. His mother's first son, Jasper thought in wonder, taken out of captivity like Daniel from the lion's den, or Joseph from the pit where his brothers had thrown him. Henry was king and the star of Lancaster had risen once again. It was a heady feeling and Jasper kept glancing at his nephew, looking to share his astonishment and joy.

Henry Tudor appeared unmoved by the spectacle of the capital's river, though Jasper could only marvel at the contrast for one who had been raised in Pembroke. Perhaps it was that his nephew had expected shouts and crowds, so had not been surprised by it all. Or perhaps, Jasper had begun to suspect, there was something off in the boy, some part that did not respond as it should. Still, he grinned at Henry, inviting him to smile. The boy had been poorly treated, no doubt, raised by cuffs and curses without parents or friends. It was no wonder he was cold in his ways and his manners. Jasper nodded to himself. He'd known a dog that had been beaten savagely for months before it broke its rope and found him in his little camp in the woods, drawn to the smell of his stew. It had taken a long time for it to stop snapping and shivering, to find its confidence again. Perhaps that would be his task for his nephew, he thought, to teach him to find a little joy, even in a raw winter's day.

Jasper followed a path away from the river around the huge walls of the palace. He and Henry dismounted with the

Abbey at their backs, looking up in awe as they entered Westminster Hall, stretching up and away. It never failed to catch Jasper's breath, the scale and the sheer brag of it. The king's councils met in the cavernous halls of Westminster, the Commons and the Lords – and beyond and above were the royal quarters themselves.

Jasper touched a wooden stall for luck, where a wizened old man sold goose quills to lawyers, a penny a dozen. It was in King Henry's gift to grant Pembroke Castle back to the man who loved her above all. Jasper hardly dared form the thought in his mind, for the discomfort it caused him. A man could hold a full bladder for a long, long time, but then be in agony as he dragged out the pot. To be close to your greatest desire could be an exquisite pain.

Floor by floor they climbed, into rooms where sound was muffled by tapestries and rugs and thick, heavy furniture, so that the whole world outside seemed to recede. Jasper and Henry were stopped again and again by king's men wearing the embroidered red-rose livery of Lancaster and the king's symbols of the swan and the antelope. Jasper stopped to examine a pewter badge showing King Henry on horseback, holding an orb and a cross. The guard looked pleased at the attention, replying to the enquiry while he stared straight ahead.

'I bought it in the market, sir. Take it if you'd like. I can get another.'

'No. Your loyalty gives me joy enough,' Jasper said. 'I will find my own. What a city this is, to be selling badges of King Henry before he has warmed his seat.'

'Nowhere like London, sir, that's true,' the man replied, pushing his chin and chest just a little further out. Jasper grinned suddenly, heading for the next flight of stairs that would take them to the king's rooms. More guards waited there, staring down at him. Jasper endured it all in good spirits, noting that his nephew seemed fascinated by everything, his eyes never still.

Uncle and nephew were thoroughly searched at the last door. Jasper handed over two daggers before they could be discovered and taken.

'I want those back,' he said, as he and his brother's son walked into the presence of King Henry of England.

Jasper found himself smiling as he followed the lad through. Some thirty yards away, the king was seated, his head turned to the sun streaming in through a window over the Thames. Though there were guards along the walls, only one herald and Derry Brewer stood close by the throne. Jasper had spent enough years in Pembroke's tower keep not to be too awed at the sheer height, but it was still hard to drag his gaze from the picture of London it revealed, a place of busy little houses and roads and markets and great fields, with the river meandering through it all at a winter's pace. It was a clear day and he tried to hold the picture as a memory.

'Master Jasper Tudor,' the herald announced as he drew closer, 'who was Earl of Pembroke. His nephew Henry Tudor, son of Edmund Tudor, who was Earl of Richmond.' The man seemed disappointed not to be able to go on further. Jasper frowned as King Henry continued to stare out of the window.

Derry Brewer stepped forward then, dressed in a fine brown doublet jacket and black hose. Jasper took in the leather strip over his eye and the gnarled-looking cane Brewer carried, more a blackthorn club than an aid to balance.

'His Majesty is not so given to speech and idle chatter as he was when you met him last, Master Tudor. His heart was broken at St Albans – and it is not healed yet. I remember you, though. You fought well and gave your archers to their fates without a backward glance.'

'We've all had our knocks and cuts, Master Brewer. I had Pembroke taken from me and given to my enemies.'

'Aye, the world's a hard place,' Derry replied carelessly, understanding that the man before him was pleased at a chance to bring up his lost possessions. Everyone who came to see King Henry had some tale of that sort. Half the lands and titles of England had been given as favours over the previous decade. It would be sorted out by the courts and in private, one or the other, though Derry suspected it would take a lifetime of wrangling.

Jasper reached over and pressed his nephew forward a pace, so that the young man stood almost touching the king.

'This is Henry. Son of Margaret Beaufort and my brother Edmund. Nephew to King Henry himself.'

'On the mother's side though, wasn't it?' Derry said cheerfully. 'You are the son of Owen Tudor, Master Jasper, not King Harry of Agincourt. That is a difference, in the blood and in the heart.'

'His mother, Margaret, is of the line of kings, from John of Gaunt,' Jasper said stiffly, recalling how irritating he found the king's spymaster.

Derry tutted at him, then shrugged.

'I remember there was a mistress? Some children born out of the marriage bed? It is all so long ago – and the legitimate male line is what matters. Henry the Fourth, Fifth and Sixth, mate, with York just usurpers, leaping and grabbing for coins like the London cripples on feast days.' Jasper saw the man's face turn ugly, his mouth twisting to a sneer. 'So, whatever you're after, you have no claim at all, beyond that too great a part which has already fallen to you.'

For the first time, Jasper's brow cleared. He wondered

how many others had come to beg for old titles and anything else in the king's gift.

'I am not here with a claim, sir,' he said firmly. It was bitterly hard at that moment not to mention Pembroke and make himself a liar. 'I have brought my nephew out of Wales and I thought it would be a fine thing to introduce him to his namesake and his blood relative, King Henry. For all your barbs, Master Brewer, my nephew *is* of Lancaster.'

Derry Brewer weighed them both in a cold gaze that took in the mended tears and hard-brushed cloth as well as the quality of the old boots Jasper wore. He nodded, seeming to relax. To Jasper's astonishment, Derry took King Henry by the hand, leaning in to look him in the eye.

'Your Majesty? Your brother is here, with your nephew, Edmund's son.'

With the slowness of a winter thaw, Henry's eyes drew in some spark. He tilted his head and turned to them, the corners of his mouth rising.

'How blessed I am, gentlemen. How blessed to see you both,' he said. His voice was high and soft, caught between an old man's fluting tone and a child's song. He reached out and Jasper's eyes tightened at seeing such pale fingers, more bone than flesh. He accepted the king's grip even so, the touch seeming to please Henry. The king turned again towards his half-nephew and Henry Tudor let himself be pressed forward once more, silent and watchful as his hand was taken and held in turn.

'Aren't you a fine boy?' King Henry said. 'I am sorry about your father. There are so many lost now . . . I don't know how . . .' He trailed away and Derry Brewer was there instantly to lay the king's arm back on to his lap and tuck a blanket in a little better. When he faced uncle and nephew once more, Derry watched them closely, protective as a ewe with her lamb.

'His Highness has not been well and grows tired,' he told them. 'I will do what I can for you, Master Tudor.'

'I did not ask,' Jasper said.

'I know, but you fought for him when his future was still golden. That deserves its reward.'

Jasper felt his breath catch, hardly daring to hope.

'Is it true, then, that York has been driven out?' he asked, dropping his voice to a whisper. London was full of lies and half-truths, without much real knowledge. All they knew for certain was that Warwick's army had gone racing off into the north and not a word had come back since.

Jasper made no move to pull away as Derry took him by the shoulder. He would not insult a man who might win back Pembroke for him. Instead, he allowed Derry to walk him a few yards out of the king's earshot.

'I heard this morning that Edward of York was made to run,' Derry said with grim satisfaction. He had worked for years to bring it about. His pride showed.

'Not killed?' Jasper said, biting his lip in thought.

'Sadly, no. He reached a ship with a few men.'

'Then he'll come back,' Jasper said with certainty. Derry Brewer looked at him, considering whether it was worth his while to argue the point. He decided it was not.

'He'll try. And we will kill him when he does. He's fat and slow now, did you know? Drunk on spirits half the day, weeping and vomiting. The throne was too much for him, in the end. No, his time is finished. Be sure of that much.'

'Have you ever been wrong, Master Brewer?' Jasper said with a bitter smile. He had spent more than a decade in exile, with strangers and enemies in his home. To his surprise, Brewer chuckled.

'I have made such errors as you would not believe, son. Just one of them cost me this eye. Still, we ain't angels, are we? We do our best, failures and bleedin' all. And we go on, without looking back.'

The last two words perhaps reminded both men that they had left the king and Henry Tudor alone. When they turned, it was to see the two of them talking together. The king was smiling, the lines of worry easing on his face. Derry felt his eyes prickle and shook his head.

'Jesus, no one ever warned me that getting old would mean weeping like a little girl whenever I saw something touching.' He glanced over to check that Jasper was not mocking him, then laughed at himself. 'His Highness has known a great deal of pain. I like to see him smile. Your nephew must have a way with him.'

'Perhaps he has,' Jasper said, shaking his head in wonder.

Edward of York stepped on to shore in Flanders, at a stone dock some hundred miles or so to the north and east of Calais. Still pale, his brother stayed close to his side. Richard had blessed his saints that the sea-illness had gone. He had never known anything leave him so weak, and yet when it had passed his strength and fitness returned almost as if they had not been stolen. The ground seemed to sway beneath his feet for a time, but then settled, his confidence coming back.

There were no soldiers waiting to capture them or hold them for ransom. Richard knew they would have outrun any pursuit over four days at sea. He felt his spirits creep upward and saw the same in Edward as his brother stood taller, looking around him with interest at the busy little market port, with scores of fishing vessels drawn up on to a shingle beach and painted a dozen colours.

'I have been here before,' Edward said. 'There is a barracks, or there was, not six miles from here. If it is still there, they will carry a message to Burgundy for us.' He looked up at the flags waving in light winds above the town. 'It seems Duke Charles has kept his gains here. I can only hope he will remember our friendship.'

'He will help us?' Richard asked. His brother nodded firmly.

'He *hates* the French king – and where have Warwick and George been in their exile? No, Brother, Duke Charles will see his interests lie with us. To frustrate the plans of his enemy has ever been his delight. They call him the Bold – Charles le Téméraire. You will see.'

Richard understood his brother was talking up their chances, sounding more confident than he felt. The truth was that they were abandoned on a foreign shore, with just a few loyal men. Edward had lost all their father had won and he was heartbroken and utterly ashamed, hardly able to meet his brother's eye.

The captain of the ship came over then, to stand before the two brothers.

'My lords, I have fulfilled my duty, but you must understand, I had to leave my cargo on the docks at Bishop's Lynn. I am not a wealthy man and in winter . . . I could lose it all. Will you pay some part of my costs, my lords?'

Richard felt anger surge. He began to step forward with one hand dropping to his sword hilt. Edward's arm stopped him like a bar across his chest.

'No, Richard. He is right. There is a debt to be repaid.'

The jacket Edward wore was studded with rattling pearls along the seams. To his brother's dismay, Edward removed it and passed it into the astonished arms of the captain.

'There, is it enough?' Edward said. The wind was cold and he was already shivering. The captain hesitated, caught between pity and greed. His greed won and he clutched the coat tightly and nodded, bowing as he backed away.

'Let me take it back,' Richard murmured. The captain still expected a reverse in his fortunes, glancing nervously over his shoulder as he put distance between them. It had been a royal gift.

Edward shook his head.

'Let him have it. It will do me good to shiver for a time. I am too fat, Brother! I should mortify my flesh like the monks who prick and stripe themselves.' He seemed to brighten at the idea. 'Yes, like those words you mutter when your back makes you weep.'

'I do not weep,' Richard whispered. He was appalled that his brother had noticed.

'All right, Richard. But the words, what are they? That give you power over your weakness?'

'*Non draco sit mihi dux. Vade retro Satana.*'

'The dragon is not my master?'

'Yes. Get thee behind me, Satan.'

Edward closed his eyes and muttered the words to himself, over and over, throwing back his shoulders and raising his head into the cold wind. To Richard's surprise, the shivering stopped. When his brother looked down once again, his grief had eased just a fraction.

'I shall train with you tonight, if I may,' Edward said. Richard nodded, even as his back sent a fresh cry of protest.

The horses had been unloaded and the merchant crew were like spiders hanging on the ropes and yards, getting their ship ready for sea once again. Edward mounted with the others, patting his gut ruefully where it poked through the shirt. 'I will master the dragon, Richard,' he called, his hair wild. The king dug in his heels and the horse sprang forward, clattering along the road south.

7

Elizabeth frowned at the monk's bald head. He had dipped it in a show of respect, but though he still trembled under her stare, he had made a point of remaining standing. As if in echo of her own seething anger, her newborn son began to squall, the sound pulling at her marrow, so that her breasts ached and a pang rushed from her womb to her throat.

'I do not understand your hesitation, Brother Paul. *All* the grounds of Westminster Abbey are consecrated and part of Sanctuary, is that not so?'

'That . . . is true,' replied the young man grudgingly, his colour deepening shade by shade under her close scrutiny. 'But this building is the safest part. The abbot . . .'

'And my newborn son must be baptized as quickly as possible, is that not also true?'

'Of course, my lady, but you must understand . . .'

'And yet you come to me,' Elizabeth went on over his weak protests, 'with this *nonsense*? This . . . lack of manners that I can only assume is a deliberate insult to my husband, the king of England?'

The monk gaped at her in misery. His mouth moved, but only to make a strangled sound. He shook his head and chose to look down once more, staring at his toes in their sandals where they peeped from under his black robe.

'I believe an error has been made, Brother Paul, perhaps one your dear abbot has not understood to the very *roots*. My son was born on consecrated ground – in Sanctuary. I would have him baptized in Westminster Abbey – on consecrated ground and safe from all my enemies. The small stretch of garden from here to there is all under the authority of the Church, is it not?'

'My lady, it is of course, but you know the abbot cannot guarantee your safety if you leave this place, even to cross to the Abbey itself. A single bolt, my lady – a madman or a traitor . . . *Please!* I have been ordained as a priest, of course. I can baptize your son here, in quiet and safety.'

In fury, Elizabeth Woodville remained utterly silent, knowing the young man would fold upon himself like a snail touched by salt. She did not need words to shame such a weakling.

When he seemed close to tears of embarrassment, she replied.

'Your abbot cares nothing for my safety, young man. Or the safety of my son, Edward. No, if you had the courage of a child, you would say so clearly. Your abbot panders to Earl Warwick and perhaps to Henry of Lancaster, that empty *sack*. Or is it that my husband has been killed? Does your abbot wish me to vanish as well? Will men come in the night for me?' All the while, she watched him, frowning at the odd twitches and shakes of the head and clenches of his jaw. The monk knew something and had almost corrected her. She would return to that. She waved a hand.

'But whatever fate has in store for me, my son *will* be baptized today – and in the Abbey. Not in this stone cell, like a prisoner. *No.* Like a boy who will be Prince of Wales, like a future *king*.' She realized her voice had become harsh and loud, each word lashing the monk so that his trembling resembled a fit. With an effort, Elizabeth gentled her tone.

'Edward the First was baptized there. My son's namesake, sir! His ancestor! The Abbey is the heart of London and I will not be kept away like a pauper. Do you understand?

Now gather your monks and line the path for us if you must. I will walk the road on consecrated ground and you will witness every step.'

The young monk could only stammer and Elizabeth reached out suddenly and took his arm, feeling the surprising strength of him beneath the coarse cloth. His eyes widened in shock or revulsion and she wondered if he had felt the touch of a woman since taking his oaths.

'Tell your abbot to expect me. I am coming.'

Brother Paul lurched and almost fell as he scrambled out of the room. Elizabeth sighed as she looked after him. He was one of those who could not bear the bustle of the world, with its noise and threats and bargains. Poor Brother Paul was suited to a cloistered life and the murmurs of prayers. He had chosen a gentle post and yet on that day he had been bullied, threatened, shouted at and forced to run back and forth between Elizabeth and the abbot until he was red-faced and stank of fresh sweat over the old.

Her mother, Jacquetta, had watched the entire scene from a chair in the corner, working a mortar and pestle to grind ginger, cinnamon, black pepper and a little sugar into *poudre forte*, or 'strong powder', to add to the insipid fare provided by the brothers. The woman looked up as Elizabeth turned to her. They broke that shared gaze only when the baby shuffled in his tiny wooden cot. One of the monks had made it from fallen wood as a gift. Elizabeth stood with a grunt and leaned over, rocking the tiny crib before her son could begin to scream.

'He's hungry again,' her mother said. 'Shall I summon that lazy girl, Jenny?'

'Not unless he cries. He might yet go back to sleep.'

'Not if we are going out into the cold, my love. He'll shake his fists and wail, I tell you.'

Elizabeth saw her mother was afraid. She had come from a quiet retirement to visit her daughter and been snatched up into a rush of events that saw the house of York tumbling down around their ears. When her mother put the grinding bowl aside, Elizabeth saw her hands were shaking before she clasped them. Jacquetta was not a brave woman, though perhaps it was in part the oppression of Sanctuary, a place built with no thought of comfort or ease.

Elizabeth made her decision and picked up her son, leaning him on to her shoulder and walking up and down. Her mother rose immediately, placing a cloth under his head in case he vomited up his milk.

'You do not have to go with me, Mother,' Elizabeth said after a time. 'Wait for me here, please. I would like to know you are safe. And I would like . . . my daughters to be protected.'

To her surprise, her mother waved a hand to dismiss the idea.

'Would I miss such a moment of your life? The girls are in no danger here, with the nurse. I think Katie would take on a Tower lion if he even licked his lips at them. Worry about tonight only, Elizabeth. The girls are safe here.' Her mother smiled at her and Elizabeth took comfort, for all she knew it was just an echo of a child's belief in her mother's love. Still, it eased her fears.

'You will have me at your side,' her mother said firmly. 'I saw a stick by the door when I came in. I'll take it up and cudgel any rude scoundrel who steps too close.'

Elizabeth felt her own heart beating hard at the thought. Had she made a mistake?

'My pride has led me to this point, Mother. Was I wrong?'

'No, don't be silly, Elizabeth. You are a queen! They will not hide you away, or your son.'

'But that monk was so afraid, he makes my heart flutter.'

'*Pfui!* He was just a boy, almost. A mere lily of a man. Not like your Edward. Think of him as you step out. Show them no fear, Elizabeth. It is just a hundred yards or so. If there are men there, they will not dare to intrude upon you.'

Her mother spoke to bolster her confidence, to reassure her, but Elizabeth's fear seemed to double and soar as they went downstairs together and nodded to the wet nurse, Jenny. Elizabeth's three daughters came rushing out of a room, scattering wooden bricks from where they had gathered them in the laps of their skirts, holding their arms out to her. The oldest, named Lisabet for her mother, was just four. That little girl frowned at the two younger ones as they sensed the tension in the room and began to cry. Mary and Cecily both sat down hard, raising their arms to be held and growing red in the face with the force of their sobbing.

'Shh now, girls,' Elizabeth said as firmly as she could. 'I am leaving for just a short time, to have your brother blessed in the font at the Abbey. I will not be gone for long, I promise you.'

Their nurse came out at last behind them, with the same doting expression of bovine love as always. The woman hardly looked up as she gathered in her charges and shooed them back to the side rooms.

Elizabeth thought she might be sick as Jenny lifted a heavy cloak to her shoulders, shielding the child from any cold wind.

'He *must* be baptized,' Elizabeth whispered to herself as if reciting prayers. 'I will not deny him heaven if he dies – and I have waited days already. The Abbey grounds are covered by the protection of Sanctuary. I will not hide him away in shame, *never*.' She saw her mother's eyes sparkle with pride and tears and Jacquetta really did take up the cudgel left by the door. Jenny stepped around her mistress to open it, the sound of the river coming in on the night air.

Light spilled across them and, for a moment, Elizabeth cringed back at the sight of men with torches, waiting for her. She heard her mother gasp, but then she understood. The abbot had decided to aid her rather than rebuke her further or continue to resist. Perhaps her trembling monk had put her case rather better than she had hoped, or the elderly abbot had just given up over her stubbornness, she did not know. She stepped out between a line of monks in black habits, each with his hood raised and a torch held in his hand. The flames lit their faces and Elizabeth relaxed further when she saw how many were smiling. This was not a mob, come to drag her out, nor even a jury sitting in judgement on her actions. They nodded to the queen and smiled at the babe resting in the folds of the great cloak.

Elizabeth raised her head and walked through them. She could not see past the light of the torches to the darkness outside it. The grounds all around her were hidden, but the path of light stretched all the way to the huge open door of the Abbey. She saw there were more people waiting there and her steps faltered. Her mother touched her arm then.

'Show no fear, my pigeon. Trust in God . . . and the abbot. They will not allow harm to come to you.'

Elizabeth forced a smile and though she felt her heart skip and race, she reached the Abbey and passed out of the night's cold into the equal cold within.

Edward looked nervous for a moment as Duke Charles of Burgundy entered the room. They had not been kept waiting and as his brother Richard rose from his seat to bow, they saw the duke tug a napkin from his throat and toss it aside.

'Edward, my friend! This perfidy! This invidiousness! I

had word of it only this morning.' Edward reached out his right hand, but the older man embraced him. When he stood back, Edward seemed to have grown in stature as his confidence continued to return.

'You honour me by coming here, Your Highness,' Duke Charles said. His gaze dropped to Edward's throat, taking in the travel-stained cloth of his shirt. As Richard looked on, the man touched a gold ornament and chain he wore as a pendant.

'You do not wear the fleece?' Duke Charles said.

'I have only the shirt on my back, Charles, I'm sorry. It is at home.'

'I will have another brought to you, that all men may know you are a knight of Burgundy as well as a king of England, eh? And clothes! I swear to you, before the sun sets, you will be dressed as a king once again. And who is this fine young fellow?'

'My brother, Richard – Duke of Gloucester, if our titles have not yet been attainted.' Saying the word seemed to steal away Edward's returning spirits, so that he dipped his head and his skin took on a greyish hue once more. Duke Charles noticed immediately.

'Edward, you have been my friend as long as you have held the crown. When that spider, Louis of France, was sniffing around with Warwick, you welcomed my father and me to London. I still remember those nights, Edward. How we drank! You were generous then, more than generous. You recognized my father as an equal and he was proud. Now that he is gone, I count you among my dearest friends. Let me repay you.' The Duke of Burgundy favoured Richard with a glance and a nod, to acknowledge him, but all his excitement, all his energy was focused on the giant English king, suddenly in his debt and under his control.

Richard wondered if they could even trust the man, though he thought they could depend on his enmity towards the French king. That Louis and Duke Charles were cousins mattered not at all – the men of York and Lancaster could testify to that. More important was that Charles had inherited his estates only three years before – and already earned the nickname 'Téméraire'. He had captured Flanders in a series of pitched battles and it was the thought of those professional fighting men that made Richard smile.

'I will not live in exile, Charles,' Edward said suddenly. 'I will return to my kingdom before spring and I will die there or make a bloodletting of all the foul humours. That is my oath to you.'

It was a fine speech from a man standing in a wet shirt with his belly pushing through and without even a coin for a cup of wine. Yet it seemed to work, as Duke Charles nodded like a man overcome with emotion. A clap of his hands summoned a dozen servants to take the guests away and tend them, with promises that he would see them when they were refreshed and rested.

Richard was happy to allow the gaggle of servants to take him to rooms where water was heated, to stand him before an enormous brass tub of steaming water and strip and measure him. He sank into the bath with closed eyes, wincing at the heat that stung his flesh but immediately began to uncoil the rigid mass between his shoulder blades. He gave a great groan, despite himself. Across the room, Edward was descending into another, though his bulk had the servants scurrying to mop the water that sloshed out.

As Richard lay back, he wanted to weep at the way his pain had dwindled. He resolved at that moment to bring home one of the baths, perhaps with a few of the servants who knew how to manage it. It was wonderful. When he opened his eyes, he discovered a platter of food had been laid out on a wide board alongside. He picked at grapes and sank a full cup of some clear spirit, choking at the aniseed warmth that seared his throat.

'That is a powerful draught, Edward,' he called. 'You'd like it well.' His brother sat back with his enormous arms resting on the edges of his bath. He opened his eyes at Richard's voice and reached for the cup, immediately filled and held out by one of the attendants. Richard saw the hand stiffen in the air, then Edward shook his head, waving the cup away.

'No. I will not take the grape or the grain until I have my England back. I am too *fat*, too slow. I sweat, Brother – and I have folds that were not there when last I fought and jousted. No, Richard, I will live like a virgin monk until I am ready to take it all back. I will not lose all I have won because I have grown soft, now or ever again. I swear to God, on my life and my honour.' As Richard watched, he saw something of his brother's old strength in the jut of his jaw, for all it was made softer by the rolls of flesh. He sent up his own private prayer that the big ox would have the will and not fail and be found blubbering into his cups.

A thought struck Richard and he grew still.

'Your child will have been born by now, surely. You could have a son.'

Edward closed his eyes once more, dozing in the heat and the steam.

'Or a daughter, or a child born dead. I need an army, Richard. Then we will see.' He opened his eyes again suddenly, staring at his brother across the room.

'Get me up at dawn, Richard. I would like to train as you do. Will you bear the bruises for me?'

The thought filled Richard with dismay. Yet he understood his brother's impulse and the truth was that back in

England, their titles and their lands were being taken away by act of Parliament. They had so little hope that he would not steal the last of it from his brother.

'I will, Edward, of course. Rest now.'

Elizabeth walked almost in a daze along the great nave of the Abbey, where kings had been crowned and Mass said for five centuries. Lit by a dim gleam of lamps above, she shivered, clutching her son close to her so he would smell her skin and feel the comfort and warmth of it. She forced herself on, looking stiffly ahead, too painfully aware of the man limping along on her left side, his stick tapping on the tiled floor. Ahead, Abbot Thomas Millyng awaited them by the baptismal font, the man an ancient with great white eyebrows and a face the colour of brick.

Derry Brewer leaned in as he tapped along.

'I do not make war on children, my lady. Don't fear for that. Think of tonight as a little truce between us, if you will. My lord Warwick is of the same mind. The news reached us of what you were about and we decided we could not miss such a thing.'

Elizabeth clenched her jaw until her teeth hurt, refusing even to look at him. She knew Richard Neville, Earl Warwick, walked behind her. Her heart had begun to trip and shudder when she'd seen him sweep low into a bow at the Abbey door. It hammered then in such a wild rattle she thought she would surely faint and spill the child on to the stones. She knew them all and she did not trust them. The only mercy was that she could not look into Warwick's face and see his triumph. She knew him best of all, had seen him straight away for the clinging vine he was, when she first arrived at court.

Elizabeth knew she was flushed and that perspiration shone and ran on her skin. Her breath had grown short and her hands were trembling about as badly as those of Brother Paul earlier. How she wished she had not left the rooms then! Her mother walked on her right side with her head down and all the light and cheerfulness stolen from her.

The Abbey church was a house of God. That was their protection, Elizabeth told herself, over and over. Yet there had been murders before in the sight of altars, good men cut down on consecrated ground, though their fall had shaken crowns and kingdoms.

As if in echo of those old quakes, Elizabeth shook her head in small denial, increasing her pace. They would have to kill her before she let them win. They would have to tear Edward's son from her arms. For her husband's sake, for her own pride, she kept her head high. They surely knew she was afraid, but she would not cringe for them.

There may have been stranger groups assembled in the centuries that the Abbey had seen, though Elizabeth doubted it. Brewer and Warwick were accompanied by John Neville, whom she had known as Northumberland. He had a cold eye and she shuddered as she felt it crawl over her skin. Apart from her mother, only the terrified wet nurse, Jenny, stood by her, though a pace behind. Three women and three men, with fear enough to curdle milk in the air between them.

When Elizabeth reached Abbot Thomas, he looked about as frog-eyed and nervous as she did herself. Warwick wore a sword on his hip and she did not doubt the spymaster was armed with vicious little blades, the sort of razors preferred by men who murdered and stepped away. It was hard not to flinch in the presence of such a man, with all Derry Brewer was capable of.

Elizabeth forced herself to look at Earl Warwick. He caught the glance and immediately dropped a leg back into a sweeping bow.

'My lady, Master Brewer spoke the truth. You will not be harmed, on my honour.'

'Poor ill, *adulterated* coin that it is,' Elizabeth said clearly. Warwick flushed, but he still smiled. He had his victory, she realized. Sitting high on his hill, he could choose not to crow.

The abbot cleared his throat, drawing all eyes to him.

'I remind you all. Her Highness, the Queen Consort, Lady Elizabeth of York has been granted sanctuary . . . by the power and the authority of God's Holy Church. God sees us all, gentlemen. Through the lens of these windows, He sees with especial clarity. He watches us now. He judges our *every* word. In His name, in this Holy place, I will not allow interruptions, nor any clamour. Baptism is the door to the Church, the first of the seven great sacraments. It is not a mummer's show. Is that understood?'

The three men all nodded and murmured that it was. Elizabeth swallowed her fear as the abbot's gaze passed over her. She dared not hope to leave that place in peace. The stakes were too high and she was already thinking in desperation what she must do if the child was taken from her.

'All children are born with the original sin of mankind still clinging to them, a stain only the clear water of baptism can wash away, as Christ himself was baptized in the River Jordan. Now, Elizabeth, hand the child into my care, Edward, your son.'

Elizabeth felt tears spring in her eyes and spill down her cheeks as she opened her cloak. She was so afraid at that moment, it was a blessing she was almost blind with tears. If one of the other three men had reached for her son then, she thought she would surely die on that spot, her heart bursting in her chest.

As she held him out, the abbot took the babe in its swaddling, smiling at the sleeping, peaceful face, for all he felt the mother's fear and was angry at the men who had brought it about. Even so, he refused to rush through the vows. Elizabeth and her mother responded aloud, their voices joined by Brewer and the two Neville men, rather than incur the wrath of the abbot.

'Do you renounce Satan?'

'I do.'

'And all his works?'

'I do.'

'And all his empty promises?'

'I do.'

Abbot Thomas touched a thumb into chrism oil and marked the baby's ears, eyelids and breast, drawing a cross on his forehead. The child began to fuss and struggle then, shocked into a moment of silence as the abbot gathered water from the font in a silver jug and held the child as he poured a clear stream over his face, murmuring, 'Then I baptize you, Edward, in the name of Jesus Christ Our Lord. Amen.' The tiny child spluttered and choked, spitting and blinking all around him.

It was a strangely solemn moment. Elizabeth felt some of her fears recede as the immediate threat disappeared. Her little boy would not be denied heaven, even if he died at that very moment. It was a relief from a burden she had borne for days and she felt fresh tears come. It was exasperating to be made to seem so weak in front of her husband's enemies.

She watched as the abbot accepted a clean cloth from her mother and wrapped the child's shaking body. The little boy was red-faced and bawling by then, but reborn. Elizabeth watched as her mother took the child and wrapped him snugly, before she turned at last to the three witnesses.

Derry Brewer was smiling to himself.

'It was my idea to come, my lady. I feel like I should

apologize now. Yet I wanted to see it. In the end, his father has run. The throne is secure and returned to Lancaster, with an heir who is a fine young man. We have some years of hard work ahead, but that was always so. Yet I had to see this, Edward's son. If he lives, perhaps it will be as a knight for King Henry's son, I don't know.' A shadow passed across Brewer's brow then and he wiped a hand over his face. 'I hope he will not be raised in hatred, my lady. I have had enough of wars.'

'He will be *king*, Master Brewer,' Elizabeth whispered. Brewer grimaced as if in sorrow.

'If he shows the size of his father, perhaps he'll be made a captain for the Lancasters. Beyond that, you should not hope, if you'll take my advice. Or you'll curdle him and ruin him.'

Warwick bowed once again, standing tall and confident as he tapped his staring brother on the shoulder and began to walk back down the long nave. Derry stood for a time, watching a woman hold her child to herself, glaring at him as if her anger alone could keep them safe. The spymaster shook his head with a sigh, bowed and walked away.

8

At dawn, Christmas bells began to sound across the city of Dijon in Burgundy, muffled by falling snow, echoing into cacophony, with the beat of a heart within. The world was at peace and in all Christendom families exchanged gifts as the wise men had done on their arrival at a stable, over a thousand years before.

Richard slipped, his leg suddenly skidding out from under him. The damned snow melted to mush wherever he trod and every step was treacherous and could send him sprawling. He was cold and he was in pain and he was close to collapse, panting fire, though the air carried a grave chill. He gripped the railing with both hands, steadying himself.

On the cloistered yard, his brother stood bare-chested, snowflakes turning to clear water on his shoulders as they touched. There was blood running down his face. Edward began each day with an hour of boxing before dawn, against any brawny lad from the city who wished to risk his teeth or his knuckles for a few silver coins. Word had spread quickly that the king of England could be knocked down without reprisal. Once that had been settled, each day began with a line of farm boys rolling their shoulders and cracking their necks, waiting for the chance to put Edward on his backside in the cold.

The last of them lay senseless on the stone flags, with Edward standing over him, smiling in triumph. As the younger man was dragged away by two of his friends, Edward felt the sting of his cut and reached up, frowning at the blood that leached into his bandaged hands. He fought in Roman style, but had decided against the studded metal gloves they'd worn. His aim had been to improve his wind, as a pony gone to pasture could be brought back to racing fitness over time.

In the two months since landing, Richard had observed his brother's determination with both pleasure and awe, seeing at last the man who had stood his ground and fought on foot and ahorse at Towton, for all the hours of daylight and into the dark.

On first arrival in Dijon, where Duke Charles had his palaces, they had sparred every day for hours until Richard was a mass of bruises and cracked ribs. His brother was still only twenty-eight and he'd kept his vow over strong drink and excess, living instead like one of the stoics or a monk of swords. When Edward had boxed and run for miles around the hills, he would return to the striking posts, hacking back and forth until the oak was cut through. His life was simple, without the subtleties of planning and thinking ahead.

Richard smiled at that. His brother would be God's own vengeance when they were ready. That was something he would not mind seeing. He knew Edward's weakness was that he worked hard only when he was oppressed and struck down. Left without enemies, Edward grew fatter and lazier by the day. Denied his crown and his newborn son, he had become a stern figure, unbending and uncaring for those he battered in his training.

Edward looked up then as he sensed his brother's gaze, his frowning glare easing. Richard was not sure it was imagination, or whether he could truly hear the snowflakes hissing as they touched exposed skin.

'It is too cold to stand there without a shirt, Brother,' he called across the open yard.

Edward shrugged.

'I only feel it when I stop. I am a Spartan, Richard. I feel no pain.'

Richard bowed his head in reply, though he felt a twinge of anger at seeing a physical confidence he would never know. The twist in his back had worsened over the previous month, with some deep part of it sending such a spike of pain that he had sought out remedies from the apothecaries of Burgundy. The damned shoulder blade winged out constantly, making it feel as if someone was always touching him on his back. He had even tried imagining it was his father's hand pressing there, but the thought had become oppressive.

At least Duke Charles had signed over a stipend of great generosity. Each month a satchel of gold and silver was brought to Edward. Richard then had to ask for his portion of the pouches, an experience that humiliated him, as if he were a child going to his father for a silver penny. He spent his small wealth then on reeking oils and herbs, on draughts and powders and prayers in the cathedrals. Richard had found a blind slave girl whose task it was to work her thumbs into the most painful points, until he could not stand it any longer. With the deep metal baths, an hour of that probing gave him some ease, so that he could sleep.

Edward snatched up a sword in its scabbard as well as a woollen vest and overshirt he had laid aside. He tutted to himself at how damp the garments were, shaking off the layer of snow. He approached the edge of the cloister where his brother had come to stand.

'Any more news from home?' Edward asked hopefully. Richard shook his head and his brother sighed. 'Then I will come in to break bread . . . unless you have a desire to cross blades one more time with me? I have another master coming in this afternoon, some friend of Charles from the south. I need to be limber.'

'And you will batter him unconscious, as you did the last one,' Richard said acidly, still feeling his most recent set of bruises. It took him longer than most men to heal and move well again, though he had never admitted it or asked Edward to hold back. His pain was his own and not to be shared.

Edward shrugged.

'Perhaps. Given what we are about, Richard? Given what we intend to do, I cannot begrudge any time spent training my feet and my shoulders – and my striking arm. Either we set foot in England – and win – or I might as well throw my wife and son on to a fire.'

Edward stood before his younger brother, his bare chest still rising and falling from his exertion, with the line of blood mixing with snowmelt so that it spread into trails down Edward's chin and on to his neck. Richard could see the desperation in his brother's eyes – and it shocked him, rocked his own confidence. Edward had always been the blusterer, the one who could laugh at death and cheerfully kick it up the arse as it turned away. Yet his ebullience had taken a terrible beating. He'd left the land of his birth without even the coat on his back. He was now dependent on the generosity of a man who had no especial love for England, but hated the king of France – and the Lancasters by default.

'It will not be long now, I swear,' Richard said. Even so far from home, he looked left and right to see if they could be overheard, leaning over the railing as Edward moved in to hear. To his pleasure, Richard found he was at the same height as his brother for once, his equal in stature.

'Duke Charles has agreed to sixteen hundred men and three dozen ships, whenever we want to go. He has no good archers, but some hundred or so will be his hand-gunners, with thunder and lightning at their call. I have said the first day of March, no later. Even if the winter blasts us still, we will go then. He'll give us ships and men and arms to make a landing. The rest is up to you – and the army you will raise in spring.'

'Will they come though?' Edward said under his breath. It was barely aloud, muttered almost to himself. Richard chose to answer it even so.

'We had barely three days before and yet eight hundred loyal men raced to your side! With two armies pinching in on us and no place to stand, they still came! If we can win a single month and an open field, they'll remember York. They'll remember Towton and what you did for them then. They will! We'll beat the bastards back in rags after that. And we will *not* stop until they have been trampled. Not this time. Warwick, Montagu, Bishop Neville, King Henry, Margaret, Edward of Lancaster and Derry Brewer. I'll leave *none* alive. They have broken faith with us – we will *break* their faith in turn.'

Edward saw the fury and the passion in his brother and he was moved by it, reaching out and gripping Richard by his neck and shaking him in affection. The big hand went almost around and Edward felt his brother's throat move as he swallowed.

'I will not fail you again, Richard,' Edward said. His voice was no louder than the sound of falling snow. 'My wife had the luck or the determination to find sanctuary. And I have a son now, an heir. So we'll not stop, once we have begun. As you say. Not till you and I are the only ones left.'

George, Duke of Clarence, looked up in gaping confusion at the stranger with the boldfaced nerve to hail him, looking for all the world like one of those who lived wild in the hedgerows, or perhaps a cave, like the hermits of old.

Seething, Clarence reined in, letting the deer he had been chasing vanish into the undergrowth.

'My lord Clarence, would you be so kind as to grant me a moment and a few words, perhaps for the sake of your dear brothers, as one who supported them in all they did?'

The duke frowned at the accent of Ireland. The man was grinning at him and George jerked round in his saddle, suddenly convinced he and his men were about to come under attack.

'Your Grace! There is no cause for alarm. I assure you, my lord Clarence, there is no threat. I am unarmed and helpless, though I bring word to you from friends.'

'If you are a beggar, you have just cost me a fine buck for my table, on my own land,' Clarence retorted. 'I believe I will have something of yours instead. Bring me one of this fellow's ears, Sir Edgar.'

The knight in question dismounted with easy grace, though the man wore half-armour and mail. He pulled one of his gauntlets off and slid a long dagger from a saddle sheath. Suddenly afraid, the Irishman blanched beneath his dirt, backing away until bracken and brambles pressed him from behind. He was about as ready to bolt as the deer.

'My lord, I was told you would hear me alone. I bring word from your brothers!'

'Ah, I see,' Clarence replied. 'Then it is a shame I do not wish to hear from my brothers. Go on, Sir Edgar. Take his ear in exchange for my buck. It will make him think twice before he ruins my hunting again.'

The man tried to jerk away but he was knocked down with one blow to his stomach, then knelt upon, crying out in agony as one of his ears was cut free. The knight held it up to Clarence as its previous owner scrambled up, staring in shock and pain. Blood sheeted down his neck and he held his hand clamped to the side of his head.

'Go on your way now, tinker,' Clarence called to him as he dug in his heels. 'Be thankful I have left you your life.'

The Irishman watched in dull hatred as the one who had cut him mounted once again. Sir Edgar peered in curiosity at the red scrap he held, then tossed it into the brambles and followed his master.

Margaret of Anjou looked over to King Louis, inclining her head to him. The January sun streamed in through glass windows, cold outside, but somehow warming the room. It was like magic in such a bitter season, with spring still on the way. She raised her face to that light, closing her eyes and breathing deeply.

'Can you feel it, Your Majesty?' she asked.

'The warmth, my dear? I can, of course. This palace is a wonder of artifice; there is nowhere like it in the entire world, I am told. It is said some buildings of the east are made of pure glass, but I think that is fancy, to be dismissed with stories of great lizards and giants.'

Margaret smiled at the little man, so full of vim and vigour. She enjoyed the king's company, though she had not seen a great deal of him during her first years, when she had had no value. Margaret was wise enough to know that she had only become useful to his plans when Warwick fell out with Edward of York. It had been the French king's plan to force a reconciliation between Warwick and herself then – and he had succeeded.

Once more, she bowed her head to him. He did not need to be told her thoughts or indeed her admiration. King Louis saw all, as he liked to claim. If he had a skill, it was simply the ability to read the emotions and lies of those around him, to see them for what they were. The knack of it might have made him a fortune in commerce, but he had been born above such grubby concerns. Instead, his talent had kept his throne for him – and sent Edward of York tumbling down from his. The thought was still a delight to Margaret. She felt her dimples appear and a faint flush darken her neck.

'Your Majesty, I meant to ask if you could feel the tension in this moment, this day. My son was married before Christmas to Ann of Warwick. The men of York are gone from England. My son and I are . . . poised now, Your Majesty, to step across the sea and take back all that was stolen from us, to be your sure and certain allies for all the years of life ahead. Who knows? To form such a bond that our two countries might remain as friends for ever.'

'And yet you are afraid, Margaret,' Louis said, his eyes crinkling in gentle amusement. 'You are just that single step away and you do not trust me yet to bring it about?'

'Oh, Your Majesty, how could I not?' she protested. 'You arranged it all – for Warwick to come to me, for us to lay aside old sins and begin anew, with fresh vows sworn on a relict of the true cross.'

The French king rose from the table and walked the length of it to take her hands in his own.

'Margaret, you have suffered greatly and borne it with the dignity of a *grande dame*. Your husband betrayed and imprisoned, yourself and your son banished. Of course you are afraid, to be so close to seeing it returned. Is it too perfect? Too great a justice for you to see your enemies cast down? To imagine Edward of York suffering and despairing as I do not doubt you suffered in the first years?'

For reasons she could not fully understand, Margaret felt some part of her resistance, her battlements crumble. Tears came to her eyes where she had thought they might remain dry for the rest of her life. Louis smiled to see a woman weep with strong emotion, though he hid from her his peculiar arousal at the sight, it not being particularly useful at that moment.

'My dear,' he said, holding her hands tighter. 'I understand your caution. You have seen so much betrayal that you cannot shake your fears. I assure you your husband, Henry, is once more in fine rooms, being tended by servants. One or two of the staff in that little palace in London write to me to pass on news, you understand? I imagine it is the same here in Paris. I sometimes think all the ships that sail between England and France are just filled with the letters of our people, all spying on each other and scribbling down what they hear.' He sighed to himself, looking away from her. Some animating spark went out of him as his desire faded.

'Now, my dear, listen to me. Send your own letters to Earl Warwick, or to those lords who loved you and were most loyal. Tell them you will come in a ship with an honour guard of my best men, a hundred, no – *two* hundred to guard your safety so you will not bruise your foot on a loose stone. My authority will keep you and your son safe, my lady, until you are in London once more. Until that day, until you are ready, you are my guest still and you may remain for as long as you wish.'

Margaret felt his grip on her hands lessen and let his dry skin slip over hers. She looked up at the sunlight through the glass once again, reminded that his concern had been to break King Edward, who favoured a traitorous duke of Burgundy over a king of France. That had been the insult Louis had repaid a thousandfold, no other. Margaret's fate, with that of her son and Lancaster, had been always a mere shadow of the rest.

She allowed her lips to part and breath to ease silently out. The king saw her acceptance and he smiled at her, unseen. Once Lancaster had settled itself and England was quiet, Louis knew he would be able to turn his hand and his power against the usurper in Burgundy, Charles le Téméraire.

Louis remembered a vase he had seen once. It had been a small thing, delicate in white and blue. It had been far too ugly for display, though it had been painted and fired in some impossibly distant realm of the east, where khans and satraps ruled. It had been secured with tiny bars of metal, a piece of pottery considered so valuable that it had been worth saving, even when shattered. Piece by piece, a master craftsman had put it back together, with glue and metal and months or years of his time. Louis nodded to himself. His reward would be greater: France unified under one crown, England a steady ally. He only wished his father could have lived to see him make so much of the pieces he had been given.

George, Duke of Clarence, opened his eyes in the darkness. He felt a cold line lying across his throat, and when a voice whispered in his ear he was consumed with such terror that he stiffened in the bed, arching up so that only his head and his heels still touched. Next to him, his wife, Isabel, slept restlessly, sprawled across the covers.

'If you move, at all, I will cut your throat. They'll find you staring at the ceiling in the morning.'

Clarence recovered slowly from his first shock, lowering back down so that he lay more normally. There was very little light from stars outside the window. There was no moon and the man in his bedchamber was just a blot, hunched over at his side. George breathed more shallowly when he smelled blood on the air, coming from the fellow. Blood and bracken. He felt fresh sweat break out all over him, forming beads.

'Now, Your Grace, I was told to pass a message to you and I will do so, though I have a mind to cut you for *taking my ear.*' Despite the need for caution, the Irishman's voice grew louder as he spoke, as if he could barely keep his anger in check. In her sleep, Isabel murmured something and both men froze.

'You don't understand,' Clarence whispered back. He began to turn his head, but froze as he felt the movement cause a sting and a trickle of warmth. 'You don't know Derry Brewer, the king's spymaster. He has men everywhere, listening. I could not let you come to me with other men there to report every word to him.'

The pressure of the knife blade increased for a moment, almost as if the man wanted him to stay still while he thought. Clarence swallowed and felt his Adam's apple move uncomfortably against the blade. Isabel groaned in her sleep, half turning without waking up, and he thought his heart would beat right out of his chest. Clarence could feel the softness of her breasts resting against his left arm. Ludicrously, with his life hanging in the balance, he could feel arousal stirring. It really could not have been a worse time.

'God knows, I'd rather kill you,' the Irish voice hissed, unaware of his burning embarrassment. 'But I've been paid and I am a man of my word. Just sit still and listen.' Silence fell once more until Clarence could hear his wife's rhythmic breathing, not quite a snore but deep and burred in her throat.

'Your brothers will come home, to roost. Soon, though they have not trusted me with the date. When they stand in England once again, they want you to remember that Warwick will never make you king. He has married his second girl to Edward of Lancaster and, by all accounts, he is a fine and fertile young man. You have tied your colours to the wrong horse.'

Clarence blinked hard in the darkness, pleased the stranger could not see him. His betrayal of his brothers had been from rage and loss – and yet he missed them still. Great passions were hard for him to keep aflame and always had been. His instinct was to forgive and let old pains drift away on the breeze. He heard Richard's dry tone in the words the man had memorized, or perhaps Edward's briskness. He yearned to be returned to their trust.

He thought again of the young woman sleeping at his side, Warwick's oldest daughter. Clarence could say truthfully that he loved her, and she him. Yet would it remain so if he betrayed her father? Who could say if she would ever come willingly to his bed again? If he turned back to York, she might hate him with the same poisonous vigour she had previously reserved for Edward and his wife, Elizabeth. Clarence clenched his fists in the darkness. His marriage or his brothers. One side or the other.

'What do they want me to do?' he whispered.

'Just to consider where your loyalty should lie. This is a passing season. It will all be settled in battle – and you know Edward of York will not lose on the field. Gather your men and be ready to march to our side. If you do, you will be pardoned and restored – or damned and destroyed if you do not. Now go with God, Brother. But come with us.' The Irishman's voice changed subtly as he came to the end of the passages he had committed to memory, becoming angry once more from the throbbing pain and sickness he felt from his injury. Clarence's eyes had adjusted enough by then to see the man's head was swathed in cloth, bulbous and misshapen in the darkness.

'There is a pouch of coins on the dresser,' Clarence said softly. 'Take it in payment for your wound. I have heard you.' There was a faint chink as the man found the silk bag with questing fingers, though the knife against his skin did not move. It was odd how he could no longer feel the cold of it, Clarence thought. His skin had warmed the steel.

'Will you send an answer?' came the man's voice. Clarence lay still, looking up at blackness.

'What? Would they accept my word? They do not know my heart and they will not, no matter what I tell you tonight. I command three thousand men, sir. They are my word, when they move. Now, goodnight. You have disturbed my sleep for too long.'

For an instant, the pressure of the blade seemed to increase and Clarence flinched in the dark, taking a breath. Then it vanished and he heard a creak as the window casement was eased open and the shadow vanished through it once more. He turned then, to run a hopeful hand over his wife's breasts until she grumbled something unintelligible and presented her back to him. After that, he lay in wakeful silence until it was time to rise for the day.

9

March opened in cold winds and miserable, gusting rain. The English Channel had been a grey hell for most of February. Storms had battered the coasts of France and England, beating at the merchant fleets so that they were forced to abandon trade and cluster in sheltered harbours, away from the open sea. French warships waited on the deepwater moorings of the Seine, miles from the ocean, ready to escort Margaret and her son to England once again. Further north and east, stung by gales, the ships of Burgundy rocked and groaned at anchor. There were hundreds of islands in the archipelago where they had been gathered. Over the winter months, dozens of ships had been towed in, one by one, hidden from view and the knowledge of man. There, on green and mildewed shores, Duke Charles had assembled an invasion force for the house of York.

The air was cold and the sunlight weak as silent regiments in mail and leather trudged aboard moored ships, all along the quays. A few of the officers wore falchion blades in tight leather wraps on their hips. The rest might take up pikes or billhooks, or even a few English pollaxes that had found their way into the canvas bundles. The weapons had gone on board in huge cloth rolls that were already stained with rust. The pitting was all on the surface then. By the time the weapons had rusted to weakness, the war would be settled.

Perhaps eight hundred men still waited in small groups to join their ships and sail to a land from which they knew they might not return. The mood was subdued at the prospect, with all the clicks and rattles of men in battle array, checking their equipment with patting gauntlets, or swearing softly as they realized they had forgotten something vital.

Edward walked up a gangplank to his flagship, the *Mark Antony*, making the planking bend into a curve under his armoured weight. He cast a nervous glance at the water as he passed over it, knowing that if he fell in, there would be no rising once again from those depths. He reached for the polished wooden rail as he stepped into the waist of the warship, looking about him with stern interest. The *Mark Antony* was the personal property of the Burgundian admiral and well appointed in whitened oak and polished brass. Some thirty men had gathered on both fore- and aftcastles as well as the main deck. Others clung to the ropes like hanged thieves, craning to see the king of England who would send them into battle on a foreign shore. He heard one of the horses whinny below, sensing some rising note in the crew that made it kick its tiny stall.

Edward met the gaze of every man with deliberate confidence, looking around slowly so that they could all say he had looked them in the eye and they'd felt the strength of his will. Some of those weighing him up would be experienced mercenary soldiers of Flanders, come for the only work that paid so well. Edward knew there would be spies among them, sending word back to Duke Charles. That did not concern him. His aims and desires were completely in accord with those of the man who had financed the expedition: to spite France and recover England. He felt a surge of excitement as he understood the men were also confident. They would not fail him. All he needed was to set foot on an English coast and plant his flag. They would surely give him that.

His brother Richard came on board with a lighter step, making the planking bounce. The spirits of both York men rose at the sight of ships tacking and manoeuvring out amongst the islands, testing the ballast and the cordage, already packed with men. Still more were heaving up anchors and spreading small sails ready to navigate the deep channels of Zeeland back to open sea.

'Like an arrow from a bow, Brother,' Richard said, making his voice carry. 'Like a falcon from a great height, we'll fall upon them.' He was pleased to see his brother grin fiercely. Gone was Edward's dull eye and great white belly. Four months of brutal training had made a hound of him again, restoring youth and vigour and speed. Edward moved lightly as the ship rocked in the swell. He reached out to draw Richard close, his smile widening as he spoke in a mutter the crew would not hear.

'Will there be a fleet out there, ready for us, do you think?' It was their great fear, that spies from home would have reported their preparations. If they sailed out into the Channel to find an English fleet waiting, the sun would set on their plans and their lives.

Richard clapped his brother on the shoulder, playing the part of two young men delighted by all they saw before them. At the same time, he spoke under his breath, leaning in.

'They can't expect us yet, Brother! It is not half a year since you left the coast of England, yet we are here, ready with ships and men. They cannot be ready for us. Nor can they know you have found your fighting spirit once again.' He chuckled then. 'And I never lost mine. I tell you, Edward . . .'

Richard of Gloucester broke off as Earl Rivers bounded up the gangplank, making it creak. Anthony Woodville had grown a dark beard that lay upon his armour like a spade so there was no telling where his chin ended. Richard repressed his irritation as the man greeted them and bowed. Rivers had inherited his father's title in the struggle for power. The queen's brother had seen his main chance in King Edward and remained close ever since. Richard nodded to the man, though he had been enjoying the quiet conversation with his brother – an intimacy rare in Edward and treasured all the more because of it. With Lord Rivers standing idle at his shoulder, there would be no more privacy.

Instead, Richard turned to the rail to look out over the docks. His brother was a fine leader in war, only a fool would deny it. Yet in peace, Edward surrounded himself with thick-limbed knights and thick-headed barons, men who owed him their advancement and were willing to waste it in drink and hunts. Richard had little time for any of them – and the queen's brutish brother least of all. Yet he smiled and inclined his head even as Anthony Woodville thrust his presence upon them, exclaiming on the rain and the cold.

'Gentlemen,' Edward said, suddenly. He still had the knack of making his voice travel, though he did not seem to shout. It boomed across them and even men on the next ship along stood still in their tasks and turned towards him.

He unsheathed a huge sword then, the priceless gift of Charles le Téméraire, resting the point of it on the wooden deck so that it dug in. Edward knelt and all the standing men sank down with him. Even those in the ropes bowed their heads and clasped hands through the rough ropes. Edward gripped the bared blade so that the polished cross of the hilt was held before him.

'I ask Our Saviour, Our Lord Jesus Christ, to guide us on our voyage and keep us safe. I ask my patron saint and all the saints to give us the strength and the will and the honour to take back what has been taken from us. "*Placebo Domino in regione vivorum*" – "I will please the Lord in the land of the living". In England, gentlemen, where I am king. On sea and on land, I ask for your favour, Lord. God grant us peace when we are done. And strength until then. Amen.'

The final word was echoed by the men. On the ships already at sea and those still tied to the shore, every head had been bowed in common purpose, though very few had heard his words. Sixteen hundred men made the sign of the cross and rose to their feet with a great graunch and clatter of armour and weapons. Edward smiled, showing sharp teeth.

'Now take me *home*, gentlemen! I would see my England once more.' The ship's crew raced about their tasks, heaving on ropes and directing clumsy soldiers when they needed them. The *Mark Antony* seemed to shiver as the last ropes were cast off. The sails cracked taut in the breeze and the motion changed subtly, becoming a live vessel on the deep. Edward crossed himself once again. Leaving the coast of Flanders was not an ending but a fresh start. He could barely contain his desire to set foot on English soil once more, almost a physical pain he had denied for the months of banishment. Even more, he wanted men like Warwick to understand who he was at last and to be afraid. There was but one king of England. As his ship broke out in formation with three dozen more, the wind and their speed increased. The great prow plunged into the sea, coming up with a beard of green water and dropping down once again. Spray surged over Edward and he walked forward into it, delighted by the sting of cold and everything it meant.

'Go on!' he shouted, though whether it was to the men aloft or the gulls or the ship herself, no one could say. 'Go *on*!' He was coming home, to settle all his debts and to take his crown, even if it was spattered with blood.

'The brave men of Parliament resist, my lord, because they think they can serve two masters.'

'Well, we must show them they cannot!' Warwick retorted. 'And I am weary of being baulked by these little men. King *Henry* summoned this Parliament. They have all taken oaths of loyalty to him – and they witnessed the execution of the Earl of Worcester for treason. A lesson for all! Yet still they seem determined to block me and make themselves a mockery.'

Derry Brewer sighed, examining the bottom of a pewter mug and raising it to be refilled. He had not grown tired of the service and fawning courtiers at the Palace of Westminster. The addition of a fine pewter badge on his tunic and a word in a few of the right ears had earned him the appearance of respect. Servants bowed when he entered a room and ran when he asked for ale or wine or a steak and kidney pie. He found he enjoyed the ease of life under such conditions.

'Richard, they are just men,' he said. 'Tutored men who know their Latin and their Greek, yes. Men who can figure a little if you give them a piece of chalk and a slate and you don't need an answer that same morning. Yet they are not above manoeuvring for their own survival, if you understand me? They have homes and hearths, wives and mistresses and brats to feed. All of which can be taken away and given to others, if Edward of York comes back.' He shrugged as Warwick looked in anger at him, refusing to apologize for what he knew was true. The men of Parliament were trying to walk an impossible line. If Edward returned they could still show him they had delayed and been loyal. If Lancaster continued to hold the throne, they would begin to scurry over one another for that favour instead.

Derry despised the lot of them, but then he always had, ever since the long-dead Speaker Tresham had set two dogs on an old friend. Dogs with tools and a brazier. Derry expected no aid from such men – and nothing but frustration and obstruction. As a result, they could not disappoint him and he found it oddly refreshing. Warwick had not had the same revelation and struggled on.

'I have half the houses in London filled with men, Derry, sleeping in every attic and basement, packed like cordwood in the taverns – and stealing the ale as soon as the owners are asleep, as I hear in some complaint and bill just about every day.'

'So build a barracks to house them,' Derry said with a shrug. 'Outside the city a way, where they can't bother the young women. Grant them a meadow where they can sweat and train.' He saw the idea sink in as Warwick drank, his Adam's apple bobbing. Warwick gasped as he finished the pint, shaking his head and raising the mug for another.

'All right, perhaps I will. That is in London though. All the while, I have a fleet beating up and down the coast of France looking for their ships, enduring winter cold and rot and broken boards – and men who fall from the rigging and dash out their brains on the decks in high winds. Others who get some fever and die screaming. Yet they remain, out there, sweeping up and down, never knowing when York will be sighted.'

Warwick paused to press a knuckle against the joint of his nose and his eyes, breathing out in a sigh or a groan.

'And all the time, as I bleed fortunes into the sea, the king's Parliament, these grain sellers and lawyers from the shires and the towns and the cities, cannot even be relied upon to see the wind has changed! York has *gone*. Lancaster has returned after a decade of their poisonous rule. My brother John appears before me each morning to announce he has had no word of his title in Northumberland. The rents from half my old lands are still pouring into the coffers of other men and when I bring it up, I am told to apply to the courts! Perhaps King Henry has been too gentle with those whitebeard lawyer bastards! It took three months just to attaint Edward of York, like his father before him. That cursed line! All I have managed for Clarence is to make him Lieutenant of Ireland, while his old titles lie in disuse or disputed. Must I spend the rest of my life in a courtroom? I tell you, the gift of Towton was that so many seats were empty after it. Edward had titles by the dozen to award his favourites and by so doing, to secure his support. Advise me, Derry! Would you send these Parliament men away, in King Henry's name? They will mutter and argue until the trumpets are blown for the end of the world, I swear, while I have a dozen men owed favours – and no titles or estates to give them.'

'The men of the Commons are just afraid of one great shadow falling across them again. We struck at Edward of York and the lucky whoreson slipped the blow and ran. Like King Arthur's return, they are expecting him home in the summer. The whole blessed country is expecting him home.' Derry took advantage of that moment of sad declaration to sink half of the pint he had been poured, smacking his lips appreciatively.

'That is the heart of it,' Warwick said softly. 'And I am ready for him.'

Derry made a snorting sound into his beer, spattering bits of froth.

'You cannot keep an army camped in London for the winter, my lord. Borrow more from the priories and build your barracks. That is my advice. The wheels of Parliament grind slowly. They'll vote you the funds you have spent in the end, but you cannot run dry, not now.'

'By God, I was the richest man in England, once!'

'Yes, my lord, my old heart breaks for the reverses you have endured,' Derry said, eyeing the gold rings on Warwick's fingers. 'I'm sure it is just malicious gossip, what I heard about you allowing your captains to take the merchant vessels of any other nation as their payment, all under the seal of King Henry. Some might call it piracy, my lord, but I am not one of those who leaps to accusations, or even cares particularly, as long as he does not have to hear complaints about it after. If you do not earn a fortune from your cut, then let it be as I say – speak to the moneylenders to tide you over this winter. You will be rich again, in a year or two, when they see the country thriving in peace. The one thing all those merchants hate, is war. Their cargoes and cogs stolen by ruthless pirates, armies eating all their food. No, son, peace is where the money is. War interrupts trade – and trade is our lifeblood. They say Henry the Fifth borrowed so much he almost broke London. If he hadn't won and captured all sorts of wealth, well, perhaps we'd be speaking French, really, *really* badly, Mon-sewer.'

'And until then, I must just depend on those Parliament old women, mustn't I?' Warwick said waspishly. His face and neck had grown flushed as he realized how much Derry Brewer knew of his arrangements. 'Just as I depend on you, Brewer, to tell me where York and Gloucester have hidden themselves – then to reach out and strike at them.'

Derry used his one good eye to effect, knowing that it had a piercing quality. He stared until Warwick looked back into the depths of his own mug.

'You used to have a . . . gentleman's approach to such things, my lord. A restraint. I admired it in you then.'

'Yes? Well, I have been attainted and my father was killed, Brewer. I am not as green, now, nor as patient. I want to see an ending – and I do not care how Edward of York is brought down. If he falls from a horse or is stabbed by his mistress, I will be as pleased. Take what chances you can. If he returns to England, nothing after that will be certain. Do you understand? I fought at his side at Towton, Brewer. I know the man. If we cannot stop him before he plants his flag, all we have won can be torn away. All.'

Derry Brewer grimaced to himself as he drained yet another mug of the fine brown ale, feeling his senses swim. He had men in France and Flanders, looking for some sign of the brothers of York. There were a dozen rumours, but the pigeons had all been sent and had to be shipped back to the Continent. It all took time and he could not escape the sense that the hourglass had already been thrown against a wall. The sea was vast, so that entire fleets were no more than splinters against that watery deep. The Continent was dark and endless, even with the spies reporting back for King Louis. Belching, Derry placed his mug down and nodded to Warwick, rising to his feet to head out into the darkness and the rain.

Daw looked over the grey sea, with the sun setting behind him. It was his favourite time of day, when gold and slate mingled in great bands across the waves, a pattern stretching into the far distance and all flecked with white. He was alone on his hill, as always. He'd kept a one-eyed dog up there for company for a while, but the village butcher had told everyone about it and they'd all said he couldn't be trusted to keep an eye out if he was playing with his hound. They'd made him leave the animal at home and then of course it had gone, vanished like morning dew. His mam had said the animal had just skittered out of the door and never come back, but Daw had an idea the butcher had taken him for those horrible little pies he sold at market day. The man called him Jack

Daw and always laughed when he did, like it was clever. Daw was short for David, that was all. He liked Daw. He might have liked Jack Daw if it hadn't been the butcher who'd come up with it.

He sighed to himself. He was fourteen years old and his leg was too twisted to do a man's work for his food, that was what they all said. All he could do was stand still and stare until someone slapped him out of it, so they'd shown him the hill watch and the tiny hut up there for when it rained. He pissed into the bracken and emptied his bowels in a little pit not far off, with a nice slender ash tree to hold on to as he dipped down. At midday, his mam would bring him a few boiled eggs, or a bit of meat and bread, whatever she'd left over – and at the end of the month, the local merchants paid his mother for his labour. It was not such a bad life, he had come to accept. In the summer, others came up the hill on fine days, to enjoy the sun on their faces and the view. He hated those times and those people, standing on his shadow, as he liked to mutter to himself. It was bad enough when the widow Jenkins came stumping up to take the night shift on the hill, but all they ever did was exchange a nod. In two years, she hadn't said a word to him and that was fine. He'd been alone so long, he knew no other way.

His mam said there were boys and simpletons on hilltops all the way down the coast, stretching further than he could even see. Daw wasn't sure whether he could believe her when she rattled off the names of towns he'd never known and would never visit. They were far-off places and he could not even imagine the fine people who lived in cities and knew stone houses and wide roads. Sometimes he dreamed of going south to see the others of his kind, imagining himself all weather-tanned and healthy like, just walking up and exchanging a nod with them, like equals. It always made him smile, though he knew he never would. No, he'd spend his life in all weathers and he'd watch the leaves grow green and then gold each year. He knew his hill better than anyone alive already and he'd come to love it in his observation, just as he loved the sea beyond with all its moods and colours.

With care, he stuck a tiny piece of pork fat to a branch, stepping away so carefully he made hardly any sound at all. He looked up into the chestnut tree for the red squirrel who made its home somewhere high above him. Each day he'd been tempting the animal closer, trying nuts and a dab of honey, anything he could snatch from his mother's kitchen. He had high hopes for pork fat. Everyone liked that.

He stepped back and turned away to sweep his gaze across the horizon – and froze. In an instant, he had forgotten the squirrel. He ran forward to the very edge of the cliff, shading his eyes though the sun was weak.

Ships. Out there on the grey, each as long as one of his fingers. He'd been standing in that spot in winter and summer for two years, with two more before that when he was the apprentice to Jim Saddler. The old man had resented his failing eyesight – and the boy who would replace him. He'd beaten Daw too many times to remember them all, but he'd taught him to read flags and banners and he'd taught him about Viking ships and how they were rowed or sailed and how French ships looked and the sort of colours they flew. Old Jim was in the ground a year, but Daw's mind flickered as he stared at them, counting and remembering. Not merchants, clustering together for safety on the deep. Not English ships. Not one or two, but a veritable fleet, more than thirty, on his oath.

Daw looked at the huge pile of wood some forty yards away from his little hut. It was part of his work to take it apart and rebuild it each week, to keep the wood dry. He had tarpaulins to pull over it in the storms, tying it all down. He knew it would light and that he had to move, but still he just stared, back and forth, fleet to bonfire.

He shook himself awake, muttering curses under his breath. The oil lamp was lit in his shed, thank God! His first task of the day and he had not shirked it on a cold morning, when he could have the pleasure of pressing his hands against the warming glass until it was too hot to hold. He snatched it up from its shelf with a sheaf of tapers, racing back to the bonfire. He went down on his hands and knees to insert the burning wands, blowing on them and stuffing in dry moss until the fire began to take hold. Flames wrapped around the balanced sticks like maypole ribbons of red, beginning to crackle and boil the sap still deep in the wood. When Daw was certain it was well set, he ran back to his hut and snatched up handfuls of tall green ferns, dumping them on the inferno to create a stream of grey smoke, hundreds of feet above his head.

He stood then, with his hands on his hips, realizing he was panting and staring at the enemy fleet crossing the North Sea along the English coast. He did not look round when a warning horn sounded in the village below, though he could imagine the butcher's cheeks growing red as he forced his breath down it. Daw grinned at the thought and then he became aware of another prickle of light.

He turned, his eyes widening. Along the coast, further than he had ever gone, another bonfire had been lit. Even as he stared, he saw an even more distant point of light twinkle. He spun in place and his mouth opened further at the sight of another gleam some dozen miles away. Men and boys like himself, who were answering the warning, carrying it further. He could only see a tiny number, but Daw had a vision that left him gasping, of the bonfires spreading right along the coast, carrying his word. For an instant, he was afraid, but pride forced out the sense of worry. He smiled and wished his dog could have been there.

Edward had been watching the coast slide by, miles away on the larboard side, with a sort of desperate longing. He had tried not to think of England in his months of exile. There had been no point to it while he was banished and unable to return. Yet then, with the chalk hills fading into brown and green, with the great curving cliffs speaking to something in his blood, he could only stare and hope.

A point of light showed, on a high chalk hill. From so far away, it was no brighter than a single torch perhaps. Yet as he watched, a line of them came into existence, one by one like bright beads on a thread, making a chain. It was a strange thing to think of the men at each one, setting the fires, warning that there were ships out, threatening the coast. Edward could see the sun setting behind the line. It would not be long before they were like drops of amber on black velvet. He looked up at the mast overhead.

'Captain! Put up my colours! The Sun in Flames, if you please. Let them see I am returned.'

It took a little time to find the enormous banner in the signal chest, but Duke Charles knew him well and it was there. The roll of embroidered cloth was attached to signal ropes and run up high on the mast, snapping out overhead. Edward heard cheers go up from the ships around him, spreading from one to another as they spotted his colours flying. He smiled as his brother Richard came out of the hold in a clatter, almost falling on to the deck in his rush.

'They know we are here now,' Edward said, sweeping his hand across the line of lights. How far would it go south before some rider carried the news inland? Or were there men racing already, galloping through narrow lanes to be first to reach King Henry in London?

His brother Richard looked up at the Sun in Flames and laughed.

'Good! Let them be afraid! They chased us out and that dishonour will not stand, Brother. Not for sons of York. Let the fires burn. We will not stop until there are just ashes left.'

10

They anchored off Cromer on the east coast of England that night, sending boat-crews in to hire horses and find friends. Edward and Richard dined together with Rivers and Baron Say aboard the *Mark Antony*, waiting for news. For the first time in months, they could gather word from their supporters without the sense of being behind events, or worse, that someone else would intercept and read their messages. Pigeons coming in from Flanders did not always fare well. Falconry and archery were obsessions in most English villages. Codes could be broken. Sometimes, the only safe way was to stand in a man's presence and ask him what he knew.

The following dawn was a nervous time for the entire fleet. Only a few ships had dared to come in close, so the rest beat up and down in constant labour, waiting for word to come back or some sign of a pursuing fleet surging up from the Channel to the south. It did not help that bonfires still smoked that dawn, replenished and rebuilt along the coast, as far as anyone could see in the haze. Thousands came out to stand and stare on the beaches, shivering in the cold while they watched the banners of York and knew King Edward had not gone quietly into exile.

Some hours after noon, the ship's Flemish captain reported seeing the signal flag. He sent a boat at great speed before their man could be killed on the beach by those who had seen him waving to the ships. It was a close-run thing and he arrived before Edward and Richard of Gloucester with a black eye and a broken lip.

Edward laid aside his plate and offered the man a cup of wine for his trouble.

'What did you learn, Sir Gilbert?' he said. Only the thick fingers twitching at the table's cloth showed how important he considered the answer.

'Your Highness, I bear the sealed word of Thomas Rotheram, Bishop of Rochester.' The knight handed over a ribbon sealed with a wax disc, containing a scrawled name in the seal as proof. 'He swears his allegiance, but he says Your Highness must not land in Cromer. The Dukes of Norfolk and Suffolk have been imprisoned on the orders of Warwick, when they would not take an oath to . . . Henry of Lancaster.' Sir Gilbert Debenham was careful not to refer to 'King Henry' in that company.

Edward winced, working his tongue into the spot where his back teeth had been drawn, a memory of great pain followed by two days of a sweating fever. Norfolk in particular had been his gate into the country.

'What else?' Edward said. The knight was clearly reluctant to go on, but Edward waved his hand impatiently, looking away in thought as Sir Gilbert spoke once more.

'The Earl of Oxford has declared for Lancaster, my lord. He has bands of men all over this part of the country, ready to join together and fight, so the bishop told me. If you summon Sir William, my lord, he'll tell you he heard the same, though from different mouths. Cromer won't do, Your Highness, as things stand.'

'Dismissed, Sir Gilbert. And tell my steward to lay a gold angel on your swollen eye. I'm told it can work wonders.'

The knight's smile grew wide at that and he bowed deeply as he left.

'That is a blow,' Edward muttered. 'Norfolk was the right spot to land – in reach of London, with good men to gather to my banners. How strange it is, Richard. You know de Vere, Earl Oxford?'

'Well enough to know he will not be a friend of ours, no matter what we offer. His father was executed for treason, was he not? Do I have the right man?'

'Yes, that is the one. His older brother too. I do not suppose he feels any gratitude to me for securing his title for him!' Edward shook his head. He had kept his hair long and it swept over his face like a cowl of mail. 'If they hadn't cut his head off, I would have had Worcester flogged for his cursed cruelty. I swear it, Richard, if the enemies he made all stand against me at every port . . . where will we be then? I should never have made him Constable of England.'

'Worcester supported you, Brother. The sight of Lancasters enraged him, as I heard it, so he could not abide them to live. You cannot concern yourself with every trial, every fine imposed or criminal beheaded! The decisions were his.'

'No longer, then. If we survive, Richard, you will be Constable, with the annual stipend and the fine apartments in London. No more of his madness.'

Richard of Gloucester smiled in surprise, genuinely pleased.

'If we survive, I believe I would enjoy the labour. You honour me, Edward,' he said. His brother shrugged.

'It will mean nothing if we cannot land. If not Cromer, then where? The south is hostile country. Not Kent or Somerset, not Sussex, Devon, Cornwall, Bristol – all Lancaster strongholds. My life would not be worth a silver penny if we landed any further south than this.'

'The city of York itself is said to be against us,' Richard said glumly, 'though Northumberland will surely stand with you, God and Percy honour willing. The Percy heir fears Warwick's brother Montagu too much, with his greedy eyes on his old title.'

'Perhaps I am not well loved in York, though they owe me loyalty, not love! Oh, to hell with them all. I wanted to come back to the same place I left, to be seen rising once more.'

'But that gate is closed. So north, then? We have to land somewhere – and our first task will be to march away from it and be seen. You know it. There will be a dozen lords who will support you only if they see it is not a lost cause. Let them believe you can win and they will scramble to stand at your side. Just land and march, Edward. You have sixteen hundred men.'

'Flemish men,' Edward muttered.

'The rest will come.'

'Or watch as I walk on to the swords of the Neville family,' Edward said.

'Well, yes. But try to avoid doing that,' his brother replied. Edward smiled, staring into his cup. He was caught between sullen anger and amusement at his own failings.

'Henry of Bolingbroke came back from exile,' he said at last. Richard raised his head, understanding immediately.

'And he won back the throne,' he said.

'He landed in Ravenspur, on the River Humber, did you know that?' Edward added, looking into the distance.

'It would ring out like a bell,' Richard replied. He met his brother's gaze and both of them nodded, having reached an understanding and staved off despair for another night. Edward rose and opened the cabin door to the servant waiting outside.

'Have the captain signal the rest of the fleet. We sail north – for Ravenspur. I will plant my flag there.'

Warwick felt again the weight of armour. Being strapped and tied into the plates held many memories for him, few of which he welcomed. St Albans, with his father; Northampton, where they had captured Henry for the first time; St Albans again, where he had lost him. Towton, over all, in terror and killing. Some of the plates of his armour had been remade in the years since, while others still showed old marks, polished to shadows on the steel. He looked at the sweat-stained leather layers of his helmet and felt no desire to put it on.

His brother John had gone ahead of him, riding out as soon as news of the fleet had reached London. Derry Brewer had become a ghost, glimpsed only at a distance and then rushing about, his stick clicking on the flags. The spymaster hardly seemed to sleep and must have aged another dozen years. He'd told Warwick he'd exposed the secret lives of men who had been loyal for decades, just to get them out and searching for news. Derry's spies might not have worn armour, but they were still vital to the cause. The word had gone out to report a landing, anywhere in England. Not a boat could draw up on the shingle all round the coasts without being described to the local sheriff hours later.

Warwick drew his sword with his right hand, inspecting the blade though his squires and servants had checked every piece of his equipment a dozen times. His horse waited in the stables that were part of Westminster Hall, ready to ride west and north. Warwickshire was the seat of his power and his primary title, regardless of all the others Parliament still withheld from him. Those petty men and their disputes would have to wait until he returned. Warwick Castle was where he had kept Edward of York a prisoner. He only wished now that he had killed him then and saved them all years of pain and fear. It griped to see the paths he should have taken, as clear as the road to Warwickshire ahead. He sighed at that, wondering if one day he would look back on this moment and know he should have gone some other way.

He caught sight of his serious expression in the dark glass of the windows and chuckled. A man would not move at all if he wrapped himself in so many doubts and maybes. All he could do was act and know that sometimes he would surely be in the wrong. But to do nothing made him just a cat's paw for other men, a pawn who sat shivering, not daring to move until he was swept away.

His sword clicked home in its scabbard, a long cavalry blade as wide as three fingers at the base and hard enough to cut through an iron plate. He recalled an old story of King Richard the First, the man they called 'Lionheart' for his valour. He had used just such a sword to cut the handle of a steel mace into two pieces. It would do.

Richard Neville said a prayer then, for his father, Earl Salisbury, for his mother buried in Bisham Abbey, for his brothers and his own fate. If Edward of York had a fleet, he also had an army – and neither man nor angels could prevent him landing. It was barely five months since Warwick had come home himself and he was satisfied. With the exception of the needle's prick of bad luck that had let Edward and Richard of Gloucester escape, he had achieved everything else he had wanted. If he could have gone back a year and said to himself then that they would have King Henry on the throne and England at peace once again, it would have been enough. Perhaps.

He smiled wryly, knowing that he was afraid and trying to deny it. If Edward landed, Warwick would have to face him in battle. The very thought was a cold hand in his innards, squeezing at him. It would be the same for anyone who had seen Edward on the field. Yet Warwick would stand against York, because he had renewed his oaths and chosen a side. And because he had a daughter married to the Lancaster Prince of Wales.

He ran his fingers through his hair, seeing strength and determination reflected back at him in a long glass. He could not remain in London while Edward landed in the north. At such a time, he had to be out in the country, riding and gathering the bands of men he had waiting for his leadership. He feared Edward, of course, though he recalled that courage needed fear or it was worthless. If a man could not see the threat, he was not brave to resist it. Once again his mouth twisted wryly. In which case Edward had made him the bravest man in the world, for Richard Neville, Earl Warwick, was just about terrified of standing against him.

He looked up as the window shuddered under a gale's breath, suddenly spattered with rain as clouds spread over the city. Warwick clenched his fist, hearing iron and leather creak. He hoped Edward was out there at sea in a storm. The coasts were cruel and ships could be blown on to rocks or made to founder in waves as tall as cathedral spires. Perhaps God would do his work for him, just this one time, and batter the ships to splinters, drowning all the dreams of York.

'If it can be so, Lord, I would raise chapels in Your glory,' he muttered aloud, crossing himself and bowing his head. The wind outside seemed to increase, rattling raindrops against the dark glass. Warwick had spent much of his life at sea. Despite himself, he shivered at the thought of men struggling over black waters on such a night.

Edward felt fear rise in his chest and swamp him as if he had been taken by a wave. He could see almost nothing with the moon and stars hidden by thick cloud. The whole world seemed to have become madness, lurching and pulling his ship in every direction. He had grown used to the gentle rise and fall of the prow, but this new motion was entirely different, each lurch snubbed and interrupted by the chaos of the waves striking the sides. His brother Richard had gone a shade of white that was almost green and yet he could not lean over the stern in such heavy seas, not without being swept away. The captain had sent a man to strap Richard to the mast with quick knots, where he puked down himself and snarled.

In the darkness, the captain of the *Mark Antony* had lost sight of the shore. From that moment, with no glimpse of stars or the moon to navigate, the great fear was that they were being driven in upon the coast, soaring through the darkness on to rocks. To Edward's disbelief, there were men still up in the shrouds, though it must have been a freezing hell with no shelter from the spray and the storm wind. Their salvation, their lives all lay in spotting the shore before they were broken on it. Those men stayed where they were without complaint, frozen and squinting, turning their heads back and forth to make out any part of the howling darkness that might be land.

Edward hated to be helpless. He and his brother had understood as the storm came in that the best they could do for the crew was to stay out of their way. The sail was brought down and a sea-anchor played out behind them, a raft of planking and old canvas on a cable thick as a man's arm to give them some purchase on the sea as it went berserk around them. Edward and Richard thought they had seen storms before, but it seemed they had not. The waves rose and rose in thunder, while lightning cracked suddenly overhead, leaving silence and blindness until half the ocean crashed down on to the decks in foam and torrents, snatching men away over the side. In the last of the light, the sons of York could only look at each other in horror and wait it out, numb and useless as the hours passed, praying that the ship would stay afloat, that the ship would swim and not be smashed on the shore and leave them all as pale fish, on beaches north and south, for strangers to pick over and steal from.

'Land there, on the port side!' came a voice from far above, almost drowned by wind and sea. Edward looked up and then ahead, straining to see whatever the sailor had glimpsed. The captain too glanced up, wrenching his steering oars over with two other men, kicking at the deck and straining at the oak handles, roaring in frustration as they fought waves greater in size and weight than the ship itself.

''Ware the shore! Land to port!' came the lone voice again. 'Bear away.'

For an instant, Edward thought he saw a light, floating and dipping on the darkness, though he knew the motion was all in the ship that held his life. He had heard of wrecker towns placing lamps on the hills on stormy nights, guiding desperate captains on to the worst rocks so they could steal some remnant of the cargoes. He did not know whether he should mention the light, gone as soon as he had seen it.

It returned, on his left shoulder – and the sailors cheered.

'Why are they cheering?' Edward shouted to a crewman passing by.

'Because the light is afar!' the man replied. He carried a huge coil of rope and staggered as the ship lurched again, half falling until Edward reached out to steady him. 'Thank you,' the sailor said gruffly, realizing who had grabbed his arm as he squinted closer in the blackness.

'It means we ain't about to strike the land,' he said. 'Captain will swing us round now and we'll run east or north-east before the gale – and come back in the morning.'

'We can't reach the shore?' Edward asked, feeling like an innocent or a child. He ached to stand on firm ground once again. The sea was a different world and not one he enjoyed.

As if to reinforce the sense of wrongness, the sailor laughed at his suggestion.

'In a storm, we'd never make it. The biggest harbour in England would kill us all if we tried to race in under sail. Without the sails, we've hardly any way of steering at all, see? So it's a death trap trying to get into shelter. No, the only way is to run before it and hope it blows itself out.'

'And if it doesn't?' Edward asked.

'It gets cold up north, past the Shetland Islands, enough to freeze the ropes if we're driven far enough. If the storm doesn't blow itself out though, the boards will spring long before that. They can't stand this battering for long, not really. We'll sink long before it's cold enough to freeze, so there's no point worrying about that.'

To Edward's surprise, the sailor clapped him on the shoulder and carried the coil of rope to wherever it was needed, disappearing into the darkness. With enormous care, he made his own way to where his brother had been tied and left. Richard's head had sagged and his hair hung in rat-tails, the picture of misery.

'Are you alive?' Edward asked, prodding him. A groan was his only answer, making him chuckle. 'We've seen a light on the shore, over to the west, Richard. Did you hear? It can't be a bonfire on a night like this. This gale and rain would snuff it out. And there's only one light tower within a hundred miles of here – at Grimsby and the Humber. I think we've just passed Ravenspur, Richard. God willing the fleet will survive this blow to make our way back to it. What do you think?'

His brother was not asleep, but was instead so ill that he had withdrawn from the world, like a man knocked unconscious. With a great effort of will, he raised his head to his brother and told him he thought he should fuck off, which made Edward laugh.

The storm passed during the night, some time before the sun rose, though little was done until light returned. It was true the *Mark Antony* had been driven to the north, but the main mast was intact and the water level in the bilges was not dangerous, though it had reached a line marked on the boards that had not been touched in a generation. The captain himself had come down to have a look and Edward had gone with him, watching the man's face closely and seeing little to please him.

The sea was rough still, showing whitecaps on the waves, turning to foam in the gusts. Yet they could raise sail and tack south against such a blow, heading back to the spit of land that made Grimsby one of the best-sheltered fishing ports in the world.

The crew were busy as the ship heeled over, heading back down the coast, checking every seam and joint, repairing and mending anything that had sprung loose in the storm. Railings had to be reseated and the carpenter and his lad were busy with damp shavings and saws, the noise oddly comforting.

By noon, Richard of Gloucester had lost some of his blue-green colouring and could be safely left to groan over the stern. The sailors grinned at the noise he made, though he saw no humour in it. He played no part in raising signals to the fleet, though the captain watched the first one or two approach with huge caution, ready to raise sail and race away if they attracted the wrong attention. There were ships on that sea who would snap up a vessel battered by a storm without a second thought. It was likely some of them had put to sea that morning in the hopes of sighting just such a vessel. Yet the fleet came back together, mostly from the north and east where they had been scattered. Edward took it upon himself to climb the mast to its highest point to count them, gaining himself a view and a memory he would never forget. Thirty-two of them came back to cluster around the *Mark Antony*. They took up station in close formation, spaced far enough apart to avoid collisions, then just waited as the day poured through their fingers and the sea began to rise once more.

The captain of the flagship waited as long as he dared, but it became obvious Edward would not cease his search for the missing ships. In the end, the man climbed his own mast and asked permission to take the rest in. In truth, they had been lucky to lose just four ships and around two hundred men and forty horses, taken to the bottom or snatched by armed force. Yet the sun was heading for the horizon once more as Edward gave up and agreed.

The captains of the fleet had been waiting only on their order. All the sail the ships could bear was sent up and they came in fast to the great opening of the Humber River, two miles across from one sandbank to another. For safety, they came in three abreast, each crew feeling the sudden drop in wind and the change in the rhythm of the waves that meant there was land between their vessel and the big ocean rollers once more. Those who had been ill felt themselves growing well again and there ahead, gold in the setting sun, was the spit of Ravenspur, an arm reaching around to shelter them all from the storms outside. A cluster of houses could be seen clinging to the outer edge, looking as if just one more storm would scour them all away.

Thirty-two ships anchored and began the work of sending boats in to shore and establishing a safe landing for horses and men. Some of them looked south to where there were docks and quays across the estuary, but Ravenspur was where a king had landed and Edward only laughed and shook his head when his brother pointed wordlessly at Grimsby on the other side. It was one of the finest fishing villages in the north, just about. But no one began a revolution from Grimsby, that was just the truth of it.

Before the dark had truly settled on the spit of land, Edward came ashore with his brother and his lords. Earl Rivers and Baron Say took station as his guards and representatives. Another two hundred or so of those who had disembarked gathered around. It was not a coincidence that those few who had been born in England and Wales had also been the first to set foot on the shore they had once called home. They had been the first to volunteer as well, when Charles le Téméraire asked for men. Many of them had not set foot in England since boyhood, or whatever crime had made them run for the sea when they were young and foolish. Their delighted grins touched Edward's mood and he smiled back at them. The rest would land the following day rather than risk drowning in the muddy shallows. As Edward looked around him, he felt the joy of it, so that his eyes shone.

'Bring me my banners,' Edward called. His brother was there to hand them to him, on poles of polished oak that stood eight or ten feet high. Edward took them reverently in his arms, resting them on his shoulder as he trudged away through the men. His brother followed with torches and the crowd came with them both, swirling around them as they stood in awe at what was happening.

A hundred yards or so from the shore, Edward found rising ground and stalked up it, with the sun setting on his right hand. At the highest point, he planted the spikes of the banner poles with great lunges, pressing them deep into the ground. He knew better than most how the men would take the omen if one of them fell, so he used all his strength to shove them into the clay. The white rose, for his father. The Sun in Flames for himself. The three lions for the crown of England. He knelt then in silence and when he rose again and crossed himself, it was dark – and he was home.

11

It took another day to land the rest of Edward's forces from the battered little fleet. Some of the captains found sandy places where their boats could get all the way in, while others had to clamber through grasses and thick mud. Despite the care they took, a few men still drowned in armour, dragged beneath mud or salt water before anyone could get a rope to them or drag them out. It was hard work and they were panting and weary by the time the sun rose to noon.

As well as the *Mark Antony*, six of the ships had brought horses over in stalls that could be knocked down in moments. Two were designed for the task, with Venetian slings and cranes to lower the animals into the water, where they could swim to shore with the boys tending them. The other four were just merchant cogs with deep holds, crudely adapted for the task. They were driven on to the beach as fast as they could go, coming to a halt with a great groan of cracking timbers, then leaning over with horses whinnying in terror inside, the noise carrying far in the cold morning. Those ships would not sail again – and their crews treated them as hulks, already dead. Teams of them battered out the planking and joists with hammers, breaking wide holes. They led the miserable horses out to stand together, pawing at the scrub soil and looking sickly after the storm. A number of them had died in the chaos and crashing of the great waves, either overwhelmed by sickness or killed by the same hammers when they broke down their stalls and threatened the ship itself. Those shiny black bodies were left in the bilge-water as daylight shone below for the first time.

Perhaps because the storm had passed, the March day seemed to have a touch of spring in it, though it was a grimy and bedraggled army that assembled on the flats. Boats continued back and forth from the ships waiting at anchor, bringing weapons and tools and pieces of armour found scattered over the decks after the storm. The men could taste salt in everything as it clung to their skin and clothes in a fine powder. They drank deeply from flasks and broached barrels of drinking water as they were floated ashore, but it was not enough to sate their thirst and no one had eaten beyond a meagre ration of dried fish and meat for two days.

Edward looked at the men who would win his kingdom back for him. They stood as if they had been defeated already, worn out and starving, like so many beggars. His brother looked keen enough and Lord Rivers too, with Baron Say standing alongside. Those men would follow him to the end, he was certain. The rest would see their own poor state as they looked around. They would begin to doubt and to be afraid.

'Lord Rivers,' he called. 'Take my banners from the hilltop and pass them out to three of your men. Let us begin with pride. The city of Hull is no more than a dozen miles away. We'll find rest and food there. Beyond that is York. We will gather more men to my colours in that place. This is just the first step, gentlemen! Captains – have your men form in column.' His orders were echoed by the twenty men with authority over the grumbling soldiers, bullying them into lines and formations, all the while snapping commands to the boys running alongside with horns and pipes and drums. The rhythms of the march began to sound across the salt flats and those who had heard them before felt their sluggish blood respond in the cold, raising their heads to scent the wind. They turned their backs to the sea and headed inland, leaving the fleet to its repairs and its return to Flanders. The sea-captains knew they would not be needed again. Edward would not run a second time, no matter what he faced.

Warwick had not disbanded his army over the winter months, though keeping twenty thousand men away from their work for an entire winter had reduced him almost to beggary. The heart of it was the chaos around his titles. There simply was no mechanism in law to bring an attainted man back into society. Denied his rents, Warwick had been reduced to selling small estates. There was no help for it. The army had to be paid – and fed and clothed and given weapons. Those men needed another host of trades to keep them in the field, from smiths and leatherworkers to cobblers, spinners, tailors, doctors, too many to recount. All of it meant that a torrent of silver and gold had to be found, even when Warwick paid as late as he could and was always a month or two behind. He seemed to spend entire days cloistered with clerks and sheaves of accounts until his head ached and he could hardly see.

Though he had not yet won the formal right to his estates in Warwickshire, it still felt like coming home. Coventry was his English heartland, the great city to the north of the county. It was not as rich as London, though he had still taken loans from all the monastic houses there, at whatever terms they imposed. One way or the other, he would have it all back – or if he died, he would not care about the debts. It was an odd freedom to feel, for a man without sons. His daughters would be protected by the Duke of Clarence or the Prince of Wales. One way or the other, his fortune was his to recover – and to spend as he saw fit.

The last of the religious men left with his ledgers, bowed over by responsibility and age. Warwick was alone for the first time in six days and he felt his senses swim. Ever since the sighting of a fleet had come in, he had been working and planning a thousand details. All for the threat of one man.

The door opened at the end of the hall. Warwick looked up at the interruption and found himself smiling in welcome at the sight of Derry Brewer. It was not a friendship he had ever expected and in fact they had been on opposing sides more than once. His brother John Neville had no liking for the man at all, though he'd formed a grudging respect for Brewer's loyalty. Yet if Richard Neville could forgive the queen who had killed his father, he could surely forgive her servants as well. Warwick felt a little smug about it, as if he had attained a sort of wise spirit that other men would never know.

'I thought you were heading back to London, Master Brewer,' he said as Derry approached, tapping along on his stick. It was strange, but for all Warwick's newfound warmth, he still became aware of the dagger he wore on his hip. He felt a twinge of weary cynicism, but kept a hand close to its hilt even so. The world had proven itself to be a hard place, of betrayals and brutal killings. He would not be one caught by surprise, not ever again.

'I am, this afternoon,' Derry replied. 'I thought as I was gathering in my little bees, that I would take a moment to visit you.'

'Your "bees", Derry? The whispers of men and women you employ, I suppose?'

'I like the image, Richard. Of my people settling here and there, all unnoticed as they listen. Or perhaps it is just that the news they bring in is honey to me.'

'You have heard something?' Warwick said, straightening.

'As you said, London is too far from the north of England to be of use to us. The news is always out of date. Coventry though – these middle lands – is a beating heart. And it has a couple of miles of good, thick city wall, which I have learned to value over the years. I do like it. Perhaps I will take a house here in my retirement. If I had a patron willing to lease a property to me, perhaps, at a fair rate.'

Warwick scratched the lobe of his ear.

'I imagine a man with useful information can make all sorts of arrangements, Master Brewer. It depends on what he has heard.'

'Yes, I'm sure it does,' Derry replied, giving up. In truth, he had a small house in the Rookeries of London and a manor house outside, in the name of an old friend and archer. He had spent barely a month there in the previous decade, but he still dreamed of tending his true hives and pruning apple trees when Henry's son sat safe and secure on the throne and York was just a black mark in the scrolls. He smiled at Warwick, the one eye seeing the younger man's exhaustion and understanding it only too well. Neither of them would survive if Edward was allowed to win, that was an absolute certainty.

'I did hear that Edward and his brother set out from Flanders with more than a thousand men. I have a reliable lad there who said they are mercenaries of Burgundy, though we could have guessed at all that. Still, the boy deserves a patron and I said you'd find him a place in the ranks.'

Warwick waved a hand.

'What's one more on my payrolls? I have thousands of men sleeping in the market place here, have you seen them? There are many more marching up and down in Warwick Castle. Each morning, I am visited by the fine mayor and the aldermen of Coventry holding their hats in their hands and asking if I would mind very much stopping my army from stealing food and bothering their young women. I had to hang a fine great bully for killing a local, can you believe that? For doing what I need him for, I had to take his life! I find myself become a nurse to them all – or a tutor, or a . . . man of accounts! All while I wait and every day that passes is a turn of the thumbscrew, tighter and *tighter* . . .'

'Calm yourself, Richard,' Derry said. 'We sighted a fleet, that's all. Yes, this is the worst time, the waiting. Won't we look fools if that great storm broke his ships to pieces? Think of that! Or if he lands up by York, think of all we've done to remind them of Towton in recent months. Lancaster on the throne means *peace*, son! Peace means trade. Trade means wealth. That's our line, when they ask. Polite and firm – tell them what they want to hear. The cities of the north don't want Edward's wars. They still remember the last one.' Derry was pleased to see Warwick was at least listening to him.

'When they land, my little bees will send word just as fast as they can and then we'll fall on him from a great height. You have Earl Oxford on your side, Duke Exeter, Earl Essex and Devon, Somerset down on the coast, waiting for Margaret to cross. You have your brother John – and I would imagine you have your own trusted men in the north with pigeons, for the moment they catch sight of our big lad?' Derry paused until Warwick nodded. The pigeons had been taken up to York months before, ready to wing their way back to London. He bit his lip and muttered a curse at that thought. The birds would pass straight over Coventry, heading for the mews in Westminster where they had been raised. It was just one more of a thousand things to consider and plan around.

Derry Brewer was rambling on as if oblivious, though Warwick knew from experience that the man rarely missed any reaction to his words, even with his one eye. In that single aspect, Derry reminded him of the French king, another man who watched rather more closely than was good manners.

'And Edward has his brother Richard and Lord Rivers, loyal as an old dog. Baron Say went with him and is likely still at his side, tasting the crumbs that fall from his great champing jaws.' Derry grinned at the image, then grew more serious. 'There are men I do not trust in these times, Richard – Earl Percy in the north, for one. You knew him when he was a lad, so I might discount him. But then your brother John keeps telling anyone who asks that he will have that title returned to his hot little hands. So Percy could well come in with the Yorks, whereas if your brother could just keep his trap shut, he might stay out of it completely.'

'I'll have a word with John,' Warwick said. Brewer shrugged.

'It's too late for that now! The whole country knows your brother has a claim, or thinks he does. What about Clarence? Can you trust him?'

Warwick considered his son-in-law for a moment, then nodded.

'Yes. I was there when his daughter was born and died at sea. He has not forgiven his brother, not yet.'

'He seems to expect a great deal for one who has chosen his wife and his vengeance though. Heir to the throne? Has he learned yet of your daughter's marriage to Edward of Lancaster? Does that not put Clarence further away from the throne? What will "second in line" matter then?'

Warwick snorted.

'He wants the Duchy of York above all – and Edward will claim that over any other right. No, I will trust my son-in-law for his ambition, even if he cools on the rest.'

'You forgave Margaret of Anjou,' Derry reminded him, prodding at old wounds. Warwick shot him a sharp glance.

'I did, because it was my way back to my own titles. I have had enough of being in the wrong.'

'I see that. But I just meant Clarence might come to feel the same way. I would not trust him on the field if the day can be turned against me, if you understand? Him and Edward and Richard – those three shared the loss of a father. You should be wary of those sons of York, that's all. Just think of your own brothers, even John with his petty anger and his sense of the world against him. He's still yours, if the knives come out.'

Warwick chuckled suddenly.

'I would not let John ever hear you say that. You'd see petty anger then, and spite. It was John who told me not to trust Clarence. You and he are more alike than you would care to admit. Twins in your suspicions! I'll tell you what does matter, Brewer – I have assembled and fed more than twenty thousand men this winter. Think of that for a moment, of sixty thousand meals a day for months and months. Of equipment and horses and weapons and land. I have paid for them to remain in Warwickshire, in the heart of England, to train and sharpen and drill. And when Edward comes against us, and he will come, they will surround his few men and they will cut them all down.' He leaned back then, blowing air out. 'I fear the man, Derry, there is no shame in saying it, not for those who were at Towton. That is why I have archers building their range outside the walls of Coventry. That is why I have ten thousand men marching to build their wind and strength, then sparring in all the fields around Warwick Castle. More here in Coventry. *More* ready to come in if Edward is sighted!'

Derry bowed a little way, easing his right leg back.

'I am glad to hear it, Richard. I would like to see this brought to an end – and you know Edward has to die for there to be an ending. He is not even thirty! You have seen how life will be if he remains alive, with days spent waiting for horns to blow and the whole country to rise up and swallow us. Five months of it has been too much for me. Can you imagine five years spent in this way?'

'No, I can't,' Warwick replied. 'And I agree, Derry. Whatever else happens, I will not leave them alive. I made that mistake before, when Edward was my prisoner in Warwick Castle – and this is my chance to put it right. My last chance.'

'Don't wait,' Derry went on. 'He will grow stronger every day, once he lands. You know how others flock to him, all the dispossessed, all the enraged, all those knights and lords who see no special future for their families under Lancaster – they will all stand with him. So you must strike out as soon as you have word. You have made your camp here, away from London. That was wise. From here, you can summon your armies and lunge in any direction. God be with you, son. Don't cock it up.'

'You won't stay then?' Warwick asked, though he knew the answer. Derry shook his head, a smile playing at his lips.

'I will keep King Henry company in Westminster. Where he is safe. I am too old to march and I always said that my work ends when the fighting begins. All I want now is a quiet retirement – and Edward's head on London Bridge. I will be happy to forgive him then, but not till then.'

'Go with my blessing, Master Brewer. I hope you'll raise a pint to me when we meet again. And pass on my prayers to King Henry.'

'Oh, His Highness won't understand, Richard. Not any more. But I will raise a pint or two of London ale, that I can promise. Until we meet again, son.'

The walls of Hull were made of dark-red brick and stood forty feet high at the lowest point, with towers rising all along the river and right around the enclosed city. Edward's double column had trudged in from the marshes for sixteen miles, at their best estimate. They stood waiting patiently to be allowed in through the closest gate, while those who lived within the walls crowded on to every open space to stare down at them in dull fascination.

Edward's banners flew proudly before the city walls, but the gate ahead of him remained closed. He knew his arrival had been observed, of course. The guards on those high walls could hardly have missed so many armed men approaching. Yet it seemed they would be denied entrance. As he exchanged a glance of fury with his brother Richard, a herald was let down to them on a wooden platform held out on a long beam and tackle. The man reached the ground and stepped away quickly, just in time as it was winched back up.

'I do not imagine this fellow is coming with good news,' Richard muttered. 'It seems Hull will declare for Lancaster, Brother. Who would have thought that?'

The herald approached and bowed deeply. He wore the livery of the city itself and was an unremarkable man, though his neck was furred with some white crust of fungus or rash. He scratched at it as he talked, making both Edward and Richard want to back away from whatever disease had its hold on him.

'My lords, the city council prefers to remain aside from any conflict.'

'If you refuse me entry, you are of Lancaster,' Edward said shortly. The man swallowed and scratched himself again, his eyes wide with fear.

'I am a mere messenger, Your Highness, I mean no insult. We are all afraid and the gates will remain closed. That is all I have been told to say to you.'

'Go back then. Tell your council I will not forget. I will

return here and hold them to account when I am finished. That is all I have to say to you.'

Edward whirled his horse around and jerked his head to his brother.

'Come on, I won't beg these people for their help. I am the king of England and they are my subjects. I have planted my fucking banners. That is all I need to do.'

Without another glance at the cringing herald, Richard rode after his brother, back to the staring faces of their Flemish soldiers. His brother rode past them, deep in his anger until he had gone a mile further down the road and dismounted.

Though there was no food to be had, Richard gave orders to camp for the night and to send anyone with the skill out to seek a local flock or catch live prey, the rest making themselves as comfortable as they could on damp ground. Only the horses would eat their fill of spring grasses. Unless they found a few sheep or cows, most of the men would go hungry, with another thirty miles or so to march the following day. Richard sent one of the captains to retrieve his brother's banners and as he did so, grew thoughtful. He rode out along the road heading west, a wide track better than the one that had brought them in from the coast.

'Well, what would you have had me say, Richard?' Edward demanded when he came close. 'Should I have begged for them to let me in, their anointed and crowned king?'

'I do not think they would, even if you had,' Richard said. 'It made me think though, of Henry of Bolingbroke once again. He was refused when he came into the north. He had to stop claiming the crown.'

'He was not king though, was he?' Edward demanded. 'Not then. These people would have thrown themselves at my feet less than six months ago and yet they tell me now they will not open their gates? I will not forget it, Richard. I'll remember this!'

'Brother, listen to me. Old Henry of Bolingbroke told them he cared nothing for the crown of England. Instead, he claimed he had come for his personal titles. The towns and the villages could not deny him those. *There* is your gate. Raise just the banner of York and the Sun in Flames when we reach the city of York tomorrow. Leave the three lions furled and perhaps they will open the gates to us. You are the eldest son of Richard of York – no man can dispute your title.'

'Attainted in Parliament,' Edward said, though he had grown less flushed. His brother snorted at that.

'Parliament which is hundreds of miles away. This is Yorkshire, Brother. A different world from all the doings down there. Raise just York and your own badge tomorrow. And pray.'

12

Edward could sense Micklegate Bar as it grew before him. His brother had told the captains that they would approach the city of York from the south because that was the tradition, and where they would ask the mayor for permission to enter. After the gates of Hull had remained closed, that was not something to take lightly. Yet the truth was darker and more complex. Micklegate Bar was where the heads of the old Duke of York and his son Edmund had been left to rot on spikes. For years, Edward had dreamed of taking them down and on the first morning after Towton, still spattered with blood and earth, he had come to that spot and ended the humiliation of his family.

Earl Warwick had stood with him on that day, retrieving his own father's head. It beggared belief that Edward could find himself standing against that man, now his true enemy, after they had shared such a moment of their lives. Edward could see it as if he stood there ten years before, just by closing his eyes and letting his horse walk closer. His brother Richard looked at him in concern, but he could not understand, having been just a child when Edward broke Lancaster and avenged their father and their brother.

Edward opened his eyes. The city of York had a more intimate connection to his family than any other place in England, so that by approaching it he was dragging up his past triumphs and disasters in a great storm within. He found himself breathing harder and with warmth, though the day was cold.

The gate was closed, though that was not a surprise in itself. The walls were there for exactly that purpose, to protect the men and women and children within from being trampled by every marauding force of soldiers passing by. Massive stone towers and gates meant that cities could thrive and grow, where once they had lived in terror of Viking raiders, or the private armies of lords in dispute. The walls of York gave them confidence and pride as they stared down at the white rose banner and behind it, Edward's Sun in Flames.

Richard of Gloucester raised his right fist to halt and the order snapped out along the column. The two brothers exchanged a glance and went forward alone, the hooves of their horses clattering and scraping, echoing back from the walls. Micklegate Bar loomed above the gate below, the broad tower pierced with windows and walkways, a symbol of power in its own right, proclaiming York as a centre of trade – and strength.

The sons of York came to a halt before the gates, reining in and waiting as a man walked out on stiff legs above them. Mayor Holbeck looked flustered, pink and shining with hands that clasped a sheaf of papers as if they would protect him. He opened his mouth, but Edward spoke before he could.

'I come here, not as king of England, but as Duke of York. You have seen my banners. My family estates are close by. I ask only to pass these walls in peace, perhaps to purchase food and rest for my men. Beyond that, I make no claim on you, though this city bears my name and kept the heads of my father and brother on the gate where you stand, sir!'

The mayor flinched from the last, gripping his papers with even more force. Yet he was not a fool, nor a weak man. Holbeck stared down at the two brothers, seeing their determination. Further back, their army stood like ravening wolves, looking at a city they would surely strip of food and ale. Holbeck shook his head at that thought, thinking of his daughters.

'My lord, I know you for a man of honour. I know your word is good. If you give me an oath of safe passage, I will order the gates opened. Choose . . . a dozen men to enter with you and gather what supplies you need. I cannot allow more without skirting my oath to Lancaster. I cannot do more, my lord, though I might wish it.' Mayor Holbeck clamped his mouth shut then and stood with his head bowed as Edward glanced aside.

'Better than nothing,' Richard murmured. His brother nodded and took a huge breath to call up his answer.

'Very well, Mayor Holbeck. You have my word, on my behalf and all those beholden unto me. There will be no clash of arms, no injury or rude action. With your permission, I will enter with my brother and a dozen other men, to gather food and water for those who love York still.' He filled his lungs again to make his voice carry further, to the hundreds who would be clustered close inside the walls, craning to hear every word. 'If any man of this city wishes to join me then, I will accept him! And if there are none, I will not forget, when I return! I am the Duke of York, my father's title. I am Edward Plantagenet, the head of my house, on my honour. I have given you my word, in the name of Christ.'

The mayor signalled to men below him and the gates were unbarred, their chains removed. Edward waited until he had a dozen of his men at his back, then rode under the tower. He did not flinch as its shadow passed across him, though he had to stop on the inner yard and turn his mount to look back at the row of iron spikes set into the stone.

'There, Richard. That Anjou she-wolf put my father's

head there. Dipped in tar to gape at the crowds below – and with a paper crown.'

Richard looked at his older brother, seeing his eyes shining. He wondered in that moment if the oath by which they had gained entrance would be broken. Guards watched them all around and some carried crossbows still, yet were abashed to see a man who had been king pointing to where his father's head had been.

'I wish I could have seen it,' Richard said. 'I was just a child when you won at Towton. I would give anything to have stood with you on that day.'

Edward shuddered. 'No, if you had been there, you would not speak with such longing. That day . . .' He tapped his head. 'It remains, bright and terrible.' He looked up at the Micklegate Bar once more. 'And when the sun rose again, I climbed that wall and took down the heads of my father and my brother Edmund. Made black by tar, they did not look like either of them, though I could see father's hair . . .' Edward broke off, his grief enough to choke him. 'She meant it as an insult, that such a man as our father could aspire to wear a crown, but be worth only paper. Yet I am his son – and I was crowned in gold, Richard! I have sat the throne and given battle under royal banners.' He breathed slowly out, forcing his temper under control until he could look at Richard and around them, at the cowed guards and the mayor still waiting to be addressed. Edward ignored them all.

'And she still lives, Richard, with her son grown to manhood – to the age our brother Edmund reached when he was cut down. Is that not a strange thing? I sometimes think we have no more say in our life's events than you and I had in that storm at sea. We are just thrown and battered back and forth. Some sink and are lost – and some rise up on great waves, all undeserving.' His voice had grown somehow to fill the enclosure by the walls, so that every man and woman watching had their gaze fastened on to him.

'Yet I am one who stands *before* the wave that will engulf him and I am not afraid! I am the house of York, Brother. I am the ancient line. I will not turn from the storm, though it blasts me down. And if it does, I will rise to my feet once more!'

There were some in that city who had not lost their love of Edward as king. They cheered his words, from the windows and in the streets leading deeper into the city. Richard joined them, raising his arms and roaring with the rest.

Through sheer labour and pain, his brother had remade the ruin he had been. It was a moment of clear joy and Richard was still chuckling as he dismounted and clapped the stunned and appalled mayor on his back.

'Come, sir. We have a loyal army of York in need of a hot meal – and there was talk of ale. Come, break out your stew-pots and your casks for us, there's a good fellow.'

The mayor flinched under the slap, still looking around at those cheering Edward of York and feeling himself flush. He had given his personal oath to a herald bearing the seal of Lancaster. That had seemed only right a few months before, though he had not expected to have King Edward himself return to test his word, standing there for all the world as if he had never left. Well, he would do what he could.

'Follow me, my lord. I will have carts and sides of beef brought, you'll see. Your men will eat well tonight.'

The small army of York had marched thirty miles that day and were footsore and starving. They gave a great cheer when the gates opened once again as the sun set, revealing a train of carts and steaming cauldrons. The captains were hard-pressed to stop the rush forward, bawling and laying about them with sticks. Those who had been born in England took some pleasure in pressing forward as one group, holding the rest back so that the queues could form. Otherwise, it would be 'bleeding chaos', as they explained slowly and loudly to the men of Burgundy and Flanders.

There was enough for all and more, so that they filled flasks and added dozens of carts to their baggage, enough for other meals to come. Some women of the town came out to walk with them, arranging to be paid by the captains or lords for their labour. In truth, all those men were grateful for their presence and there was no question of respectable women being insulted or treated roughly. They would cook and mend and any man fool enough to say a cross word to them was likely to take a beating from his mates.

The column was made greater by almost a hundred of those ladies of York, with their sleeves rolled to their elbows and their caps and shawls tied tight as they clambered aboard carts and took up the reins of sleepy old ponies. The entire setting took on the appearance of an army on the move rather than the column of refugees it had resembled before.

There could not be a general call to arms, after Edward had agreed not to summon them as king of England. Yet even so, they came. As the evening turned to darkness, men left the city in twos and threes and groups, in mail and with what weapons they had, walking out proudly to join the camp. They were greeted with humour and satisfaction, fresh ale pressed into their hands. Their names were assigned to the captains who would command them, with some new men promoted from among those born on English clay. It was true the newcomers were only three hundred or so by morning, while the rest of the city stayed safe behind their walls. Yet it was a beginning and Edward put a brave face on his disappointment. At sunrise, he marched the men south, with drummer boys rattling away and every horn blown. He needed to be seen.

Behind them, pigeons clattered into the air, released from private mews in the city. The birds found their bearings in great wheeling circles above the walls, then responded to some ancient sense and headed south, carrying news of the landing of York. Edward and Richard watched them pass with expressions of foreboding, the birds too high even for archers. It made their stomachs clench to think of word spreading ahead, bringing the news to Warwick and to London.

From York, they followed the road south for a time, passing Towton with heads bowed for all those who had left their bones there. When they reached Ferrybridge, Edward rode over a crossing he had seen destroyed and rebuilt, lost in solemn memory.

The road was of good stone as they passed Pontefract. By then Richard had scouts out in wide lines, riding miles beyond the marching ranks. It was they who reported the banners of Montagu flying over the battlements of Pontefract Castle.

Edward did not know how many men lay safe within those walls, but even so, he rode to the edge of arrow-shot and challenged Montagu to come out. There was no reply. Some of Edward's men showed their bare buttocks to the walls. The action amused Richard, though his brother was tight-faced and smiling falsely as he gave the order to march on. John Neville, Lord Montagu, had played his part in their humiliation the previous year. It would have been a grand beginning to have caught Warwick's brother beyond his walls and strung him up by his entrails. That would have rung the bell Edward wanted. Instead he could only ride past, looking back over his shoulder at the banners still flying on the battlements there, as if to spite his ambition.

Sandal Castle was a place of special pilgrimage for the sons of York, where their father and brother had been murdered by a French queen fighting with Scots against better men. Edward and Richard knelt on cloaks and prayed for the lost souls of that place, and for the guidance they would need to exact a vengeance long overdue. It was not too much to ask, not in Sandal, close by the city of Wakefield. At least there, so close to their father's estate, they were not refused at the walls. Edward put his ring to a loan of a thousand gold angel coins, then changed most of them to silver to pay his followers for their service.

Another eighty men joined him when they saw that generous act, ten knights among them, and a dozen smiths and farriers with blades of forge iron in their hands. It was such a small number that Edward came close to despair, though he greeted them as brothers and spoke to all he could. In private, he told Richard he was dreading the sight of the first army to move against his little force. He would be overwhelmed and cut down. England drowsed and Edward could not see how to wake her, or her people.

Each day brought a greater sense of spring and growing in the land. Richard sent men out ahead of them to carry word, but the people were cold and dark of heart. Few came in and it seemed they had turned their faces from the house of York.

The news of them began to spread, so that each town and city they reached knew York had returned. Some were hostile and jeered as they passed or used slings to clatter stones against armoured knights. Edward resisted the desire to leave those villages and towns in flames behind him. He was the king returned, not some brutal usurper. It galled him more than he could express, but he allowed only stern and dignified rebuke in his dealings and not the hand round their throats he would have preferred. He and his brother felt alone in the evenings, though the army grew around them like callus or armour, in dozens and scores at a time. In Doncaster, an old hunting friend brought out two hundred men, well armed and equipped. William Dudley also brought a huge quantity of claret on a cart, though he was astonished to find Edward would not touch a drop of it. His vow of abstinence was holding still, though Richard saw how his brother licked dry lips at the sight of such fine skins and casks. Perhaps because he felt Richard's probing gaze, Edward did not weaken.

At Nottingham, two men Edward had knighted years before caught up with their column, bringing fully six hundred about as road-weary and travel-stained as it was possible to be, after a hundred miles of loping along in his wake. Edward's spirits began to rise as he considered how many others owed him their livelihoods and their estates, from lowly manors and trading licences, to barons and earls by the score. Just five months before, he had been their liege lord. If some of them chafed, it seemed they had not all forgotten their oaths.

At Leicester, the first of his great magnates showed his loyalty, as Baron Hastings arrived and knelt before him, renewing his oath to the 'Rightful son of York and king of England'. Edward embraced the man in joy, at his loyalty, but also at the three thousand in steady ranks Hastings had brought with him to the London road. In all, six thousand men followed the two sons of York, with three lions held high along with the rose of York and the Sun in Flames. There were no hidden ambitions by then, as Edward strode through the camps. He spoke to anyone who asked him and affirmed he had come home for his crown.

That night, Richard and Edward broke bread with Lord Hastings, along with his captain, Sir William Stanley. Once more Edward touched no wine or ale and those who knew him well were solemn, even moved at the changes in him. He ate just a little and pushed away a plate that had not been scoured clean, looking at the newcomers with clear eyes and a fine colour to his skin, the picture of health.

'Your Highness,' Hastings said, beaming. 'I am overjoyed to see you so hale and strong. I only wish every man of England could observe you this moment, perhaps to compare you to the sickly creature and his French wife who are the alternative.'

'And men like Warwick, Your Highness,' Sir William Stanley added, raising his cup. 'Damnation and death to him.' Stanley had a wiry look compared to some of his rank, with a lustrous beard finely trimmed about his chin and curling into thick moustaches. Edward might have dismissed him as a fop, but his brother Lord Stanley had been a great supporter and it was said the younger son knew the skills of war as well as any other who had devoted his life to them. Richard nodded unreservedly to Stanley's toast, raising his cup in reply. There could be no settlement with Warwick, not again. Such men had turned traitor so many times they could never be trusted, but only put down like a mad dog.

'Your three thousand are more than welcome, Lord Hastings,' Edward replied, settling himself. 'And I will spend them well. Tell me, then, what news have you of Warwick, of the Earl of Oxford? Of all those traitorous bastards who thought they could run me out of England and never pay a price for that scorn! Tell me of them.'

Hastings gave a great bark of laughter to see Edward so fierce and full of brag.

'There are perhaps six thousand gathered at Newark, my lord. Under de Vere, Earl Oxford. A far greater force lies with Warwick at Coventry to the south. Some say he has twenty thousand there, or even more.' For an instant, Hastings looked uncomfortable, but forced himself to continue speaking. 'Your . . . brother George is to the south and west of us, my lord. He has some three thousand of his own men and they say he is loyal to Warwick, as his father-in-law.'

'Yes, Lord Hastings. They do say that,' Edward replied, with a glance at Richard. 'My brother has been tainted by Warwick's influence, that is true enough. I am not certain of him, but I will call on blood over marriage and see which way he leaps.'

Edward waved his hands to clear away unpleasant thoughts.

'I have my path then, or at least the first step. Newark, if they gather there. We will march, what, a day north? I would not leave that six thousand at my back, perhaps to join with Montagu, when he finally finds the courage to leave his castle at Pontefract. No, that will suit me well – and give me a chance to bind these men into companies. I have found battle to be a powerful bond, Hastings. I have seen too much of it perhaps, but I am not finished yet. Tell your men to be ready to march before dawn. I will see these Oxford dogs and kick their disloyal teeth back down their throats. And I will not stop then, not until it is done.'

Edward's lords and captains matched him with shouts and clatter, as he was to be seen fully dressed and clear-headed even before the sun had risen. With the king waiting on their pleasure, they raced around to rouse their men from slumber, kicking them into line. There was no time for a proper breakfast and instead they gulped water and snatched meat pasties handed to them as they passed the cooking carts.

Edward's warhorse was snorting and pawing the ground, taking its mood from the man who waited upon its back. His impatience spread to the rest of them and they set off at a pace that had them sweating after just a mile or two. Yet the road was good and there were streams across their path to take in cold water. Newark was some twenty miles from their camp, but they reached the outer lines of Oxford's scouts long before noon, sending those men racing back to carry news of their approach.

Edward slowed the pace then, enough for his captains to arrange the men in wider lines for battle. He sent the hundred Flemish hand-gunners into the front ranks, eager to see what they could do with the heavy guns they carried on their shoulders. He had seen such things before, but they still seemed more noise and smoke than actual bite.

They were to be disappointed. The ranks of hand-gunners shrugged and pinched their smoking fuses dead as the sun reached just past noon. Ahead of them, the trail of thousands of men could be seen stretching away to the south. There were always scraps left behind to mark the passage of an armed force – broken sandal straps and buttons, rotten food thrown down, broken poles and weapons gone to rust. Edward was disappointed, though he saw his men were pleased enough that they would not fight that day. His brother too seemed cheerful and when Edward called him over to ask the reason, Richard laughed.

'They will not stand, Brother! Can't you see it? First Montagu hid behind his walls, now Oxford and his captains run for their mothers at the first sight of this royal army marching into sight. Your reputation goes ahead of us like another ten thousand men. They are terrified of you.'

'Well, they should be,' Edward said, brightening. He put aside his desire to see the first blow of his return and simply accepted that an enemy haring away in bleating terror was almost as good, perhaps even better for spreading the word.

'Have the men camp here,' he called to Anthony Woodville as the big man dismounted nearby. 'But keep the scouts wide.

I will not be ambushed by some scoundrel. Make sure we can see them coming.'

Lord Rivers bowed and went off to pass on the news. The king's brother-in-law was smiling at Edward's rekindled enthusiasm, so very different from the bleak months behind them. They all felt it. The army was too small, God knew, but it was still better to be on the move than rooted in one spot.

It took a few hours to collect the camp followers who had fallen behind. Though the day was not old, Edward passed orders for them to rest and mend. They would spend the spring afternoon tending weapons and cuts and eating the vast amounts healthy men needed to march and fight. Trappers went trotting off into the local woods, while others sought out healthy cattle to buy or steal. Rivers chuckled as he hobbled his horse with an old rein and removed his saddle and tack. He remembered the fat and drunken king Edward had been. To see the great hawk returned to them, lean and fierce, was a joy.

Scouts came in and out of the York camp at all hours, working shifts of half a day to keep their eyes fresh for anyone else creeping about in the hills. At sunrise the following morning, one of them came racing in from the north, blowing his horn and yelling the alarm. The entire camp came alive as six thousand men threw off blankets and took up blades and armour. News spread as fast as it could be shouted, that the banners of Montagu had been sighted there, with thousands on the march. It seemed John Neville had come out after all, behind them.

Edward yawned as he was startled awake. He slept on his back in the night air, resting on a blanket and wrapped in two or three cloaks so that his face was bared to the sky and damp. He rose and dressed as the excited young scout stood at his side and passed on his news, proud as a cockerel at being of use.

'Thank you, son,' Edward said. He reached in a pouch for a silver penny and found a gold angel in his hand instead. The scout's eyes widened and Edward chuckled. He took a moment to search for a different coin and then gave up. He was in a strange, light mood, now that his campaign had a sense of life to it. He tossed the coin and the young man snatched it in awe, delighted. Edward looked up to see his brother Richard watching him in amusement.

'What makes you smile so, Brother?' Richard said. 'Did I not hear that Montagu is creeping around behind us?'

'He is, Richard. Don't you see it? Warwick lies ahead with his army, with his host. John Neville leans on our shadow behind, so that we are forced south. Just as it was last year, when we ran for the coast.'

'I do not see why that is cause for your bright eyes . . .' Richard replied, beginning to worry that his brother had gone mad.

'It is not the *same*, Richard. I had eight hundred before, in the winter. I have six thousand with me now, in the spring. And you know, I am not the man I was. I tell you, Brother. I will eat them alive when they come. I will call them out for their treachery and their cowardice and I will spit their bones back!'

Derry Brewer raised a silver fork with a piece of roasted pork on it. The polished implement had been the gift of the Italian ambassador, a man whose company Derry enjoyed, though he trusted him not at all. Ambassador D'Urso was clearly a spy, though he seemed genuinely pleased that Lancaster had regained the throne. Old nations preferred stability, Derry assumed. They did not enjoy usurping kings, or peasant revolts. Such things made the foundations of their own kingdoms tremble. Before he had gone, the man had said that Edward had left by the door and would have difficulty finding his way in by the window. That he would surely leave his skin behind. Derry chuckled to himself. It was amusing how foreigners talked.

'One more, Harry,' he said. 'Come on.' King Henry frowned slightly without looking at him, but he opened his mouth and Derry pressed the piece of meat and gravy between his lips, watching patiently as he chewed.

When a knock sounded, Derry arranged the table so that the bowl and the fork were in front of the king and no sign remained that he had been feeding him like a child. He called for the visitor to enter, fully aware that only the most important news could have found its way past the layers of guards at each door and stair of the Palace of Westminster.

The man who entered handed over a grey pigeon, held upside down and seemingly quite at peace. Derry's interest sharpened at seeing a tiny brass tube attached to its leg. He checked it had not been disturbed and gave the bird back to the man as he backed away, flickering a glance at the seated king, who had not reacted at all.

Derry unspooled a tiny strip of paper, standing closer to the windows to see it in the best light. He dropped it into the flame of an oil lamp then and sat back down by King Henry, taking up the fork and the bowl, long cold.

'Edward of York has landed, Your Highness,' Derry said softly. 'He is riding south, where we are waiting for him.'

He had not expected a reply and Derry blinked as the king spoke.

'Cousin York is a good man, Derry.'

'Of course he is, Your Majesty. Course he is. Come on now, if you don't mind. One more piece. You have to eat to stay strong.'

13

The sun shone and Edward inspected his new horse, the gift of a knight who had bred the massive brown destriers himself and clearly wished to impress him. Sir James Harrington had also brought forty lads from the town he owned a few miles from Leicester, a dozen archers among them. In all, it had been a princely gift and if they survived, Edward knew he would indeed find some reward for the man, along the lines of dean of his chapel, or one of a hundred posts that were a king's to bestow, each bringing wealth and status to the owner.

'I will ride him this very day and test his wind, Sir James,' he said. 'I would be pleased to have you accompany me.' The knight dropped to one knee, overwhelmed. As Edward turned aside, Sir James rejoined the gaggle of his family and servants outside, pleased as anything to have spoken to the king.

Edward turned to his brother, watching him wryly. He smiled at Richard's expression.

'Would you have dismissed him or scorned him after such a gift, Richard? England is made of such fellows. Clever, deal-making men who work all the hours of the day and kiss their wives and count their coins at the end of it. Men of good judgement and clear sight, hard to fool, who will bend the knee to me only if they think I am a man to follow.'

'Then I am pleased you are such a man, Brother,' Richard said. 'Though I worry you have let their admiration turn your head.'

Edward chuckled, rubbing his big hand along the muzzle of the horse. It loomed over even him, an animal of extraordinary strength and size. Yet it stood calmly, trained and watchful.

'You are the one who opened my eyes, Richard. Montagu hangs back, Oxford runs with his tail tucked away as soon as he sights my banners. They are afraid – and I am glad of it. I have said I will not stop. I will take risks enough to shame the devil himself! How else would you have me turn this small army into a victory? You know Warwick has a host . . .' He broke off, clenching his fists as he heard how loud his voice had become. He whistled for a servant and handed the horse over, then stepped closer to his brother.

'Richard, I have too few. If Warwick had the sense – no, the warlike manner to move against me, we would be swallowed up. I am a man who has to throw his sword! If it strikes home, that will end it. If it misses, the man will be made to seem a fool, mocked and defenceless. Do you understand? That is why I have our columns growing lean and strong on these marches. We must hit Warwick before he decides he has the strength and numbers to chase us down. Even with too few men, I can challenge him. I can call him out. Who knows, he might even face me.'

Richard rubbed at his mouth, suddenly aching for a drink to take the edge off all his worries. He had not said anything about it, but as Edward suffered on through his abstinence, Richard had quietly matched him. His appetites had never been nearly as great, but he found the lack of ale and wine had sharpened him, sometimes to an edge that cut. He felt the lack when anger and frustration overwhelmed him. That was when brown ale and clear spirits would have been a wondrous ease to his troubled mind. Without them, the world was full of thorns and irritations.

'I am at your side, Edward, right to the end, even if you throw your sword. I swear it, I will not let you down. Nor any man who has come to you here. Perhaps they are worth two or three of those who stand against us because of that loyalty. I hope so.'

'Mount up, Brother,' Edward said, chuckling. 'You think too long, on everything. There are times when you must just ride out – and be damned to all those who would hold you back.'

The warhorse was a fine mount, though Edward was sure to have his usual gelding brought along as well in case the new one was too skittish for fighting. As with men, a steady nerve was at least as important in a horse as strength or even training. He patted the blue-and-red silk that draped the warhorse, stepping on to a block to throw his leg over. His men watched him, ready and calm. Edward smiled and raised his open hand to them. They cheered, as he'd known they would, lifted by his great spirit, to joy. The city of Leicester dwindled behind them as they marched away, taking another two hundred volunteers.

The road was flat and dry and the sun rose into a sky studded with white, warming the marching men. Coventry was barely fifteen miles from where they had made their camp and the word among them was that Edward would march them right down Warwick's throat, that they would see battle that very day. Yet it was not even noon when the scouts came racing back, on mounts still fresh. The men trudging along on Roman stones glanced at one another and were not surprised when they were made to halt. The captains went forward for orders and brought back the command to form squares for battle.

Richard of Gloucester commanded two thousand on the right wing, his own banners raised there by knights in full armour. Edward held the centre: three thousand men who were the strongest and most experienced he had. The left wing, staggered back, was commanded by Earl Rivers with Hastings and Stanley as his seconds, the three men waiting patiently as their captains assembled the ranks. It was not an impressive manoeuvre from men who had not known each other even a month before. There was a great deal of swearing and shoving and loss of tempers. Yet when they had found the places to stand, they took good grips on billhooks and pikes, on pollaxe and woodaxe, like men who knew how to use them. Archers assembled on the outer wings under their own bow captains, while ahead of the front rank, the hand-gunners gathered, just a hundred with matches smoking thin trails into the air. Two dogs had followed the army as it moved on from Leicester. They were bounding along the front ranks in enormous excitement, barking at all the men who stood and looked into the distance. There was some nervous talk and laughter in the ranks then, as old friends mocked each other's nervousness to ease their own. More than a few crossed themselves and touched relics hidden beneath shirts, glancing up to heaven as their lips moved.

Complete silence fell as the three battles of men sighted an enemy trudging towards them across the fields. The sight brought a chill and one of the men sent a dog yelping with a great kick when it barked at him. Another said something wry in response and a ripple of laughter sounded in that part of the army, though the rest did not hear it and waited quietly.

Only the scouts knew how many they had seen and even then, the numbers would be the best guess of untutored boys. The only reality that mattered was to watch the ranks forming and widening with each step, though at least the day was clear. In fog or darkness, there was no way to know how many they faced. Men like Edward who had fought in snow and through the night at Towton could remember the horror of it, the sense of endless hordes of enemies who would never falter, never stop coming, while your strength and your will faded with every step. It was a memory of such fear and despair that they did not think of it, until it came upon them again.

'Hold this ground!' Edward roared across the lines. He had brought his new destrier to the front rank of the centre and drawn his sword to hold aloft. 'My lord Gloucester, you will attend me here.'

The ranks of men watched in confusion as that order was carried across the lines and Richard Plantagenet rode in from the right wing, joining his brother. The two of them called over one of the scouts and spoke earnestly to him, the young man's head bobbing as he confirmed what he had seen. Once again, men who knew each other in the ranks looked round and shrugged. They were ready to fight, their hearts pounding, all aches vanishing. They watched as a dozen senior captains gathered and trotted off together, for all the world a parley group. It made no sense to those who had come to fight for York.

A mile away, just over, some eighteen hundred yards, those with the sharpest eyes could make out banners brought up by the enemy. Whoever commanded them had matched their width, though no one could say even then how many ranks they faced, how deep the companies and squares were. The banners they saw were quartered, just as Edward's shield was, containing two squares of three lions and two of the fleurs-de-lis of France. Yet the banners held across the field and still approaching had a strap of silver across them. George of Clarence, a royal duke of the house of York, was on the field. As the men in ranks watched, the great force came to a halt, some eight hundred yards away. It was close enough to be a threat and they gripped axe-handles and retied belts and loose pieces of kit, aware that the peace of the day could be broken at any moment by wild yells and horns. It took only two minutes for opposing armies to crash together at that range, a period of rushing terror that no one who had experienced it would ever forget.

The order to attack did not come and those in the front ranks saw captains and knights ride out from Clarence. They met in the middle of the field, grim and serious men, gauging the intentions of the others. They would have talked longer if Edward and Richard had not ridden up to that central point with Earl Rivers and half a dozen guards. Edward's confidence showed clearly in his manner, as if he could not imagine being in danger.

Some of Clarence's men trotted away to take Edward's promise of safe passage and it was then that George of Clarence rode out, bare-headed, to that central point. He smiled nervously as he reined in, facing his brothers.

'I accept safe conduct and grant it,' Edward called to the men gathered around to protect them. 'You have my thanks, gentlemen. Return now, that my brothers and I may speak alone.'

George of Clarence echoed the order and all those who had ridden out turned their horses away without a word and cantered off, leaving the three men staring at each other.

'Did my Irishman reach you?' Richard asked. George nodded, his tongue thick in his mouth so that he did not know what to say. They all sensed the wrong word would have them bickering and silence seemed almost the better alternative.

'Well, George?' Edward said. He wore no helmet, but beyond that he had not unbent in any sense. He sat his warhorse with a straight back, his gauntlets resting easily on a knot of reins. 'Do you expect me to make this easy for you?'

George of Clarence made a sharp grimace and shook his head. Without hurry, he dismounted and approached. Armed and clad in iron, merely walking towards his brothers made both men straighten and ready themselves. Sensing their response, Clarence unbuckled his sword belt and held scabbard and blade out to one side. It was more a gesture than actually disarming himself, Richard noted. He would have to remember it.

The Duke of Clarence nodded to Richard, then addressed his gaze to the older brother he had betrayed.

'I am sorry, Edward. I broke my word to you, my oath. It was losing the child. In my grief . . .'

'We have all lost those we love, George,' Edward said softly. Richard shot a glance at him. He had thought he knew his brother's mind, but there was something threatening in the way Edward regarded their brother still, as if he had not forgiven him at all. For an instant, Richard had to consider if he would or even could stop Edward from striking George down. The men who had come to that field for Clarence could well be taken under the wing of his older brother. Edward lowered his head a touch further, staring down at a man who had chosen Warwick over his family.

George flinched as Edward went from stillness to sudden movement, dismounting lightly into the thick mud. In two strides, he was able to take his brother's outstretched hand, then pull him into an embrace. George of Clarence laughed in honest relief.

'You worried me, then,' he said. 'I thought when you saw I brought three thousand to fight for you, I would surely be forgiven, but I did not know. I have had so little sleep, Edward, in the last few days! Ever since you were said to have landed . . .'

Richard dismounted in turn, listening to his brother babbling. George had been more afraid than he'd let on, that much was clear from the torrent of words he could not seem to bring to an end. Edward stood back from him, still weighing him with that odd expression Richard had observed before.

'We will put the past behind, George,' Edward said. 'That's the place for it, don't you think?'

'I will make it right, Brother, I swear it. I was made a fool by Warwick, gulled by him with promises and lies. We all were! He is an asp, Edward. Those Nevilles . . . I swear your wife was right. They are a rotten heart, wherever they touch. We will put it right, Brother. I will put it right.'

'As you say, George,' Edward said. 'Bring your captains here and place them under my command – so there is no confusion amongst them.'

'Brother, they are loyal, I swear. I have marched them all the way from Cornwall, some of them. Kernow men who hardly speak English, but they know the sharp end of an axe.'

'Good, George. Bring your captains in now, as I asked you once. If you make me ask a third time, I will strike you dead on this field. You will earn my trust again, *Brother.* You do not have it now.'

George stammered and went red, nodding and backing away as he waved in his captains. They approached warily and Edward addressed them, his voice firm and clear.

'I'll place a thousand of you on each wing, the rest to support me in the centre. I expect you to follow the orders of my lords as if they were my own – as if they were your father's orders, or Almighty God come to tell you to stand and fight for me. I will reward bravery and great feats of arms, without limit of any kind. If you would earn a manor or a knighthood or a barony or even an earldom, you would do well to follow me today. Know that my enemy is Earl Warwick and he is the richest man in England. When he falls, there will be a fair share made to you in my name. Is that understood?'

There was a gleam of avarice in some of the eyes that watched Edward, but Richard saw a touch of the old magic as well. There were men there, hard and experienced men, who were telling themselves they *would* come to the notice of the giant in polished plate. They would accomplish such deeds as would impress him. Edward brought out the best in the men who came under his command, that was the truth of it. It was not even in his words, but in the way he looked at them and the way he saw them.

When the Clarence captains returned to their lines, there was an immediate lurch forward. They carried their pikes and weapons aloft on shoulders, rather than pointed out in hostile array.

Edward saw his brother George was standing disconsolately, deprived of his command and still unsure of his new place with his brother the king of England. With a visible effort, Edward spoke to him again, putting aside his disdain.

'You'll prove yourself, George, I don't doubt. You are our father's son, just as I am. Just as Richard is. Don't forget that.'

'I won't,' George replied and to Richard's astonishment, he sobbed suddenly, dipping his head into the crook of his elbow so that they would not see. Edward stared and Richard spoke to cover the muffled sounds of grief.

'Come now, Brother. Mount up before your men see you . . . We'll stop here and eat, perhaps . . .' He broke off as Edward shook his head in answer.

'No. Coventry is just five or six miles away. We still have Montagu shadowing us behind. When the new men are settled and arranged in column, we'll walk there, today. Stay at my side, George, would you? You can tell me all you know, before the fighting begins.'

George blinked at the reckless confidence in his older brother. He knew Warwick's army outnumbered those he saw, three times over, a host of a size that had not been seen since Towton. He had expected Edward to be in command of an army to equal it, just as he had been before. The reality was different enough to make him perspire.

After a moment of silence, George remembered himself. He swallowed his fear and bowed his head, accepting his brother's authority over him without another word.

Warwick felt a sudden chill of sadness as he stood in spring sunshine. The day was beautiful, the last rags of winter blown away so that the sun warmed a green earth and brought back a sense of life and desire, thinning the blood and making all things well.

He leaned forward, hunching his shoulders atop the Coventry walls. A tower loomed over him on his right and he considered walking up that last flight of steps to see to the furthest point. The bricks in the tower's shadow were still damp as he laid his hand on them, though they would grow warm as the day ended. Some part of him observed his reactions, thinking how strange it was that he could be aware of the roughness of stone while the banners of York were still lurching into view, at the head of an army. Warwick had thought they were a hundred miles to the north, building the great force Edward would surely need to reclaim all he had lost. It was nothing less than madness for the sons of York to have raised war banners before they had the numbers to support them. Yet Warwick felt cold clutch at him.

The banners of Clarence lay alongside those of York and Gloucester. Three brothers together – and one more knife thrust into Warwick's side to cause him pain. As he looked out from Coventry's wall over the fields around, he thought of how his daughter would react when she heard. He grieved as a father for her then.

Warwick himself had gone to King Edward to ask permission for that marriage. It was he who had counselled the giddy young lovers to elope to France and gone with them. It had been Warwick who rode to save George and Isabel when Edward's wrath turned on them and they had to run.

Braced on stone, Warwick pulled in enormous breaths, filling himself with clean air above the winding streets and cooking fires of the city. He had seen their child, his grandchild, born at sea and named, only to die unbaptized in the salt spray. It was King Edward's orders that had prevented their little boat from landing in Calais. It was the fleet of Lord Rivers that had hunted them on the south coast of England and had driven them out.

Warwick dragged the steel knuckles of his gauntlet back and forth across the brick, scoring deeper and deeper, unnoticed, unfelt. He had known Edward when he was just a great bullock of a lad, delighted to fight and drink and whore with the garrison at Calais. Edward of March he had been then, and he had accepted Warwick's guidance, the young man wise enough to see something worth learning in him. So it had seemed. Warwick had been Edward's guide, his teacher. He knew he was responsible in some part for the man Edward had become. He was not responsible for all he had become. The young king had married poorly and perhaps there had always been weaknesses in him, as in marble that seemed strong, but shattered at the touch of a chisel. Or perhaps the weaknesses would never have shown if Warwick had not helped him to reach for the throne, to stretch out his hand and touch a crown Edward had not earned and surely did not deserve. They had deposed a saint and Edward had become king in blood and vengeance. Perhaps his sins had rotted him. Or his pride.

Warwick scratched the metal joints harder across the stone, wanting to destroy something, wanting to leave a mark. He wished Derry Brewer could have been there to advise him. He had grown used to the man's scorn and found it oddly comforting.

Edward Plantagenet was on the field once more. Anyone who remembered Towton or had survived Mortimer's Cross would feel a twinge of fear at that news. Warwick could not deny it in himself, as he watched the army of York tramp forward in well-spaced ranks, spreading as wide as the city itself. Over a thousand yards of them in the front rank and God alone knew how many stretched behind.

On sudden impulse, Warwick turned to the watch tower and climbed quickly up the steps inside. In moments, he reached an octagonal crest that allowed him to see miles further over the great flat plain in the heart of England. It was land Caesar himself would have allowed was a place to give battle. Warwick felt his heart thumping faster. He saw Edward had not gathered the vast host that he had feared. Clarence had given him three thousand – and denied as many to Warwick by that betrayal. Even then, Edward's army was no more than ten, perhaps eleven thousand men.

Warwick could remember standing before the hill at St Albans, staring across roads blocked with thorns and broken furniture. He and his father had stood with Richard, Duke of York, and between them they'd mustered only three thousand men, a force that would be dwarfed by those of later days. Warwick knew the merchant guilds complained that trade had suffered and the country had grown poorer as a result, that they made weapons and raised men for slaughter, rather than iron and pewter – and mutton, beef and pork. War had hurt them all and as Warwick looked over the standing ranks, he thought of his father and was pleased the breeze was there to dry the brightness that came to his eyes. They were good men, those who had gone. Better than all those poor bastards they left behind.

He watched, dragging the same gauntlet across a block as Edward of York rode forward with his two brothers and half a dozen knights in armour, banners streaming out. Edward and Richard both wore long surcoats over their armour, the sword belts sitting over quarters of glorious colours: red and blue and gold, lions and fleurs-de-lis. The banners were a fine mixture of York and Gloucester and Clarence, a calculated display: the house of York returned and united against him. In many ways it was more for those who stared down from the walls than Warwick himself.

His own banners flew above his head, facing them. Warwick glanced up at the colours of his shield and thought how strange it was that every man in command that day was a member of the same order of chivalry. York, Gloucester, Clarence, Hastings, Warwick himself, his brother Montagu edging down from the north – all were members of the Order of the Garter, with the legend embroidered around their family crests: '*Honi soit qui mal y pense*' – 'Evil be to him who evil thinks'.

Warwick found his eyes blurring and he blinked, pleased that there was no one else to see and think him weak. He had been a tutor to Edward, and then to his brother Richard, when he had lived at Middleham Castle as Warwick's ward. They had been fast friends once and it was cruel to see them arrayed against him. The worst was Clarence, a wound so fresh it hurt him with every taken breath. In all, Warwick felt as a father denied by his sons and the pain struck right to the heart of him.

14

For the first time in his life that he could remember, Derry Brewer considered punching an archbishop in the mouth. He could almost feel the muscles twitching along his arms and chest. A nice little jab with the left, then drop the cane and bring the right cross in. George Neville was no white-livered clergyman, however. The man was burly and about as angry as Derry himself at being baulked. The king's spymaster knew that if he threw a punch, they would be scuffling on the floor like two schoolboys in moments, all torn collars and bloody lips. He was too old for it, more was the pity.

'Your Grace,' he tried once more with exaggerated patience. 'I am better placed than you to make this judgement. King Henry is not well enough for what you ask. If he was, truly, I would have him wrapped in a good cloak and I would have rushes laid along the street, just as you are asking. But he isn't. He won't understand what you want. He might fall. He might cry out, do you follow? It will not help for him to be seen weak!'

'Where is Beaufort, Duke Somerset? I am weary of your resistance. Send a man to summon Somerset to vouch for me.'

'My lord Somerset is not in London, Your Grace,' Derry said for the second time, with deliberately icy patience. He did not say that Margaret and her son, Edward of Lancaster, were expected any day and that Somerset had gone to the coast to escort them. That news was about the best-kept secret in the country.

The lack of explanation turned Archbishop Neville an even deeper shade of claret.

'My brother Warwick trusts you, Master Brewer. That is the only reason I have not summoned guards to have you removed from my path. I am a prince of the Church, sir! I have come here with a dire warning in time of war – and I find myself arguing with a lackey as if I had come to beg for alms? So let me say *this*, sir! It is my considered judgement that London itself lies in peril and with it, King Henry. He *must* be seen, Master Brewer! Do you understand that much? The people of London know nothing of the greater events in the land, *nothing*. All they hear are alarums and rumours of invasions, of fleets sighted. Is the king dead? Is York returned? Is Margaret of Anjou marching once more on the city that refused her, to *burn it down*? I have heard a dozen speculations just this morning, Master Brewer, and no sign of the truth. I need to show Henry to his people, to reassure them – yes, and to show them for whom they fight. The king is a symbol, Brewer, not just a man.'

'Your Grace, King Henry is . . . withdrawn. Until you see him . . .' Derry broke off, considering. He held no official role as the keeper of the king's door, but he had been so long associated with King Henry and so clearly trusted that he had become the final arbiter over who was granted an audience. The Archbishop of York may have been within his rights to call for the king's own guards, but Derry had a shrewder sense of whether they would fulfil his order or not. He was confident he could have the archbishop thrown out. That was a decision that would surely come back to bite him, however, or even Margaret and her son, whenever they deigned to take ship and actually come home. No one crossed the Church lightly. The easiest path was to give the Neville clergyman what he wanted and let him see he had made a wasted trip into the city.

With a disarming change of expression, Derry bowed to the younger man.

'Your Grace, perhaps I have overstepped my bounds. If you will follow me, I will bring you to the king's presence.'

Archbishop Neville wasted no more time on talk and fell in behind as Derry tap-tapped his way along a corridor to the private royal suite beyond. It was Derry who gave the word of the day to the guards there, men who would refuse even him if the correct signal was missed. The king's spymaster swept on through an audience chamber with four men standing to attention along the walls.

'Stand easy, gentlemen,' Derry called airily as he went through. They ignored him as always.

Beyond the public rooms, they came to a final, smaller door, guarded by one old man who had as much chance of stopping armed invaders as a small boy.

'Old Cecil here has guarded doors for the best part of forty years,' Derry said.

'Forty-two, Brewer,' the man replied, looking down his nose. He appeared to have no love for the king's spymaster. Derry sighed.

'And valuable work it is, I am sure. There is no better-guarded door in the kingdom.'

'Wait here,' the old man said with a sniff. He knocked and went inside and Derry followed immediately on his heels, making the doorkeeper round on him in spittle-flecked rage. Derry held up his hands.

'We have discussed this, Master Fosden. The king is not in good health. If I waited on his call, I would be here all night and then where would the kingdom be?'

'Better off,' the old man snapped. He bowed his head and muttered 'Your Grace' to Archbishop Neville, then left, pulling the door hard shut behind him.

'Cantankerous old sod,' Derry said, close enough to the oak to be heard beyond it. 'I should have his pay docked.'

Archbishop Neville was already crossing the room to where Henry lay in bed, his long hair unbound and spread like a dark halo upon the pillow. He looked white rather than the pale yellow of a corpse, but though the eyes were open, there was precious little life in them.

As Derry looked on, the archbishop approached and dropped to one knee, extending his hand to touch the king's coverlet, though Henry made no move to take it in his own.

'I am George Neville, Your Highness, Archbishop of York. I pray each day for your good health,' the man muttered with bowed head. 'I pray that you might be well enough to walk the streets once more, to allow the people of London to see you alive. I fear they will turn to York if they do not, in their childlike awe. They know no better, Your Highness.'

Henry sat up in the bed, appearing to listen as he gathered his hair in a long tail, then let it fall loose once more. He had eaten rather better in recent months than during his imprisonment in the Tower, but he was still frighteningly thin, like the carvings of death seen on gravestones and tombs. His bones all showed and Derry saw hope seep slowly out of the archbishop.

'If you say I must, Your Grace,' King Henry said suddenly. 'I am a servant of Christ and my people. I will rise, if I need to.'

Derry cleared his throat.

'His Highness tends to agree, when earnest men come and say they need him to sign or seal or lend them something so important it will not wait. It would be a cruel thing to take advantage of his nature, Your Grace.'

Archbishop Neville looked from man to king and back,

his gaze remaining on the frail figure sitting up in bed and watching him. He too sensed the absence of a guiding will, for the words he spoke were as much to Derry as the king.

'Nonetheless, I must ask. This is the crossroad, Your Highness. York has returned to England and he will break the walls and bring all the towers down unless he is stopped. The people of London are afraid – and right to be! If they can see King Henry walk amongst them, with the banners of Lancaster flying overhead, they will know there is still a heart to the city.'

Derry saw Henry nodding along and he winced at the sight as the king looked across the room to him.

'I would like to do it, Derry,' he said.

Derry found himself breathing out hard, surprised by grief as his face creased up and he nodded, mastering himself too late.

'Then I will make it happen, Your Majesty. I'll walk with you.' The look Derry turned on the archbishop then was one of cold-eyed fury that made the other man quail.

From the height of the north wall tower, Warwick watched in growing disbelief as a man in royal livery rode forward from the army of York, bearing a horn as long as his arm. Warwick looked down to the walls stretching away on both sides. His own herald waited there to take any reply he might wish to send.

A scrape and echo of metal on stone signalled the arrival of the Duke of Exeter on the tower roof. Warwick nodded to welcome him though in truth he would have preferred to be alone rather than share such a moment. Henry Holland was no great thinker, unfortunately. Just when Warwick needed a good tactician, he had Exeter to stare over the battlements at his side, like a short-sighted bulldog. The man's lower jaw actually did jut out further than the one above, giving him an aggressive air that suited the map of broken veins on his cheeks from years of drink.

Some sixty feet below on the plain, the York herald's voice rang out with all the volume and reach of his profession. Warwick sighed and scratched his head.

'. . . a personal challenge on behalf of His Majesty King Edward of York, in answer to injuries and insults borne against his royal person and his line.'

The list of faults was brief enough and Warwick noted the number of times the herald used royal honours and titles. The man made no mention of Edward having lost his crown, as if the house of York wished to pretend it had not happened.

'Impudent bastard,' Exeter muttered, peering down. Warwick almost sent him away then. It was not that he had no need of counsel. A choice lay before him that shook him to his foundations. However, he would not be taking that counsel from the Duke of Exeter.

'De Vere and I have six thousand men a few miles to the east,' Exeter went on. 'Your brother Montagu is as close behind, as I heard it. We had Clarence to the west, though that is wasted now of course.'

'I know very well how and where we all stand, my lord,' Warwick said, somewhat curtly. Exeter did not miss the prickling scorn and grew a darker shade of purple if anything, leaning in and prodding the air with a finger as he made his points.

'Will you consider sending a champion? Or will you perhaps go yourself, Neville?'

Warwick controlled a spasm of dislike. Over the best part of two decades, he had fought on both sides of a brutal civil war. It was inevitable that he would encounter men he had faced as enemies in battle. Some, like Somerset, he respected. Henry Holland, Duke of Exeter, he did not. The man was a tyrant with those who were unlucky enough to fall into his power, and a lickspittle with those he considered his superiors. Men like Warwick were somewhere in a middle rank, less clear. Warwick had more land and power, more wealth and experience than Exeter, but always with the knowledge that a duke could command an earl. Exeter was only too aware of such niceties, while Warwick had seen so many things that he hardly thought of rank at all, until perhaps when he was needled by a pink-faced fool.

'After you, my lord, if you wish,' Warwick said, indicating the York herald. 'I am a couple of years older than you – and you could not face him. Edward is at his greatest strength. I do not believe I have a man in the army who could carry my colours down to that field and win. No, I will not give York a life just to increase his own legend. However, my lord, I am *certain* you have pressing duties below. You should ready your captains by the main north gate.'

'There will be some who'll call you faint-hearted if you don't come out, Neville.'

'Well, I am not concerned with the chatter of fools, Holland,' Warwick replied sharply. He kept his back turned, but his anger was finding a focus in Exeter rather than the enemy calling him out on the field. It was idiocy to be arguing with one of his own men at such a delicate time.

'You have ten thousand or so in the city,' the duke went on stubbornly, 'but at least as many just a few miles south of here by Warwick Castle. Have you sent a rider to bring them up? I have de Vere, Earl Oxford, and our six thousand out to the east, ready to flank the bastards. So bring 'em in, Neville. Set 'em loose!'

'I will send my orders to you when I am ready, my lord,'

Warwick said calmly. 'Not before you have resumed your proper post by the north gate. I believe I have command of the army over you. The army I gathered and paid and fed all winter, while you took your few thousand and did what with them? You took back estates you had lost when Edward sat the throne. You dispossessed your wife who had kept some part for you – and you settled a dozen old scores in murder and torture while you could. I'm sure the results have been to your satisfaction, Holland. I would love to have done the same, instead of taking loans from every monastic house and banker to support the king!'

His voice had grown louder and harder as he spoke and he rounded then on Exeter, stepping in close enough to threaten.

'Do you understand, Holland? You saw your chance to take vengeance, in spite and ruin. I saw a chance at peace.'

'Oh yes, you are an admirable fellow, Neville,' Exeter said, mocking him. 'And much good has it done you. You'll find no gratitude from that broken thing that sits in Westminster.'

'Go down to your men, my lord,' Warwick said, struggling to master his anger though he thought it would choke him. 'I will decide whether to sally out or remain.'

'They will call you coward if you don't answer York,' Henry Holland said.

'*Coward?*' Warwick snapped, his temper breaking. 'I fought at *Towton*, you pup! I stood at Edward's side and I killed men on foot, in snow, with blood across my face and friends cut down on either side of me. I went on until I could hardly *stand* and the darkness came. And still we fought! When Norfolk crashed against the wing, when it was all screaming and dying men.' He tapped his forehead hard with two steel fingers, leaving a mark. 'I *still* see it! Ah, you don't know *anything*.'

Exeter had lost his flush as Warwick ranted in fury, close enough to leave small flecks of spittle on his cheek.

'I know I stood on the other side,' he said softly. 'I know I saw more of my friends and followers killed that day, by you and by York. Worse than any losses you think you have suffered. I know the man you followed that day denied me my estates and my houses and my villeins and my servants. And I know York is out there with an army half the size of yours . . . and yet he is the one to challenge, while you hide behind walls. I tell you, I like this not at all.'

'Go to your men. Wait for my order,' Warwick said once more. Henry Holland looked at him for a long time, biting a part of his lower lip as he considered. Warwick waited, knowing that at least one choice remaining to him was to draw his sword. He would almost have welcomed it. Yet in the end Exeter only sneered and turned away to the stairs without another word.

Warwick breathed out slowly. He could hear the noise of the descending duke and he turned back to the Plantagenet armies of York – of Edward and Richard and George. He felt the pain of it once more. To be the victor, he had to destroy three boys he had raised up to be men. He knew how they would stand together, just as he stood with his brothers. He shook his head. He was forty-two years old and he had fought for over sixteen of them. He had sinned and he had lost friends and his father. He had witnessed bravery at the moment of death, had known bitter exile and murder and great victory, all of it marking him where it could not rub off or be washed away. He had no sons of his own. He began to chuckle into the breeze, though it was far closer to sobbing than laughter.

Derry bit his lip as the king took his first steps along the wide roadway. Henry wore a simple gold crown for his stroll through London, though the buttery-yellow metal was perhaps more wealth than anyone in the crowds would ever see again. The king had been dressed in brown wool, tunic, hose and cloak. Henry seemed to understand what was wanted of him, though his eyes looked dull. He had nodded when Derry asked if he wished to begin.

The path they'd prepared was dry and wide, with royal guards on duty to prevent the rushes being stolen and turning up later in a dozen taverns. London people took delight in that sort of acquisition and it had been a challenge to keep watch on the road from before dawn. The king's path led along Cannon Street to St Paul's Cathedral, past the London Stone that the rebel Jack Cade had struck with steel so many years before. It was less than a mile through the centre of the city, Derry told himself. It would not take long, even at King Henry's feeble pace.

Drummers began their rattle at the far front, giving a marching rhythm far slower than anything suited to the battlefield. Horns blew and Derry recalled that they were not just to fire the blood of men about to charge, but also to drown out the screams and panicked yells of those who wanted to run.

Archbishop Neville had a carriage standing ready at the end to collect the king, if he fell from exhaustion. That prince of the Church had ignored Derry's continuing stream of objections, all undermined by the fact that King Henry himself seemed pleased to do it. Derry was not certain if Henry truly understood, but it was possible. The king had been given a task and told it was something he could do to help save his throne. Henry had latched on to that simple idea and could not be dissuaded.

Walking behind, Derry Brewer looked over twin lines of Londoners, all gathered in the dawn to be sure of seeing the king walk by. He wondered how many remembered Henry walking almost as a prisoner of the Yorks before, with the father of the household lording it over Henry's wife. Those were unpleasant memories, but Henry only smiled to the people waving and calling to him.

Archbishop Neville came to Derry's shoulder, looking flushed and nervous. As well he might, Derry supposed. If the king fell, the blame would land on that man alone, he would make sure of it.

Behind them and in front, the best part of a hundred men-at-arms and knights walked in slow step. They wore polished armour and carried vast royal banners that swept back and forth in the breeze like the sails of ships. Derry dared not hope as he looked down the length of road. As long as Henry did not stumble, or faint, or become afraid . . . He blinked at his own worries, dreading the half an hour ahead of them.

'Take my arm, Derry, would you?' King Henry said suddenly. His eyes were bright, like a child's. 'My steps are uncertain. Archbishop Neville? Go ahead, please. I will follow you.'

Derry leaned on his stick as he moved up. He took a grip on the king's elbow with his free hand, steadying him. Sweating slightly from strain and worry, he wondered if he could signal the drummers to slow the column further. Yet apart from the cheering, it already resembled a funeral. He dismissed the idea as Henry steadied and went on.

The noise had built to the point where no orders he might give could have been heard. On all sides, Londoners did not disappoint in their enthusiasm. They craned and heaved to catch a glimpse of Henry of Lancaster, the Innocent. Those who said Henry had died years before were dark with sullen anger, while others cheered and hooted in delight, treasuring the moment and the memory, when they saw a saint and a king.

*

Jasper Tudor stood in the first row, raised on a wooden bench he had hired for a farthing. His nephew Henry stood with him, looking down the road with the rest to where the silver knights were assembling and the banners swept back and forth. The boy was chewing a pie with a dubious expression, having found the crust rather more appetizing than the contents, which had seen better months than that one. Jasper tried to see if his brother's boy was enjoying himself, though it was always hard to tell.

They watched King Henry grow close to them and both Henry Tudor and his uncle cheered with the rest. Jasper thought he saw Derry Brewer's gaze pass over him and snag. The man missed little, so he dipped his head in greeting as the small group at the heart of the procession passed on. Jasper would have turned away then, but his nephew tugged at his arm and so they stayed to watch the ranks of knights pass with helmets open, smiling at the crowd and their own colleagues lining the road. It felt like a county fair or a market day with all the noise and bustle, but Jasper had seen how frail King Henry was and he was frowning in thought as his young ward turned away at last, satisfied.

'Must I go?' Henry Tudor said plaintively. Jasper had explained it a dozen times and he frowned at having it brought up again.

'Yes, Harry. As I have said. Still, there is one more you must meet before we leave. One who asked to see you.' They walked east along the road, skirting local people gathering the rushes, the top layer still clean enough to use or sell. Jasper waved off one woman with a full bucket in each hand and she passed on to the next fine gentleman who might want a clean kitchen floor for a penny. The road ahead cleared quickly and Jasper walked with his nephew towards the Tower and the river.

'I should not have left it as long as this,' Jasper said, keeping his voice low. 'As soon as we heard York had landed, I should have gone then, to France.'

'Running, Uncle,' Henry muttered. Jasper's mouth tightened.

'Call it whatever you wish, boy. I have stood my time in battle – and you are yet too young. And you are my brother's son and yes, you are my ward and my responsibility. I could not protect your father, Harry. So I will keep you safe, until this threat is at an end.' Jasper saw his nephew had pushed half his lower lip over the upper, a determined expression he had come to know well over the months in London lodgings.

'Look, son, if Warwick succeeds, we'll be just over the Channel, with news winging its way to France. King Louis will be delighted and we'll come back to England. I'll have my Pembroke and you'll inherit your father's estates as Earl of Richmond.'

'And if King Edward wins?' Henry asked, always prodding for more detail. Jasper sighed.

'Then we will not return and Lancaster will be destroyed. I do not believe that poor old king who passed by just now will be allowed to live if Edward of York regains his throne. Though you should not call Edward "king", Harry. His was the younger line. He never had a right to the crown, except by fear and force.'

'Which served him well enough,' Henry muttered.

'Which meant that he could not rule a year in peace without some challenge!' Jasper replied, exasperated. 'I cannot *remember* peace, boy! There have been rebels and cannon and wildfire on this very street – and battles from house to house. I have seen men dying on thorns and . . .' He shook his head, refusing to go on, though his nephew watched with greater interest. As Henry saw he would not continue, the bright attention faded and he withdrew once more, sauntering on towards the river.

'You are my nephew, Harry. You'll obey me in this, until it is safe to return. Perhaps that will be in just a month, in the summer! Think of that, lad! You wanted to see King Henry and I held my boat for you to watch the procession. Now, there is one more I hoped to see . . . ah, there she is, the dear little thing.' Jasper waved to the small woman waiting on the Thames bank for them. Henry looked at his uncle in honest confusion as they drew close and Jasper took her hand to kiss and greet her.

'Lady Margaret, this is Henry Tudor, your son,' he said.

Henry's eyes widened and he looked from his uncle to the lady staring at him with fascinated eyes, drinking in every movement he made.

'Hello, boy,' she said, smiling shyly. 'I hope your uncle Jasper is looking after you.'

Henry stood rooted to the ground, unable to speak or move. His mouth gaped and Margaret Beaufort reached out and closed it gently with her hand. It was the first touch between them since she had left him at Pembroke Castle fourteen years before. He could feel it on his skin as if she had carried hot iron and seared a mark on to him.

'I have the details of your uncle's property in Brittany now. I will write as often as I can, if you would like that.'

'I would like that,' Henry echoed faintly. He looked again at his uncle, trying to see if some game was being made of him.

'Are you . . . well?' Henry said. 'You have everything you need?'

For some reason the question made his mother chuckle, her eyes becoming slits that twinkled at him. She made a sound like a wheeze and yet seemed well enough.

'I am, my dear. I have employment as a lady's maid at court. I look after my lord Warwick's daughter Ann. It is better to be busy than idle and I . . . enjoy being close to the beating heart of things. You are well made, Henry, like your father. Your uncle tells me you are clever and quiet, with no boasting like so many other boys. I was very pleased to hear that.'

'Should I . . . stay with you?' Henry asked. His mother shook her head, firmly.

'No. Your uncle and I have discussed it and London is too perilous a place for you, at least for now. Let us see how things turn out. If my lord Warwick is successful, perhaps you will be back before the year is out. Would you like that?'

'Yes, Mother, I would,' Henry said. His eyes gleamed with tears and he knuckled them away, embarrassed in front of his uncle. Margaret Beaufort patted her son gently on the arm.

'Be strong, Henry. We will know better times than these, I promise you. Now go on. I had only a little time to meet you and it is at an end. Go with your uncle. Pray every day and resist temptation. Go with God.'

Henry stumbled as he climbed down into the boat, all the while trying to look back at a woman he had never known. He was barely aware of his uncle taking a seat beside him. When they were settled, the little woman turned and strode away without looking back.

'*Formidable* woman, your mother,' Jasper said, a little wistfully. 'If I had met her instead of your father, well, our lives could have been very different. Row on, lads.'

The six men at the oars took them out to the middle of the current, sweeping away downriver, where the *Pembroke* waited for them.

Henry Tudor looked back at the city he had grown to love, magnificent and confusing in all its noise and colours and smells and surprises. He'd experienced just one Christmas and one spring in London, but it had been more filled with events and experiences than half a dozen years in Pembroke.

He told himself in silence that he would come back, now that he had found how fascinating life could be in a great city. Now that he had met the woman he had imagined holding him through toothache and fevers, when all he had were his own arms. He showed nothing of his thoughts to his uncle, preferring always to remain hidden, where he could not be hurt. When Jasper's gaze fell on him once more, Henry nodded politely, his thoughts far away.

15

York's herald waited for an age before he rode back to the three brothers. Facing the city, they rested, silent and still for a long time, until the sunlight lengthened their shadows in late afternoon. They turned away then, marching two miles from the walls to a spot where they could make a formal camp. Their men spent the remaining hours piling thorn and brush in a great perimeter, ready to repel any attack that might come that night. Warwick could barely see the smudge of them when they began the work, the labouring soldiers made into tiny figures. He saw parties of men go into the woods with axes, to fell saplings and drag them back. Some part of Warwick was pleased at the good order he observed. He had been there for their training after all, with Edward and Richard more than George. It made him proud when they showed they were not fools.

He knew he had them even so – he was almost certain of it. It was true the loss of Clarence had been a blow. He supposed his son-in-law had passed on news of the numbers and lords at his command, that had to be assumed. Yet Edward's pride would not allow him to withdraw. The young man was depending on momentum. The error of that approach was shown when an enemy held up a spear and let you run right on to the point.

A few miles further off, John Neville, Lord Montagu, would have made his battle line with three thousand men, enough to block the north. De Vere, Earl Oxford, commanded six thousand in the east, while Warwick could bring ten thousand from the city and ten thousand more from Warwickshire behind him. The sons of York had come into his heartland, his home. He had them in irons, with only the western road as a way out.

As night crept silently across the landscape, Warwick watched until torches were lit all along the edges of the York camp. Groups of lamplighters did the same on the walls of Coventry, forming two long lines of oil and flames, a thousand yards wide, facing each other.

The Duke of Exeter had sent a number of messages during the day, culminating in another attempt by the man to gain entrance at the tower, this time refused by Warwick's own guards. Holland had gone on to the wall then, shouting up at him that he had better look sharp. Warwick had refused to reply and at the last, the furious noble had thrown up his hands and gone off to get drunk. It was disappointing that Exeter had not called him a coward in the hearing of others. Warwick would have had his head then for interfering with command in time of war and no one would have dared say a word. Unfortunately, Henry Holland knew that as well as he did and had stopped short of putting his head on the block.

Warwick slept poorly, throwing off his covers on a night too warm for comfort. He should have closed the trap he had set, once Edward walked into it. He could imagine Derry Brewer's reaction and distrust when he heard he had not drawn the noose tight. Three sides would have been enough to crush the small force and make an ending. Warwick could hardly explain what he could not understand in himself.

At sunrise, he rose from a bed soaked in sweat and wrapped a cloak around his shoulders, gripped by a strange sense of dread. He went out to the walls and stared across swirling morning mist to the dark line of brush that lay across his horizon. The torches had all gone out, or showed as embers, a dark and sullen gleam, fading even as he stared.

There was no sign of movement in the camp, no scouts of York riding out to check the fields all around. Warwick suspected then, but he gave orders even so and watched from on high as men rode out to the camp. They returned even faster, waving their arms and shaking their heads as they came at a gallop. The York camp was deserted. The army had crept away in the night and it was Warwick who had let them go.

Edward held his horse on a short rein. He would have liked nothing more than to go racing off down the road, but the men marching behind him could not go any faster. Only eight hundred of his army were on horseback, with spare animals bringing up the rear. The rest had to walk every mile – and then fight if they were challenged once again.

They had moved out in silence the night before, just as soon as it was too dark to see them leave. Edward and Richard had given the work to their captains and those men had imposed the need for silence with hard blows and whispers promising such brutal threats as to make strong men wince. Yet there were few who had to be bullied on their way. Most of them, even those who had come with Clarence, had been caught up in the cause. The difficulty lay in stopping them calling out and laughing with their mates in their excitement. Readying the camp to move had been a fraught few hours, but the reward had been to creep silently through black countryside. The moon was still at a half with little cloud – not ideal, but they'd moved even so.

The night had covered them well enough to bring them up to Oxford's camp. They'd rushed the guards on watch and staggered on across a field and tiny stream, plunging amidst tents with billhooks and axes swinging wildly. For a time, it had been terrifying chaos, but they were many. Those roused from sleep by strangled horns were driven to flight, most without armour or weapons. The panic spread quickly and Oxford's men could be seen haring off over the hills around, driven out as if by a host of devils rather than men.

Edward could have rested them then, to let Warwick discover he had broken his chains the following morning. Instead, he looked south and wondered. London lay some eighty miles from where they stood. On a good road, even weary men could walk three to four miles every hour. A night and a day on the road lay ahead, at least if he had food to feed them. They'd grown hard enough, tramping about the country since his landing. More importantly, they would understand what he wanted to do. London was Parliament and power. The city protected King Henry, the heart of Lancaster. Above all that, it held Edward's wife and daughters – and his son.

They marched down the great London road that led into the south, still with spirits like risen bread after scattering an enemy. That shine in the blood faded with each hour, until they reached the outskirts of Northampton. There, they lay down on the ground and dozed. Edward felt the same need for sleep tugging at him, making him stupid and slow. The men and women of his baggage train went into the city with purses of silver, returning with all the bread and soup they could buy. The sleeping soldiers were roused red-eyed to smile and take a bowl and a third of a loaf. They ate their fill and by then there were sausages on trays brought out on the heads of butcher boys, competing with each other to pass them out and show an empty tray to Edward's quartermasters. Silver passed into the city about as fast as the food was made to vanish by hungry men in full health, but the sun was up by the time Edward gathered them around him, standing them in ranks. They yawned, some of them, but the sons of York had proven themselves good men to follow to that point. There were smiles as Edward looked them over and he nodded, pleased.

'My lords, captains, gentlemen . . . ladies.' He said the last word with a slight bow in the direction of the women who had accompanied the fighting ranks. A laugh went up from the army at their reaction, a pleasant sound as some of them flushed and others dipped their heads or curtsied, delighted to be mentioned.

'From this morning,' Edward went on, 'I will force a good pace, one to match or better any legion of Rome before us. This road stretches unbroken, dry and wide, eighty miles to London. That is what I must ask of you. You have already shown me your strength and your loyalty. I must ask for more, for all. I must ask for your trust and your patience. You see, I am here to take back my crown. It lies in London.'

They cheered his words then, surprising and pleasing him so that he turned and laughed in delight to his brothers, standing nearby.

'Carts and supplies to bring up the rear. Captains, form columns six abreast. God bless you all for your loyalty. I will speak to you again when we stand within London walls!'

Dutifully, they cheered once more, though Flemish and English were already moving, their minds on collecting their tools and weapons and getting into position. It took another hour for the columns to form up, with scouts and hand-gunners vying for the front ranks to set the pace. All the women, old men and boys on the carts were waiting patiently to join the rear with whatever supplies the more enterprising of them had bargained out of the city. There were some women there who could create a feast from little more than a handful of herbs. They knew their value too, as they took up seats and reins and called out to favourite young men rushing past them, making them grin or blush. It was a fine April day and they had all marched or ridden from a dark sense of enclosure at Coventry, into freedom and spring sunshine. The mood was light as they set off, swinging along, with blades on their shoulders and pride in each step.

Edward and his brothers took the lead, trotting their horses abreast in the front rank, while their scouts cantered out on all sides to check the lay of the land ahead.

'Forty miles today and the same tomorrow,' Edward said. 'It can be done. That will be enough to see the London walls before the sun sets.' He smiled as he spoke, though he knew it would be hard on the men. He had a memory then of Warwick striking his horse dead at Towton, to march and fight on foot with the rest of the army – to show he would not retreat, no matter how the battle went. It had been a grand action and the memory did not sit well with Edward at that moment. He had admired Warwick then.

It was odd to consider that the very same man could have been following his tracks at that moment, charging along behind in a great froth of indignation. It would not matter, Edward decided. He would reach London first and shut the gates behind.

That thought brought back another memory, one that disturbed him and made him raise his head. He leaned over to his brother Richard, riding in the centre of the line.

'What if they refuse to let us in? Like Hull or York? What if the gates are closed, Richard?'

His brother thought for a time, looking off into the distance as if he could already see the city.

'When we are closer, perhaps on the second day or even tonight, I will send small groups of scouts or men unarmoured, to ride ahead.' He considered and nodded, tilting his head. 'They can gather around one gate, say the Moorgate on the north wall. A score of men could hold that against city guards, but I'll be sure and send in sixty or so, maybe more. It is a good thought, Brother, a vital one. When we are close, we will have men already inside to hold the gate. The mayor and his aldermen will not baulk us as they did Margaret and Henry. That was a blasphemy and I will not allow it again.'

Edward smiled at his brother's confidence, while Clarence looked on, not yet included in the bond of trust and liking shared by the other two.

'I need to reach London, Brother,' Edward went on. 'Elizabeth is there. And my son.'

'And her mother, Jacquetta,' Richard added, amusing himself.

'Yes, well, I am not so worried about her. Will you make light of this, Richard?'

'I'm sorry.'

Edward grinned despite himself, chuckling.

'London is where I was crowned before. It's London that made me king – and can again. Unless I have to scratch like a beaten dog at their closed gates.'

'They refused mere Lancaster, before,' Richard said with a snort. 'A French queen, a broken king and a great rabble of Scots. We are *York*, Brother! Our father's sons, come home. They would not dare turn us away.'

Edward smiled at him, pleased by Richard's mood and letting it raise his own. The column stretched behind them for mile after mile, thousands of men where there had been hundreds at first. Yet Clarence had described the host Warwick had gathered to him. Being the bearer of such grim news seemed to have reduced their brother George still further, though there was not much sense to his miserable countenance. He had brought them a vital part of their army. Yet after his initial pleasure at joining them, the duke seemed a downcast crow, the entire man a bad omen on a horse.

Edward raised his head in the slowly warming air. Eighty miles lay ahead, that was what mattered at that moment. He could not win all his battles on a single day. He could not know even if his wife still lived, or if his son had already perished, never to open his eyes and see his father standing in armour. Edward put it all aside and straightened, tall and strong, his eyes on the road.

Margaret of Anjou looked over the Paris dock, recalling how Derry Brewer had said that no matter what happened, she would start 'in Seine'. The spymaster had gone bright red with his own humour, she recalled, actually explaining the weak pun until he was roaring with laughter and wiping at tears. She missed him, even so.

At her back lay the Palace of the Louvre and the rooms that had become her home. Certainly it was the only home her son remembered, though young Prince Edward still dreamed of England like an Avalon, a land of mists and cold and the bright jewel of a birthright, long denied. Not far from Margaret, Edward of Lancaster wore fine armour and stood with a shield strapped to his back and two proud young squires bowed down with his weapons and equipment.

The small warship that waited for mother and son sat high in the river, the main deck some twenty feet above the dock-side and the hold. As Margaret watched, blindfolded horses were walked up a ramp on to the waist and then down another into the darkness of the stalls below. King Louis had not stinted with the fortunes they needed for such a departure. If she had not known very well how he benefited from his support of her, Margaret would have been astonished at the torrent of silver and gold he had lavished on her little group. They shared an enemy in Edward of York, that was the heart of it. The restoration of Lancaster would aid them both.

Margaret looked over her shoulder, as if she could have seen Louis watching. The sheer scale of the Louvre Palace still surprised her at times and she smiled at herself. The king would be there, certainly, his hopes riding with them. In fact, it was because of the king's sense of urgency joined to hers that she was leaving that day at all. The news that had winged its way to Paris, of York landing and gathering an army, had thrown all other plans into panic and disarray.

Margaret watched her only son step aboard, striding up the ramp and taking his place at the railing to look back in pride at the city that had taken them in. She felt the same emotion when she looked upon him, the only good thing to have come from her youth and all her first hopes of England. God, she remembered the spray in the Channel still, with William de la Pole, Duke Suffolk, at her side. She touched a silk cloth to her eyes then, rather than let tears ruin the kohl.

The River Seine was clear in spring. There were children swimming or fishing some way off along the bank, hooting and waving in excitement at seeing such a bustle, good as a play laid on for their entertainment. Prince Edward raised a hand to them, in greeting or farewell, she did not know. Margaret could still hardly believe this part of her life was coming to an end. She found herself trying to fix the scene in her mind: the colours, the great banks of flowers; understanding suddenly that she might not see Paris again for years, if at all.

She had guarded her son from all the perils of the world, waiting for the moment when the tide of York ebbed away and he could cross the Channel on the flood. Only a mother could know the exquisite torture of that spring day on the river, with all of France around – and her son reaching for the crown he should always have had. She pressed a hand to her mouth for comfort. There were so many enemies who would deny it, who would take his life without hesitation. Yet her Edward was the only son of the oldest line of kings. No one else alive had such a claim on the throne, by blood, by law – and by right of arms if need be.

Richard *Neville*, Earl of Warwick. That was a name she had said aloud in rage and pain a thousand times through the years of her exile. In a sort of madness, she had pinned her hopes on that very man, whose father's head she had taken and spiked on a gatehouse wall. Margaret had lived so long with strain and worry that she knew her beauty had vanished along with her waist, with her youth. It was impossible to live each day as a glass thrown into the air, never knowing when she would be broken into a thousand pieces. It had made her sharper and colder over the years, with disaster always fluttering at the edges of her vision.

'Your Highness, would you do me the honour of allowing me to take your hand?' said a voice at her shoulder. Margaret turned slowly, as if waking. King Louis had come down, to give her the titles and the honours she had long been denied. He smiled to see her dazed pleasure at his appearance, inclining his head a fraction. He held out his hand and Margaret placed her palm sweetly in his.

'I believe your friend Lord Somerset will be there in Weymouth to welcome you, my lady. He has communicated as much to me. I pass you into his safe hands, to your husband's realm and your home, after so long. I know you will consider me a friend still, in the years ahead. I will watch to see how you thrive amongst all those cold English farmers. Show them a little colour, Margaret, would you? They live in constant gloom without our example.'

'I will try, Your Majesty. And I am grateful for everything you have done. If there is a way to repay even some small part, I will make it my life's work, whatever years remain to me.'

Louis chuckled as he guided her up to the scrubbed oak planking of the deck and looked around with no small satisfaction.

'Many good years, Margaret, when all this will be just memories. I wish you good summers, my lady of England. And Prince Edward? I wish you good hunting. May you strike true.'

The prince was much taller than the Frenchman, showing the height that marked many in his line. Though he wore armour, he moved as if it had no weight at all. He bowed to King Louis, delighted.

'I *will*, Your Majesty, in the name of Our Lord, Jesus Christ.'

'Amen,' Margaret and the king said together.

'I am told the sea is a little rough today,' King Louis went on, 'but I do not doubt the waves will grow quiet, in awe perhaps, as you reach them.' Margaret smiled as he had hoped she would. She was dressed in fine silk and wore only a little paint on her lips and cheeks. For all the lines that marked her face, for all the pain she had seen, Louis could not remember when she had looked more beautiful.

'You will be in London in five or six days, Margaret. God willing, milord Warwick will have struck already – and taken the head of the one who threatens us all.'

'I pray for it, Your Majesty. And I have your birds on board. I will release them as soon as I know.'

Louis embraced her for the last time and took her son by

the hand in a strong grip so that the younger man would not crush his fingers in careless strength. After that, the French king bounced down the ramp and watched it taken up and the ship untied. He stood on the bank with just a few guards to protect him from the gaze and pawing hands of his people, while the little ship was towed into the main channel by two boats. As the ropes between them grew taut, they threw off drops of sparkling river water. Louis was well aware of his nickname of the 'Universal Spider'. He thought of the strands as part of a web and smiled at the sight and the conceit. It was an ending – and perhaps also a beginning. Newly embroidered banners of Lancaster would be unfurled at sea. For the moment, in Paris, the ship wore the fleurs-de-lis of France alone, in gold and blue.

16

The captain of the gate sent another boy racing off for orders from Mayor John Stockton. There was no bustle in the streets around them, that was certain. As far as Captain Seward could tell, the entire city of London was holding its breath, just about. He knew its moods, as one who'd grown up the son of a pepper merchant in Wych Street. Half of his men had come from the rookeries, but Captain Seward was a wealthy man. He showed no sign of that in the worn and faded leather and iron he wore. He had found a post that pleased him, on the Moorgate of the London wall. It did not matter that he went home to fine tables and servants, or he did not think it did. He treated his men like a father with his sons and in fact, two of them were his own lads.

Seward had sent the first runner when he'd been summoned to the wall by a report of ranks marching towards the city. The London gates were not for ornament. Closed and barred, they would protect those within from any hostile force. London could not even be besieged, not with the great river running to the south.

Locked outside, any enemy could negotiate with lords and the mayor, but that was not Seward's worry. His only concern was the gate, his world and his charge.

He had been present when the order had come to close it against the house of Lancaster years before. Seward had looked down then on a great ragged army, stretching for miles – but the gate had remained shut. He had disagreed with the old mayor over that, but followed his orders even so. He had done his duty, which was all a man could say in the end, or so he told his sons.

Captain Seward had gone grey since then, and had a great bare patch on his scalp that showed with no hair at all, like a bit of leather. His father had left him only the fine house on Wych Street, not any kind of income to go with it. Seward had fed and clothed his family for all that time by being master of the gate and keeping a close eye on the road running through it.

He could make out individual banners by then, though he turned away a dozen times to see if his youngest boy was on his way back. It took time to close the gate. Oxen had to be brought forward and made to heave against the great beams. Seward had them ready on the street below, with six of his best men, steady fellows who would not panic even if they saw soldiers walking right up to them as they reduced the bar of light to a crack and then nothing.

The merchants would howl in protest, of course. They always did, especially when Seward carried out his drill each quarter-day. Just four days a year for his men to practise closing a London gate and every single time the merchants reacted as if he'd lifted their purses or slapped their wives. Seward smiled a touch when he considered their reaction that day. Perhaps they wouldn't complain quite so loudly when they saw his gate preventing violent men from just wandering in.

It was with relief that he saw his lad at last, racing along the street below. The gate tower where Seward stood was raised some forty feet above the road, already busy with passers-by, come to gawk as news spread. He had no time for those. Seward watched as his son reached the steps up to the wall and climbed them without slowing down. The kid had a crust of snot between his nose and upper lip that never seemed to wear away, though he licked it all the time. Captain Seward nodded to him in pride as he scrambled up the last step, turning yet again to look out beyond the city wall. The marching ranks were no more than six hundred yards off by then, perhaps less. They'd cut it very fine.

'Well, Luke? Out with it! What's the word?' Seward demanded. The little bleeder was panting like a bellows and Seward began to lose his legendary calm. He reached down and grabbed his son, lifting him into the air.

'Luke! Closed or open?'

'The mayor's gone home, Dad, Captain Seward!' the boy panted. 'Gone to 'is bed and he won't come out.'

Seward put his son down. Mayor Stockton had never been one for quick decisions, Seward had always known that. It was no surprise that the man had run away from this one. Well, Seward had fought for Lancaster at Towton and he *was* a man used to quick decisions. He knew King Henry had been paraded in front of his people the day before, like a calf at auction. Seward had no idea where the king was then, but captains of the gate gave their first duty to the sitting monarch, to protect him from any and all enemies.

Seward leaned over the wall to give his order to the teams below. It would mean closing the gate in the face of those approaching, but there was still time if they moved sharp.

He felt an arm reach around him and tighten on his throat, pulling him back. He heard his son shout in surprise and fear. As Seward struggled and tried to roar, he saw his men below being surrounded by dozens of the gawkers and traders, all suddenly pulling knives.

'You'll be leaving that gate open,' a voice breathed in his ear, thick with garlic and violence. 'York is come home.'

Captain Seward was a brave man. He struggled for an instant before he felt a hard shove against his back. He yelled then as he went plunging forward, clawing at air as he fell forty feet to the cobbled road.

Edward and Richard of York came in together, both hard-faced with tension as they rode under the gatehouse and entered the city of London. In those first moments, they passed oxen teams and city soldiers standing with their heads bowed. Crossbows and longbows had been taken away from them and those who had ridden on ahead nodded or bowed to the sons of York. They had made the way safe and kept the gate open.

There were a few bodies sprawled around, proof of the brief violence that had occurred. Edward set his jaw as he rode past them. He had not asked for Warwick's French rebellion to land and drive him out of the country. He had not asked for traitors and betrayals to dog his reign. Yet he had returned and scorched through the north to reach London. His forces were too few and yet he had the capital city in his hand.

In the yard beyond the gate, Edward and Richard gestured for Clarence to rein in with them. The three York horsemen moved their mounts off to one side, to where the body of a gate captain lay broken on the ground. There were four or five of his mates standing with a weeping boy, their heads bare and their hats twisted to ropes in their hands. Richard sent one of his scouts to ask what they wanted and then gestured his acceptance. They took the body of Captain Seward away, while the army of York came in.

'Ten thousand men,' Richard murmured. 'It does not sound so many, until they have to walk through a gate. It seems then as if there is no end to them, like one of the hosts of heaven.'

'I believe we can trust George to close the gate after us,'

Edward said. It was an olive branch offered to his brother and George nodded, pleased to be counted part of the friendship he saw between the other two. His smile faded as Edward and Richard rode off together, trotting their mounts through the sucking mud to reach the front.

Both men preferred to lead rather than to follow. George of Clarence wondered if he would ever feel the same, perhaps as age tempered him. Looking after them, it was hard to be sure. Richard was the youngest, but he had spent vital years out of the shadow of his brothers. It was one reason for having young noblemen go as wards to other families – they had to learn to lead rather than to be dominated at every turn by the firstborn of their own line.

George stared down the road after his brothers until the last ranks had marched away and he was left with just the scouts, waiting on his order. He looked up, working a finger into his ear to scratch an itch.

'Very well, gentlemen. Close the gate,' he said. 'Then close them all.'

Clarence guided his horse to the very centre of the road to watch the light beyond reduced, with a pair of matched black oxen grunting and straining alongside him. The last few inches narrowed with a thump, then men stepped forward to drive iron poles into slots against the lower edge. It was no small deed, closing a London gate. Or keeping one open.

It seemed darker inside when it was done. Clarence felt the itch again in his ear and worked his finger in as deep as he could, opening and closing his mouth as he turned away and followed his brothers into the city.

'Where to, Your Highness?' Richard called to his brother, his voice strained. The crowds seemed to have thickened wherever they went, pressing in along the side alleys and standing three deep against the walls. Others darted like children or imbeciles through the marching men, always in danger of being knocked down and trampled. They were not cheering, Richard noticed. The whispers and darting movements made the York guards nervous, though the crowds did not seem hostile or even sullen. For the most part, they just watched the sons of York. Some touched their foreheads and hats out of respect. Others glared or turned aside to mutter and laugh with friends.

The roadway from Moorgate through the centre of the city was glutinous, a mixture of mud, pig's blood from butchers' shops, various chemical outpourings that stung the nose, and of course the ordure of both animal and man, sitting in forgotten piles where the original owners had left them. What sewers there were sometimes leaked back into the streets and the results were fairly eye-watering. Edward found himself breathing shallowly as he went deeper and deeper in, waiting for his lungs to accept the stronger air. It was good for you, so they said.

He considered his brother's question seriously. On entering, Edward had experienced a soaring confidence, a giddy sense almost of awe. He had not dared to imagine he would see the London streets again, not riding in at the head of an army to take back his throne. That delighted madness had drained slowly away under the stares of thousands of men and women, all interrupting their day's work to come and see him pass.

Control of London meant the Tower and the Royal Mint, St Paul's, the river itself and the Guildhall, where the lord mayor had retired to his rooms and refused to come out. It meant lords and wealth, both of which would be vital. Yet on that first day, there was little Edward actually needed in the walled part of the city, for all the symbolism of entering.

Scouts and messengers came back and forth as he walked his horse, some accepting payment. Richard glanced down at promises and oaths, at men declaring new loyalty and wasting no time in making claims against land and titles they had lost. He passed on just a few more pressing snippets he thought Edward might want to know. In that way, they learned that King Henry lay prostrate in the royal rooms at Westminster. It seemed the poor fellow had been driven almost to collapse by some farce of a walk through the city the day before.

The Royal Palace of Westminster lay away from the foul odours of the city proper, a good mile along the river – and in that cluster of Parliament and Abbey, of jewel house and Westminster Hall, lay everything that mattered to Edward. Yet he was unutterably weary and content to let them all wait on his pleasure. Baynard's Castle was a York fortress on the river bank. The thought of resting there in peace and safety made him yawn until his jaw cracked.

'The men are exhausted,' Edward said at last, gesturing his brother closer. 'In truth, I am tired and sore myself. Forty miles today, enough for anyone. Pass word for the captains to seek out warehouses, taverns, empty houses – anywhere they can find room to rest and be fed. London will have to put our good fellows up for a night or two.'

He looked around him for some sign of support, but there was none visible in the crowd. They stood, large-eyed and lugubrious, with even the usual chatter and sounds of movement dying away.

Edward raised his head. He understood the people of England had been battered back and forth over the years. Just months ago, they had been expected to cheer and pay their taxes as stout Yorkist folk, with Edward on the throne. Then he had been turned out – and King Henry was there once more, returned to their loving and bemused embrace.

Edward stared haughtily around him, responding to their scrutiny by puffing out his chest and staring them down. Though he might understand a little resentment, he was *damned* if he would acknowledge it. London was his city, the capital of his kingdom. They were his subjects. They could swallow that truth and choke on it. He felt his anger lend strength to tired muscles so that he straightened further.

'I think, Richard, that I will *not* rest after all, not yet. Call out a few score of the men to walk to Westminster with me before they settle down, would you?'

Richard of Gloucester turned his horse out of the marching ranks and gestured to Lord Rivers as he came abreast. The Woodville earl seemed pleased to be called, though he grew less pleased at every passing moment.

'My brother and I will be going on this evening, my lord,' Richard said. 'I leave the army and London in your hands, excepting only . . . eighty of our better knights to guard His Majesty.'

'I would be honoured to join them,' Lord Rivers replied. He preferred to remain close to his brother-in-law and was mulish when kept out of the councils between the York brothers. Richard found the man tiresome and it was exactly for that reason that he had brought him up short that day.

'No, I don't think so. I have given you my brother's command, Lord Rivers. Edward and I will ride on to Westminster, returning later tonight or tomorrow. I imagine there will be a crowning then, perhaps in St Paul's, where the city can be reminded York has returned – glory be to us, and so on and so on. Now, I am weary, Lord Rivers. Have you understood what I have said to you?'

'I believe I have, my lord,' Rivers replied, though the muscles in his jaw bunched alarmingly. Richard dismissed the man back to the ranks and returned to his brother, already thinking of the night ahead. He was tired, it was true, but he was also eighteen years old and he could remain awake for two days straight if he had to. He saw Edward yawn hugely, and was not sure his brother would manage quite as well.

'God's bones, we *know* where he is *now*!' Exeter roared, his voice so loud it was a weapon in itself. 'He is in London, eating slices of pink beef and murdering King Henry! There is no mystery, Neville! He and his treacherous bastards crept past us because we thought he'd come to challenge or begin a siege. I have never seen such a shit-poor example of battle offered and refused in all my life. I tell you, Neville . . .'

Exeter's whip-crack of a voice choked off as Lord Montagu stepped in between him and Warwick.

'You keep using my family's name,' John Neville said. 'Are you speaking to my brother, Earl Warwick? Or to me? I can't tell if this familiar tone is just rudeness, or a man who doesn't know when to hold his tongue. I can do that for you, if you wish.' He leaned much closer, until Exeter could feel the bristles of the man's beard against his chin. 'I can hold that tongue for you.'

Exeter's high colour deepened. He squinted at the younger Neville lord, eyeing his scars.

'I am not at fault, my lords,' he said, leaning back. 'We missed a chance to break Edward's neck – aye, and those of his brothers. We had the men, the position. Yet he slips past and leaves us holding our cocks.' He looked around the room in appeal. Earl Oxford dipped and raised his head deliberately. Montagu and Warwick looked on as if carved of stone, giving him nothing. Even so, Exeter continued, emboldened.

'My lords, I do not cry foul, or treachery, though some will wonder why we did not crush the sons of York between us when we had them here, outnumbered! That will be for a judge and for Parliament to discern, I do not doubt.' He shot Warwick a glance then, a promise of future malice.

Oxford cleared his throat to speak.

'Whatever the truth of that, it is clear enough to me now that *Exeter* should command,' Oxford said into the silence. 'He has the rank and the authority over the men. Nor is he . . . tainted by this disaster. No suspicion falls on to him and therefore . . .' Warwick shifted as if he might speak and Earl Oxford held up a warning hand. 'Therefore he should raise his banners over all the rest. The men will trust a duke and we cannot delay here any longer. In truth, we should already be on the road to London.'

'And would have been, if not for your demand for this extraordinary meeting,' Warwick replied. For all he recognized it had been his vital hesitation that had allowed the men of York to escape, he would not move an inch for a fool like Exeter, nor his weak-chinned friend.

'I believe I command still, my lords,' Warwick said. 'For good or ill. With authority granted by King Henry's seal and the approval of Parliament. I do not see any power here to remove me from my duties. Am I mistaken? That being so, I have no *choice* but to go on. Do not mutter at me, Oxford!' His voice had risen into a sudden bark as the Earl of Oxford made an unwise sound. Warwick glared at him for a moment, until it was clear the man would not voice a complaint.

'Lacking any legal authority to replace me, I must continue to fly my banners.'

'You could step down,' Exeter said, his eyes cold. Warwick shook his head.

'I have given my oath! I cannot break it merely because other men stand in disapproval of my actions! Am I a milkmaid to run in tears from the rebukes of others? No, my lord. I remain in command, with the blessing of King Henry.

I cannot lay the burden down and keep my soul. That is all there is – and you may do as you please.'

'You are releasing me from my duty, my oath?' Exeter said quickly.

Warwick smiled.

'Oh no, Holland. You gave your word to follow whomever the king placed in command, in peril of your soul. You risk damnation even by raising the *idea* to me, as if there is some interpretation that will allow you to withdraw. There is not. Is that understood, Holland? Is that perfectly clear, my lord Exeter?'

Exeter looked again to Oxford for support, but the man kept his head down and refused to look up. Henry Holland's mouth tightened, his cheeks drawing back in lines.

'You leave me no choice, my lord,' he said.

'How dare you, Holland!' Warwick snapped, surprising them all. 'What I leave you with is not your concern. Your *oath* is your concern! Do not take that begrudging tone with me! Stand, if you would stand. Leave if you would burn. *There* is your choice.'

Warwick waited until the younger man finally lost some of the stubborn resistance in his face. A subtle tension went out of Henry Holland and he bowed from the waist.

'I remain at your command, my lord Warwick,' he said quietly. To his surprise, Warwick came forward and clapped him on the back, startling them all.

'I am pleased, Henry. Your word is intact, for all our differences. What I have done in error is my concern. That is for me to answer, but I am relieved you did not break your oath and damn yourself.' Once more he patted the duke on his back, like a favourite hound.

'In truth, I am in agreement,' Warwick said, surprising Exeter further. 'We have twenty-four thousand men, all ready to march. London and King Henry are under threat of a usurping house. We should already be on the road, as I said, not risking our souls here. My lords, I give you my oath now, sworn on Mary, the Mother of God, sworn on the honour of my family line. I will stand against York, when we meet again. If I have been in error in the past, I will wash it clean then. That is my word to you, by Christ Our Lord, amen! *Amen!*'

The last word was enough of a bellow to make Exeter step back, still caught up in swift-changing emotions that he could hardly follow. He seized on the last of it and brightened.

'To London then?'

'With all we have, my lord,' Warwick replied, showing his teeth. 'We will end it there, with the whole world watching.'

Edward of York pushed open the door to King Henry's private rooms in Westminster. In the darkness outside, London's lights gleamed. He and his brother Richard brought a smell of iron and the sound of jingling mail into that quiet space.

Henry lay pale on his bed, the sheet fallen away from his chest so that they could see blue veins and the lines of his ribs. His hair was wet with perspiration and his eyes were reddened and half open. As the breath of colder air reached him from the outside, the king began to struggle to sit up.

The noise woke the only other occupant of the room, who had been snoring at the foot of the bed with his legs sprawled and crossed, in the comfort of a wide, stuffed chair. Derry Brewer startled awake and looked blearily at the two men standing by the open door. A shadow crossed his face then and he reached for his stick with hands that had grown heavy-knuckled and gnarled. The king's spymaster was sixty-three years old and he grunted as he sat up and leaned on his blackthorn.

Edward crossed the room on light steps, padding in with his brother at his shoulder. Derry watched them come and his eyes were bleak.

'He isn't well enough to be moved,' Derry said. He had known his voice would draw their attention, the two sons of York turning on him as wolves on prey. Before either of them could reply, Henry spoke from where he lay, his voice weak and as high as a child's.

'Cousin York! Thank God you've come. I know it will all be well now.'

Derry raised one hand to his mouth in grief to hear Henry's trust. The spymaster thought of the blade hidden in his stick as Edward leaned in to take the king's hand in greeting, showing a pale throat. Derry might have moved, but Richard of Gloucester was watching him still. The young man pressed a stronger hand over his own and moved him away from the king, lifting his weight from the chair as if it was nothing. Derry found himself gripped so tightly he could hardly breathe as he was half walked, half dragged out of the room. The door closed behind him.

He found his voice was rough with grief.

'You don't have to kill him,' he said. 'You just don't. Please, son. Put him in a monastery somewhere far off. He won't trouble you again.'

'Ah,' Richard said, his voice gentle. 'You love him.' He looked aside for a moment, then shrugged. 'You don't need to fear for Henry of Lancaster tonight, Master Brewer. We won't kill him, while his son might land in England any fine morning. My brother and I have come to make an ending, not raise another king on the coast. There's Earl Warwick too, with his great host. We might need a hostage for safe passage there. No, Master Brewer, Henry has nothing to fear from my brother tonight, or from me. *You* though – you're done.'

Still holding the king's spymaster in a young man's hard grip, Richard of Gloucester prodded him down another flight of stairs and out to the empty yard beyond. The Palace of Westminster had enough lamps lit above to lend a golden gleam to part of that square, with the great Abbey lying across from it in darkness.

Derry looked around at the waiting men-at-arms, standing silently as they watched him with cold indifference. There would be no help for him there. He slumped, leaning on his stick.

'I lost a daughter and a wife when I was very young,' Derry said, looking up at the clear night sky. 'And some good friends, son. I hope I'll see them again.' For an instant, he turned his single eye on Richard and smiled, looking almost boyish. 'I remember your father. He was an arrogant whoreson but still, twice the man you are. I hope you get what you deserve, crookback.'

Richard of Gloucester nodded to his captain, making a sharp gesture. The man stepped in and Derry looked up into the darkness, marvelling at the sheer beauty of the stars above. He made a soft grunt as the man struck him, then sank down, coughing once as he died. The cane fell from his fingers and rolled with a clatter that was the only sound.

17

Elizabeth felt a pang of terror at the noise of armoured men approaching. For months, she had suffered with that particular nightmare, risen like a white spark in her chest every time a grocer or a priest came to Sanctuary. Every time she heard a strange voice or a tiny bell rang, a great, dark fear would come that it was Lancaster or some lord, come to slaughter her children and herself. She dreamed of blood, spilling black across the floor.

She heard the true clatter of knights in iron and sprang awake, her heart thumping in the darkness. There were always one or two monks in the tiny cells of Sanctuary. She had grown to know them all well in the months of confinement. She recognized Brother Paul's tone and then a yell and a crash that had her reaching for her night robe and fumbling with its belt in the darkness.

She slept alone and could hear the wet nurse, Jenny, stirring in the next room along the corridor. Her mother, Jacquetta, was already moving about and appeared with a lamp and her hair in a great pile of sleep-creased curls.

Wordlessly, Elizabeth showed her the long knife she had snatched up. Jacquetta vanished back into her room, returning with a poker from the fireplace. The two women went to the top of the wooden stairs, shushing Jenny when she too came out, pressing her back into her room with their hands. Further along the floor, one of the girls began to wail. The crying would surely wake the old lady who looked after them and she was actually quite deaf, so that when she called out, she woke the rest of the house. Elizabeth bit her lip in fear as she edged to the top step and crouched to peer down into the tiny entrance hall.

Brother Paul lay crumpled against the wall, unconscious or dead, she did not know. Elizabeth drew in a sharp breath and then some part of her realized she knew the man standing over him with his back to her. She watched Edward turn in silence, though there had to have been noise.

Her husband looked up to where she stared down through the banisters and his face split into a great beam and shout. Elizabeth matched him, giving a cry of relief, though she felt as if she might faint and tumble right down the steps. She swayed as she tried to stand and felt her mother's hands on her waist, guiding her away from the fall.

Edward came bounding up the stairs, peering at his wife in pride.

'I have woken you,' he said, laughing. Elizabeth snatched frantically at her thoughts.

'Edward, I don't . . . Is it over then?' she asked. To her confusion, her giant of a husband shook his head, though he still grinned.

'No, love. Though this is a part of it. Yet London is mine at least – and I can take you out of this place. That is enough for tonight, isn't it? Now where is my son, Elizabeth?'

'I named him Edward,' Elizabeth said. 'Jenny! Bring me the baby. And he was baptized in the Abbey.'

The wet nurse came out in triumph, the bundled prince held high in her arms. To her credit, the young woman looked to Elizabeth first for permission. Elizabeth nodded, pressing down the sense of grievance that her husband had not even embraced her, though he would hold his son.

Unaware of his wife's disappointment, Edward raised the

boy into the air, staring up at his tiny, crumpled face in delight or awe. He had never seen his son before that moment.

'Light, girl!' he said to the wet nurse. 'Bring that lamp closer would you? More light here, that I may see my son. Hello, boy. Edward, Prince of Wales, who will be king of England. By God, Elizabeth, I am glad to see him whole. King Henry is returned to the Tower – and I have my wife and my son.'

'And your girls,' Elizabeth said. 'Your three daughters.'

'Of course, love! Have them brought out to me. I will squeeze them pink and tell them how much I have missed them all.' Edward had noticed his wife's growing irritation. He tried not to let it annoy him in turn, but she managed it even so, with her stiff face and wide eyes that he knew would mean an argument. He glanced at his brother Richard on the floor below, watching the happy reunion with a dark expression. Neither of them could remember when they had last slept. Dawn was close and Richard had seen enough of violence and striving, at least for a time. He wanted to sleep.

'You'll come back with me, across the road,' Edward said to his wife. 'I had Henry put out of his rooms there.'

'You went to him first? With me still a prisoner in this cold place?' Elizabeth demanded. Edward's temper snapped suddenly, too tired to wheedle and flatter his wife. His eyes grew cold and he passed his son back to the nurse hovering at his elbow.

'I did as I saw fit, Elizabeth! By God, why must you . . . ? No. I am too weary to argue with you. Have the girls brought out to me and then my men will walk you all across to the palace. You'll sleep in a better bed tonight.'

He made no mention of joining her and Elizabeth only nodded, coldly furious for reasons she did not have words to explain. She had longed to see him for an age. There he was, looking slim and younger again, but caring only to see his son, as if he had not missed his wife at all. She had not thought he could hurt her so deeply.

Their three daughters came rushing out to cling to their father's legs and look adoringly up at him. The sight of their delighted tears went some way to cheer Edward up. Still he yawned and felt sick with tiredness, as if he could just lie down and pass out.

'Yes, I am pleased as well, to see you. Yes, all of you, of course! How pretty you have grown! Now girls, yes, I must go ahead for a little while.'

The two youngest began to snivel at the merest suggestion their father would not remain with them. Edward gestured sharply to the nurse who had followed them out and still stood, beaming toothlessly at her young charges. Catching his eye, the woman dropped her beatific smile and gathered his children into her skirts.

'Come along, dears,' she said, making a clucking sound in her throat. The wet nurse, Jenny, dropped into a curtsey, then she too went to pack, the Prince of Wales in her arms.

Edward stood uncomfortably then with his wife, all the bustle and noise that had centred around his arrival dying away. At the door below, Brother Paul began to stir, a livid bruise showing where he had been knocked cold. Edward looked down without apology as the monk rose to his feet.

'You have my thanks,' he said, flipping a gold coin down the flight of stairs. Brother Paul's eyes never left his as it arced through the air and fell to the stones with a dull sound.

Edward snorted in exasperation, almost too tired to stand. 'I'll leave a dozen guards here. Come over when you have the children ready.'

'Yes, Edward. I will,' Elizabeth replied. 'I'll find you in your rooms.'

Edward went more heavily down the stairs than he had come up them. He had to duck his head to pass beneath the lintel of the Sanctuary fortress. Perhaps because of that action, he paused on the threshold and stepped back inside alone. Edward came up the flight of steps again to embrace his wife, holding her tight enough to choke against his shoulder. To her surprise, she began to weep and he was smiling as he pulled back and kissed her. He removed his gauntlet, revealing a hand dark with oil and grime, a hand more suited to a killing blow than anything more gentle. Yet she did not flinch as he eased away a tear from her cheek.

'There, love,' he said. 'I am home and all is well, isn't it?'

'Not if you have to fight again, Edward,' she said. He looked away then.

'I do. I need to be a burning brand now, just for a time. There'll be peace afterwards, I promise.'

She looked into Edward's eyes and saw the determination there. Despite herself, despite knowing his enmity was not aimed at her, she shivered still.

Edward woke from dark dreams, finding himself slippery with sleep-sweat, as if he had fought or run for an hour. He knew he lay sprawled across the very bed where he had spoken to Henry the night before. He had no memory of collapsing into it, with his armour half off and the rest digging into him. The sun was either still rising or falling, he did not know. It would not have surprised him to have slept the entire day, the way he'd been feeling, but he was still tired. He scratched himself then and winced. He also stank so powerfully he began to consider having a bath filled.

He looked up at the sound of shuffling feet, catching a

glimpse of a servant ducking back out of sight. Edward groaned and lay back. Was he sickening with some illness? His head was clear, his stomach empty. He had not touched grapes, hops or grain since taking his oath in exile, just as he had promised his brother. Like Samson and his long hair, the oath had become a talisman to him and he would not break it at that moment, not with Warwick and Montagu and Oxford and Exeter still to face, all with blood in their eyes. He sat up at the thought that he had Parliament under his thumb then. He could send orders to have the Dukes of Norfolk and Suffolk freed. Every day would secure his position and lessen that of Warwick – except for one weakness.

Margaret of Anjou would land, with her son. The whole country seemed to know it was coming, though not one of them could say when or where she would touch her dainty foot to English soil. Edward knew he could not ignore the mother or her son. Margaret had rescued her husband before. With Warwick's army, her landing could become a mighty rebellion of the south, great enough even to break London's walls.

He raised his head at the steps of a steward. The man went down on one knee at the far end of the room, his head bowed.

'Your Highness,' he said. 'Lords Gloucester and Clarence await your pleasure in the audience room.'

'Or were too impatient to wait,' Richard said behind him as they entered, 'one or the other, surely.' The steward rose to his feet in confusion, but Edward waved him off.

'Is it morning, or evening – or the next morning?' he said blearily.

'It is Good Friday morning, Brother, a few hours after I saw you last. Were you dreaming then? I hope you found a little rest to restore your humours, because I have news.'

'I am sharp set, I know that much,' Edward said, yawning. 'There are kitchens here. Have something sent to me before I am worn down to a shadow.'

He smiled at his brothers as he spoke, then stood and stretched like a mastiff, pulling off the shoulder plate he had not managed the night before.

'That damned thing was digging into me. I did dream – of a spear shoved in right there.'

Richard shook his head.

'Do not say such things, Brother. Not today, when Christ suffered the same wound. Shall I wait then, for you to dress and eat?'

Edward sighed.

'No. Very well, tell me. Did King Henry die in the night?'

Richard raised his eyebrows and Edward chuckled.

'What else would bring you rushing over to wake me?' He looked from one brother to another. 'Well?'

'Warwick's army has been sighted, Edward, coming south. They will reach London late tomorrow evening.'

Edward looked down for a moment, thinking.

'That is a little slow. I wonder if he delayed to gather siege cannon. That must be it. My old friend loves the long guns, do you remember? He always put too much faith in them, instead of the men he commanded. He expects me to hide behind the walls of this fair city.'

He raised his head then, his eyes clear and a smile spreading. Richard grinned at the man his brother had become, so much more a threat than the great pale pudding he had been before.

'And you won't,' Richard said.

'No, Brother. *I won't.* I will go out to *meet* him. You will command my right wing, my vanguard. I will hold the centre and you, George . . .' There he leaned to one side to observe his brother. 'If you wish it, you will command my left wing. It is an honour, George. Are you up to it?'

'You have what, ten thousand?' George of Clarence said faintly. Edward could see a line of bright perspiration had appeared along his hairline. He wanted to take pity on the man, but he had not yet recovered his patience with his weak-spittle brother. That particular betrayal had hurt him, sharp and worse and more deeply than Warwick's own.

'I'll find a few brave lads in London before I go, George, don't worry! I'll have myself crowned once more in St Paul's, where the crowds can see. You'll get some fine fellows then to stand with you.'

George of Clarence swallowed, raising his hand as if to give a blessing, though it trembled. He could see a mad, wild mood in his brothers, and in that moment he was certain it would lead to the destruction of them all.

'Edward, I *told* you, Warwick has two or three times as many. No one knows the true number beyond his paymaster and Warwick himself. Is it . . .' A horrible thought struck him and his voice became strained. 'Is it that you don't believe the numbers I have told you? I have apologized for breaking my word. I will redeem it in time, as I have promised. Yet I did begin by joining you at Coventry. I brought three thousand men raised from *my* villages and towns – equipped and fed by *my* funds. Will you deny me even so?'

Edward looked stonily at him and George could not bear that cool appraisal.

'If you can't trust me, trust what I told you! It was no exaggeration! I swear by the Rood of Christ that Warwick has as many as I have said. A host, Edward, a *host*, well armed and hardened. He . . .'

'Brother, I believe you,' Edward said. 'I never thought you would lie over such a thing – how could you, even, when a falsehood would be revealed the moment our enemies took the field against us? No, I accept that Warwick and his allies have an army greater than ours.' He looked aside at Richard then and Gloucester nodded. Clarence felt his eyes snap back and forth, once again with the sense of having missed some previous communication.

'What?' George demanded. Edward shrugged.

'I do not deny Warwick's numbers, George. But I have decided to attack him anyway. I will throw myself at his throat – and I will win . . . or I will lose.'

'Against so many?' George retorted. 'You *cannot* win!'

'We'll see, Brother,' Edward said darkly, growing angry. 'Either way, I will take our people out to them. I will stand in Warwick's way.'

He rolled his shoulders and called for servants to feed and bathe him, clapping his hands to bring them running. He looked at his two brothers standing there, George still in shock, Richard enjoying some dark satisfaction Edward could not trouble himself to read.

'I will give the left to Lord Hastings, George. It would be better to have you standing with me in the centre. Does that please you?' George nodded like a schoolboy. All three knew there was yet another alternative – that the Duke of Clarence might remain behind in London. Edward did not offer it and George could not ask. At last, Edward smiled, his good humour reasserting itself.

'I think I will sleep for a little longer, or perhaps the rest of the day. Meet me on the steps of St Paul's at noon tomorrow, to see me crowned. Fetch me . . . the Bishop of London, Kempe – not that Neville who crowned me before. Much good did that do me. No, I'll have a different set of omens today. Fetch me good Bishop Kempe and a simple crown from the Tower, a band of gold all unadorned. Ready my army and send out the call to good men who would rather fight today than depend for their freedom on those who will.'

Edward looked through the leaded windows then, over the city. The light had grown brighter as he'd spoken to his brothers. He could feel the ache in his joints still, from too little sleep. Yet he smiled as servants brought in a great copper bath and began to fill it before the fire in the grate. Perhaps he would doze for a while in the hot water, before he rose to challenge for his realm once more, with the life and death of all he loved as the stake.

Weymouth had been a great port once, before the Black Death had ripped through it a century before. Half the population had gone into lime pits then and the town was not yet as prosperous as it had been. It was one of the reasons Edmund Beaufort, Duke of Somerset, had chosen it for Margaret to land. There were no spies so far from London, or if there were, he had men on the only road east to intercept them, men with crossbows and black scarves. He had no qualms about telling such men to use whatever means were required. Somerset knew well the importance of his task. He stood on the docks of Weymouth and stared out over the dark sea, looking for any sign of a ship coming in, as he had done for a week straight. Each day had ended in disappointment and he was growing desperate.

News was scarce in that part of the world, so far from the cities in the north. Somerset had only twelve hundred men with him, enough to keep Margaret of Anjou safe, with her son. Yet a single rider had come from London days before, telling him that York had landed. He'd recognized the hand of Derry Brewer in the ridiculous requirement of exchanging words and counter-words with the courier. Yet the news had made him forget his irritation. Edward of York and

Richard of Gloucester, returned to England, as if God himself had snatched them out of reach and relented, bringing them home one last time.

Somerset's father had been hacked down in St Albans, by the Castle Inn, fighting to his last breath for King Henry and Lancaster. The title had passed to his older brother then – a good man who had tried to continue that loyalty. He had been executed by the house of York, by a man Somerset had been told to avoid if he could not call him an ally: John Neville, Lord Montagu, brother to Warwick. The idea that Edmund Beaufort could ever have found himself on the same side as those two cutpurse whoresons was an abomination, impossible. Yet there it was – and he was duke because his brother and his father had been murdered for a lost cause. He felt a silken touch of regret that he had ever come home from France. He would be there in peace if he hadn't been seduced by the news of York driven out at last, made to run with his brother, the Duke of Gloucester. Somerset had wept as he had reached England once again, believing that a terrible, grim period of his life had come to an end. Instead, there he was, waiting for a ship and his last hopes.

He looked out over a darkening sea, with the sun setting gold on his left shoulder, turning his head back and forth as he tried to sense anything out of place on the deep. When it came, he noticed it immediately, a flicker of metal catching the last of the sun's light. A piece of rail or a blown-glass lamp, he did not know. Edmund Beaufort crossed himself and raised a coin to his lips from where it lay on a chain around his neck. It had been his father's and his brother's and in that touch he carried them with him.

'Light it,' he called to his men. They had raised an iron cradle on a beam of oak, filled with packed straw and oil. A burning rag was carried up and the torch burst into flame, streaming six feet out into the breeze. All those who had been fool enough to stare at it were made blind for a while, but Somerset had kept his gaze on the sea. With a smile, he saw a warship tack round in the direction of the shore. They had seen the signal and been ready for it. It must have been a great relief to them as they ran so close to a coast that had been the death of so many.

Somerset called his captains to him and had them assemble their men in perfect ranks along the docks. He had a company of forty archers ready with their bows, standing to attention, while the rest were well-trained soldiers, not farm boys and ploughmen given a bit of sharp metal to hold. They were the honour guard that would bring Queen Margaret and Prince Edward of Wales back to London. Their task was to protect those two lives at the cost of their own if need be.

Somerset felt his fist tighten at that thought. His family had paid enough, if such things could ever be measured. He had no son of his own, which was an itch he could not reach to scratch. If he fell, they would have broken his father's line for good. He hated the men of York, who had destroyed and despoiled for their ambition, at a cost so great, and themselves so small they could not peer over the edge of all they had ruined. It burned in Edmund Beaufort and he could hardly stand to live.

As he watched, the French warship showed colours of Lancaster, but then dropped sail and drifted, not half a mile from shore. The sun had set and darkness had come in upon them. Beaufort craned to see, blowing a sigh when he spotted a boat lowered down and the white flecks of sweeps moving.

The waves were rising, blown to spume in a wind becoming a gale. He could imagine the coast was black as a coal pit by then, beyond the torch he had lit – and that a mere spark in the darkness. Somerset guessed a French captain would rather have his ship safely anchored than risk her closer in. Perhaps that was wise, given those he carried. Somerset waited until he was sure the boat was carrying an anchor and not those he had come to escort away. He listened for the great splash as they dropped it in, but the sound was lost in the howl of the air.

'Rest easy, gentlemen,' he called to his captains. 'Leave a couple of lads here, but I will return to the inn. I don't think they'll land a boat in this chop. Return before dawn, if you would. They'll step ashore tomorrow.'

He shivered and crossed himself as he turned away. The sea could turn in an instant, from gentle breezes and light waves to a terrifying sheet of buckling iron, so full of rage and spite as to shock a man's breath right out of him.

Edward was crowned for the second time that Easter Saturday, in a service notable for its brevity, though the pews were packed in St Paul's Cathedral. He accepted a gold circlet pressed down on to his brow from Bishop Kempe, the man of the cloth still looking flustered, yet respectful enough. The Church had supported York before; it could hardly refuse to do so again, just months after Edward had reigned in peace and been driven out by traitors.

King Edward came out to be seen by the people of London and was gratified to find so many there on the roads all around. Some of them were his own men, of course, but Richard seemed pleased and there were some new faces asking for a blade and a place to stand.

As the afternoon wore on, they took their urgency from Edward as he fretted and checked his armour and weapons and squires. He moved and spoke as if he could not wait a moment longer to be on the road. His wife and son and daughters had been brought out of sanctuary safe and alive. He had put Henry back in the Tower in his old cell and Edward wore a crown once again. All in all, it had been a good day.

All that was left was to seek out those who had turned on him and still roamed his kingdom, with iron in their hands and no right to even walk his roads. He was stern when he called his men to order at last. The command to 'Make ready' was shouted up and down the ranks, echoed by London lads in their excitement until it seemed the whole city shook with the order.

As Edward mounted his warhorse, the sun was sinking in the west. He saw his two brothers swing their legs over their saddles on either side of him, adjusting themselves and their cloaks and scabbards. It was a comfort to have them both there.

'We have come such a long way,' Edward said to Richard. 'I do not think this is the end, but if it is, I know our father would be proud of you. I know I am.'

Richard of Gloucester reached out to him and Edward took his gauntleted hand in a fierce grip.

'God loves a grand gesture, Edward.'

'I hope so,' the king replied. He looked down the lines of his men, standing with long shadows reaching out, waiting in patient ranks for Moorgate to be opened once more.

'Open the gate,' Edward called. 'Raise my banners. For York.'

18

With the vital decision made, Warwick had felt free to drive his forces hard down the Great North Road to London. If he had owed any final scrap of loyalty to Edward of York, or Richard of Gloucester, or even his fool of a son-in-law George of Clarence, he had repaid them to the last coin by letting them pass him at Coventry. He felt clear-headed. The past had been expunged and all that was left was what lay ahead. It was a pleasant feeling, like a ship cutting its anchor rope so that it floated free. All the past was ash. He saw it then.

Only a fool would make plans before facing Edward of York on the battlefield, so he did not. He had a vast force and he had taken good cannon from foundries in Coventry, to be wheeled along at a smart pace by pairs of ponies. His commanders, Exeter and Oxford and Montagu, were all experienced men in war. He knew they would give no quarter if he asked for it.

From that one order he held back. Edward had forbidden prisoners at Towton, condemning thousands who might have lived to be slaughtered in that great butchery. The memory of the ground churned in blood and snow as far as the eye could see still troubled Warwick. He sometimes woke from dreaming of it, with his hands raised against attack. He knew the men would not demur if he gave the order. It was easier for them to kill in wanton savagery, far easier than it ever was to use a man's judgement and to show restraint. He could call for the reins to be cut, for all curbs and bits to be dropped. The order would be welcomed if he did.

When he had been innocent, when he had been kind, it had come back to bite him. When Warwick had stood with Edward and stayed his hand, refusing to let him kill King Henry, Margaret had used the man as a symbol and roused the entire country against them. When Warwick had held Edward as a prisoner and not brought him to the block, his reward had been Edward restored and Warwick driven into exile. It was even said that the old Duke of York had sallied forth from Sandal Castle to save Warwick's father. The result of such an act of courage and friendship had been his execution – and both their heads on iron spikes. For almost twenty years, showing mercy or upholding honour had led to disaster. Taking no ransoms, murdering bound prisoners – delighting in red-handed slaughter – had led to victory after victory.

Warwick could not take back the moment of madness when he had stayed his hand at Coventry. That had been the payment of old loyalties and old debts – and they were paid. If his father's shade still watched him – and he hoped it did not – he would be satisfied. The Great North Road was made anew and Warwick breathed good air as he trotted his mount. He was made anew. He had been at war for half his life and it had eaten him away and made him less. He was weary of it.

He had been surprised not to catch the sons of York on the road, at least at first. He'd come to realize Edward had lunged for the city, pushing his men to exhaustion and injury just to reach the capital. Exeter had settled into a cold dislike as he understood what a chance had been missed. That young duke would not attack Warwick directly, but Exeter made his displeasure and his scorn well known through the column, with half the men whispering that Warwick should have stopped York at Coventry – and never let him past.

Warwick wished them all luck with their ability to look

over their shoulders and see exactly where they had been and what steps they should have taken. For all his awareness of his own failings, he knew that to lead was to take that single step into a dark room, then react to whatever took you up and dragged you in. To be responsible for the lives of thousands was to feel a combination of awe and pride and grim regret, all mingled together. The victories were his – and the failures were also his. Yet he would not give back a moment of it, not one.

The sun set slowly, the harbinger of a sweet and gentle spring, with all the harshness of the winter blast now a memory, as if it had never been. Yet for soldiers and for those who commanded them, spring always came with the sense of danger. It was the fighting season, where armies stirred from sleep and worked off their winter fat with hard blows and miles unfolding under their feet. Darkness would be upon them as they reached the London walls, so Warwick had a horn blown to halt the column. They made camp just to the north of the town of Barnet, so the men would eat well and some of the officers might even sleep in real beds rather than on dry ground. Yet Exeter sent out scouts and began to set guard shifts for the night. London was just eight miles away and close enough for a forced march and a sudden attack. They would not be surprised.

By the time full dark came, the stars shone in a sky that was achingly clear, the blackness perfect as they waited for the moon to rise. The first companies had been fed from the cooking carts and the rest were gathering their tin bowls and forming lines, stomachs growling with hunger. They turned at the sound of shouts going up along the southern edge of the camp, looking in frustration at the cauldrons of stew and piles of loaves as high as a man. The shouting grew in noise and breadth and those waiting for food cursed and gave up, racing back to where they had laid their kit and weapons. The captains and their serjeants were already running along the lines, calling 'Form square! Squares to form!' over and over.

Warwick felt a shudder go through him as he mounted in the dark, murmuring thanks to his squire as the lad held his horse and guided Warwick's foot to the stirrup. In part it was because Warwick knew he had to trust others. With so many men, he had been able to keep a reserve behind the three main squares. He had stood at Towton to see the Duke of Norfolk drive in against the flank at the right moment. A reserve to be directed where they were needed was vital, if you had the men to spare. He had – and he stood with six thousand as Montagu, Exeter and Oxford formed up across the North Road in three huge companies, each as large as his own. Warwick shivered again at the memories that kept flashing into his mind's eye. He had forgotten some of them over the years, but it seemed they were still there to come back and fill him with dread. Vast armies crashing against each other in the dark. True terror as the night filled with arrows and smoke and swinging metal and mere skill counted for naught. He swallowed, accepting his helmet from the hands of his squire and working the buckle under his chin so that it would stay on. He was ready. Though it was dark and he sat his horse behind the front lines, Warwick called for his banners to be raised. He could hear the embroidered cloth flapping back and forth with a noise like wings.

Edward had not expected to catch sight of Warwick's forces as close to London as Barnet. He had gone barely five miles from the walls by then. It felt as if the men who had come out of the city had just begun to stretch out when the forward scouts came racing back with news of a huge army. The sun had been setting as they'd left and Edward had intended to use the wide road to march ten or fifteen miles, then camp and eat well. He was quiet with thought as he trotted along, hardly looking up as heralds came in from Richard ahead of him and Lord Hastings behind. Those two horsemen waited patiently for the king's orders.

It was madness to attack in the dark, especially to attack a man with a history of digging defensive structures, as Warwick had at St Albans. How long had Warwick prepared the ground? Even a few hours would have allowed him to dig a trench or two to ruin cavalry, with the accompanying ramps and mounds to protect his archers from return fire. Edward reached past the leather and cloth of his helmet to scratch his chin. He grew itchy when under strain, he realized, wondering if it had always been so. Either way, he would not retreat. He had come out of London to give battle and found his enemy waiting patiently for him.

'My orders, gentlemen,' he called to the two heralds. Every man marching in range of him was craning to hear, so much so that the lines ahead began to bunch and wander off the path.

'I will not offer battle in the darkness, but tell the men to be ready to rise before dawn and strike. I will form squares as close as I can, to fall on them as soon as there is light. No torches. No sound. I do not want them to aim their cannon as we come to rest. When battle is joined, let there be no quarter offered, no ransoms taken. I will *not* face these bastards again.'

Some of the more hardened soldiers around him chuckled or murmured in pleasure at his words. Others repeated them for those who had not caught the meaning, so that it spread out before and behind his position. All the while, they marched on. The scouts had been out at three miles and raced back at full gallop between the armies they had sighted. Edward made his decision and gave his orders when they were barely half an hour apart on the road.

The forces of York marched on through the quiet streets of Barnet, cheerful enough though resigned. The news spread quickly that a great host awaited them and they would surely fight in the morning. The laughter became muted and the talking dropped to mutters or whispered prayers.

The army of Warwick was sighted outside the town, outlined across the Great North Road in pinpricks of torches. Perhaps it showed they had no fear of the enemy springing out from London, or just that experienced commanders did not want the York force to stumble into them in the darkness. The night was black all around, the land bare of all but a few trees and hedges. The road made gentle rises and falls as Edward approached, judging his spot. A mile was close enough, he decided. He gave the order and then winced as it was roared out up and down the column. The men formed with noise and clatter, each serjeant, each captain busy gathering in men they knew, forming the ranks one by one and shouting furiously as lost men called to their friends. It was complete chaos and Edward could see almost nothing, just hear it going on all around him. He was only pleased that Warwick had not thought to risk an attack over that hour or so. Yet the moon had shown and begun its creep up the sky. Even that sliver made the night a little easier to bear.

Edward was pleased he had forbidden torches to his captains when the first cannon fired, a crack of sound and a spike of light from a mile away. He did not see the ball or hear it land, but the thought of enduring a night under a barrage of iron and fire was suddenly impossible.

'Summon my captains – *quietly*,' he said to his heralds. 'Go out amongst the men and bring them all in to me.'

One man spoke to a dozen and they went out in turn so that it seemed a short time before a hundred grizzled captains were standing around his horse, waiting for orders. To the north, another three cannons spat flame and they all tensed or crossed themselves. There was a crump of sound a few hundred yards away and voices raised in fear or shrieking injury, quickly muffled by those around them. Edward lowered his head in anger, as if he wanted to charge right then.

'We cannot remain here,' he said. He could not see whether they agreed with him or not. It would have been madness to give the enemy a target by lighting a torch and the night was truly dark, so Edward spoke almost to the air. 'We could retreat, but I would prefer to advance on their lines. If it can be done in silence, they will not know we are there, the whole night. We'll sleep like children and all their shot will pass over us.' He waited and some of them acknowledged his orders with a chorus of assent, understanding that he could not see them nod.

'It must be in silence, lads,' Edward said. 'If they know we are there, they will adjust their aim. If that is clear, go back and tell your men, but let them know I will have the skin of anyone who makes a noise. Half a mile more, gentlemen, before they can lie down and sleep. Keep square formation so that we are ready to attack in the morning. Quiet and slow is the order for now. Quiet and slow.'

There was no argument from his most experienced men and a few of them chuckled at the idea of sitting safe under the wing of an enemy shooting overhead. Yet it would be a fraught position to hold. In truth, there was little chance of sleep for any of them.

'We will attack at first light,' Edward promised.

Moving ten thousand men in the darkness was its own challenge, though at least there was no resistance to the idea.

No one wanted to wait for a ball of stone or iron to come tearing through a rank of men. They shuffled forward line by line, trusting those in front to count off eight hundred and eighty yards. In the end, Richard of Gloucester found a ridge of land just ahead, some five hundred paces from the torch-line of Warwick's army. It was barely out of arrow-range and the ridge itself was no more than the gentlest rise. It would not have slowed them on the march, but it did mean they could lie down on the ground, on spring grasses growing in clumps and hummocks, finding a place to sleep with insects crawling over them in the blackness.

Cannon fire continued all night, passing safely overhead. The army of York lay down in three great squares, waiting for morning.

Margaret had not minded the roughness of the waves. It had pleased her to feel again that she had nothing to fear from the sea – and that her son felt the same, showing no ill effects from the battering wind or the lurching of the deck. She had seen the torch raised to guide her in the night before, her heart leaping at the sight. Yet the captain had refused and would not allow her authority over him when it came to the handling of his ship. Margaret had been forced to watch the man seek out an anchorage in frustration. The shore was there! She could almost have swum to it. She had endured years in exile, swallowing a thousand small inconveniences and outright humiliations. She had known poverty and debt and the shame of being utterly dependent on the largesse of another, who might at any moment cease to care whether you lived or died. Yet that final night had been the hardest of them all, with the coast of England there in the dark, with a great streamer of light raised for her – and a French captain who would not listen to her entreaties until he saw the sun again.

It had been a night of troubled sleep and ill dreams. Her son, Edward, had spent most of it awake, even sparring a little with one of the knights King Louis had sent. The clatter of their iron boots on deck woke Margaret from her doze and then she sat up, still clothed, in the foetid little cabin. There was a dim and whitish light showing, a pale gleam of dawn that had her breathing hard and calling a servant to help her lace her boots. Margaret came out on deck still flushed, shivering instantly in the breeze. The sea had died down in the night and she saw the captain was smiling and the boat was being brought alongside.

Early as it was, the shore was hidden in mist that swirled in the sea breeze, showing a smudge of green or white as a girl might swing her dress and flash a sight of her legs. Margaret smiled. She had been so young when she had seen that shore for the first time – the first of any land that was not France!

'Take my hand, Mother,' Edward said at her side, reaching out to her. 'There is still a little life in the waves, so Captain Cerce tells me.' Margaret allowed her strong young son to guide her across the deck to the break in the rail and the pitching boat below. That actually did look a little nerve-wracking, but she forced herself to smile and incline her head to the captain, though she thought him a pompous little fellow.

Edward went first and stood in the boat to guide Margaret safely down. He was solicitous of her and made sure she was settled before he took some of the chests Louis had given to her cause. One or two were filled with purses, Margaret knew. She hoped not to need them, but she had been poor enough to take comfort from the weight even so.

At last, her son took his place. There would be half a dozen trips that day, bringing out the rest of their belongings and the squires who guarded them on deck, staring after the Prince of Wales as if they had been abandoned. It was enough that Margaret would land. She peered ahead at the docks as they grew through the mists. There were soldiers there and her heart contracted with fear, though Somerset had placed his banners high and to the front to reassure her. Beaufort was a good man, she recalled. Like his father and brother before him. The war had taken too much, broken too many families. She could only hope she had come home to see it end.

There were stone steps on the docks and Margaret watched as her son jumped easily on to them and then reached back to her. The French sailors shipped their oars and rested, panting lightly from the labour. Margaret came forward and looked up to see the Duke of Somerset waiting, looking handsome in his armour.

'Welcome home, my lady,' Edmund Beaufort said. He dropped to one knee and bowed his head as Margaret reached the docks and felt England under her heels for the first time in ten years, almost to the day.

19

During the night, thick mist grew on the fields, settling like drifts of snow. The scouts lost sight of one another as soon as they stood more than ten paces apart and duly reported the danger to their serjeants. The stars vanished and the darkness became absolute, as if they had fallen into a pit. Only the roar of Warwick's cannon still firing lit the blackness for an instant, leaving smears of light to dance in gold and green. The cannon teams wasted shot and powder all through the small hours, never knowing the enemy lay almost in their shadow.

Edward had tried to sleep, had spent at least some time pretending to, so that the men would see he was calm and unworried. Yet when he sprang up it was with relief, after lying still for so long. He could see nothing of the sun, his personal symbol. No yellow gleam showed through the foggy morning, just an eternal whiteness of damp and cold.

His simple act of standing brought his army to life all around him, rising from the ground where they had lain. Some had to be shaken awake, but most were as ready as they could be. They knew what would come and the advantage they had gained for themselves by creeping up close on the enemy camp.

There was always noise when men and horses made ready for war. The animals snorted with strong hands holding their heads down so they would not call to one another. Men slipped and swore aloud, while mail and plate clanged like bells sounding. They stood, hard-faced and nervous, but resolute as they waited for the horns to blow. They crossed themselves then, raising their eyes to a heaven they could not see.

Horns blew and the archers punched out arrows on both York wings, six a minute with fine aim, ten without. There were just hundreds of them but they poured thousands of shafts into the white, answered by screams and the sound of clashing armour.

Warwick's men knew where they were by then – and that they were close. A hail of shafts began to snap out of the mists at the York lines, dropping men even as they lurched into step. Iron points clanged off armour or thumped into shields held high to present the smallest targets. Some found gaps so that knights slumped and horses collapsed slowly forward, their front legs buckling. Yet the volleys were ill-aimed and most passed far overhead. The answer came from the hundred Flemish gunners arrayed before Edward, a massed crack of shot that sent lead balls whirring into the mists. Around them a thicker cloud billowed, flecked in grey. Cries and yells of agony began in answer, going on and on.

The York archers kept only a few shafts per man in reserve as they gave a ragged cheer and retired to the rear, mocking the foreign hand-gunners for achieving so little. As they went, three great squares tramped forward in a rush, pushing on, each man concentrating on the rank in front so that they would not fall and be trampled.

That was the initial terror for those marching in mist, that they would stumble and go down and all those behind would run over them. They looked down at the ground as they went, clutching billhooks and pollaxes, woodaxes and swords. Only the first few ranks looked ahead and when they saw men gathering against them, they gave a vast growl. It was a sound of violence, of threat and animal challenge to other men. It made their hearts pound and all the petty restrictions of normal life were left behind. They carried iron and they would kill anyone standing against them. It would ruin many, so that they could not go home. Others would be given a private pride they would treasure – and the rest would be left dead on the field.

The roar they made was answered. Stung and bleeding from the buzzing shafts, Warwick's lines were there in the mists, standing with weapons raised, ready for them.

Richard of Gloucester sat his warhorse in the third rank of his brother's right wing. His company was first to reach an enemy, ahead of the rest, with the strongest knights and most experienced captains. Only the archers held ground further out and they had sent their shafts into an enemy they could not see, trotting back after that.

It was his turn. Richard of Gloucester's wing was the hammer of York, to be brought down. He exulted in the responsibility, eighteen years old and in full armour, with just a slot of vision. The mist was all-enclosing, swirling like white liquid as men appeared out of it and his ranks crashed into them. Yet he could not raise his visor. Just one arrow, one thrown spear and he would fall in his first battle. Instead, he forced his horse forward, sensing each impact as its armoured chest struck men and knocked them down or into the path of his sword. His shoulder burned and his neck spasmed in a bright agony as if he was on fire, but he swung and killed and crushed, feeling strong, as strong as he had ever known he could be.

They could not touch him. They could not unseat him. He smashed roaring men from their feet with terrible wounds and then passing him was an armoured knight, sitting a mount as massive as his own. The knight raised a great studded club of iron, designed to break helmets and the skulls within. Richard stabbed him under the shoulder plate, spearing the joint so that the man's right arm fell limp. He brought his sword across against the knight's neck, causing his hands to jerk and flail as some vital part of him was broken. The knight slipped aside and vanished into the marching men below.

Gloucester dug in his heels, forcing his mount on past the riderless horse. He could hardly believe how much movement there was. He'd seen the banners of Exeter against him and known that Henry Holland would not give him the road, but still Gloucester's wing advanced step by step, as if no one could stand against them. He could not understand it, until the mist shifted ahead and he saw his great company had overlapped Exeter's line. Sheer luck had placed their camp beyond the outer edge of Warwick's wing.

Their first advance had curled round to become a flanking assault in the initial surge, terrifying men who found themselves attacked from two directions, as if they had been ambushed. The mist had made it work and Richard dug in his heels, suddenly gleeful. He roared a challenge and cut another soldier down as the man swung an axe at his thigh.

'Push on! Push on!' Richard bawled to his captains. 'Flank them! Turn the field.'

Nothing was more frightening to fighting men than to feel their entire square driven backward, trying to hold formation as they went. Each step of failure and retreat sapped at their morale so that they could break at any moment – and they would be slaughtered as they ran. That was all that held them in line, knowing that to run, to feed the terror that surged in each man as they felt their army give way, would mean their death. Yet the fear clawed at them and the whites of their eyes showed as they were forced back, pace by pace.

'Push on!' Gloucester's captains responded, showing their teeth in delight. They knew they had broken the wing. If the mists would only burn away, they would know how the rest of the field fared. Until then, they were on their own, lost and struggling with rage and fear and triumph.

The mist had reminded Edward of Towton from the first moments, the terrifying closeness of the white damp that seemed to press on his face and throat. With his visor down, he could not breathe, so he raised it and sucked in air and the smell of iron.

From the height of his destrier, he should have had a sense by then of how the battle was going, but the mist made him blind and he could feel panic swelling in his chest. He roared orders up and down the line, crying 'Advance!' to the captains and serjeants urging their men on. Edward had felt his brother Richard's wing surge forward in the way it pressed against his own formation. Whenever the mist swirled, he could see his right square had gone ahead like a spear thrust. It put pressure on the centre to drive on with them.

Yet on his left wing, Lord Hastings had been driven back with almost the same speed. Edward had even caught a glimpse of Oxford's banners there, advancing in delight, waving above his own ranks. Edward felt himself being turned, himself the heart of the battlefield, driven south on one edge and north on another. His entire centre square had to wheel in place or lose contact with both wings and be isolated.

'Wheel left!' Edward called at last. 'York centre! Captains! Wheel left on the spot! In slow march.' It would have been a difficult manoeuvre on a parade ground. To try to turn three thousand men at the same time as they fought and strained against enemies made him bite his lip in worry until he found he could taste his own blood. Edward had been outnumbered from the beginning. Now his left wing had collapsed, was still collapsing, with Oxford's men roaring forward and Hastings falling back.

To the third rank where he sat his horse, Edward's runners darted, panting and calling out, cutting shapes in the air with their hands as they tried to describe what they had seen. He reined in, looking left and right as understanding dawned. His men had taken a position in the darkness where the right flanks overlapped, facing no one at all on the far edge. On a normal day, they would have adjusted as they attacked, but the mists had made that impossible. Both right wings had curled around in the charge and the result was a giant wheel, two armies turning slowly together in a gyre, grinding blood and bone as they went.

It was too late to make use of it. Edward saw his left wing break and Oxford's men, the very same soldiers he had sent running from him days before, came charging through, howling like wolves after deer, lost in fury and with deep and restless murder all unleashed. There was no freedom so terrible, nor so exhausting. Edward remembered the horror and delight of it and felt his entire body prickle and shiver.

He saw a great flood, a torrent of men running and heaving together, all courage gone. Edward bellowed new orders at his closest captains, but they could not hold the tide and fully two or three thousand broke and ran like hares. After them, came Oxford's horsemen, forty or so knights, with long swords to strike down and twist out, moving swiftly on to pin another. The slaughter was beginning and Edward remembered that too from Towton. He could not endure it and his answer was to shore up his withered left wing with spears, then move up to support his brother Richard. Edward's left wing had been broken and would be cut to pieces. There was nothing he could do about that but drive forward in the mists.

'Push on!' he shouted, his voice like a cannon's breath. 'We have them! Push on!' It was madness and a lie, but those who looked to him to lead worked harder in a great flurry of blows, exhausting themselves. They strode into the gap they had cut and Richard of Gloucester's right wing was still pressing ahead in order. It was hard just to keep them in sight.

Exeter's men had not routed, but had been cut down rank by rank, overwhelmed from the flank and ahead. It was ugly work, spiteful and exhausting, but Richard had seen Exeter himself fall, his banners wavering. Richard's men took heart from that and forced the wheel further round. The mists made chaos of everything and all they could do was smash staves and iron into the faces of those against them, see them fall and take a step over, stamping down so they could not rise again.

John de Vere, Earl of Oxford, considered himself a killing knight. He burned with cold pride as his men overwhelmed and ruined the entire left wing of the army of York. All he saw in the mist was to his liking: an enemy forced back, his men triumphant and cutting all before them. He walked his horse over bloody ground and even the mists seemed tinged in pink as he went. When the York wing broke he howled like a wolf, cupping a hand to his mouth and imitating the pack call as he dug his heels in. It was an old hunting signal and those men who had come from his personal estates repeated the sound in savage joy, pushing in hard to take advantage.

The York soldiers under Lord Hastings went from a determined foe begrudging every step to fleeing men, showing their backs. Those who pursued gave out a cry that put greater fear into them. They were no longer equals, but hunted prey. Oxford's men came forward swinging long-handled weapons, like harvesters in fields of grass.

In the great rush forward, Oxford rode alongside his men in their laughter and howling, plunging his long sword into the necks of soldiers running from him. He was a fair hand at killing boar in such a way and found he was enjoying the challenge. The men jinked and threw up their hands, giving him a rare chance to test his skill. He sent them tumbling and shouted in triumph at good single thrusts that dropped them cleanly, frowning only when his blade slipped and he gashed flesh like a butcher. Those he left for others, as unsporting.

He was so caught up in the challenge of his cuts that he was hardly aware of how far from the battle he had come. Oxford looked up into the grey mists only when his horse skidded on a cobbled street. He hissed a curse to himself. He had pursued the routed force right to the edge of Barnet itself, the town a maze of alleys and small roads that would take an age to search, like pulling winkles out with a pin.

The earl could hear the clatter of boots on stones all around him, even the grunt and gasp of someone struggling. It was impossible to tell friend from enemy and he had a sudden vision of being surrounded and cut down that made him shudder. He did not like to leave a force of men at his back, but they had been truly routed and he was certain half of them had been cut down in the wild run. He pursed his lips and drew a cloth to wipe muck from his sword blade. To his annoyance, the cloth snagged on chips and burrs that were probably too deep to polish out. He tutted and then shouted his orders into the mists all around.

'Form up! Oxfords! Form on me once more in good order! Captains and serjeants gather your men to me! Oxfords!'

There were answers all around and men came to a halt, panting hard from their exertions. Many were wide-eyed and spattered in blood, shocked by what they had done. Others grinned and chuckled, pleased at having lived and killed. The lines reformed slowly and with some sullen looks as the men realized they would be heading back to danger. One or two of them called out what Oxford could do with himself and the result was furious captains and serjeants patrolling the rough lines, quite ready to break the head of anyone who offered insult to their patron. Oxford was the landlord for almost all of his officers, which meant they would support him regardless. In any case, those grizzled men had no time for the sort who called insults from the safety of a crowd.

A small breeze had sprung up, giving them hope that the mists would be driven off as they marched back towards the battle. The sense of being enclosed had grown worse, making it oddly hard to breathe for some so that they panted even as they walked, like bellows working.

Oxford himself took a spot in the second rank, riding along in pride beside a dozen other men. He congratulated those he knew and in truth they had reason to be proud. All he desired that morning was a chance to strike at one of the sons of York. Failing that, Oxford hoped to strike the false king's baggage or reserve. Best of all would be the rear of Edward's centre square. That would be an answer to prayers and there was a good chance of it. Oxford knew his men were a mile behind the battlefield. He had to keep a tight rein to stop his horse prancing out, the animal sensing his excitement.

'Look for the Sun in Flames!' he called to his men. 'Pass word as you sight the enemy!' His own family badge was a gold 'estoile', a star with six wavy rays. His men wore it in badges of pewter as well as on the great banners swinging on poles above them. He considered how similar it was to Edward's symbol. Both flames and rays of light could burn.

Oxford heard sharp cries of fear and confusion sound ahead of him, though he did not understand them. His duty was to come back to the battle and he would not shirk it after a single successful action. He urged his men to press on, even as the air suddenly filled with arrows and some of those around him went falling in great crashes.

'Treachery!' he heard called ahead, the cry taken up by panicky voices. Oxford dug in his spurs, sending new blood dribbling. His horse sprang forward, knocking his own men down in his urgency.

'What is this shout? What treachery?' he called to his captains. They could only shrug in the mist, but the cry went on, loud and repeated. 'Treachery! Traitors!'

'Who is that man? Who calls? Oxford here! Oxfords!' His captains shouted his name again and again, but there was a great tumult ahead and all Oxford could do was press on to reach it.

The rain of arrows dwindled away and he saw his men were slaughtering a mass of archers.

'God, let these be the York reserves,' Oxford breathed to himself. He had done wonders that day. He could yet do more. There was no understanding the cries of traitor and treachery that were growing louder with every moment. He strained to see through the mists and then sagged in his saddle with a sense of dawning horror.

The entire battle had turned as he had reformed his ranks by Barnet. The wheeling lines had spun around in slow, trudging labour. Instead of the rear of York, Oxford's men had charged the very centre of Warwick's armies, his own side. Oxford saw Montagu's banner fall and still his own men were lunging forward, disappearing into the mists, unable to stop though some cried out and waved their arms in denial.

The effect of Montagu crashing down was that Warwick's entire centre wavered – and Edward of York drove right through the heart of it in the confusion. He had been given a single chance and he did not hesitate. His men formed a wide spear formation and hacked and battered their way through already panicking Oxfords and Montagus, not knowing where or how to pull themselves away from the murderous embrace of their own kin.

Warwick heard a long, hoarse roar somewhere ahead of him, like waves breaking on a shingle beach. The cursed mists made it impossible to know where he should strike with his reserves, but the moment had surely come. He had six thousand men, fresh and unmarked, ready at his word.

'Forward to the centre,' he called. His order and his army. He could not spare a thought for the fate of his brother John where the fighting seemed thickest. Whenever the mists swirled, Warwick turned his head and stared as far as he could before the clinging whiteness seeped back and left him with whatever he had glimpsed. The right wing had been cut to pieces by Gloucester. Warwick could see fast-moving ranks closing on his flank as he tried to bolster the centre. It was a brutal decision, but he was putting his men in the way of a dual attack.

'Spears to the flank! Repel . . . the flank! Raise pikes and spears there!' His serjeants took up the order. It was all he could do, to present a bristling edge to those who might try and overwhelm it. The centre had to hold or Warwick knew it was finished and had all been for nothing.

He drew his sword as he felt a tremble run through the ranks ahead of him. For all their fresh strength, they knew they were being hit along the flank and in time would be enveloped at the rear. No fighting men faced that prospect unmoved, but they drove on. They could not run while Montagu's square was being ripped apart in front of them.

Line by line, Warwick's reserve made their way through to the centre, while others stumbled past them, dying or holding some wound so terrible it drained them white. Over on the wing, Gloucester's victorious companies roared through the last of Exeter's men and fell on the fresher wing of the reserves. In that moment, Warwick could see Edward high on his horse in battered armour, his visor raised and his banner of the Sun in Flames flapping behind him. The young king did not seem to see his old friend.

Warwick hacked down against anyone that moved. In slow step, he went forward in a line of knights, forcing their way through with sheer power and ferocity. Some of those who went down looked up to see a horse passing over and lunged cruelly, even as they died themselves. There was no limit to the spite and rage released on that field.

Warwick's horse lurched and he felt it lean, swinging quickly out of the saddle before it could fall and trap him. He staggered as he reached the ground and crashed against a stranger, armed with a pointed billhook blade bound to an axe-handle. Warwick punched out with a metal gauntlet, but the man ducked under the blow and smashed the billhook into his side with savage strength. It jammed in the plates there and the man wrenched at it, tearing Warwick deeply so that he groaned. Unable to find his sword, he punched and punched until the man's face was a ruin, then went down on to one knee, panting hard, though it did not feel as if he could take a breath.

The battle went on all around him, a clamour of screaming and metal. Warwick shook his head, seeing blood drip from his mouth as he looked down at the ground. He knew then that death was close and with a huge effort, he tried to stand.

He pressed a hand into his side, where it ran with blood. The pain was growing worse there, opening into him like acid or flame. He coughed and spattered his gauntlet with red. He could feel himself choking and he was suddenly afraid as he looked around. His gaze alighted on his sword where it had fallen and he took one unsteady pace and snatched it up. With fading strength, he plunged it into the ground before him and rested one arm on it. Warwick knelt then on the torn grass and choked until there was no more breath in him. He saw Edward ride triumphantly through the centre, routing the rest of his army. It was magnificent. Warwick's hand slipped from his sword and he fell.

When the last of the fighting had come to an end and the rags of Warwick's forces had fled the field, Edward of York walked the battlefield with his two brothers, to see the lines they had written across the Great North Road and the cost of it. The mists had thinned at last as the sun rose. Some of the men looked up to see if it danced, as their mothers had told them it might. It was Easter Sunday morning and church bells rang out across the fields from Barnet, long and sonorous.

Edward's eyes were dry and red when he came upon Warwick's body. He knelt by him and Richard and George joined him. They said a goodbye and a prayer to a man who had been like a father to them in many ways. Yet Richard Neville had chosen to stand on the other side of a battlefield and earned himself a hard death. After a time, Edward stood once again, looking down.

'I do not regret it,' he said to Richard. 'I will be a burning brand to them, as I said. Oxford escaped me, that is my only regret.'

'What now?' George asked, looking down at the body of his wife's father.

'I will have Warwick and Montagu shown in London under guard. I'll have no tales spreading that they live yet and will restore Lancaster. You know how people are.'

'Then drawn and quartered as traitors?' Richard asked, looking up. His brother shook his head.

'No. I might for Montagu, but not for Warwick. He was . . . a good man. I'll send his body back to the Nevilles for them to bury.' He fell silent for a time then and neither of his brothers interrupted.

'I said I would make an ending,' Edward murmured. He raised his head, his eyes bright. 'And I will. They drove me out. I will not hold back now, whoever they send against me.'

20

Margaret rubbed her forehead, feeling the attar of roses smear under her fingertips. She looked at her fingers and saw a faint white smudge. When she had been young, she had possessed a physical discipline she could only barely recall in her forties, an ability to suffer any itch or discomfort without raising her hand to ruin the powders and oils on her skin. Not that she had even needed concealing pigments then, she thought ruefully. She had assumed it would always be so, but age had taken that as well, so that her own body betrayed her in its lack of control.

It was a cruel thing to be asked to face a man like Edward of York, still shy of thirty, still in the last bloom of his youth. She had been strong enough to bring his father down. The sons had undone that extraordinary victory, picking it apart with teeth and swords. She felt a sting where her nails dug into her palms and opened her hands to see fading red marks.

'Are we certain this is not some ruse?' Somerset demanded. 'Some . . . story to frighten those who might support us yet? By God, Warwick had *twenty thousand* men!'

The duke still looked incredulous, Margaret saw, all his plans broken into shards before they were begun. Her son stared off at nothing and the stranger who had come to her merely stood and waited for Margaret to give him orders.

Margaret was nervous around this unknown man, thin as a corpse, though the fellow had introduced himself with a secret phrase Derry Brewer had given her years before. Leo of Aldwych seemed a much more solemn man than his predecessor. He certainly knew he had brought terrible news, of the death of Warwick and Montagu, just when Margaret and her son needed them most to have won.

Margaret had still not dared to consider all the implications of the man's presence. She had thought Derry Brewer dead once before and she could not bear the thought of the reality. If Derry had gone as well as Warwick and Montagu, she might as well send one of her precious pigeons back to Paris for another ship to take her away.

If Margaret had returned from France alone, she honestly thought she might have done. Wherever her husband lay his head was where he could stay, after ten years apart. With all the changes he had suffered, Henry was as much a stranger as Derry Brewer's man. Yet her *son* deserved a chance – and a life that was more than just frustration and failure. She had promised the world to him, after all.

Margaret was nervous too around Somerset, as one who had lost his father and older brother in defence of King Henry and the house of Lancaster. He paced up and down, his hands clenched at the small of his back. In truth, the man seemed to have such a personal desire for vengeance as to eclipse her own cause. Somerset wanted to see York burn. She thought he did not much care who would sit the throne after that.

'If the news is true, my lord,' Margaret ventured, 'can we go on?'

Somerset stopped his pacing and approached her, his eyes as cold as the hands he pressed against hers.

'My lady, London is very far from here. The news of Warwick is three days old already – and that from a man who broke his mounts to bring it as fast as he could. It will not reach Cornwall and Devon or Dorset and Hampshire – Sussex even, though it lies closer to London, not for days more. In your son's name, I can send word and raise an army. The men of York must have taken grievous losses when they faced Warwick at Barnet. They cannot have any great force to muster, at least for a time.' He spoke faster, his excitement building. 'They must have wounded who cannot fight again – and others who will be bruised and battered, a mere remnant of a fighting force. If we are swift, Your Highness, if we are ruthless, I believe we might honour Warwick's memory by finishing his work.'

To Margaret's surprise, the spy stepped closer then and bowed.

'The count of great numbers has ever been muddled, my lady. It is not as though an army is ever considerate enough to walk past one of my lads while he tallies them on a board or puts pebbles in a jar. Yet I do trust the fellow who told me Edward of York lost two thousand men or even more at Barnet. York must be weaker now, despite his victory. He has only eight thousand *at most* beneath his banners. If you could raise as many in short time, I believe my Lord Somerset says it rightly. You could yet bring him down.'

'I have some twelve hundred now,' Somerset said. 'I expect two hundred more under Baron Wenlock, perhaps as early as tomorrow. He will not let us down.'

'You think I'll find the rest of those I need here in the south?' Margaret asked with a brittle smile. 'Shall I send recruiting serjeants with boys to bang a drum in every seaside town and village? While Edward sweeps down against me, with blood still bright on his hands?' She made her decision then, as her son turned to watch her. In time, such orders would be his to give, but not then, not on that day.

'I feel the sea at my back, my lord Somerset. Gather what men you have with you and be ready to march north. How far from here is Wales? I found an army there before. I have friends there still, though God knows they are not what they once were.'

'Wales, my lady?' Somerset said. He rubbed his chin and made his own fast decision, nodding sharply. 'For your son, of course.'

'My son who is the Prince of Wales, yes, my lord,' Margaret confirmed with cool calm. 'Prince among those who always supported Lancaster over York. Wales is where we will find our army. Let them just see my son, tall and strong. They will take up our banners once again.'

'Bristol has rejected York before as well, my lady,' Leo of Aldwych added. 'It is but sixty miles from the coast or thereabouts. There is no harm in banging the drum there – nor in Yeovil and Bath for that matter. You could make a stop in those places – and from Bristol, cross to Wales by ship.'

'I will have an army to march beside you by then, my lady, I swear it,' Somerset replied, frowning at a man he had no intention of trusting. 'You'd need hundreds of ships and not just the fishing vessels you'd find there. No, you'll need to go further to one of the great crossings of the River Severn – the toll bridge at Gloucester perhaps, or the ford at Tewkesbury.'

'If I can reach Wales,' Margaret said, 'I will take a long summer in the hills to raise a great host for my son to lead. That is my path – and yours, Edward. If you can make a victory then, you can restore Lancaster, over the bones of York. Like the Black Prince before you, all Wales will know you as the rightful heir. No more rebellions and usurping traitors. No more sudden marches and battles that have plagued us all for so long. Just peace, gentlemen, with the ploughboy and his maid, with the busy cities and all the priests and merchants and sailors and lords. All unmarked by war, all unbowed and unscarred.'

'It is a . . . grand dream, Mother,' her son said dubiously. He was seventeen and had prepared for that very war his entire life. To have his mother wish it all away and look ahead to beer and apples before he had even set foot on the field of battle was somewhat vexing.

'Wales though,' Edward said with a smile. 'It would please me to see the land that calls me its prince.'

'Very well,' Somerset said, his gloom lessening. 'Yeovil and Bath and Bristol lie on our route, while I send word to all loyal men. "Lancaster stands and calls to England" – that is the word to send, to cry out. My lady, I do not think those ploughboys will let the Welsh overmatch them for their loyalty. You will see, I swear it.'

'Oh, my lord, I have heard so *many* oaths,' Margaret replied. 'I knew your brother well and your father. They were men of honour – and their word was good. It was not enough in the end. I believe I have had enough of oaths, my lord,' Margaret said. 'Instead, show me deeds.'

Edward brooded as he sat in the spring sunshine. Windsor Castle was ever at its best in the drowsing warm and he had happy memories of hunts and great feasts there. Perhaps that was why he licked dry lips and considered the oaths and promises he had made. Warwick had fallen. It was still not something he could quite believe. How could that man, with so much cleverness in him, somehow not be in the world? How was it possible? It nagged at him, as if he had forgotten something and with just the right word, he could bring them all back. He missed his father still. He missed his younger brother Edmund, raised to an angelic presence by the smoothing iron of memory. He could not call them back, no matter what regrets ached like broken teeth and made him shiver and draw in his breath.

In the days since, Edward had not allowed himself a single frothing cup of ale, though every part of him had yearned for it. Instead, he had grown surly and snapped at those in attendance on him, until his brother Richard had ridden off to Middleham to take the news of Warwick's death to the man's wife. Clarence had gone home to an uncertain welcome from Warwick's daughter. Edward wished them both luck. His own wife was oddly cold to him and the truth was he had not won the peace and calm he had expected. Perhaps he expected too much from a single victory. By the saints, it was better than having lost! He was troubled still and though he was bright with sweat from the training yard, it had not brought the sense of joy he imagined he would find in a jug of warm froth. He licked his lips once again, though they were cracked and sore.

He slept without nightmares, he reminded himself. His stomach no longer sent him scrabbling for the chamber pot under the bed. He was healthier than he could remember being in all his life and . . . still, his mind felt too sharp, or as a piece of cloth with a cat's claw dragging at it. A healthy life was not a happy life, that was the simple truth of it, at least for a man with his blood and his ambition. Edward knew he had not been made to follow, nor to live quietly. He was loud and strong, with a look that made other knights want to examine the ground by their feet. Some women found him infuriating almost on sight, while others . . . well, the way he was had some advantages.

Yet he could not break his oath. His men had drunk themselves stupid after the battle, of course. He could not deny them and would have looked a fool and a curmudgeon if he had tried. Lord Rivers had upended a great cask of ale and spilled far more down himself than had ever reached his throat. He'd passed out not long after, reeking.

Edward found a piece of his lower lip had come away as a shred of flesh. He gnawed and worried at it, pleased to have anything to take his mind from its usual concern. He was not a weak man, he knew it. The idea that anything or anyone could be his master made him itch. Yet the danger came when he did it to himself, when he threw up his hands and decided not to be strong, not to endure.

Margaret had landed, with her son. That news had focused his thoughts and somehow brought his thirst to the surface. Of all the God-given drinks, from wine to help a man sleep, or ale to make him laugh, the spirit made from grain mash was the one he missed most. The Romans had called it *aqua vitae*, the Scots *uisge beatha* – the 'water of life'. Whatever name they used, it brought Edward to a clear and steady concentration. It allowed him to talk and talk for hours, and when it was time to sleep, he just slept. The following day was not such a fine thing, but he was used to pain, as his brother Richard said. A life without pain was like beef without salt, without savour.

He wondered what Margaret's son looked like, after ten years. King Edward of York had been a mere Earl of March when that boy had last set foot in England.

Edward knew he had run wild after his father's death. He did not speak of that year, even with his brothers. Warwick had been his friend then and Edward had drunk enough whisky and wine to kill some men. More than a few of those events were just gone from his memory, as if some other wight had lived them instead of him.

He found himself dwelling too long on the drunken stupor of those violent months. He had not washed the blood off his armour, he recalled, standing. It had flaked away in the end, like paint.

With the spring sun coming through the high windows,

Edward began to pace, raising his head when a child started to cry, somewhere close. His son. His heir. He smiled at that, crossing himself in silent prayer for the boy's health. Edward could only hope his son would rule in peace when his time came. A dynasty begun in war could become a ruling family. It had been so before and his was not a lesser line, not any longer.

As he paced, an image came to him of the huge flask of rough red wine that he knew sat on the dresser just inside the kitchen door below. He could see it and it was the strangest thing. He knew it was the rudest stuff, used in cooking, almost vinegar, yet the very thought of it made his mouth pucker and sting, as if he would have chosen it at that moment over any fine vintage.

He came to a halt, looking off at the door that led down to the kitchen. It would not matter if he spent a day drowning in that bitter wine. No one would begrudge him that. He could begin with just a little to see if his stomach might rebel and if it did not, at least it would make the waiting easier to bear. Would Margaret march on London? He had no way of knowing. His spies were on the roads, with pigeons in their little wicker cages. His birds would come home and then he would spring out for the last time, against an enemy as old as the wars themselves. The woman who had killed his father and his brother. The woman who had torn England apart for a broken, weakling king. The woman whose son claimed a title that was Edward's to award. The Prince of Wales would be his own boy, if it was to be anyone.

He would not suffer that mother and son to live. God knew he had paid enough, Edward thought. He wanted it to end.

He had forgotten the red wine in the kitchen, he realized, congratulating himself even as he began to think of it again.

*

The counties of Cornwall and Somerset were far from London in a way that had nothing to do with roads or maps, though there were precious few of those. The coast was well known, but there were parts of the west where no sheriff's men could tread without a few heavy lads bearing cudgels – and sometimes not even then. Taxes were resented by righteous men and women and spoken against in the churches with all the other sins. Villages obeyed older laws than anything London claimed for itself and may have been ancient and stern when Romans beached their ships and built fine villas. London was a different place, with fashions and customs and ways of doing that did not reach the west at all.

Margaret found her cause was alive in Yeovil, then in Evercreech and Westholme. In each small hamlet or village, a few stout men would down tools and kiss their wives and children goodbye. They saw the banners of Lancaster and they took off their caps in her presence. Margaret was bright-eyed with tears at the sight of a row of curly-headed men all standing to take an oath from one of Somerset's serjeants. They said their names slowly together and blushed to have it witnessed by a queen. They put aside thought of any judgement on her, as a woman and a fine lady, and a French lady at that. Margaret was extraordinarily exotic to men who expected to die within three miles of where they were born, like the hundred generations before them. They knew the land well enough, every tree and field and custom and boundary. They went to Mass and they baptized their sons and daughters and they had never thought too hard on the doings of London and the king there, until she'd come and asked them to.

It did not hurt her cause that her own son looked so fine on a destrier. Prince Edward might have been dwarfed on such a beast, but his legs were long and he was both lithe and strong as any ploughboy. In one place, he had wrestled their lads and gone tumbling into a pond. They'd all frozen then, unsure if they would be punished until Prince Edward had broken the surface and cheerfully held the other lad under until he'd gone limp. That had been one more to walk with them, when they'd slapped his face and brought him back to the world. That particular Devon lad had joined Edward's squires and was learning all he had to do to keep a knight in the field of battle.

Each spring day was spent marching through a countryside alive with flowers and crops, the air growing sweet and thick, with the promise of summer still ahead and everything growing and pressing on.

In Bath, they marvelled at the Roman ruins there and Prince Edward swam in the sulphurous waters, wrinkling his nose and calling out that his mother should come in. Margaret had chosen not to, but the small council had been delighted at the peaceful presence of their own Duke of Somerset, perhaps even more so than Margaret and the prince. Crowds had turned out to welcome them and with them had come the merchants and moneylenders, setting out their stalls. Somerset had secured new loans and food as well as six hundred men, all joining up together. Half of them worked in the same coal mine and the owner was distraught but forced to put a brave face on his loss for the cause. Every one of them mattered, though Margaret feared the army she needed was growing far too slowly. She left the details up to Somerset and the Earl of Devon when he came. John Courtenay owed his title to her husband's return and he would not give it up meekly. He had brought out eight hundred trained men with him from his estates and towns. They made a fine display in matched tunics and the banners of

Devon in yellow and red, complete with drummers and trumpeters. Two hundred more came in with Baron Wenlock, a knight who admitted to sixty years of age. He was by far the oldest of them and given to peering at whoever spoke with one eye squinted shut and the other half obscured by enormous eyebrows. He was white-haired from his long moustache to the curls poking from his shirts. His men though were in rude health and youth and equipped with new mail and billhooks.

For all their gains, they were still little more than three thousand as they reached the outskirts of Bristol. Word had gone ahead and as close as they were to the border of Wales, Margaret should not have been surprised at the response. Yet she was close to tears once again as young girls came out and pressed flowers on her mob of marching men, all standing a little taller as they entered the city gates and marched along the main street.

Prince Edward rode at the head of them, with Wenlock and Devon on either side. Margaret rode alongside Somerset a few ranks behind and if her heart was close to bursting with pride, she supposed it did not matter if others saw. Lancaster had known so many years of pain and loss. Perhaps it was time for the scales to be rebalanced.

As the crowds cheered, she began to imagine years ahead without the shadow of York. She had surely paid enough for any lifetime, whatever sins she had committed. She had confessed to a young priest before setting foot in the French warship that had brought her to England. Ships failed and foundered and she had not wished to drown with her soul still marked by sin. It had been the first time in ten years that she had confessed and she still felt lighter than before in all senses, as if the soft breeze that touched her hair could just lift her up and up, above the Bristol streets. Paris she had loved, but England in the spring was . . . She closed her eyes. It was perfect.

Her army was the stronger by fifteen hundred men when Margaret was ready to leave Bristol. Perhaps some of them would come to regret it by the time they sobered up, but entire streets had joined the cause, taking a pewter pin of her swan or a badge of Edward's feathers as Prince of Wales, more usually both as they were treasured and admired. The men had all eaten well and had collected new weapons forged in every smithy, or taken down from walls where their fathers had rested them a generation before. Her lords and captains had been treated respectfully by the burghers and townspeople of Bristol, though Margaret could not help feeling a pang as they waved her goodbye. Alone, she and her son could have crossed to Wales on a fishing boat that very hour. With more than four thousand men kicking stones along the road, they could cross the massive River Severn into Wales only on the toll bridge at Gloucester. The coast of Wales was there to be seen just a few miles off by boat. Yet thirty miles of marching lay ahead.

Margaret wondered again if she would lose some of those who had come with flowers still in their buttonholes and jugs of cider and ale under their arms. Or gain more, she dared to hope, forcing her chin a little higher. England had been a dark place before, but she could not fault the welcome they had given her that year.

After a day of marching along the roads and paths, they made camp by a gentle stream that first evening – and all men would have gone to war if that had been the usual way of things. Lords and knights and common men sat together on dry grass in an orchard with the trees in blossom. The cooks and carters came together to produce a fine meal from the food they'd brought out of Bristol, with fish and flour cakes, leeks and onions from dark, dry bags. It made a decent stew and they were groaning full by the time the sun was settling into colours of gold and red, the sky so clear they could see for miles.

Margaret saw her son looking troubled as he approached her sleeping spot. It did not look like rain would intrude upon them and she had not asked to have an awning rigged, nor a tent. Yet she felt a chill at Edward's expression.

'The men say they've been seeing riders galloping along the roads all around. Too far off to chase down, so they told me – and I believe them. They say one of them may have worn a doublet in herald colours – of York.'

'Did you have the archers go out to ambush and capture one?' Margaret asked softly. Her son wanted to command, but he still had the sense or the humility to ask her advice. She thanked God for it.

'I sent a dozen or so, but they have not come back. I wasn't sure if I should worry.'

'How long ago did you send those men?' she asked, more urgently. Her son leaned closer.

'Earlier on, before the meal was served . . . I don't know. I didn't say they had to race back.'

'And perhaps it is nothing, Edward. Or perhaps there are soldiers and scouts cutting the throats of anyone they find out there in the fields, keeping us blind. I would rather be too cautious than surprised and killed, do you understand?'

'Of course,' Edward said. 'Then we cannot stay here. You know, the men will groan and grumble when I order them up, especially if we are being too cautious, as you say.'

'I did not say that. I don't know yet what to make of strange heralds and missing men. Make no apology for what must be done. It's not dark yet and the crossing at Gloucester is just a few miles off. It would be better for us to rest in Wales, with the river behind us. Your men will see the wisdom of it then, when they sleep without fear of alarms.'

The sky was flaming in violet by the time Somerset and Devon and Wenlock's captains had the camp packed and more than four thousand men back on the road. There was not much grumbling, not with so many experienced soldiers in the ranks alongside the newcomers. Those who might have complained were given short shrift by the rest. Baron Wenlock was a useful man to have in the ranks, if only so the captains could point him out and say, 'If that old devil can be up and about, so can you, mate.' Armies did not move at night without a good reason and most of the men still trusted the Lancaster banners that flew in the twilight.

Perhaps another hour passed on a good stone road by the time they sighted the walls of Gloucester, with torches already lit at the great gates. Margaret allowed her mare to ease forward alongside the ranks of sleepy men, heavy-footed by then with the need to rest. They had put some twenty-six miles under their belts that day and she was desperately proud of the loyalty she saw in them.

The gates of Gloucester remained closed. An old man in fine robes appeared above and waved Margaret off in angry disdain, as if she had brought a troupe of beggars to the city. She watched the man go back inside and was left staring up at a line of crackling torches. The river bridge could not be reached from outside the city. She had to be allowed to enter before she could cross and for a time, she could not think what to do.

Wales meant safety, or at least as safe as anywhere could be to her with Edward of York on the throne. They still remembered Lancaster there, she knew, even more than the good people of Bristol. Her son would be in his heartland and they would flock to him.

Her hands trembled on the reins. She had seen too many good men killed, too many disasters. She did not think she could bear even one more. She wanted to scream out her rage at the walls and it was only her son's gentle arm around her shoulders that held her wildness in.

'This is York's doing, or his brother's, you know that?' Margaret hissed. 'Those riders you saw. They have sent word ahead to these weak, traitorous . . .' She closed her mouth on the worst oaths and wracked her mind for what Duke Somerset had said before, when they were planning their route. Gloucester's bridge and then . . . a ford across the river. She sent a runner to Somerset and he came over in stiff dignity, bowing in the saddle to her.

'You mentioned a ford to cross the river, my lord.'

'Close by the ruins at Tewkesbury, Your Highness, yes. The ford itself is Lower Lode. I know the place well. I rode across only last year.' He paused, tapping his finger to his lips as he thought. He read Margaret's concern, though he was pleased at her control, even so. Her authority would not stretch so far as to order him into action. The prince might do so in his father's name, but Somerset was twice his age and unlikely to charge the wrong way just because Edward of Lancaster told him to.

Somerset felt Margaret's eyes on him in the gloom and knew she had made the same delicate judgement and chosen to remain silent. He was willing to allow her the small victory over him.

'I wonder, my lady, if you agree with me that it would be better to push the men on to Tewkesbury tonight.'

'That was my thought, my lord, if it can be reached.'

'Oh, certainly. The ford is . . . say eight or ten miles from here. The men will be sore tomorrow but it runs shallow there and there is a fine plain beyond where they can fall down and snore like bullocks.'

Margaret reached out and touched the duke on his arm, pleased to have the support of such a man. She felt relief as the orders went out to groans and grumbling voices. Her army came back to its feet and she saw it had grown truly dark. They would enter Wales under starlight alone, where the waters ran fast and shallow – and not Edward of York nor any of his people could prevent it.

21

In the field, Edward could leave all his devils behind. He had felt it almost at the moment the messengers came in and he'd left Windsor for the west. Margaret was making for Wales and perhaps another man might have felt a touch of fear at hearing that. Edward had experienced something close to joy. He could leave behind his wife's accusing looks, though he had at least done his duty by her in the bedchamber, cold and unwelcoming as it had been. His rights as a husband had not been particularly easy without drink to ease the way, but he had managed and in truth, some of the dark cloud over him had lifted, at least for a time. He had even taken a moment to wave goodbye to his daughters, though the noise they made put his teeth on edge. A sword aimed at his head could not make Edward flinch, but three shrieking girls would have him quickly in full retreat, closing doors behind him as he went.

Out with his brothers Richard and George of Clarence, with the sun in streams of gold, he felt none of the silent pressure that seemed to squeeze his skull in Windsor or London. He could breathe more deeply in the warm country air, feel more keenly, as if his very senses had sharpened. When he observed a wheeling flock of birds, he would see immediately where a falcon might lunge and bring them down. He lost that sense in the cities and the palaces somehow, so that he stumbled and felt his way like a man made blind or dumb.

Almost all the captains and lords present at Barnet had come back to him. Only Clarence had tried to withdraw.

Edward still found the man's selfishness extraordinary, but then George of Clarence could never have been the son who became king. The death of Warwick, without male heirs, had meant a vast number of estates had fallen into dispute with previous owners. Some would return to the crown. Edward knew he would make them gifts, either whole or sold to pay a bonus to his men, just as he had promised. Other estates would be too strongly mired in law and muddled ownership to take back, but still the vast majority would fall to George of Clarence. It was for that reason his brother had asked to remain in London – and been furiously denied.

Edward took a deep breath and put aside the anger his younger brother could bring about in him. It served no purpose except to make him miserable. He took comfort instead from the presence of Richard, who had overcome his twisted back and made himself a fine knight and a royal duke. Edward was proud of him and looked across at the banners of Gloucester on his right wing with a tight smile. Clarence was a useless, weak bastard, that was just the truth of it. Richard of Gloucester, however, was a brother to make their father proud.

With the losses they had suffered on the field and from wounds after, Edward had brought just five thousand to array in ranks before Windsor. Those who had marched with them before were sorely missed.

Edward knew very well he could be rash. He had married an older woman with children on a wild whim. He had declared himself king of England while Henry VI was still alive and faced his armies in the field. Yet his preference for a sudden leap to action had served him well against Warwick. Reacting without too much preparation had its dangers, but then every day that passed meant Margaret could raise more to her banners.

She could not be allowed to reach Wales, that was the heart of it. There were too many there who remembered the Tudors, who still felt some loyalty for a line Edward had crushed at Mortimer's Cross. That battle, before even Towton, was like looking back at the memories of another man. He remembered only madness, but Owen Tudor had not survived it.

At least five thousand men could move relatively quickly across the land, Edward thought. They were the victors of Barnet and he had been sure to reward them well for that service. There was no better paid work in England that year, and for three days, Windsor had been awash with more coin than the town had seen in a century. After that, the news had come in and the horns had blown, calling them all back to the war and the fighting. It had been a grim start, but on horse or on foot, they'd settled into the miles.

Edward had hoped at first to cross the path of Margaret and her son while they were still coming in from the coast. By the time his five thousand had covered the first ninety miles in three days, she'd moved on. According to the spies that came back down the road, the city of Bristol had treated the prince like a prodigal son, killing the fatted calf rather than casting them out as traitors. There would have to be some example made along those walls, Edward decided grimly. Perhaps the mayor's head, or the sheriff's. He recalled the walls of Hull being shut against him, just when he had been at his weakest. He hoped they'd heard of his victories since that day. It pleased him to think of those city merchants all quaking at the thought of what he would do.

Edward pushed his brothers and their men on as best he could, but the border with Wales was deep into the west and they were trying to intercept an army without knowing how far it had come. He would have given a purse of gold angels to change his path further to the north, but there was only one western road capable of taking an army. His men simply could not march as many miles over broken ground. One good marsh or an expanse of tussock grass and they'd lose a day and be exhausted. The western road was the only road – and yet Edward stared at the valleys running alongside, wishing he could send the men across.

His fastest riders raced ahead to bring back information and send warnings on to the towns and cities in Margaret's path. The reward came in the news that Gloucester had closed its gates, a fact which gave his brother Richard particular satisfaction. His column was not far from the city then and perhaps that had influenced its council.

Loyalty was a fickle thing when both Lancaster and York had a claim to the crown, but it did not hurt to have your own named city remain loyal to you. Edward could only laugh and shake his head when Richard enquired if York had always done the same. None of it mattered then. The messengers reported that they had closed the gap in the last great push since morning, having force-marched thirty-six miles already. Margaret's army lay somewhere ahead in the darkness, with her son and her lords. The men felt Edward's rising mood and were lifted by it. He looked hawkish as he stared into the gloom. He had broken the Nevilles at Barnet. He would break the heart of Lancaster as well – and he would bring about peace in England, after almost twenty years of war. It was no small thing to contemplate.

The moon rose and the city of Gloucester lay on their left shoulders. They passed it with their heads high and backs straight, ready to strike wherever they were aimed. The spring grass was flattened in a great swathe ahead of them. Every man marching along with Edward knew they were close, that when the sun rose, they would land a blow hard enough to shatter a royal house.

Margaret tried not to let her son see her nervousness, though of course he read it anyway. He had spent some part of every day for the previous ten years with her, either at her father's estate in Saumur or in the royal palace and gardens of King Louis. Prince Edward knew his mother too well, perhaps. He took one look at her and his eyes darkened, as if a light had gone out behind them.

'Is the news so terrible, Mother?' he asked.

Margaret smiled tightly and dismissed the panting scout who had come in. The young lad looked as stricken as she was. He had taken away some part of her hopes, to replace them with an old fear.

'I had not expected him to pursue us quite as quickly as this,' Margaret said. There was no need to name the one who had come after them, springing out of London like a cat waiting for some tiny shift in the grasses. Edward of York had come at the charge and Margaret knew she was not ready to face him, if she could ever be. She still remembered the multitude of the dead, that nation on the field that had come to the banners of Lancaster around Towton, out of loyalty to her husband. They had been slaughtered by the young king who raced to catch her then. He'd stood in line and he had fought and killed as if he could not tire.

She shivered, crossing herself at the thought that someone had stepped over her grave. She could hear the voice of the river ahead, the sound of water rushing in a million tons over stones. As if in answer, she heard another roar sound behind, just two or three miles away across the fields. She was truly afraid then. Edward had come and she was still in England.

*

For what seemed an age, Margaret's army stood poised on the brink of the fording place, with Wales almost close enough to touch. The River Severn had narrowed with each mile inland and the water was certainly shallow there, but still black as the night over them. It was hard to be sure they were even in the right spot and Margaret had men casting lines with stones to check the depth was not too great for them. All the time they waited for the sound of horns and marching men approaching. Of all her enemies, Edward was the least predictable. He might wait until dawn, or he might just rush her lines in the darkness to create murder and madness wherever he touched.

The stars had turned around the north for some good part of the night by the time Somerset agreed with Baron Wenlock and Earl Devon that the York forces had made camp. The scouts reported no movement from the enemy and Margaret's exhausted men lay down to sleep at last in the fields. News of their arrival had spread to the town nearby and lights showed in the blackness there as lamps were lit and a deep note sounded from the bells of an abbey. Margaret did not know if it was to warn the sleeping townspeople about her army or the soldiers of York, but it seemed a death knell, booming through the night.

Somerset rode up and dismounted with Courtenay, Earl Devon, and Baron Sir John Wenlock, all three men bowing to the queen and her son. Prince Edward watched them with an expression of stiff seriousness in the torchlight, taking his manner from the more experienced lords.

'We could still cross tonight, my lady, if you wish it,' Somerset said. 'I'll put a chain of men into the shallows and guide the rest over without lights to alert our enemies.'

'But that is not what you want,' Margaret guessed from his

expression. She too was weary, her head feeling thick and clotted with the need to sleep.

Somerset smiled, pleased. He exchanged a glance with Wenlock and Earl Devon. Margaret saw that the three men had already discussed what they intended to do. Coming to her was no more than a formality and she set her jaw in irritation. She understood rather better than Somerset imagined. They needed no charade of asking her permission, not really. Margaret knew she had no great military experience. She expected men like Somerset and Wenlock and Earl Devon – aye, and even her son – to make decisions on their own wits and strength and skill, not wait on her order.

'You have the command, my lord Somerset,' she said a little curtly. 'Perhaps you should tell me what you want to do.'

'Thank you, my lady, for your trust,' he said, bowing again. Margaret decided she did not like this son as much as his older brother. Perhaps it was true that all the good wines had been drunk, leaving just the bitter dregs.

'We could cross the river,' Somerset said, 'but it would take all night and the forces of York will do it in half the time tomorrow morning. We would have exhausted our men further and gained nothing except to have them fall on us as we retreat.'

'And instead?' Margaret said.

'I would have the men drawn up here, my lady. The river will be useful cover on that flank. The men are committed to you – and to your son. I believe they will not run, though I will position them away from the fording point, so they would have to get past York to cross. After that, my intention is to hold the ground while the house of York breaks itself against us.'

'And you believe we can win?' Margaret said. Lord

Wenlock made almost a growl of assent through his moustaches. Somerset and Devon both nodded slowly.

'I believe so, my lady,' Somerset replied after a moment, 'with God's grace. No man can say more than that – and I would rather show you in deeds than oaths or promises.'

She smiled to have her own words thrown back at her.

'Where shall I stand?' her son said, his voice tight with strain as he tried to look as stern and forbidding as the other three. Somerset glanced at him and scratched his cheek with a rasping noise against the stubble.

'Edward of York prefers the centre, Your Highness. His brother Richard is likely to command a wing, left or right I don't know. I do not know all of the men facing us, but I would not like to put you in reach of either of them. Perhaps you could command our reserve companies, Your Highness. It is vital work and you'll have the river on your elbow. If you can hold the ground there, I'll be able to bring all our archers out to the left. Do you think you can remain steady under fire, without rashness? It will be a brutal day, Prince Edward. Your mother will remain behind the line, in the town of Tewkesbury. Actually . . .' He paused as if the idea had just occurred to him. 'It would be no shame for a young fellow of your years to wait with her.'

Prince Edward's initial excitement had faded as he heard where Somerset wished to put him.

'What? No, my lord Somerset,' he said firmly. 'If Edward of York holds the centre, I believe I must stand against him to win my spurs. Unless you think I can make my name while hiding behind my mother's skirts? No? Have no fear for my youth, my lord. I have waited all my life for this moment.'

'Ah, you see, that is what I fear, Your Highness. I . . . have my own desire to see vengeance, but that does not mean I will go rushing upon the enemy with a wild shout, do you understand? Battles can last an entire day and must be taken as strong spirit, in sips and drops, rather than a huge draught that might leave you senseless or break your mother's heart.'

Edward developed two pink spots high on his cheeks as he answered, his voice curt. His mother smiled to hear him speak with such clear authority.

'Well, I have heard you, my lords. The centre is where I will stand. I will simply have to try not to disappoint you tomorrow.'

Somerset shook his head, flushed and uncomfortable.

'I am sorry if I have embarrassed you, Your Highness. If I could, I would offer my life tomorrow and see you spared from harm. I have no sons of my own – and you are . . . you were my father's hope when he died, my brother's when he stretched his neck on a York block. In their memory, I would give my life to save yours – all to see the sons of York made cold and *broke*.'

There was a terrible passion in Somerset as he spoke the last and both Prince Edward and his mother looked away rather than observe his most intimate pain.

'I will command the centre square,' Edward murmured once again. He had not understood all he had heard and he wished to be certain the lords had not taken away what he wanted with their speeches.

'I'll stand with you then, if I may, lad,' Lord Wenlock said. When Prince Edward nodded, the old man reached out and clapped him soundly on the back.

Somerset came back to himself at the words and nodded. With formality, he bowed to queen and prince.

'It is settled then. My lord Courtenay, Earl Devon, will take the left wing. I will take the right – and Prince Edward and Wenlock the centre square. Very well. I will tell the men to sleep, as best they can. When it is over tomorrow, I am at your orders. I'll know better then if we should go on into Wales – or back to London to display the body of York for the crowds.'

'I will pray for it,' Margaret said. 'Go to your own rest now, Edmund. I will ask God for our victory tomorrow. We can make it all anew if Edward falls. With men like you, my lords, we can begin again.'

22

Edward could already see the sun's dim haze of gold in the east and he breathed out, relieved it would not be like Barnet. He'd understood how much good fortune had played a part in his victory there. He did not dwell on it, as he did not dwell on anything, but it had given him pause. Perhaps luck had given him Warwick and Montagu in the end. He would win the rest with strength and endurance – and he would be more ruthless than those who faced him.

His weary army had moved up at first light, bringing a dozen cannon carts trundling along with them. The teams of young men who had bowled them along the roads were just about finished, bent over and staggering, so tired they could barely stand. A few had gone down on the way, feet broken under a wheel or with an arm wrenched by the spokes. Yet the rest would still play their part.

As the mists continued to thin and swirl, it did not please Edward to see the forces of Lancaster arrayed across a wide line and somehow six or eight yards above his men, as if they floated on air. It was no more than a mild rise in the land, but still it meant his soldiers would be fighting uphill as they attacked. They were already tired after the vast distance they had marched to cut Margaret off.

Edward grumbled to himself, but there was little he could do, at least before the sun thinned the mists and he could see the landscape around them. His brother George sat just a few places away in line, looking up at the standing ranks of Lancaster in awe almost, as if they were a religious vision.

Edward tightened his mouth in reaction to seeing Clarence with his own hanging open. They made a fine, brave sight, it was true, with huge banners flying, the blue and yellow of Somerset, the red and yellow of Devon, the black and white feathers of a Prince of Wales. Edward did not know the three black heads on Wenlock's banners and had to point and ask one of his heralds. He knew old man Wenlock by reputation and was just surprised to find he was still alive. Edward wondered if Margaret had lost so many that she had to rely on boys and ancients.

His brother Richard came cantering across the marching lines, kicking up clods of loose earth and mud as he went.

'Did you see Somerset on our left?' he called. 'He bears a grudge, they say, for his father and his brother.'

'Why not?' Edward retorted. 'I do myself – and I lost better men than old Somerset and his lad.'

'Yes, Brother, I believe I am aware. Still, I heard he has fire in his blood. If you'll let me take the left wing, I would sting him first with cannon and arrow. Let me see if I can enrage and draw him out, away from that ridge.'

Edward nodded his assent. He trusted his brother – and Lord Hastings, for that matter. He understood how much a battle depended upon that trust. It could not be one great general leading his men, at least not with so many. It was a brotherhood and he realized he was more comfortable on the field of war than any quiet room in London or Windsor. He was made for the battle shout, the clash of arms. Silence and peace wore him down like a mill wheel held to him.

While Edward brooded, Richard of Gloucester raced off with a dozen captains falling in behind him, rearranging entire companies so that they halted and took up new positions on both flanks. The task was made no easier by the land they crossed. The forces of Lancaster sat serene on their escarpment, but every York company was forced down tiny paths between hedges, or made to seek out a gate at the end of a field bordered in hawthorn bushes they could not push through. It was deliberate, of course, which did not make it easier to bear. Edward could hardly blame his enemies for choosing a spot that suited them and interfered with his best deployment. Yet he found himself trotting down a labyrinth of hedge-alleys, separated from his own men as if he was working through a maze. He'd lose sight of the Lancaster forces in the mist or just by the lay of the land and overgrown banks of thorn. In armour, he was sweating like a blacksmith, lacking the vital calm he needed to command well. He could feel anger simmering in him. He welcomed it.

Edmund Beaufort, Duke Somerset, looked down on a landscape of white and dark green, broken by patches of marching men or horsemen hurrying the rest along. What he saw pleased him well enough. He'd seen the extent of the farming ditches that lay to the south of his position as he'd formed the men. It gave him some satisfaction to watch the banners of York go wandering off down ancient tracks as they tried to find their way back to the main direction of advance. If it would not have meant sending orderly ranks into that broken ground and losing their advantage, he'd have been tempted to make a dash down and surprise the enemy before they could truly form up. He did not give the order and watched instead as they found their way closer and closer. They would arrive sweating and weary, he thought.

At one point, the centre of York's army trudged up a rise in the ground so that they were almost level with Somerset's banners, but then had to watch them rise once more as the ground dropped into a culvert between the two forces. Somerset smiled at a glimpse of armoured men clambering over a stile in a field, half a mile off. He had no desire to give them the slightest advantage, not when he stood for the rightful king of England and his son.

Margaret had ridden away with just four guards at first light, seeking out a spot in the town where she would have to wait for news. Somerset did not envy her that. For all the danger he would face, he did not think he could have endured hours of silent worry, waiting for word from the field.

His men were ready, armed in good iron that would not break, clad in fine mail or the best plate. Many of them had painted the metal, so that they stood like shining beetles in dark green or red. The poorer knights and men-at-arms stood clad in shades of rust, in armour their fathers had worn.

Somerset could see their confidence. They had the rising ground and the numbers to hold it. More, they seemed to understand how right it was to consider themselves superior to the stumbling, perspiring ranks coming along towards them. Somerset saw determination in his men and he was well pleased. He saw some of them gesture mutely to those they glimpsed in the parting mists. They wanted to *begin*. Numbers were not the only coin on the scale of victory in battle, Somerset knew that very well. There would come a moment in any conflict of arms when an ordinary man would want to run. If he did, and if the contagion of his fear spread to those around him, his cause would be broken, his women taken, his land enjoyed by others. Yet if somehow he did *not*, if he could find it within himself to remain with his friends and his companions in iron, he would be Sparta, he would be Rome, he would be England.

'I believe we will break them here,' Somerset called suddenly across the heads of his men. His horse snorted and threw its head up, forcing him to walk it in a tight circle as it settled back down. 'They will come against us and we will say "Enough" to them all. Enough to their petty spite, their ambition! Call enough to all of it. We *have* a king. His son, the Prince of Wales, stands here on the field with us.' They cheered as he took another breath and his usual dour mood eased just a fraction, warmed by their voices.

'Call "Lancaster" or call "Wales" if you will. But call an end to these usurping beggars, who are not fit to wear the crown of our realm.'

The cheering grew louder as they laughed and stamped in reply, showing their approval and casting off the nervousness of waiting to be attacked. As he cheered with them, Somerset saw the banners of Gloucester come through the mist ahead, seeming close enough to touch. He looked for the man himself and saw him there, in armour of green or black, his dark-blond hair unbound and no sign of a helmet. He looked every inch a cruel knight. Somerset felt all his years as he stared down at the eighteen-year-old, riding with his hands held high and lightly on the reins, making his horse step over the rough-turned rows of clay and grass.

The mist was thinning then under the sun's warmth. Though dawn had barely come, Somerset could watch as Richard of Gloucester brought a mass of brown-clothed archers up on his wing. He saw too the black pipes of cannons held between two cartwheels, aimed and set with blocks and braziers. Trails of grey smoke carried far on the morning breeze that stole the mist away.

Somerset was aware of his captains calling orders for shields to be brought up. His men would have to endure for a time, that was what came of choosing a spot and deciding to stand there. His own archers would answer. Though Somerset had no cannon, he had yet to see one worth its name on the field. They had a place in battering down the walls of a fortress, that was proven work, beyond any doubt. Where there was movement, where men could overwhelm the cannon teams, he saw no future in the filthy things, all noise and smoke, as if brave men should run screaming from those things alone.

He watched as a thin line gathered ahead of the archers, carrying short lances over their shoulders. Somerset nodded in irritation as he understood the smoking fuses. Handgunners. It seemed he would have to stand straight through a swarm of bees that day. He did not intend to show any fear, or anything at all. He did not like his men to see him flinch, in case they thought he was afraid. Richard of Gloucester would have to attack, in the end. Somerset clenched a gauntlet in prospect. His men would have the chance then to take back any drop of blood they had lost. He wished only to have the chance to face the younger son of York himself. Under his breath, he began to murmur silent prayers.

'Almighty God, an it pleaseth you, remember well my brother and my father. Welcome them into your embrace and peace. I pray today, only to find Richard of Gloucester within my arm's reach. I ask for nothing more, Lord, but that small kindness. If I am to live, I ask for the will to see this through. If I am to die, I ask only to see my kin again.'

Richard of Gloucester looked left and right, pleased with the array of silent ranks. They still stood below the rise of the land, but the mist had withered away and the sun was rising warm. There was a reason why battles were fought in spring and they felt it then, with blood running hot in their veins. Somerset had chosen his high ground and stood still for all of their approach. His archers would have an advantage of range, but there was no help for that. Richard halted his men at four hundred yards from Lancaster, a dark line running across the ridge ahead. A challenge lay in those still ranks. It was one they wanted to answer, as stags will answer, smashing together in a great crunch of bone, antler against antler.

Richard filled his chest, sitting tall with one hand on his sword hilt, still undrawn.

'Ready, archers! Ready, cannon. Slow advance into range!'

It was the moment all men hated, when they would approach in line, staring across a field, waiting for the air to spring dark with thousands of shafts, for gunpowder to billow its white smoke across from them as they marched in.

Somerset gave no order and Richard swallowed nervously. He knew he made a fine target in his black armour. It was hard to force his mount forward with the men, but he was certain he would not die. Other men would, without a doubt. Yet Richard was touched and blessed, he could feel it. Death would not come for him, no matter how he called for it.

His archers bent their bows as they walked, knowing his next order. It came as Somerset roared and the air blackened with whining shafts.

'Halt! Archers, nock and draw! Release!' Richard's orders were taken up by the captains, each tending to men he knew well. The hand-gunners knelt to fire ahead of his archers and for the first time, Richard saw men fall in the lines above them, when their smoke cleared. Still, he did not like to be blinded as arrows dropped down at him. The range was short and brutal and he held no shield, relying instead on his armour. He knew it would take the most perfect of shots to pierce his carapace, but still it was hard not to flinch away from arrows falling. Only his horse seemed unaffected, or unaware, standing calm as shafts thumped and cracked into the ground all around them.

It showed then, what he had done. With his brother's

blessing, Richard had concentrated all his fire on Somerset's own position. Arrow, ball and shot had torn into a narrow strip around Somerset's banners, killing dozens of men who had found themselves in a hail of steel points and lead balls, while cannon shot ripped through a standing line, taking down two or three at a time. One of Somerset's banners wavered and fell and of course the York army cheered the sight, delighted by the first fruits of success.

Somerset's archers had aimed their shafts all along the advancing York line, where men waited with shields and the best armour. There had been injuries. Men in mail or plate lay perfectly still amidst their fellows, almost as if they were asleep. They were not too many.

Richard raised and dropped his hand and by then his cannon teams had reloaded. There was a visible flinch in the lines around Somerset. They had seen they were the target and not one of them wanted to stand close to Somerset himself.

Edmund Beaufort sat his mount, apparently untouched. His horse wore an armoured headpiece set with a spike for close combat against foot soldiers. It pawed the ground as his banner-bearers edged back. The duke sensed their movement and turned his head to snap an order at them.

Down below, Richard of Gloucester saw the movement and smiled to himself.

'Archers! Again. At Somerset!' They were more accurate than his cannon teams and far more frightening. Some stood in lines like foot soldiers, while others jerked forward in stabbing thrusts, giving themselves a few more yards of range as they loosed and darted back to their friends. They called out, judging each other's shots all the time, hooting when a bow snapped or a man slipped and sent his arrow plunging into the ground ahead of him. They were merciless in their mockery of poor skill, as it was all they had and all they valued.

Richard wished he'd brought more of them, that his brother had waited for another thousand bowmen. They would have torn Somerset's wing to pieces. He found his mind fastening on small details as his archers hammered the wing. Somerset still lived. His banner had been raised up once again and the man carrying it had lasted just a moment before he too fell, pierced by shafts. Somerset roared a challenge, but they poured fire up at him still, cannon and ball and arrow. The smoke of the guns went some way to make them all blind. The archers kept casting poisonous glances at the teams ruining their perfect aim, but the combination had torn great gaps in the Lancaster lines, while the rest lay untouched. No one there understood why Gloucester was driving his entire store of missiles against one man, except Richard himself and Edward in the centre. For an hour, he made that spot a hell and Somerset knew it was all at him. His armour was smacked and rocked a dozen times, so that he could taste blood on his lips. He had accepted a shield and drawn a studded mace. The solid heft of the weapon felt good in his hand. He felt anger rising like steam in him and then something snapped his head back so that his helmet rang. He called a messenger to him and the young man came cringing, so that Somerset scorned his cowardice as he spoke.

'*Enough* of this. Inform Lord Wenlock that I will charge. He must support me. I cannot sit under this fire any longer. That is my order. Support the wing. Attack when I move.'

The messenger raced off, desperately relieved to be able to get away from air that seemed to whine like hornets and terror. Somerset turned back to the beetle ranks he saw below. They had crept forward of course, in their ill discipline. He judged them and he was not completely lost in a red haze of anger, though he felt it tugging at him. Richard of Gloucester in all his youth and arrogance, who understood *nothing.* That *family*, who had stolen Somerset's beloved brother and his father! Who had taken so many good men and women and torn the country to pieces – and *still*, there they were in all their arrogance and spite, pouring in fire on his position like a storm wave breaking over him. It was too much.

Edward raised his head from his study of his saddle pommel, where it branched out and held his thighs so that he could use both hands for weapons. Some knights carried a shield, but he was big enough to bear the weight of thick plates and he preferred a sword and a long-hammer. The head of it looked small for a man of his size, barely larger than his hand. Yet he could swing it with crushing power and the iron shaft would block most sword blows.

He had been considering his weapons for an age as his brother sent massed fire against Somerset's wing and ignored the rest. Edward felt dizzied by the conflicting needs within him. He wanted to push forward up that rise and into the ranks gesturing for him to come on. They were brave enough at two hundred yards. Most men were. He wanted to see how they fared when he was there amongst them. Yet he had promised his brother and he forced himself to wait, light-headed with the blood pounding through him, standing still while his breath went out in great bursts, like a wolf bunching to leap.

When he looked up, it was in response to a roar as Somerset's battered wing came howling down the rise at Gloucester's men. Edward's eyes widened. It was perfect and he blessed his brother's clear sight.

'Advance the centre!' he bellowed, his voice carrying right across the field. 'Centre companies, advance!' They lurched off as he called, having watched Somerset lose his calm with rapt attention.

Ahead, the strongest part of Margaret's army came barrelling down the hill that had been their one advantage. Gloucester's companies met them head on and Edward of York crashed into them on the other flank, pikes and spearmen driving into them. The men in ranks coming down could not defend against that assault from the side. The spears plunged in, coming back red and pulling shrieks out as men fell and were trampled.

Somerset's red rage intensified as he looked back and saw Lord Wenlock had not moved. Was the old man asleep? Wenlock and the prince still stood in peaceful ranks while their best men and their only chance was being torn apart. Somerset could not allow the sons of York to bring all their force on to each piece of his army. That way lay disaster and death. Somerset was barely off the rise when he saw how badly his force was being mauled. He gestured for Wenlock, but the arrogant old bastard made no move at all to support him.

'Fall back in good order!' Somerset roared to his captains. A great groan went up from battered men who had endured the barrage and then trusted him enough to follow. They were being asked to retreat up a slope, with a delighted enemy pressing against them and swinging iron. It was a hard thing, but the alternative was to have York and Gloucester whittle them away to dust, so they halted and did their best to hold Gloucester's baying ranks away with outstretched weapons. There were a few spears and they made the first steps well enough before Gloucester saw their intention with astonished disbelief – and ordered his entire wing into a charge.

Somerset turned his horse to ride up the hill, knowing he could hardly back the animal up a slope. As he turned, he saw a pack of spearmen come racing out of woodland on his left, with their long weapons held down and ready to attack. He could not think of an order to answer them in that moment, except to call a warning. Spears were used in defence, or as a knight's lance. He could only blink at the sight of men running to attack with them.

''Ware left. Beware spears to the left!' he called, but his men were pressed from the front and the flank, where more spearmen pressed and heaved. They had but one flank free and all they could do was back away as two hundred of the enemy crashed into them, the spears punching right through the first rank so that the bloody heads came out to foul those pressing behind. It broke the last will to fight in Somerset's men, as if they'd been caught in a boar trap with spikes driven right through them. They tried to scatter but the slaughter went on and no quarter was given.

Somerset dug in his heels and felt his horse stagger as something ripped through it. He did not know what wound the animal had taken, but he could feel its strength begin to fail. The horse struggled up the rise, blowing and snorting blood. Somerset forced it on without expression, digging in his spurs again and again. He knew Gloucester and York would be pushing up the slope behind him and he had no care for that. Instead he trotted his dying horse right up to the terrified ranks of men in the centre square, who had stood and watched while their own people were cut down.

Baron Wenlock was there on his horse in the third rank, surrounded by messengers and heralds. Edward, Prince of Wales, sat a mount at Wenlock's side. The young man paled visibly as he caught sight of Somerset. The battered duke had blood splashed across his helmet and his horse dribbled bright red at its nostrils.

'Why didn't you support me, my lord?' Somerset snarled at Wenlock. 'I sent an order. Where were you?'

Wenlock bristled, his hair very white against his darkening flush.

'How dare you impugn my honour? You pup! I will not . . .'

Somerset hit him with the mace he held in his right hand, one great blow that silenced the old man. Blood poured down Wenlock's forehead and his mouth worked in astonishment as Somerset hit him again and then watched, panting, as the lord slipped from his horse and fell to the ground.

'By Christ!' Edward of Wales said, his eyes widening. He was not looking at Wenlock, but behind, to where the forces of York were charging. Somerset turned, and they were engulfed.

Edward looked down at the silver knuckles of his gauntlets. They were reddened, though he could not recall punching a man in his battle madness. He had come roaring up the hill as Somerset's wing collapsed, choosing the moment to make his charge into the forces on the rise. He'd seen Somerset arguing and a young man in the royal livery of Lancaster, hardly able to defend himself. Edward looked again at his gauntlet. There had been so much blood in his life. He had not asked for any of it. He knew there was at least one woman who would weep that day when she heard. All Margaret of Anjou's hopes were made ash, her son pale and still with all the rest.

He found himself weeping and grew angry even as he wiped tears. Other men looked away, having seen much stranger things. Some were sick on to the grass after a battle. Others fell into a deep sleep if they could, as if they were drunk. Still more would laugh or weep, all unnoticed as they walked the field and understood that they had survived. All the things they had forgotten in the heat and swing of murder came back in flashes and they would stop and rub their eyes and breathe deeply before going on.

Perhaps it was age, Edward thought ruefully. He began to chuckle at the vision of a weeping king, the ridiculousness of it. He could see his brother Richard congratulating the men, exactly as he himself should have been doing. His throat was dry and he grabbed a passing boy with a skin over his shoulder, upending it. He'd expected water, but it was foaming ale, thick and bitter. He gulped and gulped, like a child at a tit, breaking the seal only when he needed to breathe.

'By God, I am dry,' he murmured. He saw Richard approaching him and he laughed at his brother's stricken expression.

'Well, my oath is fulfilled, Brother,' Edward said irritably. 'And I find I am dry.'

'I know, Edward, it is not that. I heard there are some knights of Lancaster claiming sanctuary in the abbey, by the town.'

'Any names?' Edward said. A flush had come to his cheeks at the ale in him. He seemed less weighed down, brighter and more cheerful.

'I don't know,' Richard answered. 'The monks will not let our men enter to see.'

'Oh, will they not?' Edward asked. He tossed the aleskin to the waiting boy and whistled for his horse. Lord Rivers brought it up to him. Edward's personal guard formed up, all bare-headed and savage men.

'Come with me,' Edward said to his brother. Richard mounted once again and followed.

The abbey at Tewkesbury was not far behind the last lines of the dead, as they had been driven away from where they first stood. Edward's expression darkened at the sight of monks in black robes standing across the great Norman arch and door. He brought his horse into a canter then. Rivers and his guards surged forward with him, knowing there were few more frightening sights in the world than warhorses coming in iron and anger.

Edward reined in by the door, sending his horse into a skidding turn. The watching monks flinched, but did not stand back.

'I gave an order to seek out my enemies, wherever they might hide,' Edward called over their heads. He knew he could be heard within the walls and he made his voice loud.

The abbot stepped out of the huge doorway in response.

'My lord York,' he began.

'Address me as king,' Edward snapped at him.

'Your Highness, if it please you, this is consecrated ground. It is sanctuary. I cannot let your men go in.'

Edward turned to the knights with him.

'I was driven out of my own land, my wife and children forced into hiding. When I returned, I said I would make an ending. I gave no quarter. I have taken no ransoms. I consider this the battlefield still. I would take it kindly if you would enter and *put an end to anyone left alive.*'

Two of the knights walked their mounts towards the door. The monks cried out in outrage and horror, raising their hands as if they might hold them off. Instead, the knights brought blades down in sharp, chopping blows, sending blood splashing on to the stones. The abbot tried to get back inside to lock the doors, but the horsemen forced them open and rode into the abbey beyond. A great cry of fear went up from those who had gone inside as their last hope, wounded and afraid. The knights went into the gloom, and for a time, there were other shrieks and cries of pain and outrage.

Edward glanced over to his brothers. Clarence looked ill, as if he might vomit. Richard watched him, his expression almost curious. Edward shrugged. He had seen too much of death and killing. It did not seem such a great step to him.

They found Margaret the following day. She had heard the awful news and her guards had vanished, leaving her to run alone to a convent a mile or so away. The nuns there had certainly heard the fate of those who had stood against Edward. Though they cried out in protest, they did not resist the rough soldiers who came into their corridors to drag Margaret out.

Margaret went meekly enough, lost in her grief. The captain who put her on a horse and held her reins took pity enough to let her see the body of her son, laid out in Tewkesbury Abbey. He was beautiful in his youth and Margaret stroked his cheek and held his hand for a time then, emptied and dulled by all she had suffered.

Despite her pleas, they left Edward of Lancaster behind with hundreds of others when the army of York packed up and took the road back to London. The abbey nave was splashed with red that no one seemed to know how to wash away.

Margaret had expected at first to be brought before King Edward, to be forced to endure his acid triumph. Yet he was not his father and he did not call for her. His men treated her with some courtesy on the road, but no special interest. It seemed the house of York no longer cared what became of her.

Edward had been thorough in his vengeance. Not one Lancaster lord had been spared. However they had been bound to King Henry's line, whether by blood or by oath or by service, Edward of York had put them in the ground. The house of Lancaster had been brought to an end at Tewkesbury and on the headsman's block, with not even the wounded spared.

Margaret mourned as her horse swayed, taking her she knew not where. Though she did not want the soldiers to hear her grieve, she found herself keening softly even so, like a child in pain. Her son, her Edward, had been cut down before he was truly a man, all his promise, all his joy gone. She would not see him laugh again and that was monstrous, so wrong that she could not understand it. She found she had been hollowed. She had given her youth and her faith and her only child to England and she had nothing else.

23

Edward was drunk, though he made some effort to hide it with his brother Richard standing before him. He could remember the cold clarity of the last days at Barnet and Tewkesbury only in bleary wonder. His appetites had woken like a furnace door opening, as if he had stored them up. He ate and drank himself senseless each and every day and yet the flames flickered in him still, always there, an itch he could not scratch, a burning coal he could not quench in wine. He did not tell Richard about the nightmares that plagued him. He could not bear the thought of his brother pitying him in his weakness. No. Edward felt the sweat dribbling cold from his armpits, but he smiled as if there was nothing wrong with him at all.

'What news, Brother?' he said, staring intently down the length of the audience room, trying to read every change of expression and subtle shift.

'A terrible thing, Your Highness, a tragedy,' Richard replied. Edward closed his eyes briefly. He had spent all the night before in the company of sixty lords and their ladies, with juggling and illusions and great feats of arms. His brother had not been with him.

'Tell me, Richard, as we are alone,' he whispered.

'I spoke to King Henry about his son. He gave a great spasm of the spirit and he fell into a faint from which I could not rouse him. I am sorry, Brother. King Henry is dead.'

'I will have to display his body, as I did with Warwick and Montagu. If I do not, there will always be some fool to mutter about Lancaster's return. Can I . . . Is the body fit to be seen?'

Richard looked coldly at his brother, knowing very well what he was being asked.

'If he wears a cowl, perhaps one of mail, yes. I will have his body dressed in long robes and guarded well so that no man can come too close.'

'Thank you,' Edward said. He looked for some trace of guilt in the eighteen-year-old duke and found only a calm and certain confidence. 'Now have your brother brought in.'

With all the servants dismissed, Richard himself strode back down the room and hammered a gauntlet on to the oak doors. George of Clarence came in quietly, slipping through when the door was half open. He looked from one to the other of his brothers and his expression was wary.

'Thank you for coming in to London, George,' Edward said, inclining his head to his brother. George walked the length of the room almost in step with Richard. When he was close, he watched Edward in turn, seeing the flush and the sweating that meant the king was deep in his cups once again. George did not think Edward knew how often he paused and blew air in or out, his eyes dull. Yet his brother wore a simple crown and sat a throne in the audience chamber in the Palace of Westminster. Edward had broken the Nevilles and the house of Lancaster in battle. No man could criticize him. When they had drawn themselves up in vast numbers, he had gone out – and destroyed them. Not once, but twice, or even three times if Towton was added to the tally. There had not been such a famed battle king since Henry V and the tragedy was that Edward had spent his youth and strength protecting his throne in England, while France thrived in peace. As Edward sat his throne that day, the country was quiet and fearful.

'I called you to me, George, for your advice,' Edward said. His eyes looked red and as they watched him, he turned and reached for something, then pursed his lips in irritation, looking around for servants before giving up and settling his gaze once more on his brothers.

'Richard here is considering a union with Warwick's daughter Ann,' Edward announced. He saw George's eyes narrow in sharp suspicion and felt a smile come. He reached again for a cup of wine at his elbow and his fingers twitched for a moment before he remembered. Ah, yes. He had ordered it so. It was important for him to be sharp. There would be a great feast that very night, a celebration. Lord Rivers had some anniversary or other and Edward had agreed to host a banquet in Windsor. He could drink himself to oblivion then, in wine and spirits that would grant him sleep without dreams.

'She was married to Edward of Lancaster,' George said suddenly. 'Are you sure she is untouched, Richard? Edward of Lancaster was a very young man, full of vigour.'

'I will wait long enough to be sure her womb is empty, of course,' Richard said with a shrug. 'That is not your concern.' He looked up at Edward, and George of Clarence struggled with a growing sense of disaster. Richard was clearly prompting their brother and he could guess at the thrust of it. Before he could speak, Edward held up a finger and dashed his hopes.

'Richard was a vital part of my victories at Barnet and Tewkesbury. In addition, he has done great service to the crown. It is my desire to find some suitable reward. When I heard the name of the one he will marry, well, I knew you would join me in finding a . . .' Edward's voice died away as he flicked his fingers for the word.

'Reward, Your Highness,' Richard said, smiling brightly at George.

'Yes, reward. The Warwick estates – a dozen castles, hundreds of manors and towns and villages and fortresses. Some of the best land in England and Wales.'

'Which I have inherited *jure uxoris*, by right of my wife,' George said. He looked stubborn and Edward frowned at him, leaning over so that his big scarred hands rested on his knees.

'Don't fight me on this, George,' Edward muttered. His brother still looked stubborn and Edward seemed to grow in size as his flush deepened. In him, anger was a physical change and both of his brothers could sense the threat that had stolen into that room.

'Warwick's titles were all attainted, George. Have you forgotten? I could pass them all to your brother as Crown estates – and what would you do? Go running to my Parliament? To my lords? Would you say your brother was acting within the laws of England and you did not like it?'

'There are a thousand dispute cases in the courts, Edward. I have some forty of them being argued myself! All I ask is that you do not take from me what will be mine when the courts have run their course.'

'No, George. I will rule on this now. If you challenge that ruling in the courts, you will stand against my direct command as your king. Do not take the risk, George. Blood will protect you – to a point. You stand at that point now.'

Edward had risen from his chair and loomed over both of them. George stood quivering in rage and then spat a curse, turning on his heel and storming out at enough speed to make his cloak swirl as he went. In temper, he slammed the door at the end of the room.

In the astonished silence that followed, Richard turned slowly to his brother. His eyebrows were raised and Edward sat down once again, waving a hand at the unasked question.

'Yes, take what estates you would, Richard. Clarence is a fool. Perhaps that is the end of it and he will not challenge me again. If it is not . . .' He did not need to finish.

'I hope so,' Richard said. 'He's a weak man, but he's still our brother.'

'And an uncle once more, or he will be, if he has the sense to stay out of my sight for a time.'

'Elizabeth is pregnant? Again?' Richard asked. He chuckled. 'I suppose you were a long time apart.'

Edward shook his head in irritation.

'I do not like her, Brother. But she has a way of enticing me . . . She is already vomiting in the mornings. I think I must have the most potent seed. I have only to look in her direction and she is full again.'

'I will hope for a brother for your son,' Richard said. 'I would not like to have had only sisters.' He saw Edward was raising his hand to wave this off or make some jesting comment and he spoke over it.

'I mean it. I will hope for another boy, so that they can have . . . this. I have friends, Edward. I value what you and I have more than friendship. It matters to me that we have trust between us. Since our father went, especially. You know I admire you, above all others. Though God knows you are a hard man to please.'

'Thank you,' Edward said. 'I miss him still. I walk in his old rooms and his authority is not there. I can still hardly believe he is gone.' He smiled and Richard saw his eyes swam with brightness. Edward cleared his throat, sniffing. The loud noises seemed to bring him out of his reverie. 'But if George stands against me over your estates, I will not warn him again. Family or not, Richard, I am the king of England. I have seen more blood than any man ever should. I have earned this peace.'

Jasper Tudor dropped on to the stuffed cushion of his chair, as if his legs had given way beneath him. He held a single sheet of vellum in his hands, much sanded and scratched over, then refilled with black letters that stole away the last of his hopes. He wanted to throw it into the kitchen fire and he twitched to do so, before staying his hand. Henry would want to read it. God knew, it was his concern.

As if in answer, the boy came in at that moment, holding up a length of twine with the tiny bodies of sparrows threaded on to it. Jasper had taught him how to snare the birds and also how to make a pie of them. He could not help but smile at Henry's pleased expression, though Jasper's hand made the paper tremble even as he did.

'Sit down, Henry,' he said softly, indicating the second chair. The cottage was small and there was room only for the two of them. Even in the short time since they'd arrived, it had grown around them in comfort. For the first time, Jasper felt smothered by the place. He took Henry's arm and jerked his head to the yard outside.

'The woodsmoke is making my eyes red, Henry. Walk with me. I have news from home.'

He watched as his nephew laid the thread of sparrows down on the table, leaving a spattering of bright-red droplets on the polished wood. Jasper felt his gaze drawn to it and held. He shook himself free and led the way out to the evening warmth.

For a time, neither of them spoke. Jasper strode away from the little house, down the lane by the dovecote and out on to the main field that stretched away down into a valley. A naked oak stood at the crest of the hill, its bark stripped by death, the wood beneath made the colour of old cream by sun and passing time. Jasper walked to its foot and patted the smooth trunk. He held up the piece of vellum and his nephew glanced warily at it.

'I wish it were not so, Harry, but we cannot go home. Edward of York has won his battles and King Henry is gone to salvation, God have mercy on his soul. They say it was from heartbreak and despair, but I think he came to the end of the rope they allowed him.'

'He was kind to me,' Henry said. 'I liked him. Is my mother safe?' Jasper nodded.

'She says she is. I will let you read it, I promise. The king's hunters care not for the women of the line, only the men. Give thanks for that, in your prayers tonight.'

Henry nodded, his eyes dark.

'I will. Is she to come to us here, then? I would . . . like that.'

Jasper held up the paper.

'She spoke not of it. If she is threatened, you have my word I will bring her away, Harry. As I did with you.'

Some slight tension went out of his nephew. Jasper saw with fresh eyes how much faith the young man had in him. It broke his heart. The fields were green around the bare oak, the summer's beauty written on the land. Yet Jasper felt himself cold and dark in the midst of new life, weary with pity and grief. There would be no return in glory to Pembroke for him then, nor would his nephew see Richmond and the court. They had only a lonely exile ahead, with a few coins from the French king each month to pay for food and red wine.

'We can make a fair life here,' Jasper said, forcing cheer into his voice. 'There is a little money from Paris – and the dovecote earns us more. I'll find work for us both, I am sure. You have been trained as a knight, Harry. That has value and you will not go hungry. We can keep those skills sharp and perhaps when you are a little older, I'll find you a bride from the local barons. Who knows, we might find one with a fortune.'

Henry didn't blink as he looked him over and Jasper felt himself growing uncomfortable.

'Will I not go home again, Uncle? Never?' Henry asked.

'Harry, listen. Your mother is the last daughter of the line of John of Gaunt – the house of Lancaster. You are her only child and she is almost thirty. The last man of Lancaster stands before me now. You, Harry. All the rest have been cut down. Do you understand? If you go home, if you appear in London and try to live a quiet life, I would not give a bent copper for your chances. Perhaps King Edward was driven to his vengeance, but he drank deep when he had the chance, son. He has so many dead by his hands now, he would not hold back from one more, not to finish the task. I'm sorry, I really am. But you must think of your life here now. You must find a way to leave all of that behind.'

Henry had watched Jasper reach out to the oak as he spoke, stroking the rippled smoothness. As silence returned, Henry put his own hand on to the wood and let his fingers drift across it. He left no mark and he tilted his head in interest, like a bird.

'I will wait, Uncle,' he said suddenly. 'I waited in Pembroke for a long time – and you came. If I wait again, perhaps we'll see a way home. You must not lose hope.'

Jasper felt his eyes prickle and he laughed at his own emotion.

'I won't, Harry. I will dream of home, of Wales and Pembroke.' On impulse, he turned in the long grass, eyeing the sun until he thought he faced to the north-west. 'It is . . . over there, Harry, at this very moment. In the rain, probably, but still home.'

Margaret watched the lights of Paris growing brighter along the river. She had been four days at sea and she was calm and broken-hearted, as if she had a piece of jagged flint in her chest. Losing her son was a grief she could not encompass, could not even describe. Perhaps it had been a sort of mercy for Edward to allow her to return to France. She'd been told some sort of offer had been made, though for the longest time she had been so deep in grief that she had understood very little and her own life had meant nothing. She had not washed for weeks, so that her skin had gone grey and her hair thick with dirt. She'd made some small effort with a bucket and cloth as the boat made its way from the open sea to the more peaceful river beyond. The sail creaked in the breeze and the men of the crew murmured to each other, but still she was cold as ashes. She looked up from her shawls and her bags as the boat bumped against the docks. It had grown dark and there were soldiers standing there with torches fluttering overhead. She saw King Louis had come down to meet her and she found that there were still tears inside, though she had thought they had all gone. Margaret stood with a heavy bag in each hand as the little gangway was placed. She came down it and set her things on the quay-side as Louis came up and took her hands in his, his eyes full of sorrow.

'Ah, *madame*, he was a fine, brave boy. I asked for him to be sent to me here for burial, but they would not. I am so sorry. Your husband too. It is a tragedy. You deserved more, Margaret, truly. Yet you are home now. You are safe and you do not ever have to leave again.'

He kissed her on both cheeks and Margaret pressed a hand to her mouth and nodded, unable to speak as he led her away. Her bags were taken up by others, but her shoulders were bowed and her beauty had gone. No one who had seen her then would have known her for the girl who crossed to England in joy and anticipation, with William de la Pole at her side and her first glimpse of England still ahead.

PART TWO

Christmas 1482

Eleven years after Tewkesbury

We will unite the white rose and the red.

William Shakespeare, *Richard III*

24

Edward knew he drank more when he was maudlin. He'd heard an archer refer once to the 'bowstrings of a man' – the strands that made him who he was. Edward shared at least one of his strands with a certain type of Northman, prone to melancholy. The darkest moods drove him to the jug – and the jug made them worse. Sorrows could not be drowned. They swam.

The music did not touch him. Dancers swept by his table as he stared out, unseeing. On a raised dais, Edward sat on a high-backed chair of velvet and oak and propped his chin on a hand. A jug of clear spirit lay by his side and a servant stood behind him to judge the perfect moment to refill his goblet. Both of them had lost count of how many times the cup had been emptied.

The Christmas celebrations at Westminster were a feast of light and music, of gifts to the poor and banqueting tables set for hundreds. Lit by candles, the crowds were entertained by troupes of musicians, conjurers, knife-throwers and two acrobats wearing spotted furs, who seemed to have skin made of night. The evening had started well and grown ever more raucous as the drink flowed.

The old men and women had long retired and the night had worn into the small hours. The sun would rise again – and only that reappearance would call an end to the revels, with all the scars, scratches and scuffs revealed once more. Candles suited them all, while the drums rattled and the pipes played another reel.

Edward watched three of his daughters dance together, all awake when they should have been in bed hours before. His eldest, Elizabeth, was swan-necked and red-haired, with a fine, upright carriage. The sight of her happiness could pierce Edward's gloom as nothing else. Seeing her gathering the others and calling a measure to the musicians had their drunken father beaming at them.

Her sister Mary had died earlier that year, fifteen and headstrong. The children had wept piteously when she was found and for weeks afterwards. Edward had only winced at the keening sounds they made. His own brother had been killed at seventeen. Death was a part of life, he'd told them. His wife had called him heartless.

Edward had seen more of death than she ever would, he thought grimly. He had brought a great deal of it into the world that would not have come without his call. Perhaps it was fitting that it reached then for his own children. God knew, he had enough of them, if he included those of his mistresses. He sometimes thought he had won the throne only as a way of securing livelihoods for all his get and kin.

Young Elizabeth should have been married by then, of course. The French king had reneged on that little arrangement, blaming his son's illness. Edward's head sank a little further at the memory of his one campaign season in France. He had landed from Calais and by God, if Burgundy had supported him properly from the first, they'd still have been ruling France together. Richard had put it best: not bleeding *téméraire* at all, not when it mattered. Poor bastard. They called Louis the Spider, Edward recalled, or some such name. In just a dozen years, the man had unified France and taken back all the lands of Burgundy.

Edward felt a surly anger come upon him at the thought, somehow made worse by the sight of so many young men and women laughing and singing and dancing together, without cares. At such times, he had to struggle against a desire to spring up and scatter them, to remind them to whom they owed their lives and livelihoods. They never remembered. They went on with their lives and there was disdain or resentment in their eyes when they looked at him.

He saw a sparkle of new love or something more roguish between young ladies of the court and their admirers, bowing to one another and holding hands as they danced. They flirted and preened and Edward watched them all and lifted his goblet of pale-blue glass, blown in swirls to represent the ocean. Case after case of the glass cups had been brought in by ship, commissioned for that night's occasion. Every one of the guests would take a goblet home to treasure as a reminder. It was the sort of extravagant detail Edward demanded from his seneschal, backed by his silver flowing like a river. They would know a royal feast from any other by the time they went home! The tables groaned with hams and poultry and every manner of thing that flew or swam or grazed. Yet they were not grateful. They bowed and kissed his hand, but the moment he looked away, he knew they had forgotten him.

Edward emptied his cup in a great gulp and put it down, belching and wincing at the rise of acid in his gut. It was his proud boast that he never drank water, that he considered it a poison. Water could spoil and carry some taint that would have him marooned in a royal privy for a day, groaning. That had happened far too many times and he had learned to blame the water he had sipped with his meal. Wine and small beer seemed to have no similar effect, though they could not make him drunk any longer. For that, he had grain whisky, or on this night, French Armagnac brandy.

His children came past once more, laughing and shrieking

as they wove through the dancers. Elizabeth with her red hair in a plait down her back. God, he loved her, more than he had ever expected. More perhaps since Mary had gone into the tomb, her own hair of gold brushed a thousand times, as bright in death as it had been in life. Edward felt his eyes sting as he glared at the crowd. The dancers seemed to sense his darkening mood, so that they swung a little further away from him, as geese will make a path for a farmer's tread.

Edward's sons expected rough humour from him, if anything at all. He could not find an ease of manner with them, coming it always too loud or too clumsy. Prince Edward was still too slim at twelve, his father thought. The boy was taller than the sons of other men, but all elbows and thin arms. It made him wonder what Lord Rivers was feeding the boy on the borders. The prince certainly wasn't thriving on it.

By all accounts, Prince Edward did as he was told, whether it was learning his declensions or his sword work, or the command of a trained warhorse. Yet he seemed not to have an urge to *succeed* that his father might have understood. Edward looked for it in both his sons, but they were too meek. He did not want to break their will with hardship, but it seemed to the king that he had been a big, rough brawler by the time he was twelve. Edward recalled betting on himself in light-hearted wrestling contests against men of the Calais garrison. Those bouts had been brutal, with few rules. Though he had lost against the regular soldiers, they'd put him up then against the French dockmen and merchants. He'd surprised one or two and won enough to get truly drunk for the first time. He shook his head at that, lost in fumes of spirits and memory. The people in those halls knew nothing of such things. They ate his food and drank his beer and lived lives of softness and ease.

Edward raised his hands suddenly, looking at the thick

fingers. Two were crooked from old breaks. His palms were thick slabs of callus. A knuckle had been pushed back in on his left hand, from some blow he could not remember, so that it lay smooth. They were a warrior's hands and they ached most days, in a way that made him think he would not see an end to the pain. He clenched his right fist and heard a clink as the servant refilled the blue glass cup. Edward sighed and picked it up as he leaned back, raising it to his eye so that he bathed the dancers in the colour of the sea.

He felt a pressure then, so wrong on the instant that he was suddenly afraid, though it came without warning and passed just as quickly. He closed one eye over a sharp discomfort, more a sense of falling than an actual headache. It had come and gone so fast he could not even be sure it had happened, but it had unsettled him. He put the cup down on the small table at his side, frowning at a tremble in his fingers.

He did not know if he had been a good king. He had been a good son, first. He had avenged his father and that was something that either didn't matter at all, or it mattered a great deal. He smiled at that, an old phrase that he had come to appreciate. It didn't matter at all, or it meant the world.

He had been a good brother, though to Richard more than George of Clarence. Poor George had kept a foolish spite and sense of injury alive for far too long, as if he was owed something by the realm, as if he had some special claim on King Edward. George had sent fools into Parliament even, to claim he had been treated poorly and illegally. Edward had warned him then, for the last time. He would not allow his brother to humiliate him in public.

'Be warned,' Edward had said to him, but George had not understood. The source and root of law lay on the field of battle. The rest was just fine dreams for the years between, too good for an age of feud and bloody vengeance, perhaps.

Edward had given Clarence a chance to leave the court, to leave London, to just live quietly with his wife and his children on their estates. Perhaps the death of his wife had driven him mad, as some said. George had accused almost everyone, including her maids. In the end, it had been like putting down a mad dog, more a mercy than a cruelty. That was what Richard had said.

They'd left George of Clarence uncut at least, unmarked for a Christian burial. Richard's men had drowned him in a vat of Malmsey wine and it had been quick enough. In the end, George of Clarence had been his own executioner, no matter who had tipped him in. The poor fool just could not find peace.

Edward felt again a strange pressure that made him grip the arm of his chair. This time he could not seem to take a proper hold, so that his right hand slipped and curled in on itself. What was *wrong* with him? He had not drunk as much as the evening before, even. He should not have been leaning and mumbling words, with vomit rising in his throat. God, he should stand up before he was sick. It had been a long time since he had drunk so much as to fall down. His muscles were cramping and he leaned back, looking up at the ceiling and closing his eyes.

In Scotland, one son had ruled while the fellow's brother, Alexander of Albany, had turned against him, like Cain and Abel. That younger brother had brought a dozen bottles of some fine liquor down to London and when they'd seen it was not poisoned, Edward and Richard had matched him cup for cup over three days until it was all gone. They'd never been so ill before or since. In their drunkenness, they'd promised to support him. Edward was proud of Richard as he recalled those days. Alexander, Duke of Albany, brother to the king of Scotland. Edward had liked him in drink, though not sober, not as well. The Scot had promised he would be a vassal to England if they won him the throne. Edward had shaken his hand and solemnly given his word.

Richard had taken Edinburgh, Edward remembered. God, they'd said he would never manage it, but he had. He'd held the Scottish king prisoner and waited for Albany.

Edward twitched his hand, though he thought he had waved away a bad memory. The fellow had let them down, of course, too meek at the end to do what had to be done. Richard had freed the king to exact his own vengeance, taking his army south once again. He'd left a garrison at Berwick and that at least would remain England. It was only fair, for the expense they'd undertaken. Edward wished George of Clarence could have been alive then, so he could have pointed to Berwick-upon-Tweed, a city that had been English and Scottish and was English once again. Where was the law for such a thing, if not in the power to hold it? Where would his brother have looked for his fine sentiments, his rights and wrongs, if not in the swords of hard and cruel men, ready to fight for it?

The king was leaning sideways in the chair. His manservant hovered nervously behind as two legs of oak came an inch away from the floor. The chair was heavy, but so was the man in it, even without his armour. Edward wore a doublet tunic of gold velvet and white silk over hose. It was a bright creation that cost as much as most of his knights would see in a year. It was almost certain Edward would wear it once and not again, but still he would be angry if it was stained, when he woke the next morning.

The serving lad tried to rest his weight on the chair arm unobtrusively, rather than let his master topple right over in front of hundreds. The king would not remember his small act of kindness, but he did it anyway.

Standing closer, the young man saw that the king's brandy had not been emptied. It was an unusual sight and he blinked and hesitated.

'If the brandy is poor, would His Highness prefer wine, or ale?' he asked, expecting a rebuke. Edward did not reply and he edged closer and further around the chair.

'Your Highness?' he asked, then stood very still as he saw the king's face had twisted and reddened in an apoplexy, sagging on one side so that his mouth hung open and made odd, choking sounds. The music played on behind and no one else seemed to have seen it. One of Edward's eyes had closed, while the other swivelled in panic, unable to understand what was happening or why his serving man was peering at him and mouthing words. Edward gave a great lurch then, kicking out so that the servant went flying and the chair fell, spilling the king on to the wooden dais with a great groan that went on and on.

Edward sat up in bed, his legs hidden by a vast coverlet of purple and gold. His face had recovered its usual shape, though his right arm was still no stronger than a child's and caused him great distress. If he had lost the left, it would have been much easier to bear. His right arm had carried him through the great trials of his life and he hated the way it curled and lay limp. The royal physicians said there was hope of regaining some movement in it. One of them had disagreed and offered only to cut it cleanly. That one had been dismissed from service.

The king lay in the royal rooms at Westminster, in the bed where he had once seen Henry of Lancaster. Yet Edward spent time each morning clenching and unclenching his right fist. He thought he was improving, that he could hold it closed for longer and longer. He had not told the physicians, not yet. He wanted those doubting bastards to see him hold a sword again.

'Very well, I am ready,' Edward called to the master of the bedchamber. The man bowed low and disappeared to call his guest from outside. Edward grumbled that Alfred Noyes fussed over him, but he was secretly relieved to have the man tut and bother those who came to see the king. Since his collapse, Edward tired easily and he did not like to admit it.

He brightened at the sight of his brother.

'Richard! Now why would Alfred hold you outside with the rest? You are always welcome here, of course.'

Richard smiled as Edward made a show of shaking his head in rebuke at his servant. He understood his brother better than Edward realized at times. Nothing would change.

'I am pleased to see you looking so strong, Edward,' he said. 'Your maids said you fell again last night.'

A spasm of peevish anger crossed Edward's face.

'Well, they should know better than to carry tales! Which ones opened their little beaks?'

'I won't tell you, Brother,' Richard said, his expression still wry. 'They care for you, that is all.'

In that moment, Richard suddenly understood that his brother could not force him to speak. Their friendship had changed and was still unfolding in a new pattern. He thought he saw the same flash of awareness in Edward, but it came and went.

'I fell because my balance is poor, that is all,' Edward said. 'There is nothing I can do to improve it.'

'Can you not catch yourself?' Richard said. His brother looked bleak.

'No. I have begun to fall before I even know it is

happening. I am black with bruises now. If I could reach out, I would, believe me.'

'And you are not drinking? The doctors said your great appetite did not help, as it worsens your gout and inflames the liver.'

'Oh, I have been a good boy, do not fear for me.' Edward spoke in irritation, then relented. Richard had come to see him almost every day for three months. Even his wife and children had not come as often, though he grew frustrated at times and roared at them, which may have played a part.

He and Richard had known each other before the court, before his wife, before the teeming brood of his children that had come into the world. Edward thought at times that only Richard could look upon him and see him truly. It was not always a comfortable thing.

'Richard, I have put my seal to some new papers and sent them to Parliament. There, in the satchel, is a copy for you. In case I die.'

His brother snorted.

'You are, what? Forty? Older men than you recover from these apoplexies, Brother. You have grown somewhat fat about the loins, it is true . . .'

'A little . . .' Edward admitted.

'And you were drinking that foul Armagnac like water. A bottle a day? Two?'

'It is like mother's milk to me,' Edward said. 'I could not deny myself brandy.'

Richard chuckled at the wounded stiffness of his brother's manner.

'Edward, you were taking back the realm when I was eight years old. I went into exile with you, when we had nothing. I have fought at your side and I have seen you triumph over all our enemies. I trusted you – and I trust you still.' He saw

Edward would interrupt and held up his hand, sitting on the edge of the bed. 'You have been an older brother and a second father to me, you know it. I am *always* on your side. By God, if you don't know by now! I went on that wild adventure into Scotland, did I not? "Go north, Richard! Put my lad Albany on the throne and we'll win Scotland!" And I went! Though I knew it was madness.' Richard began to chuckle and his eyes filled with light as he did so. 'God, whatever you want, I will do, Edward, because you are the one who asks. Do you understand? I will not talk of your death, that is all.'

Edward reached out with his left hand and held his brother's fingers awkwardly. It served to remind them both how diminished the king had become and he did not look at Richard as he spoke.

'There are some things I must say, even so. No, listen to me. The papers are to appoint you Lord Protector. Our father had the title many years ago, when Henry fell ill for the first time. It grants you the authority you will need to stand over the wishes of all others. It makes you king in all but name – and you will need it to keep my son Edward safe.' Edward held up his hand to forestall any objection. '*If* I die, make yourself his regent until he reaches an age where he can rule. I would . . . I hope you can be kind to him. He has not suffered as you and I have, Brother. Perhaps that is why he is so gentle. I sent him away with Lord Rivers to make a man of him, but it has not worked.'

'This is madness, but yes, very well,' Richard said. 'I will guide your son if the worst comes. You have my word, are you satisfied? Now, your hand is shaking. Can you sleep, do you think? Shall I leave? Your wife is outside, waiting for me to go.' Edward turned his head to one side on the pillow and waved his hand in the air.

'She comes when she wants something else from me, some bauble or post or title, some piece of land that will end a dispute and make one of her cousins happy. I think at times . . . it doesn't matter. I am tired, Richard. And I am grateful that you come every day. If not for you, I seem to speak only to women. They wear me down with their chatter. You know when to be silent.'

'And when to leave,' Richard murmured. He saw his brother's eyes were drifting closed and he stood slowly. Perhaps he would tell Edward's wife to wait until morning, though she was a hard woman to refuse and always had been.

Richard left in good spirits and retired to his rooms in Baynard's Castle on the bank of the Thames. He was woken in the pale light of dawn by his wife, Ann Neville. He looked at her in sleepy confusion as she leaned in and took his hand.

'I'm so sorry, Richard. Your brother is dead.'

25

The wind was cold and filled with specks of frost that rattled off armour. The horsemen bore no banners as they might have done on a battlefield. Of the dozen men with Earl Rivers and his charge, three wore the livery of the earl and the remaining nine had gone out from London with the prince. Though the boy was just twelve years old, the prince was tall and slender, a reed among oaks on that road. The news of his father's death had reached them only a day before and still showed on their expressions. No one had expected that tree to fall. As the oldest son and heir, Edward had become king in that moment. In time, he would be surrounded by the trappings and men of his rise in status. For the moment, it was as if nothing had changed and he was hurrying back to London. He would not be crowned until he stood before the Archbishop of Canterbury and all his lords.

Edward had wept the night before, until Earl Rivers took him aside and had a stern word with him. His father was not yet in the ground and if his shade still hovered close about them, he would certainly not want to see snivelling. Rivers was not at his best when comforting a child, though it had an effect. Edward had rubbed away his tears and worn a stiff expression ever since, so as not to shame his father's memory.

The prince had been at Ludlow Castle for a little over a year, not counting the previous Christmas when he'd met his sisters and seen his father fall in that great paroxysm. He had seen the king drunk before of course, weeping or singing, then dropping into slumber like a great bear, snoring where he lay. Young Edward had not thought it was the beginning of a decline, that his giant of a father would not somehow leap up again and laugh at all their fears. It was impossible that such a man was not there, even to scorn his weak arms and tell him to use the sword posts more often.

Edward twitched his head as if a fly had settled on him. He could not afford to weep, Uncle Rivers had made that clear. From that moment, men would no longer look to him to see how he developed into a man, but to see whether he had the strength of will to be a king. It was an entirely different judgement and Edward could only stare back and try to hide the way he quailed from their gaze.

'Riders ahead,' one of his uncle's men said suddenly. The words of warning had the effect of changing their formation on the road. Two of them lurched forward and drew swords, while the rest made a diamond around Edward, pressing so close that even an arrow would hit them before it struck the boy. He could smell their sweat and the oil of their armour and he was afraid, made more so as they reined in slowly and steadily, coming from a trot to a walk, then halting in the road. Edward peered through those ahead, watching as Rivers clicked in his throat and took his great black warhorse a few lengths further.

Beyond their small group, a line of horsemen blocked the road. They too wore armour, painted dark-green or black, it was hard to tell in the fading light. Only one carried a torch aloft and the rest vanished into blurring darkness. Edward craned around the bulk of one of his guards to see Earl Rivers approach two men sent out to meet him.

'Stand aside,' Rivers ordered clearly. Edward saw his uncle had drawn a long-handled mace from his saddle loop. Rivers spun it in the air, making a humming sound. It was no idle threat, though the two knights facing him did not flinch from it. One of them made a half-grab to catch the thing, missing it by some way. The other pointed to where young Edward watched and Rivers leaned forward and bellowed in anger at him. A furious argument began and Edward called out in shock as one of the knights kicked his mount against his uncle's leg, trapping it. The mace was better used at a distance and Rivers had grown old and slow without realizing. He brought the iron head down on a shoulder plate with a terrible crack, but the young knight shrugged it off. Earl Rivers had his head rocked back by a swinging punch, then another. Blood spattered as his eyes rolled, dazed. Swords were drawn then, as he fell, both by the first pair and all those behind. That grating whisper said more than anything else how many of them waited out of the torchlight.

The captain of Edward's guards turned in the saddle, leaning as close to the prince as he could.

'Step down, son. Quickly now. Just walk into the trees and bracken by the road. There's a chance they won't even see you go. Go on. We'll fight to delay them.'

Edward stared, wide-eyed and unable to move as the lines ahead came spurring forward, filling the road. If there had been a moment to escape, it was gone.

'Don't fight, Sir Derby, please,' he said. 'I do not want to see you killed.'

The knight grimaced, but he was already surrounded. Reluctantly, he bowed his head and held out his sword to one of the dark armoured men, hilt first in surrender. At Derby's nod, the rest of them dismounted with varying degrees of frustration and dismay showing. They handed over their weapons to those who reached for them, moving with the captain to stand at the side of the road.

Richard of Gloucester came forward then from the

second rank of his men. Unlike the rest of them, he wore polished armour, gleaming like silver moonlight and making a fine show. He wore no helmet and as he looked down on the slim figure of his nephew, he breathed out, pleased.

'Your Highness, I am so very relieved I was in time. Oh, thank *God*.'

'I do not understand, Uncle,' Edward replied. Richard gestured to the knights who had come out from Ludlow with the prince. His gaze rested on Earl Rivers, carried over to lie in the ditch where they stood. Edward's uncle was still unconscious, though stirring.

'Some of these men were under orders, Edward, not to let you reach London alive. I thank the saints I was not too late to save you.'

His words were not spoken quietly and the knights in question responded in immediate anger and disbelief. They gestured and shouted, until they were surrounded by a far greater number of knights bearing swords and axes. They quietened down then, under that threat. One or two had not moved at all, understanding that they had heard their own death sentence.

Earl Rivers had risen to one knee and then regained his feet in the middle of the shouting. He stood, a little shaky still. As a man who had fought in tourneys all his life, he was used to coming round from a blow.

'What is this?' Rivers called. 'Gloucester? Is that you, Richard? Let me pass, my lord. I am bringing the prince to London to be crowned. No, by hell, my wits are half knocked out of me. I am bringing the king! King Edward. Get out of our path and I will say nothing more of this madness.' The earl looked wary as he spoke and Richard tutted at him, making him narrow his eyes further.

'My lord, it is no good,' Richard said in reproof. 'Your plan has been discovered. Your conspirators have betrayed you – and the foul murder of my nephew that you planned.'

'You lying bastard,' Rivers said clearly. Richard shook his head in sadness.

'I must protect my brother's son, my lord. You will be taken from here to a place of execution, as a warning to all men who might conspire against the royal line.'

'You *dare*, Gloucester? Where is my trial? My right to speak before my peers? To even know the accusations made against me? Why should anyone take *your* word, Richard Plantagenet?'

'These are dark times, Lord Rivers! Dark days. I have discovered this cruel conspiracy before it is too late, or so I hope. I must move as quickly as I can to protect the rightful king of England – my brother's son – so that he can be crowned.' He reached out to the twelve-year-old boy watching the exchange in shock and confusion.

'Come to me, boy,' Richard said softly. 'I will keep you safe.'

When she had been very young, Elizabeth Woodville had known a secret cave on her father's land, a deep pool overhung by mossy cliffs on all sides. It had been a favourite pursuit in the summers to run miles over the Northamptonshire moors with her brothers and sisters, a great laughing troupe of them. They ran until they were hot and sweating and then, without stopping, they would run right over the edge and fall down and down into the green water below. The rest of the afternoon would be spent drying clothes on flat stones or criticizing the young one who had taken the lunch basket into the water with him and ruined the food. It all merged into one memory as Elizabeth looked back, but she could recall that feeling almost perfectly, of rushing up to an edge, of falling, and of fear.

Her stomach clenched in the same way when she heard what Richard of Gloucester had done. The messenger had come on his own initiative, just a young man who had learned something she might want to hear and raced down the London road to deliver it. She had given him two gold angel coins with her husband's face stamped on the metal. The young lad had been delighted, stumbling as he tried to bow and back away at the same time.

Elizabeth remained sitting, looking out over London from the royal rooms in Westminster. Her husband was laid out in Windsor, dressed in armour and white for the last time. She had been to pray with him and kiss his cold cheek. She had held his hands, though they might have been wax without warm blood running through them. Edward had looked smaller in death than in life, the vital spark clearly absent. Yet he had been so much of her youth and hopes that it broke her heart to see him. He would never age.

She touched a locket at her throat, the gold clasp containing a piece of his hair that she had snipped away with silver scissors. She'd tied the lock in a ribbon and it comforted her to know it was there.

She stood then, clapping her hands loudly. Two of her maids came immediately from the room outside, curtseying before her in neat, pressed skirts and blouses.

'Now don't make a fuss,' Elizabeth said. 'Just gather up the girls and young Richard. He is somewhere on the grounds here. Bring them back to me and pass word to Jenny that I will need to pack clothes for them all. Very quick it has to be, girls. Quick and silent, as if we are running away from home. Do you understand? Can I trust you to be discreet? I don't want to rouse the whole palace and half of London.'

'Of course, ma'am,' they both said, bobbing down again. Elizabeth nodded to dismiss them and they raced away. She was twelve years older than the last time she'd run to Sanctuary, though she had not forgotten those five months spent with monks. To her shame, she had hardly thought of them since then. Was Brother Paul still the guardian of the door? Her great bullock of a husband had knocked the monk down for standing in his way when he'd come for her, she remembered, recalling some of that old joy, now always accompanied by grief. How could Edward be gone? How could it be that she would never hear his booming voice again, or hear his arguments, or watch in astonishment as he kicked some item out of the way when he paced around and caught it with his foot? For all his noise and presence and reluctance to bathe, she had loved him. Perhaps not as well as he'd deserved, she did not know. It was a private thing and she'd borne ten children for him, which was love enough for most. She'd seen how their daughter Mary's death the year before had hurt him, though he'd tried to be cold and careless, telling them all that death was just a part of life.

She found herself weeping suddenly, without warning, so that her children came in to find her clutching a handkerchief and dabbing at her eyes. Young Elizabeth came to her side immediately, embracing her and making her smile through her tears. The rest of them crowded around her, trying to add their strength too so that they formed a great bundle of arms. Five surviving daughters and young Richard. God had blessed her beyond all measure, she realized. If she could only keep them all alive.

The youngest girl, Bridget, was only three and had toddled in with a nurse in tow. Elizabeth smiled at the young woman, pink-cheeked, who brushed a tendril of hair from her face with the back of one hand, while expertly steering the child away from the fireplace.

'Did Lucy and Margaret say, dear?' Elizabeth said. 'I'll

need clothes and toys for them all, packed up immediately. Within the hour.'

'Shall I call for carriages, my lady?'

'No, dear. I will take the children on foot into Sanctuary, across the road by the Abbey. Unfortunately, I do know the way.'

Elizabeth comforted her daughters Cecily and Catherine, sending them to gather their most important dolls and toys, whatever they could not bear to leave behind. They came running back to pile items together where they were packed up by serving men from the kitchens and workshops, coming in by the dozen to take the bags away.

Elizabeth was able to stand to one side and stare once more out of the windows. Her son Edward had been saved by Richard of Gloucester from a plot against his life. That was what she had been told by the messenger. The young rider had been delighted to discover he was first with the news, though it had clutched at her heart like those moments in the air above the water, just falling, falling.

Her brother Anthony Woodville, Earl Rivers, was so steadfast that the very idea of him plotting against his sister's children almost made her smile. Anthony doted on them all and he had been utterly loyal to Edward, even when Warwick's Nevilles were entwined about the king like some pale and stinging vine. Elizabeth did not doubt her brother's loyalty, no matter what was reported. That meant she was in danger – and that her son and her brother might already be lost.

She bit her lip, hard enough to make the tissues swell as if she had been struck.

Richard Plantagenet, Duke of Gloucester, had revealed himself as the danger. Worse, she had not seen it in him. His adoration of his brother had been so completely innocent and without guile that she had sensed no threat from that quarter at all. The thought of young Edward in Gloucester's grasp, in his *power*, made her breathe shallowly, struggling to hold back panic.

Her gaze fell to her second son by King Edward, the boy Richard grinning at something his sister Cecily had said or done. As his mother watched him, he nudged Cecily so that she fell over a pile of bags with a squawk, then launched herself after him as he dodged all the servants coming in and out, laughing as he went. Elizabeth feared for them all.

'Faster, please,' she called to the servants. 'I believe I will take my children on before. Please follow after us, with the rest of our things.'

Elizabeth took young Richard's hand as he raced past her, pulling him up short. He was nine years old and could be as rude as any stable boy when he chose, even to his mother. Yet he sensed something of her seriousness and stood still, glowering in expectation of some punishment. There was no point beating him, she had realized. The boy soaked it up like a rug and did a superb job of appearing not to care. It stung her hand more when she slapped him and she hardly troubled to any longer as a result. She still *threatened* to slap the cheek out of him, of course. In turn, he pretended to take her more seriously than he actually did.

She felt his hand squirming and took a stronger grip. Young Edward had been so much easier than this little devil, she thought. God, let him live. Please, let him survive his uncle.

'Come along, children, all of you,' Elizabeth said firmly. 'Pick up young Bridget, would you, dear? It's too far for her to walk and I cannot wait.'

With all her Plantagenet children following like geese, Elizabeth kept her head high as she walked out of the room, heading for the Abbey across the road and the little fortress that was both a refuge and a prison, for a second time. As she went, she prayed, and all the while she struggled not to sob.

Richard of Gloucester returned to London at the head of two hundred knights, a force of men that could charge down any threat that faced them. Lord Buckingham waited with another forty men at the Moorgate, keeping it open. As a result, Gloucester came through without slowing from a canter, though Londoners had to scatter or be trampled. Richard had learned from what had gone before. The mistakes of the past could be avoided and it gave him a grim satisfaction to plan his counters before the obstacles even came about. Life went more smoothly when he saw the ditches coming, Richard had realized. He had a moment to nod to Buckingham as he shot past him.

Nothing cleared a street quite so well as the clattering roar of two hundred horsemen coming in fast and hard. The uncrowned king sat a horse in the centre of the column, head down and staring ahead as they drove on across the city, riding for the Tower.

Gloucester was the Lord Protector and in a crisis, his word was the closest thing to law. He had three men race ahead at full gallop along narrowing streets, yelling for the traders and people to get out of their way or be trampled. Cries of pain dwindled behind as the rest went on, the sound changing as they crossed on to stones. That was a tumult that built and built as more of them came off the mud of the smaller streets and reached the cobbles.

Those at the Tower gatehouse had seen them. The riders Richard had sent ahead had done their work so that the gate stood open there as well. There was almost a joy to it, to see the whole world falling into place like a puzzle solved.

The Lord Protector and his royal charge crossed the drawbridge and the gatehouse and clattered into the courtyard beyond, going deeper in towards the White Tower to give the others room to halt their mounts and stand, panting.

Richard dismounted and walked to where his nephew sat high in his stirrups, his horse still wanting to bolt after such a terrifying run through the close streets. The Lord Protector stroked its nose and patted the animal, soothing the horse and perhaps its frightened rider.

'There now, there now, you are safe here. There is a royal apartment that has not been used for a few years. Your father preferred the rooms in the Palace at Westminster, though I always liked the Tower more, I think.'

'What about my mother?' Edward asked. 'My brother and my sisters?' His voice cracked as he spoke, though he was trying hard to be brave. Richard held up both hands and helped him down to the ground, then brushed some specks of mud from his shoulders and his cheek.

'I cannot say they are safe, Edward, not yet. When I heard there was a threat to you, I rode north, just as fast as I could. I went to save you first. You are the heir – the king.'

'But you will find them as well? You'll bring them to me?'

'I will do my best, Edward, yes,' his uncle said. 'I promise you that. Go on with these men now and let them search your rooms before you enter them. Oh, have no fear, lad! I am jumping at shadows, nothing more. I will rest easy when you are crowned, but not till then.'

He patted his nephew on his shoulder and kissed the top of his head. Edward looked back, trying to be brave as he was led away by strangers, stone walls looming over them all.

26

Richard of Gloucester paced the length of the table, so that the six seated men had to turn their heads back and forth to watch him. They had come at his summons to the Palace of Westminster and its Painted Chamber. Despite their great status, therefore, they waited on the Lord Protector's pleasure. Richard strode up and down before them like a schoolmaster, with his hands clasped behind his back. He wore a fine doublet of gold and black over hose, with a silver-hilted sword at his waist. At thirty years of age, he could still stalk like a furious swordsman, threat radiating from him. The Archbishop of Canterbury was put in mind of his cat and almost looked for a lashing tail as Richard passed by. He kept his peace however.

As Lord Protector, Richard of Gloucester had been given royal power with no clear limits, or rather limits he could define himself in emergencies, which amounted to the same thing. The documents with his brother's Great Seal had been lodged with Parliament and the Tower archives days before the king's death. Richard's authority could not be denied. His source of irritation was that somehow it had been denied even so. Three of the Council at that table answered to a higher authority even than the Seal of England and the Lord Protector.

Richard stopped suddenly, his glare an accusation in itself. Archbishop Bourchier of Canterbury was eighty if he was a day, an ancient who seemed to have retained his wits, with enormous white eyebrows. The archbishop could communicate much with just a glance at Archbishop Rotheram of York. It was rare for the two most senior churchmen in England to be summoned to the same room, unless it was to crown a king. Both of them seemed to understand very well what was at stake.

Lord Buckingham was there to support Richard against the others, to cast a vote or simply provide another voice to win a point. At twenty-nine, young Buckingham had simply appeared around the new heart of power in London. He seemed willing enough to be led by the nose. He and Richard had been born around the same time, the archbishop decided. Perhaps they shared a sensibility, a kinship or an awareness that some of the whitebeards in that room had forgotten. Or perhaps Buckingham merely saw an opportunity to rise, like a man putting all his wages on a particular dog in a fight.

Neither Richard of Gloucester nor Archbishop Bourchier liked the Bishop of Ely, John Morton. The man was too worldly to please the archbishop – and too religious to please the lords. Either way, Morton was certainly too clever for his own good.

In the same way, Richard had little sense of support from Baron Hastings, still his brother's Lord Chamberlain until a new king chose another. Hastings had been there for the battles of both Barnet and Tewkesbury. The old sod really should have been on Richard's side, arguing for him, not crossing his arms and narrowing his eyes like a suspicious old washerwoman. It was infuriating.

The last of the men at that table was Thomas, Lord Stanley, with a beard that was still dark brown, though it rested on the table and was at least as long as those of the archbishops. Richard smiled on him as a man of great wealth who had been one of his brother's supporters in the later years of his reign. Stanley had secured a French payment of seventy thousand each year in return for not invading them again. The baron liked nothing more than to speak of his private force of men, which he maintained all year round as Warwick had done years before. It cost Stanley a fortune but he had been unusually skilled at the gathering of wealth to his coffers. For his understanding of finances alone, the man deserved respect and Richard intended to flatter Stanley to his side, so that he might benefit as his brother had.

The Painted Chamber was some eighty feet long and thirty wide, with enough space up to the vaulted ceiling to echo back the sounds of conversation. It was odd then to have so many men of power and influence look uneasily at one another in silence rather than answer his points. Hastings and Stanley in particular seemed willing to defer to the men of the cloth, though the three of them had proven quite unable to answer him.

'In this room,' Richard said, 'I see assembled before me some of the most senior men of the Church in England. The Archbishops of York and Canterbury – and a bishop renowned for his fine understanding! I would have imagined I'd be spoiled for learned opinions and rulings, not forced to endure this awkward hush. Perhaps I should have asked how many angels could dance on the head of a pin, or the exact nature of the trinity. You would not have been so quiet then.' Richard leaned over the table and it was no accident that he had come to rest opposite the Bishop of Ely. Of all the men there, Morton had the sharpest mind. Richard had heard he was tipped for Archbishop of Canterbury when the post came free, perhaps even to become a cardinal in Rome.

The bishop cleared his throat under the pale scrutiny of the Lord Protector. Morton had no desire to make a ruling that might later be shown to be wrong or illegal, but it was also clear that no one else would be drawn on the matter.

'My lord, it is my understanding that there are *no* exceptions to the protections of sanctuary, not that I have ever heard. You say you have been informed of a threat to the young Prince of York in Westminster Abbey with his mother and his sisters.'

'I say that because it is true, Your Grace,' Richard replied sharply. He could see the objection coming as the man formed it.

'Yes, so you have said. The difficulty is not in my assessment of that threat, as I am trying to explain. There are no exceptions in canon law over sanctuary, not once it has been granted or accepted. Even if the prince is truly in danger and that danger might be averted by taking him out of sanctuary . . . I'm sorry, my lord. The means to do it do not exist. I would be happy to write to Rome, of course, to seek advice and guidance in this matter.'

'I rather think it will have been resolved by then, one way or another,' Richard snapped. He found he was breathing hard in his anger. He watched as the bishop spread his hands as if in apology.

'The boy is nine years old,' Richard added suddenly. 'He was taken into sanctuary at Westminster Abbey by his mother, without any sense of the dangers they might face. At the Tower, I have hundreds of guards and high walls – at the Abbey, why that small stone block could be overrun with half a dozen men. So tell me why I cannot remove *my own nephew* for his safety? If you need a decision from the authority of the Crown, I rule that his mother protected *herself* when she ran to that place. Her children are not included in the shadow of sanctuary, how could they be?'

'They are inside,' the Archbishop of Canterbury said suddenly, sitting up. 'They have crossed the boundary. It matters nothing whether their mother intended them to come along or sought to protect them. Sanctuary is consecrated ground, intended as a place of safety for those who are oppressed by enemies. It is an ancient and valuable tradition and certainly not one that can be set aside when it is merely inconvenient.' His mouth worked in anger, as if he teased a piece of meat from between his back teeth. 'If there is so terrible a threat to the boy, you may try to persuade his mother to give him into your care. You may *not* enter yourself, however. Nor any man bearing a weapon. You may certainly not bring out the boy by force.'

Richard shook his head, half exasperated and half amused at the source of the resistance. He was a little surprised to have such an old man wake up long enough to challenge him in anything.

'Your Grace, I have a son of my own, not far from the same age. If he was surrounded by men intent on his murder, and if I had a chance to save him, I would dare anything. I would take him from his mother's own arms.'

'And you would be damned for all eternity.'

'Yes, Your Grace. I would be damned, but I would have saved my son, do you see? This Richard is my brother's son. Every day that passes brings whispers of new plots. Yet I cannot keep him safe in a place where only good men fear to tread! I have young Edward behind the Tower's walls, aye, and with a hundred men to watch those walls and each other. The most skilful assassin could not reach Edward where he lays his head tonight, but his brother? A few monks will not stop evil men, Your Grace.'

'I understand what you have said, I think,' the old man answered. He pulled at his beard, tugging unconsciously at the locks in old habit. 'You wish to protect the boy – and perhaps to give both sons the comfort of one another's presence.'

'In the safest fortress in England, yes, Your Grace. My

brother Edward made me his Lord Protector and left all he had to that protection: his goods, his heirs and his realm. All I ask is that you retrieve the missing part, before more blood is shed.'

The old man blinked at the last of Richard's words, not quite ready to ask if it was a threat or a reference to the plots Richard had mentioned. The archbishop could only imagine the horror and condemnation he would face if he refused and then the child was slaughtered with his mother and sisters. Yet even to allow that sanctuary could not protect the family without armed men was to weaken the authority of the Church.

He was silent a long time, so that the others fidgeted. At last, Archbishop Bourchier nodded into his beard and his hands became still.

'I will enter Sanctuary, my lord. I will enter and I will speak to Queen Elizabeth about her son. If she refuses, I can do nothing more.'

'Thank you, Your Grace. I am certain that will be enough,' Richard replied.

In the darkness, the Archbishop of Canterbury found his path lit by men bearing torches. He could not carry a crozier, with its shepherd's crook. The weight had become too much for him over the previous year. Instead, he rested on a walking stick of oak. The tip was of coiled leather and he tap-tapped along the damp and shining stones, looking ahead to Sanctuary with the Abbey at his back.

Archbishop Bourchier had found little to like in Richard of Gloucester, though he supposed the fellow was admirable enough for the care he was taking to protect his nephews. It troubled some part of the old man how little mention had been made of Elizabeth Woodville and her daughters. They could not inherit, of course. The female line was the weaker of the two, as it had been since Eden. Archbishop Bourchier nodded his head as he followed the stone path, thinking of all the evil seeds women had created since then. Poor benighted creatures, he thought. His mother excepted, of course. She had been a stern and wonderful woman, free with her backhand, but so proud when her son had taken holy orders that she could hardly see for tears.

Ahead, Archbishop Bourchier saw the glint of men moving in armour, like beetles creeping away, over and under each other as the lamplight came close. He hesitated, unwilling to approach and pleased to take a moment to just stand and catch his breath before all the young men around him who had never known weakness or old age.

'Who is that there?' he said, pointing with his stick. 'By the Abbey Sanctuary? What violent fellows are those?'

'Lord Gloucester's men, Your Grace,' one of those around him replied. 'There is word of an assassin from the land of the Turks or the Tartars.'

Archbishop Bourchier touched a hand to the crucifix at his throat. It contained a tiny fragment of the true cross and he took comfort from it. He had read much in his lifetime and had heard of such men and their cruelty. He set his jaw, taking a firm grip on his stick. He could play a part, still.

'Lay on, gentlemen,' he said, shuffling ahead.

The archbishop approached Sanctuary with bulldog stubbornness, bent over his stick, but never slowing until he reached the door and saw the young monk watching from inside. Two men-at-arms in mail stepped back as he approached, waiting patiently. Archbishop Bourchier saw the Lord Protector's men were two or three deep in all directions. There had to have been two hundred soldiers around that Sanctuary, presumably with more nearby for when the shifts changed. The old man understood afresh what it cost the Lord Protector to split his resources between two parts of London, each a mile from the other.

Archbishop Bourchier looked up at the stairs in concern as he entered. He was relieved when a monk ushered him along a corridor on the ground floor, panelled in some dark and polished wood. The old man had never before entered that place and he was intrigued by it. Most small churches or chapels set some constraint on giving refuge to criminals. It was usually a month or forty days, after which they could choose exile. Such things had to be, he knew, or they would have been overrun each winter with poor men who had fallen foul of the law. Yet the Abbey at Westminster was the greatest church in the land. Sanctuary there had no limit, once admitted. Such a place was a hallmark of civilisation, he thought, a shining light.

The archbishop clenched his jaw at that thought, recalling the abbey at Tewkesbury, where King Edward had broken faith with one of the oldest traditions of the Church and sent men to murder his cowering enemies. The entire building and grounds had needed to be reconsecrated after that. It was not just the blood that had to be scrubbed from the stones, but the mortal sins committed within its walls. Edward had paid a fortune in reparations in the years afterward. Archbishop Bourchier had been rather disappointed when the Church had accepted those vast sums. It seemed to him to have been a rather tawdry exchange for the breach of trust.

Such were the archbishop's thoughts as he entered through a door held for him into the presence of Queen Elizabeth and her children. The old man's gaze flickered from one to the next until it rested on the nine-year-old Richard of York. The boy's status had been recognized by his father from birth. Young Richard had been the recipient not just of the

Dukedom of York, but of the Earldoms of Norfolk and Nottingham as well.

The child was well made, the Archbishop noted, without pox scars or any sign of diseases. It meant perhaps he would endure them yet, of course. That was the great balance-scale of a life, that to be marked was to survive. Those who were not marked could yet be snatched away in the night. Death was always there in the laughter of children. Every parent knew that only too well.

Those particular children were a most attractive group, the archbishop saw. A chair was brought for him by a crackling fire and he sank into it gratefully. With a smile, he accepted a bowl of walnuts and a glass of brandy against the night's cold. He sat back and remembered when he'd had enough blood in him to sweat instead of being the dry old bone he'd become.

'Your Grace, you are most welcome,' Elizabeth said. 'Do you have word of those men who are ringed around this place? They will not speak to me, nor will they let anyone in or out for days now. I have had no news at all of the world.'

'Perhaps you should send these dear, delightful children away, my lady, yes? I think that would be best.'

Elizabeth's face grew strained at that, but she did as he asked, sending them all to other rooms so that she was alone with the old man. She cracked another walnut for the archbishop and placed the pieces where he could easily reach them.

'Richard of Gloucester is a most determined young man,' Archbishop Bourchier said into silence broken only by flames and crackling sap. 'It is not easy to discern his most secret heart. I offered to hear his confession, but he said he uses some country priest for such things. That is a shame. It would have helped me decide what I have to say to you.'

'He wants my son,' Elizabeth said, her face crumpling. 'That much I learned before the soldiers came here.'

'He wants to keep him safe, my lady,' the archbishop confirmed, chewing carefully on a piece of nut.

'From whom? His own men? Who else could come against me here, with all his soldiers clanking and muttering all night? I tell you I have not slept a wink since they surrounded Sanctuary. If this place can deserve such a name when it is encircled by iron and cruel soldiers!'

'Be calm, my dear. There is no point in . . . shrill voices. There is no need to panic and allow our thoughts to run to madness. No. Let us decide instead what is best for your boy. To remain here, at a cost I can barely imagine, taking vital men from the defence of the city and England, or to go to the Tower to be with his brother Edward.'

'You have seen him?' Elizabeth broke in. The old man nodded.

'I insisted on it, yes. Your son is in good health and spirits, though lonely. He sees no one and though he reads, there are only a few of his father's books there. He is enjoying some history of the Caesars, I believe. Such terrible lives of violence and betrayal! Yet boys feast on such things, of course. There is no harm in it.'

Some tension went out of Elizabeth at his words.

'Would you trust Gloucester in this, Your Grace? To put my son on the throne and keep safe the other? That is the heart of it, is it not?'

The old man looked into the flames for a time. His mouth worked all the while and he spat a small piece of shell on to his palm when he was done.

'I do not see that you have a choice, my lady. The Lord Protector was insistent and you'll recall that his brother did not hold back from entering consecrated ground before. It grieves me even to say such a thing, my lady, but I fear for your son if he remains here. It has become an obsession of Gloucester's to bring him out. Listen to me. You must trust someone. I will be there to see all is well, never fear for that.'

Elizabeth glanced at the white-bearded old man, wondering what hindrance Archbishop Bourchier thought he could possibly be to violent men. She had not said how close the soldiers came at night, when the monks were all asleep. They truly were creatures of blood and filth and violence and they stood beneath her window and crept about, clanking and whispering threats until she thought they would surely come in. She knew they could, that such things had happened and been covered up. She feared for herself, but also for her daughters. The men at her window made worse and worse threats. She had told no one of that, but she could not bear it any longer. Elizabeth could hardly remember when she had slept for more than a few moments, startled awake by calling voices and ugly laughter.

She stared back at Archbishop Bourchier as he reached for the nutcrackers and fumbled them in his old hands. The decision was hers, though she felt squeezed as well, gripped perhaps to breaking. Sanctuary was surrounded by armed men and it was too easy to imagine an assassin amongst them, a man run berserk for some old imagined slight or injury. If she was murdered, if her daughters were injured and killed like lambs, it would be the talk of the realm and all fingers would point to the Lord Protector – but that would not undo a single wound.

On one side, she had such terrible fears that stirred like creeping things in her thoughts whenever she pressed her exhausted head on to a pillow. Yet it was all unproven! Her son Edward still lived and would be crowned. Had she misjudged Richard of Gloucester? He had called her brother a traitor and all news of Anthony had ceased from that point. She swallowed at the thought that Rivers might not be alive even then, unknown to her.

'These men who surround me here,' she said softly. 'Will they go with my son?'

'They are here only for his protection, my lady. I will insist on it, if you wish.'

Elizabeth felt her eyes fill with tears at his faith, as if the old priest could simply wave a hand and of course evil men would walk away and never threaten her again. Still, she grasped at the chance. She chose: all her daughters over one more son. In hope and uncertain desperation, she chose.

'Very well, Your Grace. I will pass Richard into your care. I will trust you, and the Lord Protector, to do honest duty by a nine-year-old boy.' Tears spilled from her and ran down her cheeks in two streams though she wiped at them. She called for her son and Prince Richard came running in, seeing his mother's distress and looking in anger at the old man who seemed to have caused it. The little boy clambered into his mother's lap and curled up there, holding her tightly as she wept into his hair and kissed him.

'What's wrong? Why are you crying?' he said, looking close to tears himself.

'I'm sending you to see your brother Edward, that is all. You're not to cry yourself now, Richard! I expect you to be strong – a warrior and a soldier. You are the Duke of York, remember, like your father before you. He trusted you to look after me and your brother.'

She held him tightly for all the time it took for Archbishop Bourchier to rise and gather his stick. The old man smiled and gestured to the boy.

'Come, lad. You're to go with me, it seems. You may have to help me, you know. I am very old. Come now, no snivelling! You must be brave for your mother. Has he a coat or a cloak?'

'By the door,' Elizabeth said. She watched as Richard placed his perfect little hand in the old man's grip, rubbing his eyes clear. She could not bear to see him go, but it was right, she hoped, the best decision she could make. It broke her in two even so, as he turned and waved to her, smiling to raise her spirits. The boy pulled free of the archbishop and raced back then, almost knocking her over in his enthusiasm and the strength of his grip.

'I'll bring Edward back, if they let me,' Richard whispered to her. 'Don't be upset.'

Elizabeth reached down and held him so tightly he could only squirm, then let him go.

27

The Bishop of Bath and Wells looked uncomfortable in such surroundings, or perhaps in the presence of more senior men of the Church. He seemed a timid creature and Richard had not explained his presence, though he sensed the curiosity in the Archbishops of York and Canterbury in particular. Still, they would have to wait on his pleasure.

He had summoned them once more as a Council, as was his right as Lord Protector. On this occasion in June, he had called them across London to the Tower itself. It was busy with repairs and a new barracks being constructed on the central green. London itself was alive and thriving in the warm, with all the signs of a fine summer to come.

Richard watched each man as they arrived: Hastings, Stanley and Buckingham, Bishop Morton of Ely, the Bishop of Bath and Wells and the two archbishops. No one there could say he had not assembled the most senior men of the Church for such a serious occasion. For the oldest men of the cloth, just reaching the council room in the White Tower had been a trial. Archbishop Bourchier mopped his brow freely, making quite a performance of it to show what he had suffered for his duty. Even so, they were all tense with expectation. Private Councils were called rarely enough, to advise the monarch in times of disaster or war. Parliament had been summoned to Westminster for later in the month, but until it sat, the men in that room were the only power in the land. It was true too that each of them was aware of the two princes, not too far from where they sat. There had been no news of them for days, beyond glimpses at the high windows of the Tower staterooms.

'My lords, Your Graces,' Richard began, 'I asked for your presence here in part because I have news that will need to be discussed by wise heads before the mob hears and runs wild with it. I may hold a burning brand tonight. I must be careful where it falls.' He looked around the table at the men he had gathered.

'Archbishop Bourchier has my gratitude for his aid. Thank you, Your Grace. Due to his intercession, when every other path had failed, I was able to bring my nephew to a place of safety. At the same time, I saw no more need to keep such a great presence of armed men on the Abbey grounds. I have heard of no threat to my brother's wife nor to his daughters – certainly nothing that would allow me to interfere in Sanctuary once again. I have already stepped too far on ancient liberties.' He waited for Archbishop Bourchier to nod into his expanse of beard.

'I withdrew all my soldiers, gentlemen. But I left one man to report on anyone else who might slip in and out of Sanctuary, expecting to be unseen. That decision is what brings you here. I am sorry to say there are men who have been observed to carry news and whispers to Elizabeth Woodville. Men who do not yet understand I know their names. Though they will in time, Your Grace.'

'I don't understand,' Archbishop Bourchier said, his eyebrows rising in confusion. 'You are surely not accusing me?' Richard sighed.

'No, Your Grace, of course not. I had not thought to bring this news to you today . . . but perhaps it is time. I find my hand is forced, though I might wish it was any other way but this.'

With a gesture, Richard indicated the quaking Bishop of

Bath and Wells, Robert Stillington. In ordinary times, the man looked like a wise cherub, with wisps of white hair and a round-faced pinkness. In that council chamber, under the gaze of another bishop and both archbishops of England, he was white about the lips and completely out of his depth.

'These men have come at my summons to hear the truth, Robert,' Richard said, indicating the others. 'You must tell them what you told me. This is the moment and the truth must come out, though it breaks my heart. Yet I will insist on light! Carried into all the shadowed corners, so that nothing is left hidden. Nothing!'

'What *is* this?' Bishop Morton said, leaning forward. He seemed more irritated than intrigued and Richard could only stare at the Bishop of Bath and Wells and urge him on in silence. If the old fool refused to speak, he could yet lose them all – and everything else that might follow.

'M-my lords, Archbishops Bourchier and Rotheram, Bishop M-Morton . . .' The recitation of titles seemed to have dried the bishop's mouth. Stillington raised a hand and ran it along the sinews of his neck, as if struggling to swallow. 'Gentlemen, it has fallen to me to bring ill news . . . of an old marriage contract between King Edward IV, or the Earl of March as he was then, and an Eleanor Butler.'

'Oh, Brother, no,' Bishop Morton murmured suddenly. 'Thou wilt be damned for such a lie, for such a calumny.' The man at whom he had spoken went pale and his eyes swivelled left and right in panic.

'Go on, Your Grace,' Richard said in irritation, glaring at Morton. 'You say you witnessed this? A marriage promise, a betrothal. Were you the celebrant?'

The bishop nodded with his eyes shut.

'Two lovers there were, very young, who came before me, laughing and asking to be blessed in marriage before they went to bed. I was but a young priest then and I thought I might prevent a greater sin. I recall their names, though I did not see either of them again after that day. In Northamptonshire, it was.'

'Very *well*,' Bishop Morton snapped. 'Then you must summon this Eleanor Butler before us, that she may be questioned, or put to the irons. For an accusation of such import, I would have it confirmed beyond the meandering memories of an old man.'

'An old man of your own age, I believe, Bishop Morton,' Richard said smoothly. 'Now, I asked the same thing exactly when I heard. I would not believe it. Bring her before me, I said. Sadly, Your Grace, Eleanor Butler died some five years ago. If we had known – if we had *only* known, my brother King Edward could have remarried Elizabeth Woodville and declared all his children legitimate.' He shook his head in sorrow. 'Yet he did not. I can hardly bear the grief I feel, but I will not allow anything to be hidden, my lords! Let us hear the truth and *all* of the truth about this youthful madness of my brother's. God knows, he had mistresses! You all know the truth of that. He had little concern for the wives or daughters of other men and he would tumble them at a whim. In drink, I do not know if he could say himself where he had lain.'

'You have the word of one man for this entire tale?' Bishop Morton asked quietly. 'No witnesses, no wife? Yet if true, it will mean not just that the king's marriage would be annulled, but that his children, *all* his children would be illegitimate.'

Lord Hastings rose slowly to his feet as the full import of the news sank in. Not so nimble of wit as Bishop Morton, he had not jumped ahead as quickly in his understanding. Instead, he had been sitting in growing anger, turning his head back and forth as the men of the cloth debated points as if they were esoteric matters of faith and morals. Hastings could hardly believe what he was hearing.

'You would disinherit them all!' he said, pointing a shaking finger at Richard of Gloucester, the Lord Protector. 'His wife, his heir, *all*. What madness is this? What lies are these?'

'Would you call a bishop of the Church a liar?' Richard responded with equal passion. 'You knew my brother well, Lord Hastings, almost as well as I did myself. Are you saying such a manner of persuasion would have been beyond him? That he would never have talked a young girl into bed with a mere promise, with such a ruse? Can you swear to that?'

Hastings said nothing, though his colour deepened under the stares of the other men. He knew as well as they did that such a thing was possible. It was exactly the sort of error a young man like Edward might have made. He did not believe it even then, simply for the gain it brought to Richard of Gloucester. It was just too perfect, too convenient.

'Be that as it may, you expect me to believe that this doddering old fool came to you when he heard King Edward had died and never before? That he had kept this vile secret for twenty years?' Hastings turned on the Bishop of Bath and Wells, the old man curling in on himself in fear. 'Stillington, did your conscience finally cry out so loudly that it could not be silenced any longer? Does this not have the greasy feel of lies to you?'

'You cannot intimidate a bishop of the Church, my lord,' Richard said firmly. 'Nor should you try. Now listen to me, all of you. Perhaps Hastings has shown us a path, in his anger. There are no servants present. No one but those of us in this room know my brother's marriage was false, his children illegitimate.' Lord Stanley stirred uncomfortably at his elbow and Richard turned on him. 'Oh, I hate to say those words as much as anyone! Yet we could swear an oath, a pact, as solemn as any order of chivalry, or sovereignty, or oath before God. We could swear in blood not to reveal what we know of the succession. To keep it in this room and never beyond this room.' He paused, taking a deep breath and lowering his voice.

'Westminster has known secrets before and will again. Swear this oath with me never to reveal what you have heard – and I will go from here and bring out my nephews from their rooms in this fortress. I will take the elder prince from this place to Westminster to be crowned King Edward the Fifth. Only we will know. Yet if but one of you dissents, I must let the news go out, though it breaks my heart in two.'

The men at that table exchanged glances, but both archbishops were shaking their heads before Richard had finished speaking.

'I cannot give my word to such a lie,' Archbishop Bourchier said firmly. 'My oath of office prevents me, even if I could allow it as a man.'

'Nor I,' Archbishop Rotheram of York added. 'What you ask . . . is impossible.'

Bishop Morton said nothing at all, though he was tensed as if to spring to his feet. Richard closed his eyes and sagged in despair.

'Then there is nothing I can do. I had hoped . . . but, no. The word is out.'

'As you *intended*,' Hastings said suddenly. 'Why would you have this little man bring his accusation to this room if you hoped for it to be suppressed? Why not just keep the secret yourself?'

'My lord, you seem to see my guilt in everything I do,' Richard said, growing angry once more. 'Yet all I have done, all I have *tried* to do is to support my brother's memory and secure the life of his son as he ascends the throne. With an open heart, I read the archives and spoke to hundreds of men who knew my brother and what he might have wanted. This is the result and I did not desire it. Your foul suspicions . . . well, perhaps I understand them well enough.'

Hastings rested his hand on his sword hilt.

'You do? You understand me? Well, to the *devil* with you.'

Lord Stanley and Bishop Morton came to their feet in the same instant that Hastings moved. All three of the men pulled blades, though Stanley cried out for them to stop at the same time. Bishop Morton held a slender dagger and held it to defend himself, backing away a step.

Hastings ignored the shout. He had drawn his sword and he thrust with it right across the table, aiming at Richard's heart.

The tip of the blade reached the Lord Protector as he threw himself to one side, snagging in the gold stripe of his tunic. Speed and his relative youth had saved Richard, though Hastings had not remained still as his first blow failed. Without hesitation, he stalked around the table to finish the work.

'Guards! Treachery!' Buckingham roared. He too had come to his feet at last. Though he looked like a rabbit before a fox, he drew his own sword, lowering it at Hastings to block his path.

'Treachery!' Richard of Gloucester called in turn. His eyes glittered and Hastings scrambled to reach him in a fury as the doors slammed open and men poured into the room. Hastings knocked Buckingham aside, but he was grappled from behind before he could take another step, his sword falling on to the table with a clatter. The Bishop of Bath and Wells cried out in fear at the sudden presence of so many armed men. Lord Stanley almost fell across the old bishop when he too was grabbed and sent sprawling, his sword torn from his grasp. Bishop Morton stood very still with a sword at his throat, handing over his dagger to the hands that reached for it.

The crashes and shouting came to a sudden halt, leaving only the sound of men breathing hard, or groaning under the weight of five or six bearing down on them so they could not move.

'I am the Lord Protector of England,' Richard said clearly. 'Appointed by my brother, King Edward. On my order, arrest William, Lord Hastings, on charges of treason and conspiracy against the person of the king.'

'You lie so easily, I wonder if your brother knew you at all,' Hastings said.

Richard's colour deepened. He stepped closer to Hastings and though the man struggled, he was held so tightly he could not move an inch.

'How many times have you gone into the Sanctuary fortress of Westminster Abbey, William? Since the death of my brother at Easter? Before and after I had my men surround that place – over these six weeks or so, how many times would you say?'

Hastings curled his lip.

'So you have spies watching the place. What is that to me? I am a free man and no conspirator. It is no business of yours how many times I have entered that place.'

'And your mistress?' Richard went on. 'Jane Shore? How many times would you say she has crept along those paths and slipped inside, at all hours, even with the stars overhead. I wonder what messages she held that could not bear the light of day, like any conspiracy. What do you say about her, my lord?'

Hastings had swollen in the grip of the men holding him, as if he held in soaring emotions. His face had darkened almost to purple and those around him could see the webs of veins on his cheeks and his nose.

'I say it is no business of yours, Gloucester, no, not even if you make it sound like an accusation! My mistress, my sister, myself – no one who knows me can say I am anything but loyal. Your brother trusted me. How can you accuse me now? What does it gain you? For God's sake, Richard, *please*. Let us forget today and what has been said.'

'I wish I could, my lord,' Richard said. 'But you have not walked your way to the end of the path, do you see it yet? Do you see?' There was only desperate confusion in Lord Hastings and Richard shook his head in sorrow.

'You would put my brother's son on the throne.'

'I *would*, I swear it,' Hastings said.

'Ah, but my brother's son is not the heir. Neither Edward nor Richard. We know now that their father's marriage was a lie, so my nephews cannot inherit. Without them, who stands next to be king of England, William? Who is it who stands before you and calls you traitor? Can you see it yet?'

'You,' Hastings said. He seemed to deflate as he spoke, as if that one word had taken all the passion out of him.

'Me,' the Lord Protector confirmed. 'Though I might wish it was any other way but this. I cannot undo my brother's mistakes. All I can do is accept his crown and may God have mercy on my soul. I would rather this cup be taken from me, but if it cannot be . . . I will drink from it.'

Every eye in that room was on him and Richard bowed his head, visibly exhausted and saddened.

'Take my lord Hastings away now. By his own word, he has admitted to conspiracy against me. I do not know how many stand with him, or what power they have gathered. Wait for me below, gentlemen. I will speak to him again before I leave this place.' Hastings was taken outside. He went in stunned disbelief, leaving the room without looking back.

Richard turned then to Lord Stanley and signalled to the soldiers to let him stand. The man spoke as soon as he was up.

'My lord, I had no part in any conspiracy, of any kind. I have always been loyal and your brother trusted me completely.'

'My brother trusted Hastings,' Richard said.

'Even so, I have not been anywhere near Westminster Sanctuary since the king's death. I have played no part. If you have spies there, you know I speak the truth.' Lord Stanley waited, sweating, knowing that his life depended on the answer he received. After a time, Richard nodded once.

'I had no intent to arrest you, Thomas. You drew your sword, however. Morton too, waving his eating knife around. What was I to think?'

The Bishop of Ely had watched in fierce concentration. He saw his chance and stepped forward.

'I must apologize, Your Highness. I did not understand all that was going on around me. Like Lord Stanley, I drew my knife in fear and stepped back, thinking only to save my own neck.'

Richard smiled at the bishop as Stanley went on quickly. 'The bishop has the right of it. I moved only in reaction to Hastings. I thought nothing of it until I held my sword in my hand.'

Both men were sweating, Richard could see, very aware that he could have them killed with just a word. Yet Morton had called him 'Highness' and as for Stanley, his brother had said he was to be trusted. Richard made a quick decision.

'You are both men of action then – and that is to the good. Morton, any hurt is forgiven. Stanley, I have need of a new treasurer in England, to raise the funds that make possible all the rest. Will you accept?'

Stanley's eyes widened and he went down on one knee.

'I will of course, my lord. It would be my honour.'

The men around him shuffled back a distance, aware that they had laid hands on a man of considerable power who was clearly going to leave the room with more. There was suddenly not one soldier present who would meet Lord Stanley's eyes. Richard smiled to see it. He turned then to Buckingham, who had watched it all.

'There are conspiracies to be burned out still, my lord Buckingham. I will need a Constable of England, as well as a treasurer. Without gold, there can be no law. Without law, there can be no safety. It is all of a piece.'

Before Buckingham could do any more than stammer his pleasure and thanks, Richard crossed to where the Archbishops of York and Canterbury still sat. Neither man could rise easily, nor walk without a cane. Richard leaned on his fists and then lower, so he resembled a hawk or a wolf tensing to leap.

'Your Graces, Archbishops Bourchier and Rotheram, you have shown your integrity here today. When I contemplated keeping a false oath, it was a moment of weakness that shames me. I fell short and I will confess it as a sin. Yet you both held firm and showed me the moral strength for which you are renowned. Now there are no shadows left, no plots and secrets.' The old men were watching him closely, Richard saw. He looked back with wide and innocent eyes.

'My brother's sons cannot be king, not now, Your Graces, not after what we have heard. If there was a moment to cast a shroud over it all, that has passed, before all these witnesses. Yet if I am to be king, I am still Lord Protector today. There are plots still – men who call Lancaster their master, though some think they are left in rags. My nephews are safe in the Tower – and I am safe with armed men at my back. Archbishop Bourchier, will you crown a son of York, Your Grace? If I ask, will you crown me as King Richard the Third?'

The archbishop had seen events whirl past with astonishing speed, but he understood there was one man in that room who would not be denied. The fate of Hastings could hardly have been a better lesson for anyone with eyes to see.

'Of course, Your Highness,' he said softly.

The more elderly of the men within the White Tower left with care down the steps to the ground below. Richard had waited behind until he was alone with Robert Stillington. The Bishop of Bath and Wells had been terrified as Richard put an arm around him and summoned a writing table and a jug of good ale to give him strength. The Lord Protector had left the man scribbling away and came lightly down the steps to the great yard of the Tower. He paused on the lowest step and breathed in the warm day, turning his face to the sun. Old men died only too often and he needed Stillington to testify to Parliament. Richard knew he would yet face argument and dissent, there was little doubt, but as with the gate to London he had kept open, such things could be foreseen. He would have Stillington kept under close guard until Parliament gathered in Westminster. If fate or some enterprising murderer found a way to reach the old man, the Lord Protector would still have his sworn testimony, sealed with his ring and signature. All obstacles could be avoided, he thought.

A little way beyond the White Tower, Richard saw a group of soldiers had waited on his orders, as he had asked. Lord Hastings stood with them, disarmed though standing without any obvious restraint. Richard made a tutting sound. It was astonishing how the common soldiery stood in awe of his lords – or perhaps they were men who had known Hastings personally. The baron had high standing, so it was said.

Richard approached the group with confidence. Hastings raised his head, ready for some new accusation or perhaps a deal to be brokered between them. Richard smiled, enjoying the sun.

'I am sorry, Hastings. Sorry to have kept you waiting. Sorry for what you must now endure.' Richard signalled to the soldiers at Hastings's back. They took his arms and though he shouted in surprise and anger, they walked him a dozen yards and kicked his legs out from under him. He fell forward in their grasp, staring in astonishment at the builder's beam left out on the grass in front of him.

'What is this? Gloucester! Where is my trial, you whoreson? Where is justice?'

'This is justice for a traitor, my lord. As I said, I am sorry, but I must send a message to all those who think me too weak. This will serve.'

Hastings tried to speak again, but the men holding him pressed him down so that his throat lay across the beam.

'Wait,' Richard said. 'My lord, would you like to confess? I can fetch a priest for the task.'

Hastings was allowed to rise up on his knees. He saw no mercy in Richard's gaze and he became resigned, nodding briefly. He too turned to feel the sun on his face for the last time. The Lord Protector removed himself some distance while a priest was found and knelt with William, Lord Hastings, hearing his muttered sins and offering forgiveness. It took an hour before the man rose on stiff legs and bowed to Hastings and then to the Lord Protector. The priest did not like what he saw in the faces of the soldiers and he hurried away then.

When Richard returned, he saw a kind of peace had come to Hastings. The man looked up calmly enough when he saw it was time. He stretched his neck well on the beam and did not flinch as the axe was brought down.

'God be with you,' Richard said, crossing himself.

28

London seemed quiet that June, though the sun was hot and trade was brisk enough on the river. Not many of the common subjects knew the discussions that went on right across the capital in every great house. The men of Parliament had been called to Westminster from all the shires and cities and market towns, as so often before. Yet the talk did not begin as they arrived in dribs and drabs. It went on and on in private. In many senses, the true conversation would end as they took their seats in Westminster.

On the Sunday before they met, the Lord Protector rode out with his friend Buckingham and a great procession of lords and senior men. They gathered first at the Tower, where the princes were observed by all in the central yard, shooting arrows at a butt and tipping their hats to any lords who peered in at them.

The riding party set off at noon, with the Lord Protector and his personal guard at their head. Richard's banners were held high enough to be on a battlefield, though they rode only to the west of the city, up Aldgate Street to the stocks market at Cornhill then the Poultry and across to the wide road of Cheapside and Ludgate Hill, where fifty-two goldsmiths had fine establishments along the row. At St Paul's Cathedral, they halted and dismounted, a great lively group, lords and captains mingling with priests and aldermen.

They put aside jesting and laughter as they took their places to hear the speaker, a friar who was brother to the mayor and known to be sound. He was in the middle of an exhortation to the crowd on the nature of forgiveness when he saw the men who had entered. Friar Shaw lowered his great head for a moment, collecting his thoughts. When he spoke again, the words were from the Wisdom of Solomon, in Latin first and then in English.

'And glorious is the fruit of good labours, and the root of wisdom that faileth not. Yet the bastard slips shall not take root! No, brethren, the seed of the unlawful bed will be torn out.' Friar Shaw had already gathered an audience of hundreds for his Sunday lecture. They nodded along with him, though some looked behind at the Protector and his lords, all come to listen.

'In such a manner will the fate of York be decided, I am certain,' Friar Shaw went on. There was a hush then, a perfect stillness. The crowd knew very well who stood at their backs with armed men. They watched the friar closely, though he smiled. If he had gone mad enough to challenge the Lord Protector, they wanted no part of it.

'Of the sons of York, only one was born in England, making him of English blood and clay. The Lord Protector, whom I see before me. Richard of Gloucester, who was born at Fotheringhay Castle, Northamptonshire, a wild and verdant part. His brother the king was born in France, I believe. In Rouen. And Clarence, that poor benighted soul?'

'Ireland, Father,' Richard said clearly from the back. 'Dublin. What you say is true.'

'And has that sole Englishman of York come to hear my judgement upon him?' Friar Shaw asked, his voice booming out across the lowered heads. 'On his brother's marriage?'

'If it please you, Father, I have nothing to fear from the truth,' Richard replied.

'And I will not shrink from the truth, Lord Protector! Not even with you staring at me now. You heard the words of

King Solomon. Your brother's marriage was a false thing, made false by his own hand and dishonest desires. Is it true that he made a promise to another? For the usual purpose of minstrels and courtiers? Long before the marriage to Elizabeth Woodville?'

A moan of discomfort came from the crowd and Richard spoke over them all.

'It grieves me sore, but yes, Father. Yes, it is true.'

'Then all his children are bastard slips of green, Lord Protector. Bastard-born. Yet poor Clarence has a son, does he not?'

Richard found his mouth pursing in irritation. He had not planned this part.

'His father was attainted, Father. That part of the line has no claim.' The crowd murmured once again and Richard stared at the white and tanned necks of working men.

'Then who stands next in line, Lord Protector? If bastard slips cannot take root – and attainted slips cannot, who else shall stand?'

'I shall, Father,' Richard said. 'I shall stand. For my brother's sake and to honour his memory, I shall be king.'

The crowd began to cheer, beginning with those who had been paid, perhaps, but spreading quickly to all the rest. Richard basked in their approval. He wondered if the sound of their cheering would carry all the way to Parliament. Probably not, though they would hear it anyway, passed in whispers and held behind hands, but with the force of a weed growing through stone. They would accept what they could not stop, if only because England had seen too much of war.

Buckingham had said it best, perhaps. The country had been torn apart from the moment Henry of Agincourt died too soon and left a child to rule. The cities and the lords would not allow another child to take the throne, not with a better man waiting. Richard of Gloucester was of York – and a name they knew. He had also shown he would take it from their bloody hands if they stood in his way. There was no other choice in that year. The entire country would choose to crown the Lord Protector, rather than some stripling boy.

'My mother says they are much reduced,' Henry Tudor said to his uncle. Jasper grunted in reply, leaning back in his chair with his legs crossed to enjoy the Paris sun. The gardens at the Palace of the Louvre were particularly bright that year, with entire beds of iris and lily in yellow and purple that scented the air in fragrances so heady as to be dizzying.

Jasper had never been a particularly willing listener to his nephew's letters. It seemed that he had opened a floodgate of words by arranging their little meeting with Margaret Beaufort in London all those years before. From that point on, the little woman wrote almost constantly, reporting everything that went on at home. She was well placed to do it too, Jasper conceded. Her new husband seemed to have risen with Richard of Gloucester as a trusted man. Perhaps some of that changing status lay behind the delight King Louis now took in them. They were not often invited to the capital to be feasted and fitted with new garments, after all. Jasper scratched himself at the thought, hoping the cloth would itch a little less in time. King Louis's stipend had sufficed for a dozen years to keep them, but hardly in luxury.

It was true the French king no longer paid seventy thousand in gold to England, not since the news had reached him of King Edward's sudden death. Louis had thrown a great banquet in celebration of his victory over an old enemy, spending some great part of the payment on so many courses and rounds of fine wine that he had been reduced to a vomiting old man for three days afterwards. At sixty, it seemed

King Louis had become a rather elderly spider, more grey-legged than black. Still, his pleasure was infectious. It was only a shame that Margaret of Anjou had passed away in her sleep a few months before on her family estates. She had been denied even the satisfaction of outliving King Edward.

Henry Tudor had grown from the withdrawn boy Jasper had rescued at Pembroke Castle into a tall and saturnine man. They ate most evenings together and fenced for exercise in the yard of the small farmhouse they had been given, close by the city of Rennes, far to the west of the bustle and energy in Paris. They had become close enough in their years together, living peaceably, almost as father and son. Neither one had sought out a family or even many friends beyond each other. In his private pursuits, Jasper went from serving girl to lady's maid, if one took his fancy and seemed willing. He had no idea if his nephew sought out such vices.

On summer evenings, his nephew would sit by the naked oak on the hill and stare into the north and west. It was the only sign of restlessness in him and Jasper thought Henry had become resigned to a simple life. It was true Henry read voraciously in Latin and English, studying law and exchanging books with a local abbot, who had them sent from Paris. The young man seemed hardly to spend his stipend at all and had often made loans to his uncle without appearing to notice that they were not repaid.

Though Jasper felt the frost of age, he was still thin and energetic enough on most days, or so he told himself. Yet the chance to return to Paris and doze in the sun had been too good to resist, even with all the bruises and inconvenience of travel to reach it.

In the winters, Jasper still dreamed sometimes of Pembroke, his dream-self wandering its halls and standing atop the walls like a ghost. Summer was a happier time, and in the heat he slept more soundly.

Jasper cracked one eye and watched Henry pace up and down the long hall, its windows open to the magnificent gardens outside. A soft breeze blew in the scent of flowers and if he had been asked to describe heaven at that moment, it would have been that spot, with a jug of English ale waiting at his elbow. The long hall was said to have been created for the act of pacing. Some previous king had discovered the action aided him in his thinking. Henry seemed to enjoy the practice.

'My mother says . . .' Henry stopped suddenly, his eyes moving back and forth over the lines of dense script. It was unusual enough to make his uncle sit up and repress a yawn.

'Your mother was a sweet girl when I knew her,' Jasper said. 'Sharper than she looked as well. Certes I am surprised how many husbands the woman has found for herself.'

'Wait, Uncle . . . she says King Edward's son will not inherit.'

Jasper sat up straighter at that.

'Why not? Did the boy die? Come on, Harry, you've caught my interest now. Tell me or read it aloud or just hand the letter to me and let me read for myself. Don't gape at it.'

To his surprise, his nephew did just that, dropping the letter in his lap as he passed by, pacing faster. Henry was twenty-six years old and he had not seen his home for half his life. As Jasper read, he looked up from the letter and saw the young man brushing a mane of dark hair away from his face, then securing it with a leather strip. Henry looked a great deal as his father had done, reminding Jasper of his brother in moments of surprising pain when they came. It was one such instant, in the way he looked at his uncle. Jasper held up a finger in response, reading the entire letter carefully. When he looked up again, he was breathing more shallowly.

'Is it a chance?' Henry asked. '"The house of York is much reduced this year" – are they not, Uncle? There was no hope at all with King Edward on the throne, a man at forty years, with his brood of sons, and daughters to marry away for titles and wealth. Even now, even with his death, he has two strong sons. And yet . . . and yet! Did you read to the end?'

Jasper scratched his chin. It had been a while since he had visited the barber and he knew his bristles came in white and aged him. Perhaps it was time again to be smooth-shaven.

'I did. If your mother is right and has not misunderstood.'

'Uncle, she attends court. Her husband is the royal treasurer. She would know how important this was to me. Tell me! Is this a weakness in them? Instead of a strong line, they have this Richard of Gloucester ascending the throne. If we can strike when it is all new, before they settle into a long line of traitors and usurpers, who knows but we might win it all back. Is it madness, Uncle? I have thought so long on this that I no longer know what is real and what is not. Lend me your judgement.'

'It is enough to speak to King Louis, that much is certain. With respect to your mother, he'll have a dozen ears in that court and he can confirm what she says. I imagine this is why we have been summoned to Paris. King Louis will ask you the same questions. Is this a chance? I will not be found asleep if it is, Harry! I swear that much. I will not be found wanting.'

'It would be worth losing all this, Uncle, wouldn't it?' Henry said, gesturing to the magnificence all around them. The Palace of the Louvre was a place of great beauty, but not one tile, not one pane of glass belonged to them. Henry meant safety and peace. They were considering throwing to hazard every part of their quiet life.

'It is worth any risk,' Jasper agreed. 'Come, let us see what Louis has to say to your mother's letter. Perhaps we will write back and give her good news.'

Richard came out on to the balcony at Baynard's Castle, looking down on a great throng of lords and wealthy merchants, Members of Parliament, knights, captains and men of the Church. He wore doublet and hose in gold and blue, with pineapples embroidered as a pattern. Over such rich colours lay a gown of purple velvet trimmed in ermine. He was very taken with the effect.

He smiled on them all. The great and the good had made their way to his family home on the banks of the Thames to acclaim him as king. Parliament had debated his right to the throne without him the day before, his presence expressly forbidden. Yet they had known his gaze was upon them even so.

He caught the eye of Buckingham, who had spoken so well on his behalf that very morning and in Westminster the day before. The young duke had gone too far when he'd begun explaining to London crowds that King Edward himself may have been illegitimate. Buckingham seemed not to understand what a grievous insult it was to Richard's own mother, Cecily. Richard had tried and failed to shut Buckingham's mouth on the subject. The young duke was just bursting with his own importance and had insisted on addressing great gatherings of commons on Richard's behalf.

What mattered was that the Members of Parliament had nodded their wise old heads: men of the shires, serjeants-at-arms, justices of the peace, representatives from every city in the kingdom, barons and earls and dukes all drawn together in one great assembly in Westminster Hall, all present to vote on his right to ascend the throne.

They had agreed to accept the Lord Protector as king. Richard was still giddy with the knowledge. It was not three months since his brother's death and he had not wasted a day of it, not one.

The crowd below were cheering him in the great hall of Baynard's, packed in and spilling out through every open door and window, with men and women there craning just to see him.

'I have been told of good tidings,' Richard announced, causing them to laugh. 'I have been told I should turn my steps to Westminster, to sit on a chair and be crowned!'

They roared in response and he patted the air, euphoric. He saw his wife appear at the edge of the balcony, standing shyly. Ann Neville, second daughter to Warwick. Richard only wished her father could have lived to see him crowned. He wondered briefly if Earl Warwick would have been delighted or appalled.

'Come, Ann!' Richard called to her. 'Let them see you!' She was a few years younger than him and pale in her white steepled headdress, almost ethereal, so that he worried for her health. Against his ruddy tan and swordsman's hands, she looked as if he could break her in two. Yet he stretched out and she came to stand by him, causing another great roar from the crowd below.

'My queen, Ann, will be crowned at my side,' he said to the crowd. 'My son will be Prince of Wales.' He dipped his head to speak in a lower voice to his wife. 'Where is the boy, Ann? Can you not do that much for me?'

'Ned ran off,' she said sharply. 'I don't *know* where. He pulled away from my hand. All this wild shouting and cheering frightened him.'

Richard turned away from her rather than begin an argument in full view of all those watching. It was a source of constant irritation that his nine-year-old son seemed to weep and reach for his mother when he should have been growing strong. There was no sign of King Edward's towering great height in him either. It made Richard wonder if Buckingham wasn't right after all.

As his wife glared at him, Richard beamed down at the crowd once more.

'I tell you, we begin here, by God's grace, a new reign. Yet we continue a royal line that will reach a hundred years. Let there be peace now, under a white York rose, under royal lions. I awoke as Lord Protector this morning. I will sleep tonight as King of England.'

As they cheered, he took Ann by the hand, leading her down the steps to where a horse-drawn litter waited for her and a warhorse for himself. Buckingham had arranged eight pages for the king elect, men all perfectly matched in height and wearing robes of red-and-white satin. Ann's pages wore the same red and also a tunic of dark blue to honour the mother of Christ. They made a great cornucopia of colour on the drab streets, with swelling crowds heaving all around to watch them set off.

The lords and Richard's guests were already streaming away in a great surge to Westminster, if they had not already left servants to secure a good seat. Richard saw his wife was looking strained and nervous and he reached down to kiss her. To his irritation, she turned so his lips brushed her cheek. He could not snap at her as he desired with so many still cheering all around them. Yet it was typical of her to take the shine from his moment of triumph with some petty act.

Ann stepped up from the mounting block and took her place on the litter, waiting with her neck bent and head down as maidservants arranged her dress so that it spilled well and hid any sight of leg or thigh beneath.

'Thank you, Lady Beaufort,' she said to the gentlewoman overseeing the rest. Richard glanced at the miserable old trout tending to his wife.

'Look after her well, my lady. She is my greatest treasure.'

Margaret Beaufort dipped into a brief curtsey, though she still looked sour. Richard gave up. It should not have been too much to ask that his wife shared some of his joy and satisfaction. God knew, he had worked hard enough to bring it about. His back hurt like a bastard and he could feel the shoulder winging out like a gate opening under his tunic, bringing a sense of wrongness as well as an increase in pain. He would be shifting uncomfortably all the time the archbishop prayed over his head and the monks sang the *Te Deum*, he just knew it. Yet he could at least smile for the crowds. It would be pleasant if his wife did the same, he thought.

It seemed their son would not be there at his father's own coronation. Edward, whom they called Ned to set him apart from the host of boys named for the king. Richard's only child – who would be Prince of Wales and, one day, would be crowned himself. It was infuriating to think of him off playing somewhere at such a moment in his father's life.

'Lady Beaufort,' Richard called. 'Would you send someone to find my son, Ned, for me? The little . . . fellow has run off somewhere, I am told. I would have liked him to see his father crowned, that small thing. I'll instruct a man at the door in Westminster to keep a seat for him.' To his irritation, his wife's companion looked first to Ann and received a tiny nod before she curtsied again. Richard raised his eyes. A man could be king, could actually be king of England – and still be scorned in his own household. He vowed Ann would not deny him the marital bed that night. He would insist, whether she agreed or not. His son needed brothers and sisters, after all. There would be no more talk of headaches and coughing illness.

As he mounted a young gelding, Richard wondered idly if his son would be Edward the Fifth or the Sixth when his turn came to be crowned. He thought then of the two nephews in the Tower. Richard looked east where he could see the White Tower in the distance, standing above all the rest. Could the cheering be heard over there? He thought perhaps it could.

Once he was king, he would have to consider his nephews again. He would discuss it with Buckingham, perhaps. The young duke had become devoted to him over the previous months, showing an enthusiasm for the cause that was sometimes embarrassing. It was difficult to believe the man's grandfather had fought for Lancaster and been killed at Northampton. Or perhaps that lay at the root of Buckingham's attacks on King Edward, Richard did not know. It had been Buckingham who had added the details to the petition in Parliament of Elizabeth Woodville being a sorceress, ensnaring King Edward with her wiles and magic. The man spoke with such great feeling that he had almost written King Edward out of the record, despite his accomplishments, as if the poor man had been nothing but a cat's paw.

Richard frowned at the thought. For all he wanted to encourage Buckingham, he would still have to rein him in. Richard had been utterly loyal to his older brother while he was alive. It might have been his proudest boast, if he would ever have said such a thing aloud. He had adored Edward, revered him as a man much greater than the crown he wore. Edward's loss still wept in him, hidden deep. He would not give his trust again, to anyone.

At last, his wife appeared to be ready. Richard dragged himself out of his gloomy reverie and nodded to his guards and the pages ready to walk in step ahead of them all. With some of his good feeling left behind, he and his wife set off through cheering crowds. Trumpets and drums began to sound ahead, raising his pulse. Knights in armour rode along before and behind, their armour shining silver.

Richard felt his spirits begin to recover and he raised his hand to the crowds, though it made his back ache. It was worse every year, he thought. Pain he'd thought he could bear all his life became less easy to endure as he aged. It was a frustrating thing to acknowledge, but the physical power and certainty of a man in his twenties saying 'This, I can stand for ever', would not itself last. A brother and a beloved king could die. A vow could wither, a back twist further and his pain might never ease at all.

29

Richard sighed, sitting back from the table. The summer had lasted for an age, longer than he could ever remember. As late as November, the fast-shortening days were still gloriously warm. The leaves had turned to gold and red, in a thousand shades, but the sun still shone and, by God, it only seemed to rain at night. His wife, Ann, had accompanied him on a Royal Progress with judges and lords in grand procession, as far north as York. It had been a little different to his memory of entering with Edward and a dozen more. As if to make up for that cold welcome, he had been presented with a chalice full of thick gold coins, while Ann had been given a gold plate brimming with silver. They had been feasted and fêted on every side. Richard had been so pleased with the generosity of that second city in England that he'd overseen his son being crowned there as Prince of Wales, in York Minster, the great and ancient cathedral.

An ambassador from Spain had joined him and proved delightful company. Over months of drowsing warmth, Richard had carried on the business of state while going from city to city of the realm. He had affirmed peace with Spain and France and dispensed justice for just under a thousand criminals, some of whom had waited years for judgement. More important even than those things, he thought, was that he had been seen around the country. Not as a pretender, not even as a lord, but as king, giving justice and rewards, executing criminals or pardoning them as called upon. His wife and son had left him at last as he'd headed back to London. They'd gone together to Middleham Castle, after his royal physicians had said both of them were exhausted and suffering from congestion of the lungs. His wife's cough had certainly worsened, so he did not suspect her of flagging enthusiasm. If anything, Ann seemed to have enjoyed his first months as king. When she and his son were stronger, they would come back to London with him.

Richard upended his cup of wine and felt the warmth seep into his muscles. He had high hopes of a new unguent for his back and had found a little Dorset woman with thumbs of iron to apply it. He looked forward to her attentions that evening with a mixture of dread and anticipation.

He felt his back twitch as his steward entered and bowed. The twist there was becoming like one of the old wounds he'd heard about that could predict rain or bad news. The idea made him smile.

'What is it?' he asked the steward.

'Your Highness, there is a messenger without. He has grave news of Lord Buckingham.'

Richard looked along the table to where Lord Stanley had put his plate aside. Stanley shrugged, though as royal treasurer, he felt perhaps he should sit up and take notice.

'Send him in then,' Richard said. He could not shake the prickling sense of unease, whether it came from his back or just his intuition.

The messenger entered and spoke for half an hour, longer, as Richard questioned him. The news was bad indeed, though the king took the time to wipe his mouth and hands with a cloth as he stood. His guests rose with him, exchanging glances.

'Well, gentlemen, it seems Henry Stafford, the Duke of Buckingham, is not the man I trusted after all. By God, I gave him everything! To have him turn against me . . . he is the most untrue creature alive. So. You have heard all that I have. Do any of you wish to question this young gentleman further? No? Then I will send out a demand to assemble in my name. I will raise an army to defend against this rebellion, these threats and insurrections. Perhaps Buckingham has lost his mind, or fallen under some spell, I cannot say. No, I will add this: I offer a reward for his capture. If Buckingham has decided to act like a common criminal, that is how I shall treat him. For capture, alive for punishment, I will say . . . a thousand pounds, or land to the value of a hundred a year. That for Buckingham. For Bishop Morton, a man whose advice I thought I could trust, five hundred pounds, or land worth fifty pounds a year. For any knights who are such fools as to believe their promises . . . forty pounds a man.' He looked around at those who had been expecting nothing more than a relaxed banquet in Lincoln, on their slow way back to London. Many of them were smiling, reflecting Richard's own clear confidence.

'Gentlemen, I have witnessed battle at Barnet and Tewkesbury. I have seen rebellions before. I have no patience for another! Summon the men of England to stand for me. I will answer.'

They gave a cheer then and raced out as fast as they could in dignity. Richard sat down once more, raising his eyebrows at Lord Stanley, his treasurer.

'This will empty the coffers,' Richard said glumly. 'Though perhaps it will leave a healthier state – after the letting of bad blood. I suppose I would rather know now that Buckingham was a false-coat, than fear his knives in the night. At least he has taken the field and not tried to have me poisoned. Oh, damn these *inconstant* lords! I tell you, since my brother

Edward, there has not been another fit to clean his shoes. No, not even me. We have all seen too much of war. It costs too much.'

'It does indeed, Your Highness,' Lord Stanley replied with emphasis. Richard looked up.

'Yes, of course. Well, borrow what you need to, in my name.' He thought for a moment, his expression darkening.

'I wonder if Buckingham is Bishop Morton's pawn? Have they risen to put my nephews on the throne? It cannot be for *Lancaster*, surely? What rags are left of that house, after Tewkesbury? Some servant? Some faithful hound?'

Lord Stanley smiled dutifully at his patron, pleasing Richard as the king went on. 'I had not thought Buckingham would be such a fool. He is a fine speaker, but no great leader of men, I would have said. Though perhaps they are one and the same in the end.' He saw that Stanley wished to be dismissed and waved his hand.

'Go, my lord. Be sure my commissions of array go out before me. My army is to assemble in ten days, at . . . Leicester. Yes, that will do. I can strike out from there, wherever they gather against me.'

As Stanley bowed and left, Richard looked up at the rain spattering against the windows of the Lincoln hall. He had been driven out of that very county once, with his brother Edward and not two coins to rub together between them. Edward had given his coat to a Flanders captain for their passage! Did men like Buckingham think he was some innocent, some fool to be surprised by their petty insurrections?

For all his light words to the men at the table, Richard was furious with Buckingham for his betrayal. He would not be driven forth again, not as king. He had enjoyed one glorious summer – and it was not enough. The rain struck more strongly in gusts against the glass and Richard smiled. The summer was at an end. Let Buckingham fear the autumn winds and winter cold. Let sly Bishop Morton fear the rain that made roads a quagmire for marching men. Richard would answer them – and anyone else who stood. He thought once more of his nephews. While they lived, they would always be a rallying cry, an old wound still unhealed. He set his jaw. There was an answer to that as well.

Buckingham had overreached himself. He knew it as soon as he sent men to ask Bishop Morton's advice and they came back confused and empty-handed, saying he could not be found. The duke felt ill then as he watched the royal army that appeared at sunset, a dark tide of armour, marching against him for King Richard.

The men who had come to Buckingham's banners were grim and shivering as the rain poured down. They had not eaten well for days and they were worn out by damp and cold.

By the time the sun rose, there were thousands fewer than the night before. Lords and their men had simply crept away as soon as darkness hid them. They'd watched the massive royal squares taking shape, ready for the morning – and their nerve had failed.

It had not helped that rain had fallen almost without respite from the moment Buckingham took the field two weeks before. It was as if the long summer had saved up every drop of water only to unleash it all in torrents, like the Flood. Roads and paths were not just muddy but hip-deep in rainwater that would not seep back into the earth. His men slept wet and woke shivering, and even their food was always cold and sopping fare.

Buckingham felt eyes on him as he rode along a path between hedges, seeking out flat ground. He was certain he saw avarice in his own knights and the few lords who still remained that morning. The idea of King Richard putting a price on his capture was so insulting that Buckingham still burned with it, but it had had an effect. Morton had vanished, after all. Buckingham could no longer ride or walk anywhere without eyes following him, as if he was a fortune to be watched in case it disappeared. It was infuriating. Yet even then, he did not think his plans would have fallen apart quite as quickly without the whispers from London.

One piece of news had ruined him, more than the reward on his head, or the damp, or the fear. Buckingham cared nothing for the two sons of King Edward, but half the lords who had risen against King Richard certainly did. Some had come to his rebellion to restore the rightful succession, to throw down the usurper who had moved against his brother's widow and her sons with indecent haste, with the old king's body still warm.

Buckingham had not worried overmuch about their reasons – just as long as they came to the field. It would not matter in the end why they had come. A rebellion grew in power and ambition and when Richard was dead, they would be swept up and see the outcome as he did. The forces of Lancaster should have landed by then, to join them in triumph. It would all have been settled on Richard's corpse – and those Buckingham had lost could rest in peace.

The news that the princes had been killed in the Tower, no one knew how, had dealt a mortal blow to his campaign. Without them, there *was* no cause of York, no rallying point. In desperation, Buckingham and Bishop Morton had argued that their lords should change their alliance and fight on for Lancaster. If there had been some sign of the damned

Tudors, they might have swayed the gathered lords. Yet there was not – and there were nobles on that field who would not keep their titles if Lancaster returned. They had said little as darkness came, but they'd all been gone by morning, taking thousands of soldiers away with them.

It was perhaps the most disastrous and short-lived rebellion of his lifetime, Buckingham thought ruefully. He did not think he had eight hundred men left on the field that morning, a thousand at most. God alone knew how many he faced. He had been outmanoeuvred almost from the beginning and he felt a grudging respect for King Richard that had not been there before. The rising tide Buckingham had felt for a few exciting weeks had become a still pool. He liked the image, in part because the heavens had opened yet again and the rain was hammering down, drumming unpleasantly on his armour. His iron plate was already brown with rust, though he had squires and servants to polish it each evening.

He saw a farmhouse ahead and pointed it out rather than shout over the downpour. The king's army was a mile or two away over broken ground of fields and ditches and a river. With the rain making it all a morass, Buckingham did not think they would be advancing that morning, no matter whose banners flew, unless it was to demand his surrender. He had a little time, either way, and just the thought of a hot cup of milk made him want to groan.

He dismounted in the farmer's yard and walked towards the door. He did not see one of his men raise a cudgel as he ducked to pass below the lintel. When the blow came down on the back of his head, the Duke of Buckingham fell senseless across the threshold. The family within were astonished and terrified at the crash of armour bringing rain and wind into their home.

The men with Buckingham said nothing as they dragged him up and tied his unconscious form to his horse, his arms securely bound behind his back. He lolled there as they looked at one another in wild surmise. Even shared between six of them, a thousand pounds was a fortune for poor knights.

The ship no longer rose and fell with the waves, but shuddered like a wounded boar. The white crests showed above the rails as they came hissing in, breaking into foam as they smacked against the sides and across her deck, sending deep groans through the whole structure. Sailors ran bare-footed along the waist, grabbing for ropes or wooden sides whenever they saw a wave coming at them, calling and pointing to one another in warning. Again and again, one of them saw the threat too late and was thrown from his feet, shooting across the boards in a flood of white until he struck something else. Some struggled to stand, bedraggled, hair streaming with salt water as they fought for breath. Others took friends away with them and went over the side into the foaming, breathing deep.

Another danger, worse than the great waves that threatened to tip the entire ship over, lay in the ships struggling along on either side, lost to sight in the unnatural darkness under the storm. The wind would fall without warning though the sea continued to plunge, leaving men to pick themselves up and search the grey for some sight of land or their own fleet. The air itself was thick with spray and there was no warning as one ship appeared on top of another, rising up and up across the waist as men screamed. The masts snapped on the ship below and it turned right over as the other shook itself like a wet dog and leaped on as if it had not just murdered scores of men.

Jasper Tudor watched in horror. He considered himself a sailor, but the open sea between France and England was one of the most dangerous stretches of water he had ever known. The storms there came out of nothing and the coast was black rock or cliffs of chalk, with no gentle harbours visible from the deep water. He prayed as he saw one ship destroy another and heard the great wail of the men on the surviving vessel as their ship broke free and went on. It looked almost untouched at first, but then began to list and the second cry was one of unending terror. There was nothing anyone could do, though he saw men dropping into the water like stones as the ship leaned and bucked. The waves would not give them a respite and the wind increased, whistling, and freezing those who watched and those who drowned.

He turned away from the disaster and saw his nephew watching with no trace of emotion. Henry Tudor had not lost that peculiar detachment that had dismayed his uncle from their first meeting. It was not that he felt nothing, though he could be cold when he chose to be. To Jasper's eye, it was more that the young man lacked some deep connection with other men. He was subtly different from them, though he had learned to hide that difference wondrous well. In all the usual patterns of life, a stranger could not have told Henry from any other young knight or lord. Yet there were times when he was not completely sure how a man might be expected to act, times when he looked completely lost.

He did so then, staring blank-faced as one ship mounted another in terrifying union and both were torn open and went down. Heads bobbed on the water and some of the men waved, though there was no hope for them. God only knew where the coast lay, even for those few who could swim. They would be as likely to head out into the North Sea as towards any hope of shelter. There was no chance of rescue. The rest of the fleet were too intent on their own survival even to think of anyone else. Each ship had nailed wooden battens on to their hatches, preventing the breaking waves from filling the hold and dragging them all to the bottom.

For those in the water, the cold would reach into them soon enough. Either that or they would be killed by the sheer battering of waves rising and falling like ships themselves, such leviathans as to make all men no more than broken reeds and flotsam.

Jasper saw the captain yelling new orders and two of his sailors leaning their weight on to the steering bars, calling more over to fight the waves. On one side of the ship, crewmen heaved on a rope to turn the yard above. More men waited there, clinging on for their lives in the gale that plucked at them or froze them where they gripped on.

'We're going back!' Jasper shouted to his nephew. He was only surprised they had gone as far as they had. The storm had come up so quickly it had smashed their fleet in all directions, racing in from the east as if it had funnelled and increased its speed all the way along the Channel coasts. Jasper only hoped they could limp to the French ports. He dreaded what he would see. King Louis had given them eighteen ships and twelve hundred men. The intention had been to land in Wales and join Buckingham's rebellion. Jasper could only shake his head in frustration. The storm even seemed to be lessening, so he could hear the sailors above yelling to each other over the wind's howl and the crack and slap of wet ropes against wood. It was as if they had been driven off and the storm would ease with each mile further away from the coast of Wales.

'We're going back to France,' Jasper said again. 'The storm was . . . well, we could not anchor or find our safe harbour, not in this. Is it easing, do you think?' He closed his eyes and touched a cross hanging at his throat, praying for all the crews and ships that had dared the open sea in the season of storms. For those on land, he imagined it had meant a downpour, perhaps a few tiles dislodged from their roofs. Out on the grey deep, it had been one of the most frightening experiences of his life.

'When can we try again?' Henry shouted in his ear. Jasper Tudor looked at the younger man, knowing he was as intelligent as anyone he had met, but still at times, so cold as to appear unbearably cruel. Jasper was exhausted and half frozen. He had seen hundreds of men drown and for all he knew, theirs was the last bark afloat on that hissing, spiteful sea. He could not think of trying again, or even if King Louis would replace all the ships and men they had lost and think it worth the cost. Yet his nephew stared at him, waiting for an answer.

'Soon, Harry,' his uncle said, giving up in exasperation. 'Let's get back to land first and then we'll see. Not today.'

'Be of good cheer, Uncle,' Henry said, smiling at him. 'We are alive – and we are the last of Lancaster. We should show a brave face to the storm, I think.'

Jasper wiped seawater from his wide eyes and his hair, where it streamed still.

'Yes,' he said. 'Well, I'll do my best.'

In the marketplace at Salisbury, Richard looked in distaste at the young fool who had brought himself to such a point. The block lay waiting, and the executioner stood ready with a wide axe. Though the sun was barely above the eastern hills, the town had turned out to witness the death of a duke. They stood in wide-eyed fascination, watching and listening to every aspect.

Henry Stafford, Duke of Buckingham, was still Richard's Constable of England, a man trusted with great power – and the authority to command others to come to a field of battle. Many in that crowd would take a small satisfaction from seeing a man of such estate brought low. It showed that the law applied to all, to the sheriffs and the mayors and the aldermen as well as poor and common folk brought before the king's judges.

King Richard stood on one side of the market square, watching the proceedings. Young Buckingham had squandered his trust, and yet there was something unbearably foolish about his pitiful rebellion. Richard sighed to himself and rubbed the stubble along his jaw. His back was hurting once again. There was no help for it. Buckingham would not grow old and wise to regret his youthful foolishness. There would be no second chance for him.

Richard made his voice ring across the square.

'It is my belief, my lord Buckingham, that you are Bishop Morton's fool, more than the author of your own destruction. I have reports of him – and of ships sighted from the coast and forced to turn back. Your patrons will not escape my hunters, my lord, be sure of it. Yet I must punish you for your treason. You have cost me more than . . .' He forced himself to stop, rather than begin to complain. The duke regarded him with an intent expression, not yet hopeless in his bonds.

'If you truly believe that, Your Highness, then please, forgive me. Mercy is in your gift. Say one word and this fellow will cut these ropes and set me free. I would live to serve you once more.'

'I know, my lord. What you say is true. I choose not to set a traitor free. You chose this fate when you took arms against your king. Gentlemen, carry on.'

Buckingham struggled, but he was lowered on to the block by two strong men who then stood back to give the axeman room. He was a local man, sweating with the need to make a perfect blow while everyone he knew looked on. He cut a huge arc in the air and Buckingham gave a groan of fear that ended in an instant, leaving silence behind it.

30

Middleham Castle had been Earl Warwick's home, and his father's before that. It had been the very hearthstone of the Neville clan. That was part of the reason Richard had made it his own, when his brother George could no longer make a claim. He had spent years of his own youth at Middleham and it had many happy memories for him. His son had been born there, when his marriage had been happier and full of laughter. Further north than the city of York, it was true that Middleham was a bleak place in winter, but when spring returned, the rambling estate could be found in green fields, streams and orchards, an Eden of the dales.

He had been king almost a year, Richard thought, as he dressed himself once more. His ritual of the heated bath by the fire in the late morning had become more a part of his normal life with each passing month. He kept each step of it the same, so that he could know on the instant when something had gone awry. His back and shoulders were a mass of ridges. On damp days, he could feel the bones twisting. He woke sometimes in darkness, convinced by some spike of pain that something had broken. It passed, so that he slipped back to dozing once again, but it came more and more often.

He hissed as some ill-judged movement sent pain through his upper body to the point of making him pant. Anger helped, always, though his growling and swearing were best kept private. He was forced to show another face to the world, then kick a gauntlet across the room when he was alone. He left the rest of his tunic fastenings untied and went out into the sun.

A suit of armour waited on his pleasure, tied and braced in leather to a pole of iron about the height of a tall man. Richard glared balefully at the thing. He practised on such a device whenever he could. Each stroke he landed sent a jolt through him, burning and stabbing at his spine and shoulders. Yet he needed the strength it lent him, when the sweat had dried and his servants had oiled his muscles like the old senators of Rome, working back and forth with strigils of brass or ivory. He had a grip to crush another's hand, if he chose to. He could not afford to be weak, of all men.

He stood before the armour, seeing its strengths and where to put a blade. The battlefield was the only true test, of course, where an enemy would be moving and countering. Yet it helped to know where plates were weak, where a stab might break through under a raised arm, say.

The household seneschal at Middleham said nothing as he handed over Richard's sword, gripping the scabbard to retain it as Richard pulled the blade. The old man stood respectfully to one side then, though Richard knew he would watch every stroke.

'Go inside, sir. I would be alone today,' he said suddenly. The seneschal bowed and moved swiftly away so that Richard was left to turn slowly in place, looking around him at the wooden balcony above and the open square below. There were no other faces peering down, no one standing in the shadows to stare at him. He was alone and he found he could not breathe.

He tore open his tunic and dropped it almost in two halves on the ground, kicking it away. Being bare-chested usually deprived him of some feeling of support so that he could not revel in it. Yet on that day, he felt choked, confined. He looked through the walls of the upper floor, beyond, to where his son lay still. The Prince of Wales had coughed and coughed while his lungs filled with blood and dark phlegm.

Richard turned to stare at the armour, an iron knight standing brokenly before him, mocking him. He attacked, landing blow after blow, left three times, then right three. Each one made him gasp as the pain built, but he kept on. It felt as if someone had pressed a burning brand into his bones and he welcomed it, telling himself in his stinging sweat that if he could only bear it, perhaps his son would be alive when he went back in. Perhaps the fever would have broken and the chamber pot of red urine that looked so much like a bowl of blood would have been healthy and yellow once more.

He stabbed, though the armour resisted the full range of his thrust. Once, twice, thrice, then up into a butcher's cut, then backhand against the armoured throat. He swore under his breath as something shifted during the swing, so that the blow was an inch off as it landed. It happened at times and he could not predict the jarring clunk of his bones before it occurred. Instead of smashing through the throat, his sword skipped off the helmet, breaking the visor hinge. It would have left a man reeling with blood on his face even so, Richard thought. He was still strong, still fast.

The boy's mother sat with little Ned in that other room, washing his son's chest and arms. He had become so thin over the previous months. Ann had placed a bowl of water on the bedclothes and dipped a cloth into it. Richard had stood in grief as she smoothed wide circles over her son's flesh, already growing cold under her hand.

In the yard, he began to weep as he continued his labour, spinning on his heel and crashing the blade against the other hinge, so that the helmet visor fell to the dust and left an open darkness. He stabbed into it immediately, gashing the iron, wanting to kill, wanting the pain to end that stung his eyes and made his back such an agony he could not breathe. It had begun to feel as if one of his ribs had speared a lung, so that every breath pushed a knife deeper into him. He stopped, panting, crying, watching drops of sweat fall to the dust.

Ann hadn't seemed to hear him when he'd tried to call her away. She'd sat like a corpse herself, about as pale as his son. His only boy, who had been the one living thing he loved in all the world. The lad whom Richard had watched as he'd swung and clambered in a willow tree, just a little distance from where he stood. It did not seem right to have such a child of laughter and noise grow cold in silence, or with just Ann's soft coughing as she leaned over him in that room.

Ten years old was the wrong age to die. It was better when they went very young, so Richard's mother had always said, before they were much more than a name and a squalling face. When they had years in them and memories of a thousand nights talking and carrying them around on your shoulders, well, it was a hard winter in Richard, though the spring had come outside.

He would see the boy again, he told himself. Ann would see him first though, he knew that. He had been staring at her, unsure how to deal with her grief; she would not weep and would not leave. He had seen the cloth crumpled in her hand and the great red wetness clutched within it.

He struck the throat-piece of the armour more cleanly the second time. It broke the joints and the entire helmet went whirling across the yard, bouncing and scraping until it was still. He looked up at the pole and its collection of battered bits of metal, but there was no enemy there any longer, no threat. It was just an old suit of armour and he was tired and in so much pain he wanted to cry out until he had no breath in him. He tossed the sword away then and sank to his knees, staring at the dust.

He had thought for a time that he would ask Ann for another child, but he knew then she would not live long enough to bear one. He would be alone. His brothers were gone. He would be without a wife, without sons and daughters. He would have no one at all, with all the empty years of his rule stretching ahead of him.

After a time, as the household servants began to bustle around on the balconies, peeping over at the king who knelt motionless, Richard came to himself. He sensed their eyes on the ridges of his back and it was that which returned him to awareness. He stood and gathered up his sword, seeing how the edge had been ruined beyond the skill of any craftsman to grind out. His muscles had stiffened as he had knelt there and he grunted as he put his tunic on, though it was a more ordinary pain.

Standing, he looked up at the open windows that led through to the rooms where his son had breathed out and grown still. Richard did not need to see the boy again. He did not think he could bear it. Instead, he filled his lungs with spring air and thought of London and the laws he would pass that year. He thought of Elizabeth Woodville, who lurked even then in Sanctuary, almost as an insult to him. As if he threatened her still. What could he offer, to tempt her out of that damp little place?

It helped just a little to concentrate his energies on the statutes and laws. Men could not be free, he knew. They had to be constrained in fine nets of threads. None of it mattered much, not compared to what he had lost. He just wished his brother Edward could have been there. Edward would have understood.

*

Richard had not entered Sanctuary before. Archbishop Bourchier had lectured him for an age on the rules of the place, granting the blessing of the Church only when Richard allowed a man-at-arms to search him for any weapon. It was a dance, a game, and he went about it with a lighter heart than had been his more recent practice.

Richard acknowledged the monk of the doorway as he entered. The man did not introduce himself and though he bowed, he spoke not a word. Richard saw a sort of sneering spite in his expression that made him want to kick the monk ahead of him down the corridor. He recalled his brother Edward had knocked a young one out when he'd come to Sanctuary for his wife. Richard hoped it was the same fellow.

He followed, but a little too fast so that the monk had to trot to stay ahead of him and announce his presence. It was petty, but Richard enjoyed irritating those who thought they might sit in judgement upon him.

He came when he was called and swept into a finely panelled room that was much better appointed than he had been imagining. Richard had expected rough monks' cells of stone, not a warm study with lamps and rugs and stuffed cushions on the chairs.

Elizabeth Woodville came to her feet as he entered, dropping deeply into a curtsey. He bowed in return and took her hand. He had executed her brother Lord Rivers, and he could see an awareness of that in her eyes, or so he told himself. Yet he had come to leave such things in the past, with an offer of peace between them. She had allowed him to enter, after all.

'My lady, I came to you because your daughters must surely be stifled in this tiny place.'

'They are comfortable enough,' Elizabeth said warily.

'Though they have wronged no one and deserve the freedom of their estate. Their father was king, after all.'

'Of course,' Richard agreed. 'And it is my intention to bring them out into the city once more, if you will permit it. I have arranged for a fine estate to be signed over to you in retirement, with a pension of seven hundred a year. I have brought with me a document to be copied and made public – on every street corner if you wish. It holds my promise to make good matches for your daughters, for their benefit and England's. I would bring any enmity between us to an end, my lady. Having you and your daughters in this cold place shames me.'

Elizabeth looked into the eyes of the younger man who ruled in place of her husband. Richard had overseen the passage in Parliament of a document declaring her marriage null and void, her children made bastards. She was not certain even then if it had been a lie or some old foolishness of her husband. Both were possible. Yet a day in Sanctuary was like a month in the outside world. The stillness seeped in, over time. Even the breath of fresh air Richard had brought on his clothes made her ache. He may have been the devil himself, but she was not sure – and she could not throw his offer in his face. For her daughters, she kept peace. Her girls would be found some quiet earls or barons Richard wished to please and flatter. They would be left to grow in winters and summers, to have families and find paths of their own.

It was not such a terrible vision, Elizabeth thought. Neither was the prospect of a fine country estate and a very generous sum each year to manage it. Compared to the shuffling, whispering presence of monks, it was almost a vision of heaven. Yet there was a bone in her throat that she could not shift. She saw no guilt or shame in the man facing her, but the question was there even so to choke each breath. She could not let him go without asking it.

'And my sons?' She cleared her throat and tried again more firmly. 'What of them?'

'I am sorry, my lady,' Richard said, shaking his head. 'I do not know for certain, though I believe it was Buckingham. He was Constable of England and always in and out of the Tower. No door could be closed to him. Perhaps he thought he served me, or Lancaster, I don't know. I do know I failed to protect them and now my own son is in the ground.' He broke off for a moment as his voice thickened. 'I do not doubt they are at peace, all three of them. There is great cruelty in life, more than I ever knew when I was young.'

Elizabeth raised her hand and curled the fingers over her mouth, holding her lips and chin as her hand shook. She made no sound, but closed her eyes on tears, unsure whether it was better to know than not. For a long time, she could not speak and Richard did not disturb her. She did not sob or weep beyond the brightness under her lids. She had years ahead for that. At last, when she could trust herself to speak, she nodded to him, making her decision. She could not go back.

'I will come out of this place, Richard, if you will have your promises read on the streets of London. I would like to see a golden harvest once more, with apples ripe on the trees. I would like to know peace, for my daughters and myself.'

'And you deserve it and so you shall,' Richard said, his eyes dark. 'And I am sorry for all you have suffered. You know I speak the truth when I say I loved your husband. Edward saw the best of me and I was always true to him. Always.'

The new French king had abandoned the Tudors, Jasper was certain of it. If Louis had lived a year longer, he thought the little man would have shrugged off their losses and tried again. Louis's son Charles was only thirteen when his father collapsed in the middle of a great speech to his lords. The new king's advisers were clearly of a cautious sort and would not agree to the appalling costs in men and ships and gold that they needed.

It was true the Tudors had lost half a fleet in the storm. More than six hundred French soldiers had gone to the green depths in a single night. From that moment, as King Louis's health began to fail, Henry and his uncle had been abandoned in Brittany once more, their letters unanswered. Some ninety men of England had made their way to the city of Rennes to join them. Most were those who had escaped after Buckingham's failed rebellion, or men and women who still hoped for some restoration of their families they could never find under York. They came for old glories and took rooms around Jasper and Henry's modest lodgings. Whatever they had expected was not there. Instead, they found poverty and debtors gathering outside the Tudor house, waving papers for the interest they were owed.

On the coast, ships still waited for nails and beams and sails, with sailors falling foul of local magistrates so that some of them ended up swinging for petty crimes. The torrent of gold and silver from Paris dried to a complete stop. Even the regular stipend they had received for years came to an end and there was nothing Jasper or Henry could do about it.

Jasper doubted the new king even knew their names. He had always found Louis pleasant company, and for the first time, both Henry and Jasper appreciated how difficult it was to gain an audience with a king if he, or more likely his courtiers, were not willing. As the months passed, the Tudors had to sell every item of value just to eat. More letters went out from Jasper by messenger to Calais, to be carried to

Wales and London. He hated to beg, but the alternative was to starve. Jasper had one or two friends left in Wales, but the Stanleys were the best hope in lean times. As a reward for service, Sir William Stanley had been made Lord Chief Justice in Wales. He sent news and occasionally a purse of silver at the request of his older brother. Lord Thomas Stanley seemed to want to please his wife, Margaret, and her exiled son. Henry's mother sent a pouch of her own when she dared to, though she thought she was watched. She had kept her place at court, but King Richard had spies all around, just making reports and notes, gathered in at the Tower.

Jasper and Henry survived – and if their meals were spartan and their clothes were no longer in fashion, both had known and endured worse. At least talk cost nothing. Their little community of English and Welsh had grown to a couple of hundred and they could laugh and talk the evenings away. Some of them had taken work in Rennes, settling into the life.

Along the coast, they were still able to see the broken ribs of warships driven in upon the shore. Of the eighteen, nine had reached safe harbour and Jasper and Henry had shown their visitors the sight, walking along the cliffs every few days to watch men clambering about them, busy with tools. One by one the great ships had vanished, just as soon as they were fit enough to limp away under sail.

An entire year passed in royal disapproval before a smart young herald appeared at the door of the Tudor house. Jasper Tudor felt his heart give a great thump as he caught sight of the man in brushed cloth and embroidered gold, wearing a panel of fleurs-de-lis. Jasper ushered him in and took the scroll he was given. He unrolled it and peered at tight black lettering without spaces of any kind, filling one side to another. Jasper heard himself breathing as he nodded and used the tip of a finger to trace along a line so as not to lose his thread of understanding.

'Yes . . . oh, good boy . . .' he said. For the first time, he heard that King Richard had lost both his heir and then his wife, a few months later. The throne of England was vulnerable and it seemed someone in the French royal court had recalled two Tudor men waiting on just such an opportunity. In growing delight, Jasper read permission to draw on royal funds once more. He could take it to any moneylender and empty the man's coffers. His hand began to tremble and he heard a rattle of cartwheels on the cobbles outside, making him look up. He rushed to the cottage door and looked down the hill.

The road from the east was filled with carts and marching men. The fourteen-year-old King Charles of France had decided to act. Jasper turned to his nephew in astonishment.

'It says two thousand men, well trained and armed. These are just the first of them.'

'We'll need many more than that,' his nephew said. 'I'll start in Wales then.'

'Where in Wales?' Jasper asked him. It was a strange thing to look to his nephew in a new light. Henry's claim was so weak that it would never have stood the light of day in a good year. Yet there had been no good years since Tewkesbury. Henry's mother was Margaret Beaufort and four generations before, John of Gaunt and the house of Lancaster appeared in the family line. It would do.

Jasper looked up as he remembered the little woman he had taken from Pembroke all those years before. After all the pain and grief she had known, Margaret was happily married to Lord Stanley – and she had kept an eye on her son all his life, waiting and hoping for the perfect moment. There had been a dozen houses with better claims than the Tudors, but then they had not survived the slaughter of thirty years of war. Henry Tudor was the last of the house of Lancaster who might yet claim the throne of England. It was a thought to conjure with, a thought to make a man stand in awe.

The advisers to the French king certainly thought there was a chance. Over in England, Richard Plantagenet was weaker than he had ever been, his line broken. If he could be brought to the field before he fathered another heir, the crown could be taken from his hands, from his *head*. It was a chance, a wild and desperate gamble. It would almost certainly cost them their lives. Yet they would go anyway. They would risk it all. Jasper grinned at his brother's son, knowing only too well what he would say.

'Pembroke, Uncle,' Henry Tudor said. 'I would like to go home.'

31

The ships eased away from the coast of Brittany in full summer, over a hot and sullen August night. The Tudors had agreed that much with the king's men and the Duke of Brittany. There would be no repeat of the previous disaster, sailing into the teeth of an autumn storm. With time on their side, they'd waited for calm seas, clear skies and a good moon to light the way. There was always the chance of encountering an English warship or even a customs boat or two, out on the deep to watch for smugglers. Those were the risks, though if a captain of any such craft saw their fleet, he would surely turn tail and run for home.

With the sea unthreatening and gentle, they slipped across. The warships backed sails though there was so little breeze they were practically becalmed. They anchored out on the shining water, coming one by one in order, right up to the quays of the port to unload men and cannon and horses, then moving away, back to the open water.

French soldiers set foot for the first time on Welsh soil, at Milford Haven, standing in tense groups while their force increased. There had been a scuffle with some local men at first, with one or two left to go cold on the cobblestones. At least one boy had gone yelling for help, racing into the hills. Before the last ship disgorged its soldiers, there was a bonfire on a local crag, with another springing into life a mile away.

The villages of that coast had known raiders and slavers since before the time of Rome. By the time the sun showed, they were gone like shadows into the thick forests, with bows and axes to protect their women and children. They knew only too well that raiders took what they could carry and left the rest burning.

It was not the same with the soldiers the Tudors had brought to Wales. They set up an armed boundary and patrolled it. In full view on the docks, they used blocks and tackle to assemble wheeled carts, lowering cannons on to them with a few smashed fingers and a deal of swearing. Scout riders galloped away in all directions, summoning those who had not forgotten the Tudors.

Pembroke Castle lay just a few miles away, closer than it had been in a dozen years. Jasper could feel it there as he raised his head to face the dawn. The woodland and road-sides of Brittany and Paris never smelled quite the same as the home he remembered. Just standing in that spot brought a thousand memories back, from his father's smile to swimming a freezing lake in the Brecknock mountains – or the 'Break Necks' as his father, Owen, had called them.

His old haunts were calling to him, tugging him away from the sea. Jasper had spent about as much of his life in France as he had in Wales, but he knew where home was. Home was the great grey stone fortress that had never been breached, where he had once been earl. He prayed that one day he might yet enter Pembroke once more as its lord. Stranger things had happened in the history of the world, he thought. One of them had happened that very night, with an army ready to march through Wales in support of his nephew – to challenge the last Plantagenet.

Around Jasper, English and a few Welsh voices murmured amidst the French. Those who had come out to join them in Brittany had not been left behind. They had landed with the rest and as he watched, one or two of them dipped down and picked up a tuft of grass or a few small stones, just to hold. There was a love there that was difficult to describe to anyone who did not feel it. He smiled to himself, touching a smooth stone in his pocket that had once been part of Pembroke's walls. He understood well enough.

Strangest of all was seeing his nephew walking amongst them. Henry Tudor wore a set of fine armour that had been the personal gift of the new French king. It covered every inch of the young man, but allowed a perfect range of movement. He had worn it endlessly since it had arrived from Paris, understanding that he needed to be able to move freely and to build the strength to run and fight. In such things, Henry followed his uncle's advice without question, accepting his experience. For the rest, there was a part of him that could never be persuaded or rushed into action. If Jasper overstepped, he would see his nephew tilt his head and consider, then reject his advice. It could be infuriating, that coldness, but by Henry's age, Jasper had been an earl with battle experience. It worried him that Henry had never seen arrows fly in anger, not once.

Jasper shook his head in bemusement to see how Henry had grown into his authority. Ever since the remnants of Buckingham's rebellion had found their way to him, they'd made a crude court, pinning their hopes to the last Tudor, as if he had been born to command. They looked to Henry as a young King Arthur and some of the Welsh had even taken to calling him the '*Mab Darogan*': the Man of Destiny from the old tales, the one who would conquer the white dragon and restore the red. It could not have been a coincidence that the house of York bore a white rose. The house of Lancaster had a dozen badges and symbols, with a swan featuring most prominently. Yet the red rose was there too – and more importantly, Henry's ancestors had carried the red dragon on a battle banner. Jasper could only stand in wonder at the perfection of it. Would an uncle know if his nephew was the *Mab Darogan*? He saw the way the men looked to Henry, and of course, the young man never faltered, never made himself a fool or spoke too loudly or in drink. His peculiar coldness served him well, so that he seemed something more, rather than something less, at least to men looking for a leader.

His uncle watched from the side and wore both pride and grief when he thought of what Owen Tudor would have said, lost so many years. The old man would have beamed at them both to see them back. He would have said he'd known all along that his line would save Wales.

It had been too great a risk to let anyone know they were coming, or so Henry had said. It would mean days lost as word spread and their friends and supporters heard they had come. The delay would be difficult to endure after so long, but it was better than finding a vast English army waiting for them as they landed.

Jasper tried not to stare as his nephew spoke a few words to half of the men standing in small groups on those docks. When he moved on to the next, they turned to follow him with their eyes in the pale morning. Perhaps it was just that he carried the last, desperate hopes of those families.

Though he would never have said so, Jasper suspected the young man lacked the subtle shades of understanding that might undermine his confidence. In some ways, his nephew was extraordinarily quick, yet there were parts of him that were still almost childlike, obstinate in his refusal to see the world as it was.

Henry Tudor had accepted that others would follow him. He'd understood he had a tenuous claim that might just carry him as far as a battle, with the throne as the stake. Beyond that, he seemed to think no more on the matter. As far as Jasper could tell, his nephew had grown into authority because he saw no possibility of an order being refused or his cause denied. Men sensed no doubt or indecision in him because there truly was none. Jasper wasn't sure whether to admire this peculiarity or to find his nephew's confidence terrifying.

They faced a king who had known success in battle at Barnet and Tewkesbury and in putting down Buckingham's rebellion. No one who had landed at Milford Haven thought they would have an easy time of it. The days were long and sultry, with the scent of pollen on the air, but they would be met by a cold and implacable enemy, with nothing left to lose.

As the sun climbed, the last of the ships returned to sea, leaving two thousand men and a dozen cannon to be rolled along the roads. The men breathed a little faster as they shuffled and stood, gathering anything they had laid down while they waited. Jasper saw his nephew speak to a herald and the man raised a horn to his lips, blowing a single note that echoed back across them all. Men-at-arms raised the banner poles embroidered over months in Brittany, tugging loose the ties that would allow them to unfurl, then swishing them back and forth until they opened out to their full length. The *Ddraig Goch*, or red dragon, swirled above them all. With it opened up the red rose of Lancaster and the portcullis and chains of Beaufort, but the dragon was the symbol that had men crossing themselves and bowing their heads in prayer. They were few, but they would stand.

In the early afternoon, the scouts came back in to report a force of soldiers and archers barring the road ahead. Henry and Jasper came to the front and brought their horses alongside to talk in low voices. The messengers had reported the colours of Rhys ap Thomas, a warlike soldier who had pledged to the house of York, so it was said. It was also true that he had exchanged letters with the Tudor men over the previous year, but the real test would come only when he either knelt or took up arms against them. Jasper had the sinking feeling that for such a grim warrior in his prime, the moment would be one of true decision. It did not matter what had been said before or what promises had been made. Only when Rhys ap Thomas looked at Henry Tudor and made his choice would they know. Jasper gripped the hilt of his sword and wondered if he would see blood that day.

They could not appear weak, that was clear enough. The news went back to be ready for attack or ambush and then they went forward in good array along two narrow roads the scouts said would bring them up against the Thomas force.

For Jasper, it was one of the hardest miles he had ever ridden. From the vantage point of horseback, he could see before the marchers that a great force lay ahead of them, across the road and stretching over the fields. There were certainly hundreds of men in mail, carrying axes and hammers and a great host of pikes. The fields and hedges could have hidden a thousand of them. At the head sat a bare-armed and burly figure with a great mass of red hair, tied into a braid. The man wore a tunic and mail rather than full armour, though there was no question who led those men as he gazed balefully along the road. Rhys ap Thomas was the captain charged with keeping that coast safe from any invasion. He had been trusted by the York king to respond with utter savagery against anyone landing. The bonfires had been lit to summon him, no other. And he had come.

'Show no fear to this man,' Jasper murmured to his nephew. Henry looked curiously at him.

'Why would I show fear?' he said. His uncle clenched his jaw, unable to explain the danger then, as close as they were. He had tucked a relic from Brittany into his shirt, a tiny flask containing the blood of a saint. He wished he could have reached it then, to pray that Henry would not say the wrong thing to a man like Captain Rhys ap Thomas.

As they reined in, Jasper saw the Welsh captain was larger than he had realized across the shoulders, a great door of a man whose gaze was fixed on the red dragon flying a little way behind them.

'That is a grand claim, my lords,' Rhys called to them, indicating the swirling banner. It was a good start, if he would allow them their titles. The earldoms of both Pembroke and Richmond had been denied and attainted over previous years. Yet the greeting seemed unaffected and natural.

Jasper cleared his throat to reply and Henry turned to look at him, saying nothing. It was a reminder that he had agreed to keep silence unless it was to head off disaster. There could not be two red dragons, two men of destiny. Jasper knew that and had accepted it. It was still hard.

When Henry was sure his uncle would not speak, he turned back to the man watching so closely.

'Who are you to block my path?' Henry said clearly.

'I am Rhys ap Thomas, son of Thomas ap Gruffyd ap Nicolas,' he said, in the manner of those parts, naming his forebears. 'This coast is under my authority, see? When you land here, you must answer to me.'

'I am Henry Tudor, son of Edmund Tudor, son of Owen.'

'And you sit under the red dragon.'

'I am a descendant of Cadwallader; it is my right.'

The two men faced each other with identical frowns. Neither seemed to have expected the meeting to go the way it had. Jasper fidgeted, but he had promised to be still and he kept his word.

Rhys ap Thomas shook his head.

'I do not think you are the Son of Prophecy. I'm sorry. Perhaps you are of the line, but I do not see greatness in you.'

Henry Tudor kicked his mount closer by a step. All the men tensed as he came within arm's reach of the captain. Rhys ap Thomas made a great show of sitting relaxed with his hands on the reins, but there was strain around his eyes even so.

'I do not depend on what you see in me,' Henry said. His voice was low, but his uncle could hear nothing else around them. The birdsong and noise of other men seemed to have vanished and he listened in cold fear as his nephew went on.

'Perhaps you thought to test me, Rhys ap Thomas. I am not interested. You bar my way – and I have business beyond, with King Richard of York. It is my belief that you took a solemn oath to him, so hear this from me: if you thought you might walk with me, my answer is no. I will not have an oath-breaker. If you thought you would keep your oath, draw your sword and I will see you broken on the road. Either way, I do *not depend* on what you see in me.'

'I . . . don't . . .' the captain began. Henry talked over him, his voice growing louder with every beat.

'And I stand under the *Ddraig Goch* because I am the last of Lancaster, the *red* rose. I am the red – and I go to take the field against the white rose of York, the *white dragon*, Captain

Thomas! Now, what is it to be? Will you break your oath, or will you give up your life?'

'I cannot break my oath,' Rhys ap Thomas said. He had gone pale and Jasper wondered whether it was from anger or fear. Some of the best men he had known were those for whom their word was something rarely given, but then given unto death. It could not be broken lightly, at the cost of their soul. Seeing Rhys ap Thomas was one of those, Jasper despaired. They could have used his men.

'I swore I would not allow an enemy to enter Wales but over my body,' Rhys ap Thomas said, ashen. 'Will you choose a champion, my lord? Or face me yourself?'

'Over your body?' Henry said. 'Can I not just step over you, then? And let you keep your oath?'

Captain Rhys ap Thomas blinked at him.

'Step over me?'

'If that is the oath you took. If you gave an oath to let me in only over your body, then you should lie on this road. My army will step over you – and your oath is unbroken.'

'I am not lying down on the ground,' Rhys ap Thomas said. 'It would be a great burden to watch your men step over me. I think I won't do that.'

A little way behind, Jasper's smile of incredulous delight began to fade. He'd thought for a moment that Henry's odd way of looking at the world had achieved the impossible. To see it snatched away once more was a cruel blow. As Jasper watched, one of the Welsh captain's men brought his own horse in and leaned to murmur in the ear of Rhys ap Thomas. The man's eyebrows rose in surmise.

'There is a bridge nearby, so my lad says, where the river has run almost dry this summer. If I stood in the riverbed, your army could ride over the bridge. I could keep my oath in that way – and still let you in.'

'I accept,' Henry said, as if it had been a definite proposal. In that moment, he made Rhys ap Thomas consider it as if it had been. At last the man nodded.

'Very well, my lord. You can say you came to Wales over my body.'

'I will not say that, Captain Thomas,' Henry replied. 'I will say you delayed me half a day with foolishness.'

The man's pride wilted at the rebuke and Jasper felt a twinge of pity for Captain Rhys ap Thomas, having come to like him.

'How many men are yours, Captain Thomas?' Jasper called, in part to distract him. The man turned away in something like relief from the cool gaze of Henry Tudor.

'Twelve hundred in all, my lord, though I have only eight hundred of them with me here. I'll bring the rest tonight and they will send the call for more. Wales will give its sons to your care, my lords, to follow the red dragon.'

Richard sat alone in the audience chamber at Westminster, looking out on the Thames as it wound its shining path through the clusters of buildings and warehouses springing up all along its banks, new ones every year. From that high room, he could see the marks of man spreading out into virgin fields, taming the wild moors with roads, felling trees for charcoal and construction, cutting great swathes through land that had grown nothing more than nettles and beggars before. Lines of smoke rose from a hundred bonfires, or chimneys browning malt for beer, or forges melting iron in a greater heat, or town houses standing proud on clean streets of stone. It was all rather beautiful, he thought.

The room was silent, with even the servants who might have stood to answer his whims dismissed. He had never been a solitary man, but it had crept upon him even so. His father had been in the ground for more than twenty years, killed in the struggle against Lancaster. His three brothers had gone, murdered or executed for treason or at the last, broken by some great paroxysm of the brain. The only other man Richard had admired had been Earl Warwick. He had fallen in battle, standing against Richard as his enemy, bent on his destruction. That had been as cruel as all the rest.

His son had been the sharpest cut of all, he thought. He had adored the boy, though he had not shown too much of that. It had been the strangest thing, to take such joy in the mere existence of his son, Ned, yet still have wished not to show it, for fear of ruining the boy. Gentleness and love did not make a strong man, certes not a strong king. Richard knew that well enough. He had been made the man he was by pain and by loss, so that when his wife died, it was no more than a sting compared to all the rest. Of course Ann had slipped away. How could such as he be left with anyone to love? It seemed of a piece, that somewhere it had been decreed that King Richard must be utterly alone.

He missed them all. He was the last man of his line, he thought, savouring the sadness of it. He was the last Plantagenet.

'Your Highness, there is a herald, asking to be admitted to your presence.'

'Has he been searched?'

His steward looked affronted.

'Yes, Your Highness.'

'Send him in then,' Richard said. He turned away, leaning his chin on his palm and his elbow on his knee. He looked out over the setting sun at London, the warmth still in the air as birds came to roost.

He did not look round as the herald came into the room, bringing a scent of fresh mud and the outside into that still air. Richard heard him kneel and waved a hand for him to speak.

'Your Highness, I have come from Ludlow. A man came in from the western coast, exhausted almost to death.'

Richard felt the great sluggish weight of his thoughts pinning him down, so that it was hard to do anything but stare out at the golden light of sunset over the capital.

'Go on,' he murmured.

'He said a great force landed on the coast, of French and Welsh, he was not sure. He said they were Tudors, my lord, come under a red dragon.'

Richard raised his head, pulling in a slow breath.

'What news of my captain there? What was his name? Evans? Thomas?' he asked. The herald apologized and muttered that he did not know.

It did not matter, Richard knew. He would send for his most loyal lords, as he had during Buckingham's rebellion. He would summon the greatest army he could put in the field and he would . . . He stopped the rush of thoughts and considered.

'The Tudors? For Lancaster, is it? But they have no right of claim. Why would anyone follow that family?'

'I do not know, Your Highness,' the herald stammered.

'You have done well enough, sir, with what you have told me. How long is it since the landing, did you discover that much?'

'I was six days on the road, Your Highness. I believe the man who reached me at Ludlow had ridden for four or five.'

'Eleven days then, or thereabouts,' Richard said. 'Go now, with my thanks, sir. I will make myself ready.'

The herald made his way out of the royal rooms and

Richard sat in thought for a time, letting the silence seep back into him. He had no one: no wife, no heir, no brothers. He was utterly alone. If he fell in battle, it would be the end of his house, his family, his line. In that instant, he accepted it, however it turned out. He called for his steward once more. The man appeared instantly, having been standing just outside.

'Bring me my armour,' Richard said. 'I have been challenged.'

32

There was the faintest haze in the air as the sun rose. The army of Welsh and French soldiers had tripled in size since their first landing almost a month before. As they'd come east, Rhys ap Thomas had proved the most earnest advocate of Henry Tudor, calling on men to follow the red dragon, or the *Mab Darogan*, in every village they passed.

Six thousand marched along the road at the end of August, in a great triple column across the land. The Earl of Oxford reached them, bringing horsemen and archers as well as his own much-needed experience. There were simply no other great names, which made Jasper Tudor privately furious. He'd sent letters to every lord who had stood for Lancaster in the past, but the replies had been few. Perhaps it was that they were afraid of King Richard, who had triumphed at Barnet and Tewkesbury, who had made Buckingham's rebellion look like a child's challenge. Or perhaps it was just that too many of them owed estates and titles to the house of York and were loath to gamble once more with all they had won.

Whatever the reasons, public and private, the Lancaster force was weaker than it might have been. The scouts said King Richard had gathered ten thousand to himself, or even more. Jasper still hoped the tallies were exaggerated, but it did seem as if he and his nephew would be outnumbered. As a result, Jasper Tudor could not escape the sensation that they were marching cheerfully to their destruction.

Apart from the men under Rhys ap Thomas, the rest of

those who had joined them were untrained Welsh lads. They were strong enough and fit, of course. Any man who had butchered a hog or cut down a tree could wield a falchion blade or a billhook with some sort of ability. The most valuable of them carried longbows and a quiver of arrows fletched by their own hand. Yet such things were not sufficient preparation for war.

Trained men knew when to seek cover, where to strike a man in armour to kill him or render him helpless, how to respond to a horseman bearing down, to give you some small chance to survive. They understood discipline on the field and the giving of trust to those who led them. An army was not a rabble, not a mob. They would slaughter a mob.

There was also a reason soldiers trained to brutal fitness, far beyond the wind and stamina of farmers. The ability to stand when others were dropping in exhaustion would save their lives, it was as simple as that. It was not enough just to swing a piece of iron with strength and courage. War was a hard trade, a brutal craft. Jasper had seen the results once before, when an enemy had all the advantages. He could still recall Edward, Earl of March, stalking the battlefield of Mortimer's Cross in red armour, shining with it. A giant of an earl who had eaten meat and fish and trained hard all his young life, with weapons and armour and horses. Jasper did not talk much of that day, but he remembered it only too well.

Henry Tudor sat in full armour, with his uncle alongside him in the centre. Captain Thomas oversaw the left wing and de Vere, the Earl of Oxford, held the right. The ranks had fallen silent as they moved across the open land. They could already see the forces of King Richard on the rising hills ahead of them. They had manoeuvred for days in the approach, but the royal force of King Richard the Third had found themselves a fine hill and plain before it.

Henry Tudor was the one who had come to take his crown from him, after all. The king of England could choose a spot anywhere that suited him – and they would still have to come. Richard had understood that only too well and had scouted the ground for forty miles. He had found a perfect spot to offer battle, with green wheat turning gold in the fields.

Jasper turned his head back and forth and narrowed his eyes, but he could not make out the banners at over a mile distant. He saw Richard's force of knights on the hill as a blur and it hurt him to have to ask his nephew for details he would once have seen like a hawk wheeling above a field of stubble.

King Richard had gathered his army on a ridge almost, a natural rise of the land that allowed ten thousand men to stand in ranks of horsemen and archers. Jasper swallowed at that, thinking how much further the arrows would soar when they rained down. He knew the sound better than most men, as he had endured the battering of them against his armour, his life in the hands of fate and luck and curved iron. He could not help wonder if the French men-at-arms had heard of Agincourt as they marched along beside the men of Wales and England. They had not fared well before against bows the height of a man.

'It looks like Percy arms on his right. Northumberland,' Henry said, squinting. 'That is a blue lion on the coats of arms and shields there. I thought they might stand for Lancaster.'

'They should have,' his uncle said sourly. 'They did before, from the beginning. I thought they would now as well. I do not doubt Richard has their sons as hostages back in London, held as an earnest of loyalty. It is what I would do.'

'King Richard holds the centre then, with Northumberland on his right and . . . Norfolk on his left.'

Jasper shrugged. 'That is a withered line, that once was greater. I do not fear the Norfolks, not at all.' He spoke to raise his nephew's spirits, in case Henry was feeling over-awed at approaching a force on superior ground and under royal banners, a force that outnumbered them by almost two to one.

Henry appeared completely calm. Once more, his uncle could not decide whether the young man was an innocent fool, a master of appearing confident to the men, or some strange third choice perhaps: a man who believed he truly was the Man of Destiny, the Red Dragon returned out of Wales to fight for the throne. As he watched his nephew staring up at the great ridge and the army there, Jasper saw a spark in Henry's eyes, a savagery he had not expected.

They had marched just a few miles from their camp the night before. The men had eaten and emptied their bladders and bowels before setting off. The day was fine and the sky remained clear. They did not stop as they approached the army on the hill. As Jasper watched, parts of it began to creep down the slope. The men there were eager and he could hear the thin voices of their captains and serjeants, calling them back, telling them to wait and wait. They knew they had the advantage and he could imagine them readying their blades and axes, leaning forward like leashed dogs, wanting to run in. For some young men, it would be the most exciting morning of their lives. They did not fear death; it would not come for them. They trusted in their vigour and their strength, never yet tested as it would be that day.

Horns sounded to halt the Tudor columns, half a mile out. They formed in good order into fighting squares, ready to push up the hill. Jasper felt a shiver run through him and he crossed himself and said a silent prayer of penance for his sins. It had been a while since his last confession and he could only ask for mercy. He had seen war before and he was no longer young.

On Henry Tudor's right, the Earl of Oxford rode along the face of his fighting square, two thousand men in all and composed half and half of French soldiers and Welsh. The French at least were experienced, well armed and armoured. The Welsh had been given long spears and heavy-bladed cleavers any butcher would have recognized.

Eight hundred archers gathered on the outer wing, already seeking targets and pointing them out to friends. There was a slight breeze blowing and they did not look content with the sight of an army on the ridge. It would be no easy task and they had no wooden mantlets to stand behind as they shot. There would be a great band of ground where they came within range of the enemy but could not reply.

Oxford saw the danger and was considering his best approach as they advanced. He had known the confusion of battle in the fog at Barnet and he was determined to make the best decisions, only too aware that the best commanders were not those with a plan, but those who made the right choices when opportunity presented itself. As he rode in the second rank, surrounded by knights and burly men-at-arms, he saw Norfolk's forces begin to come down the hill ahead of him. Earl Oxford looked left and right along his own lines. They were moving along in good order, spears held out like sharp spines. He was slightly ahead of the Tudors in the centre, but not overly so. Further over, Oxford knew the last of their army was marching along under Rhys ap Thomas, the Welshman keen on the fight.

Oxford was pleased to see the enemy vanguard give up the advantage of high ground, though it spoke of their confidence. The line of Norfolk soldiers seemed to leap ahead.

The slow and measured approach became a rush down the slope as those behind pushed forward and those ahead went in fear of being trampled. They were at three hundred yards when Oxford roared for his archers. They had been ready, staring at the commanding earl and willing him to snap out of his trance. Whatever forces of bowmen King Richard had were up on the ridge and out of range. It was every archer's dream to face a charging line with just a quiver and a bow – and an army to fall behind when they were done.

The arrows snapped out in a great clatter, as fast as the men could put a shaft on the cord and pull. There was no great skill in aiming at that closing distance, but they showed their training in the huge strength that didn't fade after a few shots.

Norfolk's men were running into a hail of fire. Worse, as they tried to push past it, those who fell brought down the men behind. For a few vital moments, it was the sort of slaughter Agincourt had been, with piles of howling, dying men crushed under the weight of those trying to climb over them, desperate to get past.

The arrows rattled away to nothing, until there were no more than a dozen of the slowest archers left, older men who wet thumbs on their tongues and fitted shafts with slow precision. They were fearsome in their accuracy and men still died as they closed the gap, but the great breaking of lines and massed slaughter had come to an end. The rest of the archers fell back at a run, laughing and calling to the men-at-arms to try and match that. Those soldiers looked on in envy at the peculiar status of such men, without armour and without shame as they loped off and left others to the work.

Oxford's lines bristled again with spears. Many of those who still came down the hill had been wounded by arrows and marched with shafts still in them. That part of the battered charge was cut down in turn. His men used their spears until they were broken, then took out the falchion cleavers.

Oxford had no idea how many hundreds his archers had ripped from the royal ranks – and he knew any advance on the hill would suffer at least as much. Yet his men had started well. Some of those who had come racing down had so disliked the welcome he had given them that they had retreated, creeping away around the hill with their heads down in shame. In comparison, Oxford felt pride soar as he looked along the lines, hoping the Tudors had seen.

The Duke of Norfolk had come down with his men in that reeling charge. His armour had saved him from the barrage of arrows, but his coat of arms had been torn and there was blood showing on his thigh, though whether it was his own or another's was unknown. He was still ahorse when Oxford saw him, cutting wildly down at men-at-arms. They had little answer against armour of that quality and Norfolk had smashed a gap for himself. His men were rallying to him, seeing his coat of arms and calling each other to that spot, to support their feudal lord.

Oxford made his decision. He had a chance to tear the heart out of Norfolk's entire wing, not twenty yards from his position. He sent a messenger racing off to the Tudor centre and slammed his visor down, drawing his sword and spurring his mount forward. It reared as it went and the kicking hooves made his own men fling themselves aside rather than be struck.

Norfolk looked up to see the Earl of Oxford coming, trampling and knocking soldiers from his path with the horse's plating of iron. Norfolk was in full armour and yet the first blow unseated him, sending him tumbling out of his saddle in a great crash. His horse bolted and his leg was held for a breathless heartbeat before the leather snapped and he fell to the ground. Norfolk landed awkwardly and hard, with his helmet buckled and broken. One hinge of his visor had snapped and he could not see as Oxford dismounted and battered him with blow after blow.

'Wait!' Norfolk shouted furiously. He backed off and yanked at the twisted visor, heaving it back and forth until the second hinge snapped. He tossed it away then and stood tall, panting, to see Oxford waiting for him. Norfolk could feel blood seeping from a dozen gashes, stealing his strength. He swallowed.

One of the last archers on the field was no more than a dozen paces away, still thumbing his last two shafts. Old Bill had held back to watch the lords fight because he liked the idea of taking a fine nobleman with his old bow. He didn't understand why Earl Oxford had stopped attacking, why he stood there waiting for an enemy to recover enough wind to go on fighting. Old Bill closed one eye and sent his last but one at the Duke of Norfolk. The archer laughed in delight when it flew like a bird into that open visor.

The duke stood stunned for a moment and Old Bill had the sense to turn away and lower his hands as he felt Oxford's gaze searching for whoever had done it. Bill pushed his last arrow into the ground then, as an offering. You didn't do better than that and none of his mates would believe him, more was the pity.

On the ridge, King Richard watched with a resigned expression as the Duke of Norfolk fell and more of his vanguard turned away from the carnage and destruction. Norfolk had lost the slope, then the men and finally his own life. It saved Richard from having him executed afterwards, that was the only fine thing about it.

The king scratched in thought at one side of his mouth, stretching the part of his back that ached the worst that morning. Even without Norfolk's wing, he knew the force he had gathered still outnumbered the rebels. Around him on Ambion Hill, he had a personal guard of fifteen hundred knights and men-at-arms in full armour, a great tide of silver metal on the most powerful horses ever bred by man. He *wanted* to charge with them, just to hear that thunder. The very thought made him smile.

Yet he had Lord Percy, Earl of Northumberland, still on his right, in command of three thousand men, waiting in silent ranks with the flags fluttering overhead. They were not dismayed by Norfolk's failure. Battles could be won in the first charge, or they could be slow and bruising things that took all day and came down to will. The king's left wing may have been battered back, but his right wing was ready to move. Richard shifted in his saddle, straining his eyes to see into the distance.

'And there you are,' he whispered to himself. His brother Edward had taught him the power of a reserve, used properly. The Tudor forces had been so intent on his army perched on the ridge that they had marched straight at his position. Yet his entire army was not on the ridge. He smiled at the sight of marching ranks shimmering. Lord Stanley was about two miles away and he doubted the Tudors were even aware of them. Richard had the man's son secure in London. Lord Stanley would not falter. Very well. It was time to bring the Tudor dreams to nothing.

Richard gestured to a herald, so that the man came racing on a light gelding.

'Lord Percy is to engage immediately,' Richard said. 'My orders are to sweep Rhys ap Thomas from the field and then turn against the Tudor centre. I will meet him there.'

The young man raced away and Richard could only envy him his youth and enthusiasm. His back was growing worse in the cold wind. It would need a good soak that night, with oil and wine to sleep. If he could sleep at all, of course.

He waited, staring down across the plain. The Tudor army looked too small to be a threat. They had no more than six thousand and he had as many approaching them on their flank. He only wished his brother Edward could have been present to see it, or perhaps their father.

Down on the plain, a small group broke off from the centre, no more than fifty men. Richard's attention fixed on it immediately. They carried the Tudor banners and he felt a twinge of cold in his gut as they rode straight at Lord Stanley's force. He had missed something, or been betrayed.

In sudden panic, Richard looked up. Northumberland's wing had not moved an inch, though Earl Percy had surely received his orders. Yet they stood there, on horse and on foot, with the wind blowing across them and not a face turned his way, all looking down at the movement of men below.

Richard swore to himself. He sat a destrier with fifteen hundred horsemen in armour, an iron mace greater than any force on the field. He called left and right to his captains, needing them to pass on the orders.

'Close formation on the king! Engage the Tudor centre. Ready!'

He waited with his eyes closed as they repeated his orders and the riders gathered in their reins and lances. Horses whinnied and stamped and still Lord Percy's right wing remained in silent ranks. Richard cursed them as he dug in his heels, drawing his sword and pointing it at the small group riding across the Tudor lines. He would crash through them before they reached Lord Stanley. He loosened his shoulders as he leaned over the saddle, letting the horse build speed to a canter on the gentle slope down. He had picked the ground just for this and he revelled in the speed.

Fifteen hundred horseman came down off the slopes in a single mass like a spear, aiming for the suddenly terrified Tudor centre as it came to a halt. No one there had ever seen such a charge before and the thunder of it shocked men to stillness. The soldiers of France and Wales below were already bowing back from the massed line of knights and iron coming in at terrible speed towards them. They raised spears and dug shields into the earth to crouch behind, but they were afraid.

Out ahead of the Tudor centre, Henry and his uncle turned to face the silver horde pouring off the ridge. There was no doubt where they were aiming and they could see King Richard himself riding at the head, his surcoat quartered in red, gold and blue. Jasper felt his mouth dry in fear and it was Henry who halted and called up the biggest men, with shields to take the first blow. They could not reach the Stanley forces, not then.

They waited, and as they waited, the army behind them suddenly came forward. Henry and his uncle had been out in front, halted ahead of the rest. In one sudden movement, the captains and serjeants stepped forward and the line enveloped them. Men held up shields and closed their eyes for an impact they knew they could not withstand. The long lances would break the lines and the horses would smash through, half a ton at full speed.

Henry held his breath and drew his sword. The man in front of him raised his banner high, though it meant he could not hold a weapon. It was an act of madness and bravery. On Henry's right hand, a huge warrior loomed, Sir John Cheyney. The man nodded to him and winked as he pulled down a visor and turned to face the galloping wall of horses and knights, spitting clods of earth into the air that fell like rain. They could see King Richard there, behind the front rank then, hemmed in by knights who had driven themselves to exhaustion to stay out ahead of him.

The world grew quick, for a time, though Henry saw clearly enough. He did not flinch or look away as men went flat, suddenly, smacked down so hard it was as if they disappeared into the air. Horses bore iron plates against the spears and crashed past them only to collapse and skid on broken legs against crouching men behind. The speed and power of the charge was soaked up in death and broken things, and sound enough to fill all Bosworth Field.

33

Richard saw the Tudor banner flutter down from where it had streamed overhead. He and his knights had punched right through the first few ranks, smashing them down. Some horses had fallen, some of his knights had been impaled or spun from their feet, but the rest had plunged deep into the Tudor centre, against their strongest knights.

Richard could *see* the man they followed, waiting like a statue while others fought to keep him alive. Henry Tudor sat with an expression of infuriating calm while lives were ripped away within his arm's reach. The very last of the breed.

Richard jabbed his spurs in, though his horse was held tight in the press of men. In fury, he hacked down at someone as they squeezed past his stirrup. The man crumpled under the hooves and Richard looked up to see his view of Henry Tudor had been blocked by a huge mounted knight, broad as a door and sitting a horse of astonishing size.

The giant's visor was up and Richard knew he would expect a thrust at that weakness. The fellow was ready for it, his eyes bright with pleasure as he saw he faced the king himself. Sir John Cheyney had an advantage in that almost every man he faced was smaller than he was. Yet Richard had learned to spar against his brother Edward. He had more practice than anyone else alive in withstanding the force of a big ox in armour.

The fighting went on around them and both men had to keep some part of their awareness for a chance spear thrust, or a mace blow from the side. Battles could turn on luck or slipping in entrails as much as loyalty and strength.

'Get out of my way,' Richard snapped to Sir John Cheyney. As the massive warrior began to reply, he hacked down at Cheyney's sword arm, aiming for the hand or wrist to break small bones and perhaps disarm him. The blow struck well enough to make the big man curse and grumble, but Sir John kept a grip on his blade and stabbed back with it, aiming to break the plates at Richard's hip and groin. Their horses lay alongside each other and Richard's point of view was filled with the larger man. He batted the blow away and struck out with his gauntlet, jamming outstretched fingers into the open visor. Three of his ironclad fingers scrabbled within and Sir John Cheyney roared in pain. When Richard pulled his hand back the man's face was running with blood. The giant knight flailed in panic as he tried to blink some sight back. His sword struck Richard's horse on the head and left a terrible wound so that the animal staggered, dazed.

Richard ducked under a blade and struck his sword against the knight's helmet, a blow with all his strength behind it. It knocked Cheyney senseless and tumbled him from his saddle, sending him to the ground.

The battle was whirling all around him as Richard felt his horse fail. He dismounted quickly and the animal went to its knees, snorting blood. On foot, Richard roared for his knights, praying they would see him before the men-at-arms of Henry Tudor. Down in the chaos of the fighting line, he lost his sense of how the battle was going and he was alone, with men fighting and snarling on every side.

In the distance, Richard caught a glimpse of Lord Stanley's banners, swaying over the heads of those on foot or still ahorse. He took hope from that. Yet on the hill above him, the Percy ranks still stood unmoving. Richard prayed then only to survive, so that he could bring a fine vengeance on to them.

'The king!' Richard heard. 'There! There he stands!' He turned to face the sound and was attacked by two knights in Lancaster coats. In anger, he batted away their swords. He needed a horse, anything to take him away from jabbing punch-blades and the mud that sucked at his feet. He spun and ducked, using his armour as a weapon, crashing any part of him that was encased in iron against the enemies he faced. None of them were so large as the giant knight had been, but they were many and their armour meant it was hard to land a killing blow, so that they kept coming against him. He could feel no pain from his shoulder, which was a relief, though he knew he was growing weary. One of the knights attacking him slipped and screeched at a broken leg. Richard kicked at the man's helmet and smashed it free, knocking him on to his back.

He was breathing so loudly he could not hear the steps of those around him. He could see only a little through the visor's slot and he turned in place, sword cutting the air, surrounded by enemies. Richard could not see the Tudor position any longer and it seemed his armoured knights had moved on, leaving him to stand alone in the chaos. He only prayed then that Lord Stanley would crash in from the wing and save him. It was his last spark of hope. He did not hear the man who swung a pollaxe hammer in a great looping blow against the base of his skull, shattering the bone. His eyes turned up but there was no life in them as he fell. A dozen men darted in then, hacking and stabbing at the dead king.

Henry Tudor was breathing hard, muddy and battered as he rode the last hundred yards to Lord Stanley's forces. He was pleased to be out of the blood and death he had witnessed. Six thousand fresh men watched the maelstrom he had left behind, staring in grim fascination and knowing they could be asked to march right into it at any moment.

Lord Stanley came out from the ranks on a glossy brown mare. He wore armour but no helmet, preferring to breathe freely unless he was actually under attack. His beard hung down the front of his surcoat, almost to his navel. At his side, his banners were held by a knight and two more held war-horses on tight reins just behind him, ready with weapons in case of treachery. Jasper and Henry looked at each other.

'Welcome home,' Lord Stanley said. 'Your mother sends her love, Henry.'

'Thank you, my lord. Will you accept my command?'

Lord Stanley inclined his head.

'As I have given my oath, yes, Henry. You know my son is in King Richard's custody in London?'

Jasper saw his nephew grow still and his heart sank. There was a moment of silence from Henry as he considered.

'Is your loyalty conditional then, Lord Stanley?' Henry called to his stepfather. 'Are you mine only if I save your son?' Lord Stanley stared for a moment, then shook his head.

'No. My loyalty is promised, however it comes out. I have other sons.'

Henry smiled tightly.

'That is the right answer, Lord Stanley. However, if it is in my power, I will see your son returned safely to you.'

'Thank you, my lord,' Lord Stanley said, blinking.

'Now. Lead us in,' Henry said.

Jasper and Henry turned their mounts and rode back in a line of marching men, readying axes and swords as they went. A great roar went up in challenge and King Richard's knights looked up in dismay from the fighting.

The armoured knights who had come down that hill had been battered and overwhelmed by too many men. Without the right wing of Lord Percy, they had been hard-pressed from the beginning, a last desperate gamble by King Richard to reach the Tudor heart. At the sight of Stanley's vast force of six thousand coming in against them, many of them turned and raced away or threw down their weapons. Some were allowed to surrender.

They found Richard's body, broken and battered in its armour with a dozen wounds. The helmet had borne a circlet of gold and one of the welds had come loose so that it hung askew. A knight tugged it free and it went rolling under a stunted bush. Sir William Stanley stabbed it through with his lance, lifting it so that it spun around and down to his hand.

They brought it over to Henry Tudor and Lord Stanley. The younger Stanley handed the twisted ring to his brother. Lord Thomas Stanley took the simple crown and pressed it over Henry's long hair. His uncle Jasper was the first to kneel, with tears bright in his eyes. The men began to cheer the name of Tudor and Lancaster, together, in a great sea of sound.

Epilogue

Jasper Tudor swallowed uncomfortably as he looked across Westminster Abbey. The open space was lit by huge numbers of candles and so crowded that even that vast and vaulted room had become warm. He felt a line of perspiration trickle down his neck and wondered if he could possibly hand the crown of England to one of the servants while he dabbed at it.

He turned his head when he smelled violets and, at the same moment, felt cool fingers against his throat. His collar was so tight and high he could hardly look down, but he smiled even so at the sight of Margaret Beaufort reaching up to dry his gleaming skin.

'Thank you,' he whispered. He still remembered the girl she had been, so many years before, with no friend in the world and all the world in flames. He had thought then that he had saved that green slip of a thing, when he found her another house and a husband. Margaret had outlived his brother Edmund and her second husband to find a third. That man, Thomas Stanley, had been made an earl. He stood not forty yards away at that very moment, resting the sword of state on his wide shoulder. Jasper could only wonder at how well Margaret had managed.

'Thank you for looking after my son, Your Grace,' Margaret said softly. Jasper smiled, still delighted by his new title. A king's uncle could be Duke of Bedford, it seemed. He would never want or go hungry again. He had been to Pembroke Castle and found it abandoned, with all the fine tapestries taken away. He had not yet decided if he would restore it.

'You gave him hope over the years,' he said, turning to her. 'With your letters.' At the heart of the crowded hall, a psalter of bishops laid hands on Henry Tudor, blessing him. The Bishop of Bath and Wells was there, with Morton, Bishop of Ely, back from disgrace to help the elderly Archbishop Bourchier fulfil his duties.

'And it is my hope to know him now, Jasper. Now that I have the time. England is at peace, after all, long may she remain so.'

Jasper looked across the hall, waiting for the moment when he would be summoned. The crown was very different from the rough circlet his nephew had worn at Bosworth Field. The men had cheered the sight, but that battered ring had not been a crown for a coronation. The one Jasper bore glittered with pearls and rubies studded on crosses of gold. It rested on a velvet cushion and was the work of master goldsmiths and enamellers.

It was very heavy, seeming to weigh more than the mere metal. Jasper looked along a lane laid with carpet, between rows of seated lords and ladies. He knew if he tripped and fell, it would probably be the only thing they remembered.

'There can be peace from exhaustion, my lady, of a sort. I do believe these people are wearied by thirty years of war.'

'As they should be, Jasper. Either way, we shall give them a fine royal marriage to join my son with Elizabeth of York. Her mother is a . . . practical woman, I believe. And she has lost more than anyone. It is my hope that seeing her daughter safely wed to Henry will bring her peace as well. There is no one else left, after all. My son is the last of Lancaster and Elizabeth is the heir of York.'

'Ah, your son is many things,' Jasper said. 'A leader of

men, to my surprise. A gentleman and a scholar-king. But he is a Tudor, my lady, and he will make his own house now. It is only right. He is the *Ddraig Goch*, after all, the Red Dragon – and perhaps, just perhaps, the *Mab Darogan* as well.'

'The Man of Destiny?' Margaret replied, reminding him that she had spent years amongst the Welsh. 'Why of course he is, Jasper. He won. That is all that matters in the end.'

Jasper was turning to whisper a reply when she pushed him and he realized hundreds of faces were turned his way. He swallowed and stepped out into the hall, bearing the crown for the young king.

Historical Note

Henry Tudor was born in Pembroke Castle in 1457, to his thirteen-year-old mother, Margaret Beaufort. His father, Edmund Tudor, Earl of Richmond, had died of plague after being captured by Yorkist enemies. His uncle, Jasper Tudor, helped Margaret to find a new husband in Sir Henry Stafford, though she survived him as well and went on to marry Lord Thomas Stanley, later made Earl of Derby. It is interesting to note that Henry's mother was as English as eggs – and his father was half Welsh, half French and born in Hertfordshire. Still, Henry Tudor had a good claim to being the *Mab Darogan*, the long-predicted 'Man of Destiny' who would come from Wales and rule England.

It is true that when Henry was fourteen Jasper Tudor returned to take his nephew away to France with him. It is not known if they used the huge cave under Pembroke Castle, but that would have been perfect. It is also true that there are tunnels under the town of Tenby, a dozen miles east of Pembroke – and local legend has it that those tunnels sheltered Henry and his uncle as soldiers searched for them, before the two Tudors dashed out to a boat and got away.

Warwick and George, Duke of Clarence, made a great landing from France in September 1470. They moved swiftly to London, there to free King Henry VI from the Tower and to restore him as figurehead for the house of Lancaster. For this sort of action did Warwick become known as the Kingmaker.

They were extraordinarily fortunate that Edward of York made it so easy for them. It is true that he was away in the north as his wife, Elizabeth, was about to give birth. It is well attested that Edward was a man of huge appetites for food, wine and hunting. Yet there is a certain amount of mystery about this period. The king who acted so decisively before and during Towton was caught with too few men and quickly surrounded – by an army in the north and Warwick coming up rapidly from the south.

Warwick had gathered between twenty and thirty thousand men in his campaign to restore the house of Lancaster. Edward settled around Nottingham and sent out the call – and barely three thousand came. The charismatic leader of Towton had been written out of the story. In an age of no mass communication, such a thing would have required shoe leather and volunteers by the hundred to spread the word. Lancaster was coming back. The old crown was to be returned. The house of York would fall.

Outnumbered to such a degree, Edward ran for the coast with just a few men, his brother Richard among them. Even then, the move had been expected and his boat was almost captured at sea. Edward had no money with him and it is true that the king of England had to give the boat captain his coat to pay for passage. He did so with a smile, though it must have been a moment of extraordinary bitterness. Like Warwick before him, he was heading into an uncertain exile.

Yet King Edward IV was an unusually determined man. He came back, fitter and restored. He had faced impossible odds before – and won, in the snow at Towton. He was, simply, one of the greatest battle kings in English history.

For all those who have imbibed a romantic view of King Richard III, I think they have cause to be grateful to Shakespeare, for all the bard's delight in making him a hunchbacked villain. Without Shakespeare, Richard Plantagenet was only king for two years and would have been just a minor footnote to his brother's reign. There is not one contemporary mention of physical deformity, though we know now that his spine was twisted. He would have lived in constant pain, but then so did many active fighting men. There is certainly no record of Richard ever needing a special set of armour for a raised shoulder. Medieval swordsmen, like Roman soldiers before them, would have been noticeably larger on their right sides. A school friend of mine turned down a career as a professional fencer because of the way his right shoulder was developing into a hump from constant swordplay – and that was with a light, fencing blade. Compare his experience to that of a medieval swordsman using a broader blade, three feet long or even longer, where strength and stamina meant the difference between victory and a humiliating death. Richard fought in 1485. He went out even though he knew his wife and son were dead and that he had no heir. I could not resist an echo of *Macbeth*, Act 5 Scene 3, when the king calls for his armour. King Richard knew that if he lost, the male line of his house was finished – and yet he went anyway. He was brave at the end. May we all be so.

The Duke of Burgundy, Charles the Bold (or the wonderful-sounding Charles le Téméraire), was initially reluctant to commit himself to the cause of the exiled brothers York. Duke Charles was only too aware of the power of King Louis of France. Yet Louis and Earl Warwick were openly arranging a massive attack from Calais into Burgundy lands over the first months of 1471 – forcing Duke Charles to support their key enemy with thirty-six ships and around twelve hundred men, some English among them. The flagship that held Edward and his brother Richard was merely the *Antony*.

I made it the *Mark Antony*, after the noble Roman who gave Caesar's oratory speech. It must have been a horrible gamble for Duke Charles to give up such a vital force at the exact moment he needed them most, yet it paid off.

Note: '*Placebo Domino in regione vivorum*' – 'I will please the Lord in the land of the living' – was the first response line from fifteenth-century congregations at a funeral. Some mourners came only for the food and 'Placebo singers' was already an insult by 1470, used in Chaucer's *Tales* a generation before as a description of false mourners who gained a benefit without being truthful. I find that word origin fascinating, so include it here.

Edward landed first at Cromer in Norfolk, but learned only that the Duke of Norfolk was a prisoner and that the Earl of Oxford was against him. A Cromer landing was impossible at that time, so he and his brother Richard decided on Ravenspur on the mouth of the River Humber, close by Hull and not far from the city of York – the exact landing spot where Henry of Bolingbroke had come ashore seventy-two years before, to usurp Richard II.

This particular campaign began badly, with Hull refusing to open its gates. Edward was only allowed into York with a few men and progress was slow and grudging as he passed Sandal Castle. No one today can be certain why John Neville, Lord Montagu, decided not to sally out against him from Pontefract Castle, but he didn't – and a chance was missed to nip the Yorkist return in the bud.

Instead, Edward and Richard continued to gather men to them until they had around six to eight thousand, still hugely outnumbered by Warwick's forces. Lord Hastings was actually one of those who accompanied Edward to Flanders.

I wrote him joining Edward at Leicester as I wanted to show names coming in, one by one, an avalanche that began slowly but could not be stopped once it had begun.

Warwick remains a fascinating character, five hundred years later. I doubt I have done him justice, for he was a truly complex individual. His skills in diplomacy are undeniable. To survive and thrive at the forefront of the Wars of the Roses, he had to have been a man of fine judgement in personal matters. He clearly relied upon his family for loyalty and expected it in others. He turned against Edward only when that younger man made it impossible for Warwick to support him, with attack after attack on the Neville clan. Warwick was essentially loyal to two generations of York. He was driven away and the results were extraordinarily tragic. Elizabeth Woodville must bear some of the blame, though Edward IV must also take a share.

In battle, Warwick was nowhere near as talented as he needed to be. He lost the second Battle of St Albans when Margaret's forces went around his entrenched position and attacked from the rear. Warwick then made the monumental error of capturing Edward and holding him prisoner without a real plan, eventually having to release a spiteful and vengeful king. When that blew up spectacularly, Warwick could not prevent Edward's escape with Richard of Gloucester.

It is true Warwick refused to engage the Yorkist army at Coventry, though he had vastly superior numbers and position. Hindsight is a wonderful thing, of course, but something odd happened at Coventry. It is my suspicion that Warwick saw Edward IV and Richard of Gloucester on the field – and regretted his choices, at least for long enough to stay his hand. He had them boxed in: Montagu behind, Earl Oxford to the east, twenty thousand or more in and around Coventry. If Warwick had attacked, he could have written his own ending.

Yet Richard of Gloucester had been his ward. Warwick had known Edward from boyhood and stood at his side at Towton, an event of such savagery I am sure it marked all those who survived it. Perhaps it is just a coincidence that Warwick, Edward IV, Gloucester, Clarence and Montagu were all members of the Order of the Garter, yet it is a strange thought.

We will never know for sure what went through Warwick's mind in early April 1471. He died at the Battle of Barnet just days later. Warwick may not have been a great battle tactician, but at Coventry he didn't need to be. He had them cold – and he let them pass. The man who fought at Edward's side at Towton was not a coward and that is the only other explanation that fits the events.

Note: George of Clarence did indeed change sides again, betraying his father-in-law. Edward, Richard and George met on the Banbury road and there was 'right kind and loving language betwixt them' – at least for a while.

For a long time in English schools, Clarence being drowned in a 'vat of Malmsey wine' was one of the famous deaths everyone knew, along with Henry I dying after consuming a 'surfeit of lampreys' (eels), or Nelson struck down at the Battle of Trafalgar. I am not certain that is true today, though I hope it is. Stories make culture and may be more important than we know.

Note on the Battle of Barnet: Over Easter 1471, London became the gathering point for the house of York. Estimates of numbers are always tricky, but sources agree that Edward's army was still fairly small, with between seven and twelve thousand men. Warwick is generally accepted to have outnumbered them at least three to one. Edward cannot have expected his run of luck at Barnet, so was it madness for him to leave a defensible city and attack? He was with his brothers and they were all young men. It is possible they pushed each other on – and that could easily have led to disaster. Yet Edward was also the victor of Towton and a near-mythical figure in battle. At twenty-eight and restored to fitness, he would have been terrifying to face, his presence worth thousands in terms of morale. As Henry V had fought at Agincourt, so Edward continued a tradition of martial kings and the highest stakes.

Today, Barnet is a part of London. In 1471, it was a spot on the London road about eight miles from the Tower, a town with open countryside all around. Neither Warwick nor Edward IV would have chosen it as a battlefield. It was just where they clashed on the road and where, at last, Warwick was killed, a great and turbulent career brought to a violent close. He had chosen between kings more than once – and had both Edward and Henry in his personal custody on one occasion. Warwick had made disastrous decisions as well as great ones – and yet he truly forgave Margaret of Anjou and worked to restore Lancaster to the throne and undo all he had brought about. It is my suspicion that, for all his faults, he was actually a great man.

I hope I have covered Barnet with some accuracy, based on my reading of the events. It is true that Edward approached under cover of darkness and that his army was too close to be troubled by Warwick's intermittent cannon fire all night. It is also true that when Edward attacked at between four and five on Easter morning, the thick mist meant he did not see the armies had overlapped. His right wing plunged forward, his left fell back – and tens of thousands of fighting men turned with Edward at the hub of the wheel. On Warwick's side, Oxford routed the York left wing and drove them back to the town of Barnet. His return would prove utterly chaotic, including the fact that his estoile symbol was similar-looking to Edward's Sun in Flames. Cries of treachery went up on Lancaster's side and men simply panicked. Edward took advantage and Warwick's brother Montagu was killed, causing a collapse at the centre that dragged Warwick in as well. It was an inglorious end to Warwick's extraordinary life. It is true that the bodies were displayed in London and also true that Edward did not have them cut into pieces as was common, but instead had them returned to the family for burial at Bisham Abbey.

Queen Margaret of Anjou and her son Edward of Lancaster, Prince of Wales, did indeed set foot in England for the first time in ten years on the same day that Warwick was killed in battle. They'd set out almost a week before but been driven back by storms.

It is not difficult to imagine Margaret's initial despair when she heard Warwick had fallen. Yet she allowed herself to be reassured by Edmund Beaufort, Lord Somerset. He knew the south of England and was vital in raising a great army there in what would truly be Margaret's last throw of the dice.

King Edward sent out his own commissions of array for fresh soldiers, having lost some decent part of his army at Barnet. The only difficulty lay in that he didn't know where Margaret would strike and had to pursue her over vast stretches of land. He knew she had gone to Wales once before and suspected she might head north to the River Severn and cross into Wales somewhere around Gloucester or Tewkesbury.

Margaret reached Bristol and found great support there,

gaining men and funds and equipment, including cannon. Edward chose a good spot to array for war and was then informed that Margaret had not stopped to face him but gone on. Once more, he had to march in pursuit.

In the race to reach Wales, Edward had sent messengers ahead and Gloucester and its bridge across the Severn remained closed to Margaret, just as Hull had been closed to him a few weeks before. Margaret's lords and forces pushed on to the next great crossing, the ford at Tewkesbury. They arrived after a march of twenty-six miles. Edward's army force-marched thirty-six miles to intercept them before they crossed. Both were exhausted, but Edward was determined to repay the humiliations he had suffered.

The ford across the river by Tewkesbury could not be attempted by night, or with a hostile army in range and ready to attack. The Lancaster forces had to fight and it was a close-run thing.

Edward could not lay claim to any great tactical skill at Tewkesbury. He did keep a reserve of two hundred spears and they proved useful, but the decisive tactic was a missile attack by Gloucester on the person of the Duke of Somerset, who had lost his older brother and his father to the Wars of the Roses. He responded with an enraged charge downhill, giving up the advantage of terrain. Edward's centre was then able to break up the Lancaster forces piece by piece. There is a surviving story that Somerset made his way back up the hill and killed his ally Baron Wenlock for failing to support his position.

Prince Edward was killed as the York centre broke through, taking with him the last hopes of Lancaster and effectively ending the wars in that one stroke.

*

I jumped from 1471 to 1482 in Part Two. This was not because nothing of interest happened in between. The invasions of France and Scotland in particular are fascinating. My focus though was on the Wars of the Roses as a whole. It is true that, in some ways, this is Edward IV's story, but it is also the story of Margaret of Anjou – and York and Lancaster. For those interested in a vivid historical life of this half-forgotten king, I recommend *Edward IV* by Charles Ross for all the details that would have been out of place here. I also recommend *Richard the Third* by Paul Murray Kendall. Both are wonderful reads, full of details I could not find space to include. For example, Kendall mentioned that Richard and his wife, Ann, would have been stripped to the waist for part of the coronation service, to be anointed in oil. Not only does this raise the question of how female nudity was considered at that time, but also has a bearing on the fact that no contemporary source ever mentioned Richard having a hunchback. As I have said before, he was a renowned swordsman, and even bare to the waist, he caused no especial interest. My feeling is that he actually would have been slightly twisted, with one shoulder raised – as we can see from the scoliosis of his skeleton – but that a mass of muscle would have been ordinary to a medieval swordsman, as would scars and marks of all kinds on the skin.

At a distance of five centuries, it is impossible to know for certain what killed Edward IV. We know he drank prodigious amounts, astonishing visitors to his court. We know Edward had suffered any number of blows to the head in his life. Some sort of haemorrhage or stroke seems most likely. One contemporary source suspected poison, but a clot is more likely.

He was forty at the time of his death. It seems a tragic

loss, even today. If Edward IV had ruled for fifty years like Edward III, there would have been no Richard III and no Bosworth Field – but then also no Tudors and no Elizabethan age.

A note on names: King Henry VI had a son named Edward, who became, briefly, Prince of Wales. As did King Edward IV, as did King Richard III. Their brother George, Duke of Clarence, also had a son named Edward, who became Earl Warwick and was in the care of his uncle Richard for a time as one who had a better claim to the throne than Richard himself. Just as there were too many Richards, for a while, there were just too many Edwards. No writer of crime or romantic fiction ever had such a problem. I do not know if Richard III's son was called 'Ned' or not.

It is true that Duke Richard of Gloucester intercepted Prince Edward as he was brought home to his coronation in London. Gloucester moved so swiftly and so calmly that it supports a diagnosis of a double stroke in his brother, which gave Richard time to prepare.

There are few men in history with so many ardent fans, some of whom will believe no wrong of Richard at all. Yet he moved to have his brother's children declared illegitimate just days after Edward IV breathed his last. Why then would he have them killed, some ask, if they were no longer a threat to him? Because Richard of Gloucester had lived through the triumphs and disasters of the Wars of the Roses. His father had been attainted. Richard had been attainted himself, with King Edward – and they had gone on to recover their power and titles. Of all men, Richard knew the danger of a potential enemy left alive. King Henry VI of Lancaster had been allowed to live. The result was there to be seen and judged.

Richard had one of his brother's sons in the Tower. He gained the other with a deputation to Sanctuary where Elizabeth had fled with her children. No less a figure than the Archbishop of Canterbury led the boy away, after a discussion over whether it violated Sanctuary or not to remove the boy. His mother apparently acquiesced, but what else could she possibly say or do with the Protector's armed men surrounding the fortress in the grounds of Westminster Abbey?

Richard had the wit and flair to dispose of his enemies by accusing them of plots against the boys, whereas the likelihood was that they were involved in plots against him. He had Lord Hastings executed as well as Lords Rivers, Grey and Vaughn. Lord Stanley was also arrested for a few days but then released. Richard put far too much trust in a man married to Margaret Beaufort, as it turned out.

Julius Caesar had a son with Cleopatra. The boy was known as Ptolemy Caesarion and he should have inherited twin empires. He would have done, in fact, if Augustus Caesar had not had him executed when he was just seventeen. That same benign Augustus also had his grandson killed so that the young man would not interfere with the peaceful handover of power to Emperor Tiberius. Such events can be called tragedies, of course, but not really a surprise.

In regard to his nephews, Richard would have quietly rid himself of those future threats some time during the summer of 1483. Richard had a wife and a son at the time, though as was so terrible and so common, both would die not long after. In those first warm months of his reign, Richard would merely have been securing his own bloodline. He was no vacillating Hamlet, but a man of action who had moved with vigour to take a chance few others would have seen.

The murder of the boys would have been done quietly,

without evidence. It would have been seen as a shameful act and certainly a sin, but a necessary one. At least one potential uprising was averted when the whisper went round that the boys were not alive to rescue.

There are some who say it was Lord Buckingham, perhaps in answer to a cry from Richard, not unlike that of Henry II in an earlier century when he said, 'Who will rid me of this turbulent priest?' – and four knights went to Canterbury to murder an archbishop. History can be a dark and bloody story. In the end, the princes were murdered by or at the order of only three candidates: Richard III, Buckingham or Henry VII, clearing his own decks for the house of Tudor.

I am confident Richard gave the order. Buckingham's 1483 rebellion was at first an attempt to restore the house of York through the princes in the Tower. The news that they had been killed completely hamstrung his coalition. Buckingham tried to change horses to a Lancastrian rebellion, but failed completely. He may even have intended to support Henry Tudor all along, but the key point is that there is a motive for Richard to have ordered the deaths of the princes.

King Richard was never the hunchbacked murderer of Shakespeare's play, delighting in his own evil. I would be surprised if he wasn't the one who killed Henry VI in his cell, though again certainty is impossible. Richard was not a saint, any more than his brother Edward was. Henry VI could well have been, but history is not kind to saints.

As a final thought on Richard, he showed his power and perhaps a touch of greatness after the 1483 rebellion. He executed only ten and attainted ninety-six, and then went on to pardon around thirty of those. He was back in London only four months after leaving on his first Great Progress around the country. His reign was then rocked by the death of his son and, a few months after that, the death of his wife. Tuberculosis is the most likely cause in both cases, a scourge. If Richard had won at Bosworth, there is no real reason to suppose he couldn't have recovered it all – a new wife, new children, a long reign. He fought hand to hand and unhorsed Henry's giant bodyguard, Sir John Cheyney, with a broken lance. Cheyney survived the battle and was present for Henry's coronation in London.

Richard Plantagenet was just thirty-two when he was brought down. Who knows what he might have done if he had lived? I recommend the fascinating book *Bosworth: The Birth of the Tudors* by Chris Skidmore.

A note on dates: The Battle of Bosworth was famously fought on 22 August 1485, but that was under the Julian calendar, created by Julius Caesar and a Greek astrologer, Sosigenes. It was extraordinarily accurate for 46 BC and set the length of a year at 365 days with a leap day added every fourth year in February – then the end of the Roman year. (Which is how September, October, November and December were named: they were the seventh, eighth, ninth and tenth months in a calendar that began in March.) Over almost two thousand years, unnoticed extra hours on the length of a year added up; this was eventually revised in the Gregorian Calendar of 1752, when the calendar had to be advanced by eleven days. However, the fifteenth century was only nine days wrong. Bosworth was therefore actually fought on 31 August 1485, by the calendar we still use today.

Whatever his weakness or illness was, Henry VI was a good man. He certainly deserved better than to be murdered in his rooms at the Tower of London. I have stood where he was killed. I am sorry he could not have been spared a life that saw his son cut down before manhood and his wife broken and humiliated in her attempts to save her husband. Somehow, it is part of the exquisitely painful nature of her story that Margaret died in 1482, in France, with King Edward IV still strong and apparently ready to rule for decades. If Margaret had lived only a few years longer, she would have seen all her enemies destroyed and at least some part of the house of Lancaster returned to the throne. Yet she did not. In some ways, this was her story – and her tragedy.

Conn Iggulden
London, 2015

WITNESS THE RISE OF THE TUDORS

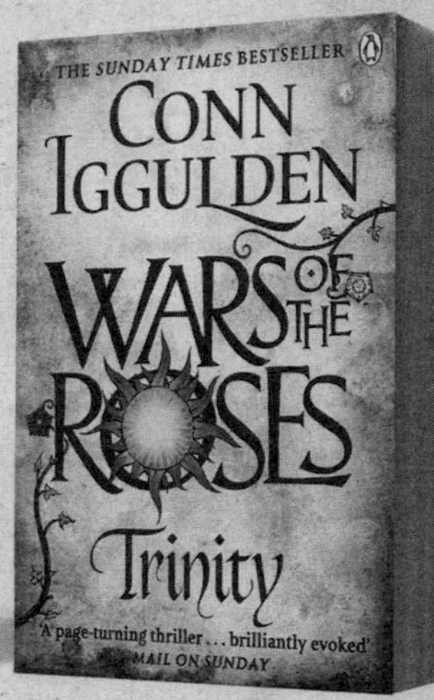

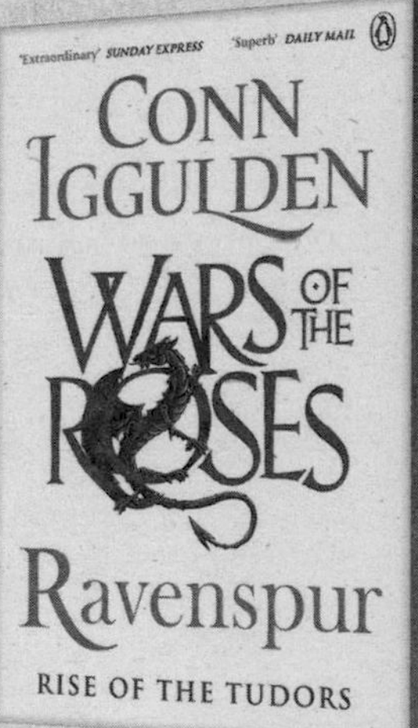

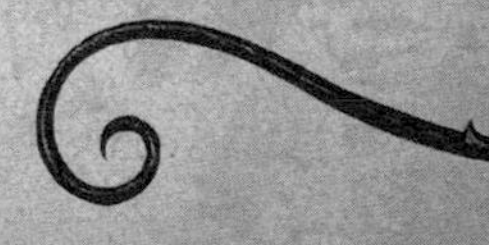